MW00878201

# CHRONICLES
## *of*
# ALETHIA

Enjoy the next adventure!

R. S. Gibb

# CHRONICLES
*of*
# ALETHIA
*The Lord of Darkness Returns*

# R.S. GULLETT

*Chronicles of Alethia: The Lord of Darkness Returns*
Copyright © 2018 by R.S. Gullett. All rights reserved.

No part of this publication may be reproduced, stored in a retrieval system or transmitted in any way by any means, electronic, mechanical, photocopy, recording or otherwise without the prior permission of the author except as provided by USA copyright law. This novel is a work of fiction. Names, descriptions, entities, and incidents included in the story are products of the author's imagination. Any resemblance to actual persons, events, and entities is entirely coincidental.

Published in the United States of America
ISBN: 978-1-73-092806-2
1. Fiction / Christian / Fantasy
2. Fiction / Historical / Medieval
16.06.10

# ACKNOWLEDGEMENTS

First and foremost, I wish to give honor and glory to Jesus Christ, my Lord and Savior. Without Him, this story would have no foundation. I also wish to thank my loving wife, Stephanie, for her encouragement and all the time she spent editing this book. Finally, I wish to thank my parents for always encouraging me to pursue my goals.

# A NOTE FROM THE AUTHOR

The Chronicles of Alethia is told through the eyes of individual characters who are sometimes hundreds of miles apart from one another. Some chapters may cover an hour, a day, or may even take place over the span weeks.  As such, some chapters may overlap or take place simultaneously as others. As the tale has grown in the telling, utmost care has been taken to ensure chronology between characters, chapters, and even books. The events in *The Lord of Darkness Returns* take place twenty years after the events in *The Heir Comes Forth*.

# ALETHIA

- ◉ Major City
- • Minor City
- ▣ *Castle*
- ▢ *(Ruined Castle)*

SEA OF AEAR

*Rysling*

*Coldwater*

Ridgeshire

MOUNTAINS OF EODAR

KINGDOM
OF
NORDYKE

Ytemest
Fortress

Stonewall

Ironwall
Fortress

GRAY MOUNTAINS

Vedmore

Castel

*Johann*

OAKWOOD FOREST

*(Ruins of
Ardaband)*

Elengil

Forest of
Roxton

Rein

Ethriel

Shadow Vale

Rockhold

Estelhold

*Westmont*

Whitewood

*(Deadwood
Fortress)*

Abenhall

IRON

Windham

DEADWOOD
MARSHES

*Belwash*

HILLS

PASS OF
STENC

BAY
OF RYST

EASTERN WASTES

Fortress
of Noland

Norhold

Dyn
Forest

Westhaven

Dy

*Nenil*

RYST

*Dy*

Farodhold

GREEN MOUNTAINS

Elmwood

Nen
Forest

Elmloch
Castle

*Elmbrook*

Nenholm

Eastern
Woodlands

REALM
OF
DONIA

Fairhaven

*Waterdale*

GAP OF DONIA

SOUTHRON MTS.

KINGDOM
OF EDDYNLAND

PLASSE
2016

# PROLOGUE:

# METHANGOTH

The Southron Mountains, a long chain of dark jagged peaks rising high like the wicked jawbone of a monstrous beast lying discarded upon the land. This range of mountains marked the border between the kingdoms of Alethia and Eddynland, and was one of the least assailable mountain ranges in this part of the world. Yet within these mountains lay a secret. Long forgotten by all save the most learned loremasters, lay a ruined fortress; a foreboding place even in its ruined state. The crumbling towers and battlements still bore the mark of evil inflicted upon them so long ago.

It was here, on this inhospitable night, that he arrived. Upon the edge of a cliff near the ruined fortress, a billowing burst of black smoke erupted. The wind dispersing the smoke, revealed a man, shrouded in a black cloak and hood. The figure stood silently gazing upon the fortress and the jagged peaks towering above him. Though his face was hidden, he could not contain his exuberance. He raised his arms to the sky, shaking his fists in defiance of those who'd tried to keep the knowledge of this place from him. He had seized the Book of Aduin, searched its pages, and found its hidden secrets. His enemies had marched against him, defeated his forces, and destroyed his own fortress far away. Yet they could not keep the knowledge of this place from him. They had failed. He had found it and soon the ancient power contained within would be his alone.

A sudden gust of wind interrupted his revelry, nearly knocking him off his feet. The man turned. A storm was blowing in from the north. Billowing clouds rolled in, bringing bitter winds, blinding flashes of lightning, followed by roars of deafening thunderclaps.

Pulling his cloak tighter around him, the man moved forward toward the shelter of the ruined gatehouse. He could feel it, the faint echo of the power that had once abided here. Yet he knew the source of the power was ensconced elsewhere. He placed a hand on the stone wall of the gatehouse. Around his hand the stone glowed violet for a moment, then flowed down the wall and onto the rocky floor beneath his feet. The glowing trail shot outward towards the mountains behind the ruins. It ran up the mountainside, terminating in the cleft of a rocky ledge several hundred feet above. There was a brilliant flash, then the glow faded into the darkness. From within his robes, the man pulled something and hurled it at the ground. There was another burst of black smoke, and the man vanished, reappearing on the ledge above the fortress.

His robes whipped wildly in the wind. Lightning flashed, casting grim shadows for an instant, then were swallowed once again by the pitch darkness a second later. In the rock face before him lay a cave, its entrance like the gaping maw of a monstrous dragon. Stalactites and stalagmites ran on either side of a path leading inside the mouth of the cave. The man took a step forward, then stopped abruptly before crossing the threshold. There was something in front of him. The air seemed to pulse with energy. There was a barrier of some sort here, which he could not see. Thankfully he had other senses attune to the presence of magic. He took another step and placed an outstretched hand just before the cave's opening. The air grew thick and took on a transparent blue hue. He withdrew his hand and the air before him returned to normal.

The man's face twisted into a grim smile. This was it. He'd reached the forbidden tomb. He withdrew several paces, then turned and drew his hands together until they were a few inches apart. The space between them crackled and pulsated with twisting red energy that formed into a fireball. With a sudden thrust of his hands, the fireball shot forth at the cave entrance. The fiery blast impacted the barrier, which shook the ledge beneath his feet. Struggling to keep his balance, the man shot another volley, larger than the first, at the barrier. This time, the impact shook the ledge, the cave entrance, and the mountainside above him. Frustration billowing up from inside him, the man released a final, massive volley, and this time the fireball shattered the barrier. Yet, the blast also sent shockwaves throughout the entire mountain, and he felt the ledge giving way. The man ran forward as the stone crumbled beneath his feet, just making it past the threshold before the ledge fell onto the fortress below.

The man leaned against the cave wall, panting for a moment from the effort required to remove the barrier. After a few seconds, he staggered forward, unwilling to wait another minute, even to catch his breath. He pressed on into the cave. Pulling from his robes a black wand, he gave it a simple flick, and from its tip issued a red light that filled the cave. He paused to glance at the rough stone walls. It was obvious that this cave was in fact a hastily dug tunnel, only six feet in diameter. The tunnel descended at a steady pace, downward into the heart of the mountain. After walking for some forty or fifty paces, the man stopped in front of a dead end. A wall of stone stood before him, and above his head was an archway, upon which was written runes in an archaic dialect. The man pulled back his cloak, revealing long black hair and black eyes that gleamed menacingly in the red light from his wand. His eyes narrowed, then he spoke words from an ancient tongue. There was a rumble from beyond the stone wall. The man pulled his cloak over his eyes as a blinding flash filled the tunnel.

When the darkness returned and the rumbling ceased, the man uncovered his face and saw the wall had vanished. Beyond the archway lay a large room with high walls and ceiling. In the midst of the room stood a high stone dais. Shallow steps led up onto the top of the dais, where a large stone sarcophagus lay. Fighting to control his excitement, the man ascended the stairs and stood before the sarcophagus. Etched into the black stone were the same runes in the archaic tongue. The man stretched out his hand and touched the hard stone lid. He quickly withdrew it, for it was ice cold. In the light of his wand, he saw his hand had changed to black. His panic was short-lived as the color gradually returned.

He waved both hands over the sarcophagus, muttering in the same ancient tongue and the walls and ceiling of the room rumbled. Soon the whole room shook, and the man fell backwards down into a crumpled heap at the foot of the stone steps. Getting to his feet, he saw a dark form rising from the sarcophagus. The light issuing from his wand went out, and the entire room was filled with an impenetrable blackness. Fear threatened to overwhelm him as a voice spoke from the blackness. The voice was thin and harsh, like the hiss of a snake mixed with the sound of nails upon a chalkboard. The man wanted to cover his ears and run from this place, but his purpose in coming steeled his nerves.

"The barrier is broken," said the voice, as speaking to itself. "But my body remains imprisoned by these stones.

"I sense a dark presence nigh. Your desire for power is familiar to my own," the voice said. The man could feel attention shift towards him. He felt an overwhelming presence attempt to penetrate his mind, commanding him to reveal all he knew. The man fought back, and at length the voice spoke, "Speak your name."

"Methangoth," the man growled, unable to resist any longer.

A violet light emanated from the top of the dais. Methangoth glanced up to see a shadowy specter floating there. Its eyes like deep pits, filled with impenetrable darkness.

"You came here seeking my power?" the shadowy form laughed.

Methangoth did not speak, but stared defiantly up at the specter.

"Pathetic fool. You believed in coming here you would somehow lay hold of my power. You are unworthy of such a gift," boasted the specter. Then as if speaking to itself it continued, "For countless ages, I ruled the known world. I controlled the fate of millions, during a time when this kingdom was but a minor province in my vast empire. Then, I was betrayed by my subjects and slain during a siege of the fortress below. Yet my guilt ridden subjects feared my power, so the loremasters imprisoned my bones in this tomb. Here I have waited for a thousand years for my revenge."

"I came to free you. You cannot escape your imprisonment without me," Methangoth shouted.

"I need no one!" the specter shouted, its eyes flashed red in rage. Its harsh voice echoed off the cave walls, forcing Methangoth to cover his ears and cower. "You impudent fool. I should destroy you."

Methangoth stood rooted, staring boldly up at the specter, but also sure of his imminent death. They stared at one another for a long moment.

"Yet, you may prove useful to me, Methangoth," said the specter at length. "Lay your hand upon the sarcophagus and I shall be freed. Then you will swear fealty to me forever, and I will grant you power beyond your wildest dreams."

Methangoth hesitated.

"Choose," The specter hissed, its eyes flashing once again. "Serve me or die."

Methangoth climbed back to the top of the dais. The specter moved to hover beside the sarcophagus. He laid his hand on the ancient stone and spoke the words he'd read in the book. The specter vanished, and darkness filled the cave once again.

Methangoth withdrew his hand as the entire cave began to shake. He fled back down the stairs to the archway as the sound of cracking stone filled the cave. A great beam of violet light burst from the top of the dais, shooting up through the ceiling. A giant claw emerged from within the sarcophagus, followed by a long powerful arm. It reached out and grabbed the side of the dais, the stone steps shattering under the claw's powerful grip. Methangoth fled back up the tunnel, the sounds of shattering stone and then a fierce roar followed him as he ran. He skidded to a halt at the mouth of the cave, just before the threshold where the fallen ledge had been, and he peered out into the dark night. The storm was still raging. Lightning flashed and thunder boomed. The wind rushed passed the cave entrance, whipping his robes and threatening to carry him away.

Then a sound came to Methangoth's ears. Stones were falling from above him onto the ruined fortress below. He turned upward to gaze at the mountain's summit. There was a rush of wind, a flash of lightning, and a thunderous boom, and he saw the silhouette of an immense winged creature swoop across the sky. The beast dived toward the cave entrance, and Methangoth made to reach inside his robes, but his hand froze in place. The creature slowed and hovered before the mouth of the cave, its great bat-like wings sending wind gust that threatened to knock him off his feet. Massive claws hung from its arms and legs, and to Methangoth's astonishment, the creature's mouth opened in a wicked smile, revealing giant spear-like teeth.

"Not so fast, Methangoth," the beast spoke, its voice deep and harsh. "You have freed me, now you will swear fealty to me."

Methangoth gazed into the beast's intense eyes, then bowed his head reluctantly. He may have failed, but somewhere deep inside his mind a little voice spoke and reminded him that this creature's power might eventually be his. Perhaps the Book of Aduin held the secret.

"You have released me from my prison of stone," the creature growled. "Now we will make Alethia burn."

The beast let out a deafening roar, as it flew forth and scarlet flames issued from its mouth, scorching the mountainside. Methangoth cowered in fear as he watched the beast fly back and forth across the mountain, the smell of molten stone wafting from the ruins of the fortress. What had he done?

*Twenty years later…*

# 1

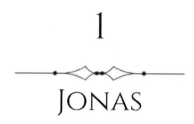

# JONAS

Winter had come. East of the Waterdale River lies a wide area of land between the Green Mountains in the north and the Southron Mountains in the south  known as the Gap of Donia; the long disputed border between the kingdoms of Alethia and Donia. The gap was sparsely populated with only a few homesteaders dotting the empty lands. There were no villages or towns. Very little evidence of civilization existed beyond the Waterdale River. This was the wild country. The borderlands between civilization. Only the companies of the king's Border Guard dared to travel far, and here on the edge of the Eastern Woodlands, one of the small companies of Bordermen lay encamped.

It was the coldest winter in living memory, yet they had a duty to patrol the borderlands and protect the kingdom. These men were hardy and brave, yet this did not keep them warm. The cold wind howled through the trees with such ferocity that it was all the men could do but try to keep warm. They huddled closer to their camp fires, rubbing their hands and pulling their hoods and cloaks tighter over their bodies.

Yet even the limited warmth of the campfires was denied poor Jonas Astley. He stood sentry along the southern perimeter of the camp, struggling to keep his cloak and hood pulled tightly around him. Yet he could not help but cast an occasional glance behind him at the nearest camp fire some thirty feet away. The warm glow of the fire was so inviting that he caught himself staring more than once and had to shake himself and turn back to the cold darkness. A sudden gust of wind caught him off guard, seeming to cut through his layers of clothing and threaten to freeze his very bones. Though he was only seventeen, it was the coldest he ever could remember being. Yet here he was, standing guard while the rest of the company huddled together for warmth.

Jonas shook his head in disgust. By his count it was two days after Christmas, though there hadn't been any hint of yuletide celebration out here on guard duty. There were no carols, only the howling of the wind. There was no warm fire for him, only bitter cold. There was no Christmas feast, only the stale bread and water.

He turned back towards the fire behind him as the sound of ruckus laughter rose up. While the other men laughed jovially, one of the men was standing and apparently giving a lively telling of a funny story. Jonas stared at the man, making the animated gestures and he was suddenly stricken with envy. Seemingly alienated and feeling ostracized, he scowled at the group of nearby Bordermen.

So far, he'd been traveling with this company of Bordermen for three weeks. His father, Lord Peter Astley, had decided that his son needed some "toughening up." Jonas, who was slight of build with sandy brown hair and green eyes like his father, was more studious than athletic; a trait his father was loathed to accept.

So Jonas had been sent out from Farodhold with the company, making their way southwest toward the border with the kingdom of Donia. On the first day, Captain Flint, the leader of this company of Bordermen, pulled him aside and explained his situation. Allegedly following the orders of Jonas's father, the captain made it clear that Jonas would be treated like any other recruit. The captain even forced Jonas to trade his clothes for the garb of the Bordermen: a simple brown tunic, pants, boots, and a long green cloak and hood. The stench emanating from his "new" attire nearly made Jonas vomit. It was clear that the former owner of these clothes knew as much of hygiene as any of his current traveling companions. In addition to his new garb, Jonas was also outfitted with a short sword, a shield, and a crossbow.

Jonas, who'd spent many long hours studying and reading safely within the castle of Farodhold, had little experience with cold or hard work. His father, though a strict and forceful man, gave little notice to his less than satisfactory son. The captain also seemed to take a special interest in making Jonas's waking hours miserable, personally assigning him to the most menial and humiliating tasks, as well as assigning him to more night watches than any of the others. As such, Jonas had been forced to endure two weeks of constant ridicule and abuse, the likes of which he'd never experienced before in his life. He'd often overheard the other members of the company taking bets as to how long it would take for Jonas to collapse from exhaustion.

As he stood there in the freezing cold, Jonas wondered if he could take much more of this. It was nearly midnight, which meant he still had two more hours before his watch was over. He pulled his cloak tighter about him as another gust of wind sent him scurrying behind a large tree just inside the tree line. The forest was silent. As he stood there, he wondered why they even bother setting a watch at all. They were at least some fifty miles from the border and there were no Alethian villages east of the Waterdale River. Even the wild beasts were probably holed up in their dens on such a bitterly cold night.

Jonas let out a long heavy sigh, sending a cloud of vapor into the night air. He leaned closer against the tree, trying to shield himself as much as possible from the howling wind. He closed his eyes for a moment, then turned once again to the nearby fire, longing to join the others but also knowing they'd send him right back out here to weather the cold alone. As had become his custom for the past three weeks, Jonas wonder if the others would even notice if he just up and ran off one night. It wasn't the first time he'd wondered this, but he also knew that leaving the company and trying to cross the wilderness alone would most likely result in his death. In all reality, he simply had nowhere else to go.

The sound of a twig snapping behind him caused Jonas to start. He spun around, bringing his crossbow up, but a shadowy figure seized the weapon and forced Jonas against the tree.

"If you are gonna keep watch, you must watch with more than your eyes," his assailant said in a low voice.

He released Jonas and stepped back, removing his hood and revealing a scruffy, but familiar face.

"Geez, Caleb!" Jonas said, with relief and annoyance. "What are you doing out here?"

"Looking out for our newest recruit," Caleb answered with a chuckle. "If you're gonna to make it as a Borderman, someone's got to teach you how."

Jonas eyed him suspiciously. So far, Caleb had not joined the others in their constant hazing of him, but neither had he stood up for him.

"Why do you want to help me?"

"Let's just say that I'd rather have a trained and grateful young man watching my back than a harassed and resentful one." Caleb said with a smirk.

"I wish that you'd decided this sooner," Jonas muttered.

"You're seriously complaining?"

"Sorry." Jonas said quickly, holding up his hands. "You're right."

"You're a long way from home, Master Astley. In a way, we all are. Well, all of us except Captain Flint. Most of us believe he was born out here."

They both shared a laugh and Jonas felt his guard lowering, if only for a moment.

"I was," came a gruff voice from the darkness.

They both turned and fell silent as a burly figure came towards them.

"Captain Flint, sir." Caleb said in alarm.

"I was born in a village along the border called Greenvale. Do you know it?"

Both Jonas and Caleb shook their heads.

"It no longer exists because of a Donian raid decades ago," the captain growled, menacingly, "a raid that could have been prevented and that should have never happened. Now, get back to camp, Caleb."

"Sir." Caleb said, moving off at a jog.

"And you," The captain rounded on Jonas. "Since you seem to be having such a nice time out here, you will take the next watch as well."

Jonas could not hide the disappointment on his face, but was afraid to speak so remained silent. His silence seemed to infuriate the captain, who shoved Jonas back into the tree behind him.

"You think you're better than the rest of us, but my men and I know better," he yelled, getting in Jonas's face. "The only reason I don't tie you to a tree and leave you for the wolves is that your father would kill me for letting you die."

Jonas remained silent, but felt anger and resentment rising inside him. He averted his gaze, unwilling to meet the captain's eyes. Suddenly, the captain grabbed Jonas by the shirt and hurled him to the ground, which was frozen and felt like hitting hard stone.

"You will learn some respect, boy, if I have to beat it into you."

Jonas got to his feet, preparing to defend himself. He knew that he was no match for the captain, but he had to at least try. Flint advanced on him and Jonas winced as he anticipated the coming pain, yet the captain stopped short. There was a strange noise coming from the camp, and both men turned to look. Jonas felt his jaw drop in horror to see every tent set ablaze.

"No!" he heard the captain shout as he ran off towards the flames.

Jonas was close on his heels until they skidded to a halt just outside the perimeter of the camp. He felt the heat of the blaze on his face and watched the billowing smoke rose high into the air. The he gasped as his eyes, following the smoke, fell upon a man hanging helplessly some ten feet in the air, held there by some unknown power. He saw the look of horror etched on the man's face as it was thrust into sharp relief by the light of the burning tents below him. Standing beneath the man, stood a dark figure whose features were shrouded under a long black cloak and hood. One of the figure's arms was outstretched towards the man in midair. In a swift motion, the figure dropped its arm and the man's entire body spasmed, then went limp. His body hung there for only a moment longer, then fell into the fires below and vanished.

Jonas turned to see the same shock on the captain's face that he felt, then he turned back only to find the dark figure had vanished too. He felt a tug on his sleeve, as the captain pulled him cautiously through an opening in the flames toward the midst of the camp. Jonas thought he heard shouts up ahead, then the captain stopped short again. He turned to see several Bordermen surrounding the dark figure. Two Bordermen attacked at once from opposite sides. Jonas gaped as both men were cut down by a single stroke of the intruder.

"XtaKal," Jonas heard the captain whisper as he drew his sword.

"Who?" Jonas asked, also drawing his sword.

He didn't hear the captain's answer as he tried to catch a glimpse of the intruder's sword, but it flew through the air so quickly that it remained a dark blur. In seconds, all the remaining Bordermen had been cut down, then the figure turned to face the captain and Jonas.

"Stay behind me." Flint said, pushing Jonas back.

The figure stood staring at them menacingly, in the midst of the burning camp. Fear gripped Jonas's heart and he took a step backwards.

"You'll pay for the murder of my men, phantom!" The captain exclaimed, lunging at the intruder

The dark figure quickly raised its left hand, and the same unknown power caught Flint, stopping him dead in his tracks. Jonas starred up in horror as the captain dropped his sword and was hoisted into the air. The captain's hands were clawing at his throat as if some invisible hand was strangling him. He rose higher and higher into the air, and Jonas winced as he heard a loud snapping noise over roar of the fires. Jonas saw the figure drop its hand and the captain fell to the ground in a crumpled heap. Then the figure turned to Jonas, who stumbled backward and fell as terror gripped him. His sword fell to the ground with a clang and the world around him began to spin rapidly as the figure advanced on him. In the measure of a breath, Jonas felt the darkness swallow him up and he knew no more.

# 2

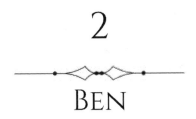

# BEN

"The answer is no, Ben."

The storage cellar rang with his father's angry voice. Benjamin Greymore glared back at his father, but he didn't dare argue. Though he could match his father's stubbornness, Jon Greymore was taller and stronger than most men. Even his personality was overwhelming at times. Ben, on the other hand, was shorter and skinnier than most and was quieter and more reserved. Yet he was resolved and stood his ground despite his disadvantage.

"They will never take you, Ben," his father continued, heatedly.

"You and Sir Eric were members of Ethriel's City Watch when you were my age," Ben stated plainly, trying to contain his own anger.

"I was stronger and tougher in my youth than you, son," His father retorted, angrily. "We both served during the Second War of Ascension and saw too much death and suffering. Sir Eric Teague was inducted into the Royal Guard because of his service, but I lost your mother because of my career choices. I will not lose you as well. Besides, the City Watch needs strong men, not skinny boys who've never even held a sword."

His father's words wounded Ben greatly, and his face fell as he hung his head. His father seemed to regret his harsh words and his expression softened slightly. He walked over and placed his hands on his son's shoulders, but Ben refused to look up at him.

"Look Ben, Eric is an honorable man, but a warrior's life is not what I want for you," His father said, consolingly. "That's why I left that life behind and we opened this shop. Then your mother died..." he trailed off. Ben saw in his father's eyes the same sorrow and regret that he always did when he spoke of her. His father shook his head and continued. "I had hoped that you might one day you and I could run this shop together."

Ben didn't answer. He had no desire to work in some storefront for the rest of his life. He wanted adventure, but his father just couldn't understand. There was a long, awkward pause, then his father turned to go.

"Since you're already down here, stop standing there and move those sacks of crates over to the far corner." His father called over his shoulder as he climbed the stairs to the ground floor. "Once your done, you can come up front and help me with today's orders."

His father left, and Ben stood brooding silently over his father's blatant insults and condescension. After a few moments, he shook his head as he fought back tears of frustration. He stomped over to the crates and slammed his fist against the topmost lip, then winced as his hand began to throb. Cursing, Ben began sorting through the crates and restacking them over in the far corner. They were heavy and he had to carry them one at a time so it took a while.

When he finally climbed the stairs and entered the main store, his father glared at him reproachfully. Another man was standing next to him who was taller than his father. The man had a short brown beard and wore a long white cloak and tunic with a shirt of chainmail underneath; a sword was at his side. On his chest was a small badge bearing a golden sword pointed down in the center of a crimson field bordered in gold—the badge and symbol of the

Royal Guard.

"About time, Ben," His father said, causing a new surge of anger and embarrassment to rise in Ben. "You remember Sir Eric Teague?"

He and Sir Eric exchanged nods.

"We're headed for the tavern for a bite. Tend the counter while I'm out."

His father and Sir Eric walked out of the store, leaving Ben behind feeling sulky. He'd just sat down on a stool behind the large counter when several young men entered the store, led by a large rotund boy with arms the size of large tree limbs.

"Look who it is, guys," said the larger boy. "It's wimpy Benjie. Still dreaming of joining the City Watch, Benjie?"

"What do you want, Jacob?" Ben asked, glaring as the other boys laughed. "On an errand for your mommy?"

The boys stopped laughing and Jacob glared menacingly at Ben.

"You watch your tongue, Greymore, or I'll have to knock some sense into you." The larger boy retorted, cracking his knuckles. "Now get me a sack of potatoes."

"Two bronze shields." Ben said sourly, dropping the sack on the counter.

Jacob tossed the two small coins so that they fell behind the counter and onto the floor.

"Oops," the large boy said, with mock remorse. "Guess you'll have to pick those up, Benjie."

Ben grumbled to himself as he bent over to retrieve the coins, then suddenly he felt someone kick him from behind sending his head smashing into the shelves. Ben's head spun and waves of pain surged through his throbbing skull. He got to his feet, somewhat dazed, as the other boys' laughter filled his ears. As he stood there rubbing his throbbing head, something in Ben snapped.

He leapt over the counter, and tackled Jacob. The impact sent them flying into the other boys and they all fell to the floor. Jacob righted himself first and grabbed Ben by his tunic, throwing him into the counter. Ben crumpled in a heap, his head spinning even more. He heard a booming voice, which was unintelligible in his dazed state, the sound of many moving feet leaving the store, then the sound of heavy steps moving closer. Ben shook his head and looked up to see the angry face of his father glaring down at him.

"And you think you could make it in the City Watch." He growled, stooping to lift Ben up off the floor. "You can't even handle a bunch of rowdy boys."

Ben shook his aching head and saw Sir Eric standing by the door assessing the situation with a look of disappointment. Though Ben didn't know the man well, Sir Eric's opinion of him was important because of his membership in the Royal Guard. He felt instant embarrassment at his lack of fighting skills and hung his head in shame.

"What hope can I have of you being able to manage this store without me one day, when you can't even handle it for a few minutes? Those boys would have pummeled you if I hadn't needed to return for my money pouch. If you can't even defend yourself, what hope do you have in joining the City Watch?"

There was a long pause before his father spoke again.

"Pick up this mess and watch the store. See if you can't handle an hour without me."

His father walked out, shaking his head, and Ben found himself alone once again. His mind was racing and his temper fuming. His mind was made up. He was leaving, tonight.

❋　❋　❋　❋

Ben awoke with a start. The night was waning and a faint light was growing. He rolled out of bed and pulled on his clothes. The residence above the shop was silent, save his father's snoring coming from the adjacent room. Ben quietly gathered his few belongings into a small sack and closed it tight. He paused for a moment to survey the room. A sudden movement near the chair in the corner caught his eye. Ben turned and saw the silhouette of a man seated there. Ben started, but the man held up a hand and removed his hood to reveal a pleasant face. The man had brown hair that fell to his shoulders, a short brown beard, and Ben could have sworn the man's face glowed slightly in the dark room. His eyes were brown and there was a kindness in them.

"Who are you?" Ben whispered.

"You and I have never met, but your father has spoken of me on occasion. You are Benjamin Greymore, son of Jon Greymore."

It was a statement and not a question, yet Ben nodded slowly.

"You are currently running away to join the City Watch."

Again a statement which Ben felt obligated to confirm. He was unable to hide the shock on his face.

"Why?"

"What?"

"Why are you running away?"

"I want a different life than the one my father wants for me." Ben managed after a long silence.

"You want adventure?"

Ben nodded.

"But your father wants you to be a shopkeeper."

He nodded again.

"And your solution is to run away?"

"I don't have a choice," Ben answered, shaking his head.

"There is always a choice, Ben," the man said, his voice rising slightly. "You always have a choice."

"You would have me stay!" Ben said, turning away in exasperation. "Who are you to ask such questions? I won't stay and waste my life as some shopkeeper."

"You have a choice to make, Ben," the man said kindly. "And remember that your choices also carry consequences. Not only for you, but for your father as well."

"What consequences?" Ben asked.

He turned back, but the chair was empty. Ben looked quickly about the room, but he was alone. He stood rooted for a long moment, questioning what had just happened and even his sanity.

As he did so, the man's words eched in his mind. At length, he made his choice. He opened his bedroom window, pulled his sack of belongings over his shoulder, and crawled out into the semi-darkness.

It was freezing out in the dark street. There was little wind between the buildings, but the still air was cold enough to bite even through the layers Ben wore. Ignoring the cold, he ran down the empty street leading to the main road leading to the city gates, known as the Citadel Way. He paused at the corner to stare at a poster hanging on the street post.

*City Watch Recruiting*
*Eligible candidates report to the East Gate at dawn on the 28th*
*Knowledge of swordsmanship a must.*

Ben turned and gazed up and down Citadel Way, taking in the wonder of the city of Ethriel. He'd heard his father and Sir Eric speaking of the history of the city many times.

The city itself was built into the side of Mount Earod and was divided into three levels. Above Ben stood the Citadel, which sat a few hundred feet below the mountain's summit on a wide plateau that extended out from the mountain to overlook the city below. Upon this plateau stood the Citadel of Ethriel. The Citadel itself consisted of the old fortress, originally built by Aden Aurelia long ago, and the new great hall and courtyard built later when the Aurelians ascended the throne and the capital moved to Ethriel over two hundred years ago. A forty-foot high wall ran around the perimeter of the plateau, broken by a number of high towers that gave Citadel defenders the clear advantage over any enemy that broke through the rest of the city's defenses.

Below the Citadel sat the upper city, where most of the city's more affluent people lived and worked. The lower city extended from the outer city walls, which ran like a great ring around the perimeter of the mountain and up the side of Mt. Earod. The Citadel Way was the main thoroughfare through the city, running from the main gates of the Citadel down to the main city gates far below. The Citadel Way was well traveled by the cities inhabitants and visitors, but unbeknownst to even the most observant citizen, there existed many hidden guard posts and defenses all along the road.

Ben, realizing he was wasting time, took off down the Citadel Way. After everything that'd happened yesterday, Ben was not going to miss this opportunity. The gates were just beginning to open when Ben finally skidded to a halt in front of the gatehouse. A group of young men were already gathered there, and to Ben's dismay, one of the boys turned out to be Jacob.

"You must be a sucker for punishment, Benjie," Jacob said, gleefully. Several other boys snickered, but Ben simply glared back defiantly.

"What?" Jacob said advancing on Ben, and shoving him. "No witty retort?"

Ben stumbled backwards, but didn't fall. Gritting his teeth, he ran at Jacob, who simply stepped aside. Ben lost his footing and fell face first into the cobblestone street. His eyes closed from the pain, but his ears heard the ruckus laughter of the other boys die away abruptly. He opened his eyes and saw a pair of booted feet. He lifted his gaze to the cold face staring down menacingly at him. Ben scrambled to his feet and backed away, taking in the grim figure before him. The man was stocky and his arms and legs were the width of tree limbs. He had a long bushy brown beard and mustache and wore simple blue garb, a sword at his side, and a long blue cape that distinguished him as a member of the City Watch.

"Stop staring at me, boy, and join the others," the man growled. His voice was gritty and deep. "Form ranks!"

Ben and the others obeyed, though their lines were sloppy. The others pushed and shoved Ben until he stood front and center. His knees were shaking slightly.

"Another sorry lot of boys instead of men," the man said, shaking his head. "My name is Saul Gunter, Captain of the City Watch, and I'm here to turn you sorry lot into a fighting force that can defend this city. Those of you who make it through training will be inducted into the Watch under one of my lieutenants. If one of you demonstrates exceptional skills, I may recommend you to the Royal Guard but I doubt that will happen with you lot."

Most of the boys were stunned into silence, but Ben heard Jacob whisper, "I wouldn't bet on Benjie here."

"You!" The captain shouted, pointing at Jacob. "Bring your sorry backside up here."

Ben had barely suppressed a smirk when he found Saul's cold eyes locked on him.

"You too, wee man," he said with a grin.

Ben joined Jacob in front of the other boys.

"Noticed you two seem to have a fondness for one another," the captain said, still grinning.

Ben and Jacob both opened their mouths to protest, but stopped short at a glare from Saul.

"Seeing as you two seem prepared to come to blows already, let's see how you fair in a real match. All of you follow me."

The captain led them past the guardhouse, through the gates, and turned towards a small cluster of buildings. In the midst of the buildings was a sandpit encircled by a wooden fence. The captain led the boys to the pit, and instructed them to line up along the fence. To Ben and Jacob, he ordered into the pit and then tossed a wooden practice sword at their respective feet.

"Pick up your weapon," he ordered, and both boys obeyed.

The practice sword was heavy in Ben's grip, but he was determined not to show weakness.

"First to land a blow with his sword wins the match." The captain said with a wicked grin.

Ben's heart was pounding. This was his one chance to prove his worth and to show his father that he could be more than a shopkeeper.

"Fight!"

Jacob had already started forward before the captain had finished speaking. Ben brought up his sword just in time to block the initial blow, but Jacob was already swinging at Ben's legs. He jumped just as Jacob's swing missed his heels. Ben backed away quickly, but Jacob was right in his wake. Ben hit the wooden fence and rolled to the left as Jacob's blow glanced off the fence. He ran to the middle of the pit, but Jacob was right on his heels. Ben took on what he thought was a defensive stance as Jacob brought his sword up for a skull-crushing blow. Ben lunged forward, tackling Jacob to the ground, but Jacob knocked him off and grabbed Ben by the neck.

"Enough!" The captain's voice boomed over the tumult.

Jacob released Ben, who fell to the ground gasping.

"Sorriest display I've ever seen," He growled, as he entered the pit and he hoisted Ben to his feet. "Rematch in two week, loser goes home. Hit the barracks!"

Ben was still trying to catch his breath. He glanced at the group of boys leaving the pit area. He saw Jacob turn and shoot him a malevolent grin as they walked away.

*The loser goes home.* The captain's voice echoed in Ben's mind. This was his one and only chance to prove that he was more than the son of a merchant. He had two weeks to improve his skills and beat Jacob. Ben's face contorted with resolve as he stared at Jacob's back and muttered, "I will not be going home."

# 3

# MADDY

As Maddy emerged from the shelter of the trees, a powerful gust of cold wind greeted her. It was a freezing, biting wind that froze her to the bone. She pulled her hood over her light brown hair, held her cloak tightly around her, and stepped out on the road leading to the village of Windham. The ground fell steadily before her giving a grand view of the village below, which lay in a cove nestled along the north shore of the Bay of Ryst. It was a cloudy afternoon, giving the village a bleak look. Long columns of smoke drifted above the small cluster of houses and shops in the village below.

Despite the cold, Maddy could hardly suppress the smile spreading across her face, as her thoughts drifted to her tryst with her beloved David, which had ended only moments ago. She felt elated and as light as a cloud. She could hardly keep from skipping down the road as she went, her feeling of elation so strong. Even the bleak weather and cold wind could not ruin her good spirits.

It was this feeling that carried her into the village towards a large house west of the town square. It was made of the same gray stone as most of the other houses were, but it was much larger, being two stories tall and twice as wide as any other. Maddy was still caught in a daydream as she crossed the threshold. As she closed the large oaken front doors, two hands reached out and shook her back to reality. Maddy was spun on the spot to see her mother glaring down at her. She was a middle aged woman with graying hair tied up in a tight bun and the same light brown eyes as Maddy.

"Where have you been!" She demanded in a loud shrill.

Maddy's smile quickly faded to be replaced with an expression of guilt. Her gaze fell under the scowl of her mother.

"Answer me Madeline!" Her mother shouted in barely restrained anger. "Were you off with that blacksmith's apprentice again?"

"His name is David," Maddy muttered, indignantly.

"What has addled your brains, child?" Her mother continued, enraged. "I forbade you from seeing that boy, didn't I?"

"I love him, mother!" Maddy shouted, finding her voice. "Don't you remember what it was like to be in love?"

Her mother's eyes narrowed, her nostrils flared, and Maddy's hope to garner sympathy was quickly dashed.

"Do you intend to ruin us, Madeline? You know we are coming to the end of our money. If your father was here..." Her mother fell silent for a moment, then collecting herself she grabbed Maddy by the arm and led her to the stairs leading to the second floor. "You will go up to your room, quickly freshen up, and then join me in the parlor."

"Why?" Maddy asked in protest.

"Just be quick," Her mother snapped.

Maddy turned and flew up the stairs, slamming the door behind her. She crossed the room and flung herself onto her bed and sobbed into her pillow. It just wasn't fair. Why couldn't her mother understand? She and David were meant for each other. Couldn't she remember how that felt? Had father been gone so long that her mother had forgotten what love felt like?

There was a loud thud. Maddy's eyes jerked towards the

window, the shutters were closed to keep out the cold. There was another thud and Maddy rose and went to the window. She threw open the shutters and saw a young man standing below. A smile broke over her tearstained face as she recognized the shoulder length brown hair and scruffy face, which bore a crooked smile. His eyes were brown and full of warmth. Maddy's heart leapt as she called to her beloved David.

"What are you doing here?" She whispered.

"I couldn't be away from you, Maddy," he called, making no effort to be quiet.

"Shhh," Maddy hissed. "If mother finds you here…"

"I don't care," David called. "I have to be with you."

"Madeline! What is taking you so long?" came her mother's voice from the hall.

"Go!" She cried, closing the shutters. "I'll see you tonight."

"Madeline!" came her mother's voice again.

"Coming!" She cried, running over to the water basin by the door.

She washed her face, removed her traveling cloak and quickly dressed. She pulled her long brown hair back, took a long look in the mirror, and then went downstairs where her mother was waiting for her by the entrance to the parlor.

She stood letting her mother survey her, and braced for a stern critique. After a few long moments, Maddy's mother simply placed a hand on her cheek.

"I love you, Madeline," she said, then turned to open the door. Maddy was so taken aback by this sudden statement of affection that she failed to register who was seated on their parlor couch. As they entered, Maddy did a subtle double take as Baron Gethrin Windham rose from his seat, flanked by two guards. Maddy glanced at the swords, thankfully still sheathed in their scabbards. A sudden fear gripped her heart and she had the momentary desire to flee.

"Baron Windham," her mother said with a slight bow. "May I present my daughter, Madeline Brice."

The man needed no introduction. Everyone around Windham knew the baron. Maddy's eyes followed the long scar running down the left side of the baron's otherwise handsome face. He was middle-aged, clean-shaven and wore his light brown hair short like most military men. His sharp blue eyes seemed to pierce Maddy, as if they could see through her. She found this very unsettling, but was unable to look away. This might explain her momentary forgetfulness in courtesy as she stared back into those deep blue eyes. A soft cough from her mother drew her attention. The severe look on her mother's face awoke her from her musings. She quickly remembered herself and curtsied. The baron inclined his head and moved to take her hand.

"A pleasure," he said, lightly brushing his lips on her hand. His voice was soft and kind.

"T-Thank you, my lord," was all Maddy could muster.

"I was hoping I could convince you and your mother to dine with me at Windham Manor this evening," he said with a smile.

Maddy was dumbstruck.

"We would be honored," her mother answered, not waiting for Maddy to answer.

"I will see you this evening then?" He asked, looking at Maddy, who nodded wide-eyed. "Wonderful. I will send a coach for you both. Until then." He kissed her hand again and her mother led the baron and his men to the door.

"An invitation to dine at Windham Manor," her mother sang as she returned to the parlor. "You know what this means, Madeline?"

Maddy didn't answer.

"It means the baron has taken a fancy to you. You could be the next Baroness of Windham," she continued with a look of utmost glee. "We must get you ready for tonight. I want you to look your best."

She took Maddy gently by the arm and led her bewildered daughter back up to her room. As they climbed the stairs, all that Maddy could think was: *what about David?*"

＊　＊　＊　＊

It was nearing dusk when the coach arrived at the front of the Brice house. Maddy peered out into the cold half-light which hid none of the coach's elegance. A beautiful white carriage with gold trim. Even the wheels and runners were gold. The side closest to her bore the Windham family crest. The driver and two footmen were dismounting and busying themselves with preparing the coach. The driver moved to check the horses, while the footmen checked the coach itself. It was then that Maddy realized that their efforts were for her and her mother. A startling realization that a man so powerful as the baron would take such concern for them.

After staring for a few more minutes, Maddy pulled back from the window and went to the hall mirror. She hardly recognized the girl looking back at her. She was wearing a pale blue dress that her mother had pulled out of her own closet; a family heirloom that somehow remained in style despite its age. Her long brown hair was pulled back in a three plait braid that swept back from the front on one side over the shoulder on the opposite side. Blue ribbons were braided into the hair to accent her dress. Her face bore makeup, a luxury that her mother coveted and only begrudgingly shared with her daughter for this occasion. She pursed her lips and, through half-closed eyes, gazed at herself seductively, then suppressed a small giggle at how ridiculous she felt.

"You look perfect," came a voice from behind her.

Maddy turned and saw her mother standing beside the stairs. She gaped at her mother who was wearing an emerald green dress with her graying hair tied up in an elegant bun. Maddy had never seen her look so beautiful. The most striking thing was her mother's smile, which seemed to take ten years off her face. Maddy beamed back at her.

There was a knock at the door and her mother crossed the room and opened it. The baron's footman bowed and ushered them outside, helping each of them into the coach. They were soon on their way, rolling through the streets of Windham and drawing stares from onlookers. Maddy waved to the passersby at first, but her mother pulled her back inside with a stern look. They soon left the village behind, following a winding lane that led to a large hedge that towered ten feet on either side of the lane. At the far end lay a gatehouse with several guards standing watch. The coach paused for only a moment before they were waved through and Maddy first beheld Windham Manor.

It was the largest house she'd ever seen. Sitting on a large hill overlooking the surrounding lands, the two-story building was constructed of brownish stone with battlements running atop its length and width. Maddy gaped at the grandeur of the manor, marveling at the real glass windows and large oaken front doors, where the coach came to a stop and the footmen helped them out.

They stood before the imposing front doors for a moment, noting the intricate carvings etched upon them, then they were led inside. A servant took them through the foyer and down a hallway decorated with many large portraits and paintings. When they reached the far end, two more servants were waiting to open the doors that led into a long dining hall. Maddy forgot all decorum as she gaped unapologetically, overwhelmed at the grandeur of the hall, in which sat a long oaken dining table which ran the length of the room. Two ornate chandeliers hung overhead but remained unlit, leaving the room lit only by a roaring fire in the large stone fireplace directly across from the door in which they stood. The fireplace was flanked on either side with stone griffins. Maddy only had a moment to take in all of this before the servant closest to her announced their arrival. She glanced down the long table to see Baron Windham, who stood upon their announcement. She saw that he was smiling and gesturing to the two seats on either side of him. The servant led them down and helped them into their seats.

The meal felt awkward to Maddy. The food was excellent, but she found she had little to contribute to the conversation. Her mother filled the air with flowery words, thanking the baron and praising everything from the food to the wine to the décor. When the baron turned to her, Maddy answered briefly, but found his gaze unnerving.

After dessert, the baron interrupted her mother, who was going on about the beauty of the chandeliers, with a strange request.

"Madam Brice, may I have your leave to speak with your daughter in private?"

"Yes, of course, Baron Windham," her mother replied. Maddy saw her mother's eyes twinkling with suppressed glee.

The baron stood and moved behind Maddy's chair. "May I?"

Maddy couldn't help but blush with awkward embarrassment as she nodded. She stood, took the baron's arm, and he led her out of the Great Hall and into the hallway decorated with portraits. She stole a glance back at her mother, pleadingly to call her back, but her mother merely smiled approvingly. The servants closed the door and Maddy found herself alone in the hallway with the baron. There was a long awkward silence before the baron spoke.

"I must confess something to you, Madeline," he began, and Maddy noticed his voice was shaking. "I have never married. All around you are portraits of my ancestors."

He walked away from her and faced the portrait of a man in military uniform. The baron stared up at the portrait for so long that Maddy wondered if he'd forgotten about her. *Was he nervous?*

"My father," he said at length, gesturing at the portrait. "A brave man and war hero. A man I've tried to emulate."

"Everyone knows you fought at the last battle of the Second War of Ascension," Maddy interjected, and saw the baron involuntarily touch his scar. "Some might consider helping a king claim his throne is being a hero."

She heard the baron let out a long sigh.

"Some might," he said, clearly unconvinced.

"Baron Windham…" she began.

"Please call me Gethrin."

Maddy blanched. The baron came over and took her hand.

"Madeline, I will come to my point. I am alone here in this empty house and of all the women in Windham, I have come to appreciate your beauty and spirit. You've grown into a fine woman. I know I am a stranger to you, but would you be willing to get to know me?"

She stared at him bewildered and unable to speak.

"I am hosting a party to celebrate the start of the new year in a few days. I would be honored if you and your mother would attend. You could even stay at the manor until the party."

He gazed expectantly at her until, feeling she had no other option, she nodded.

"Wonderful," he said, extending his arm. "Shall we tell your mother the good news?"

She took his arm and he led her back to the Great Hall. As they crossed the hall, Maddy glanced around at the portraits and wondered what she'd gotten herself into.

# 4

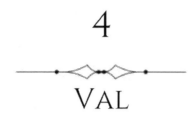

# VAL

"You've left me no choice but to kill you."

Val opened her eyes as the dark room swam in and out of focus. She tried to shake her head, but the movement caused her intense pain on the left side of her skull. She flexed her arms, but found that she couldn't move. She closed her eyes tight, as if she could force the pain away, then she reopened them and looked around. Val found herself in a dimly lit room, tied to a small wooden chair. Across from her sat her brother James, also bound to a chair. His face was beaten and bruised, and his right eye was swollen shut. Dried blood was caked to his otherwise handsome face.

"You keep trying to escape," said the same sinister voice. "If I tried to sell slaves that keep trying to escape, I'd go out of business."

Val looked up to see a middle-aged man, tall and thin. The man's sharp eyes were focused on her as he stroked his goatee, that looked like it had once been black but was now flecked with gray. The man stood over her, taking sips from a silver goblet and sneering at her. The man she knew to be Lord Silas Morgan, the infamous ruler of the city of Nenholm and the man who'd bought her and her brother a week ago.

"Since acquiring you both, I've had nothing but trouble. It's time to make an example of one of you." Lord Morgan nodded towards one of the men standing beside her brother, who took out a long knife and put it to her brother's throat.

"Wait!" Val said, struggling against her bindings. Her heart was pounding. "Wait, please!"

"You've left me no choice." Lord Morgan said with a sneer.

"No! Kill me instead! Please!" Val pleaded.

"No," groaned James.

"You would take your brother's place?" Lord Morgan's sharp eyes grew wide and an evil grin broke across his face.

Val nodded.

"Interesting," Lord Morgan answered, stroking his goatee for a long moment. "But I think not."

He nodded at the man with the knife, who made a quick movement, and her brother slumped forward in his chair. Val screamed so loudly that she woke herself up.

✳　✳　✳　✳

She sat bolt upright and glanced franticly around the room, only to realize that she was alone in a dark and dingy cell. She sat breathing hard and shaking all over, hugging her sides and shaking her head from side to side trying to empty her mind of the painful images and memories. This unfortunately only made her head ache. It had only been a few days since her brother had been murdered right in front of her. Ever since then, she'd been plagued with vivid dreams of the event. She closed her eyes tightly again, but nothing could make the images fade. Waves of sorrow and loss began to wash over her. Unable to keep it inside, Val began to weep softly. Her quiet sobs the only sound in the dark and silent cell.

A sudden noise behind the cell door to her right drew her attention. The door opened and a familiar face entered the cell. She rushed forward in blind rage, but Lord Morgan swatted her down like a fly. Falling backwards and hitting her head on the stone wall behind her, Val lay slumped over in a daze.

"Bring her," she heard Lord Morgan say as stars twinkled before her eyes.

A pair of rough hands grabbed her and hoisted her over a man's shoulder. She shook her head to clear it, as the man carried her through the door, down a dimly lit corridor, and out into the blinding sunlight of early morning. When her eyes finally adjusted to the light, she found that she was in a large courtyard enclosed by a high stone wall. A high gate sat on the far side with several guards posted. On this side of the courtyard stood a platform, which the man carrying her climbed onto and deposited her roughly in its center. She laid there for a moment, her body aching from the rough treatment. Gradually, she pushed herself up on her hands and knees and gazed about her surroundings. A large crowd was gathering before the platform, most of whose eyes were ogling her. She slowly got to her feet feeling very uncomfortable. She sensed someone come up beside her and place his hands on her shoulders. She flinched at the man's touch, and glanced around to see that it was Lord Morgan. Four guards stood, two on either side of Lord Morgan.

"Now," came his harsh voice in her ear. The smell of his breath nearly made her gag. "Perhaps you will bring a good price and I will finally profit from your purchase. So make yourself desirable."

He pushed her towards the front of the platform and stood beside her, addressing the crowd with a loud voice.

"Gentlemen," he said, smoothly. "As you know, I normally don't take a personal interest in the selling of my slaves, but I think you'll understand why I've made an exception. You've all come here today to purchase workers, but now I ask you, what of comfort?"

The crowd was alive and Val shuddered as all the men's eyes raked across her body lustfully. She glanced over to see Lord Morgan leering at her. She felt naked, though she was fully clothed.

"Who will start the bidding at eighty silver lions?"

Val did not wait for anyone to respond, but leapt from the platform into the crowd, crushing several people underneath her. Jumping to her feet, she pushed her way through the shocked onlookers towards the gate on the far side of the courtyard. She continued forcing her way through the crowd, yet as she did so she could hear shouting and felt hands try to grab her from behind. Val was undeterred, and upon reaching the gates she dove under the legs of the guards and sprinted up the street.

There was no looking back or stopping to catch her breath. She knew that the guards would be on her heels. Her only choice was to run. Heart was racing and legs begging to stop, Val forced her body onward, her long brown hair whipping behind her and her hazel eyes stinging with angry tears. Her only thought was escape. Nothing else mattered at the moment.

Leaving the gate far behind, she came to one of the main streets and found it crowded with people. Her legs pounded the road, pushing her forward as fast as possible. The street turned sharply to the left and as she neared the end Val attempted to round the corner at full speed. Her feet stumbled as she was unable to control her momentum and her inertia carried her headlong into a crowd of people, knocking several of them to the ground with her. Without hint of remorse or apology, she jumped to her feet and kept running, the yells of her pursuers loud in her ears.

Val darted around another corner and skidded to a halt as two more of Lord Morgan's men appeared at the other end of the street. She glanced around hastily searching for a place to hide. In front of her stood a tall, seemingly abandoned, building. Val hesitated for a moment, then jumped through the only open window.

Once inside, Val moved quickly through the semi-darkness trying to find a place to hide. Not finding a suitable place in the room she was in, she moved into the main hall just as the front door burst open and four of Lord Morgan's men entered the building. She moved backwards, but as she did so two hands grabbed her from behind. Val tried to call out, but a hand was clamped down on her mouth.

"Shh!" hissed her captor, and Val noted the voice was female.

Val was pulled further back into the room and behind an old dresser before her captor spoke again.

"In a moment, I'm going to release you but you must promise not to scream or run."

Val nodded quickly, and she felt the woman's hands release her. Val instinctively tried to dart away, but the other woman was too fast.

"Nope," she whispered, seizing Val and putting a dagger to her throat. "So much for your word. Give me one good reason not to kill you now."

Val stopped struggling and froze as she felt the cold metal against her throat.

"Now that's better," the woman whispered. "Now tell me, who are you and what are you doing here?"

"My name is Valentina," she answered, feeling honesty was her only option at this point. She swallowed, causing the dagger to cut into her slightly. She winced, but the other woman didn't remove the dagger so she continued. "I was trying to hide. There are men chasing me."

"Why are they chasing you?"

"I'm a slave. I was trying to escape." She answered, and felt the woman's grasp on her lessen.

Just then, Val's pursuers entered the room. The woman removed the dagger and darted forward from shadow to shadow. The group of men had separated to search the dark room and Val saw one of the men draw close to the woman's hiding place. There was a sudden movement and the man disappeared. Val gaped as the woman reappeared and moved quickly behind one of the other men and grabbed him. The woman subdued the man and moved him behind some furniture stacked in a corner. Val's other two pursuers seemed to realize the absence of their companions and moved warily toward the other side of the room. Val watched in amazement as the woman dispatched the remaining men in two fluid motions, and they collapsed to the floor.

Stunned, Val watched the woman move towards her and helped her to her feet.

"You okay?" she asked.

Val nodded then asked, "Who are you?"

"My name is Annet," the woman answered, curtly. "So what's your next move?"

Val stared back blankly. She hadn't thought that far forward.

"I see." Annet said, seeming to read Val's thoughts. "I suppose you belonged to one of the slavers. Ever since Silas Morgan was granted lordship of Nenholm, the city has become the center of the slave trade for the entire kingdom."

At the mention of Lord Morgan, Val was suddenly filled with anger and fear. *Did this woman save her only to sell her back to Lord Morgan?*

Again, seeming to read her mind, Annet said, "Don't worry. I have no intention of returning you to your previous owner. Under the previous ruler, Lord Nen, slavery was illegal, but now..." she trailed off for a moment, as if in deep thought, then turned back to ask, "Who was your previous owner if you don't mind me asking?"

"Lord Morgan," Val said, angrily. "He bought my brother and me from slavers out of Kusini."

"Kusini?" Annet said. The name clearly meant something to her, but before Val could ask, Annet cut her off. "So why didn't your brother come with you?"

"Lord Morgan killed him," Val said, looking down to hide her tears.

"I'm sorry," Annet said quickly.

Val shook her head as the tears burned and her face contorted with sorrow and rage. There was a long silence before Annet spoke again.

"Val, what if I told you that I am part of a group that fights against injustices like slavery?"

Val squinted up at her through tear filled eyes.

"And what if I told you, that if you joined this group you might have a chance at revenge on Silas Morgan and the rest of his ilk?"

Val wiped her eyes and stared up uncertainly. "You would help me? Why?"

"I was in a similar position to yours once upon a time," she answered, gravely. "I was rescued and given a chance. You remind me of how I was long ago."

There was a moment's silence, then Annet spoke again.

"I can train you so that one day you can exact revenge for your brother's murder," Annet replied with a knowing smile. "It's not an easy path, but it may provide you with your chance for vengeance."

Val got to her feet and took a deep breath. "When can we start?"

# 5

# SELENA

The slave market courtyard was packed and alive as the eager crowd anticipated the impending auction. Hidden amongst the enthusiastic onlookers, a young woman pulled her hood over her long, dark brown hair and tucked it carefully away. Beneath the hood, her piercing blue eyes scanned the crowd for a mark. The only part of her face that was visible was her narrow nose, full lips, and sharp chin. The young woman preferred to act in anonymity; refusing to trust her natural beauty to achieve her ends, but instead preferring to use her guile and honed skills.

As she continued scanning the crowd, her ears perked up upon hearing the jingling of a coin purse nearby. Finding the source of the sound, her eyes locked onto the belt of a portly man in a crimson robe. A sly smile appeared on her face as she moved slowly through the crowd toward her mark. The auctioneer was taking bids and she stole a glance at the platform where another young woman with brown hair and fierce hazel eyes was standing defiantly. She paused, as she felt a tinge of sympathy for the woman on the platform, but quickly pushed it aside and reacquired her target. The man had moved forward towards the platform and she followed, slipping behind the man and sliding a small knife out of her robes. Her heart was racing but her hand remained steady. The crowd pressed in on her as she slid down alongside and pressed the blade against the belt holding the heavy money purse. Her eyes widened in anticipation as the knife began to cut through the belt. *Halfway there.* There was a scream. She glanced up to see the young woman upon the platform leap into the unsuspecting crowd.

"Hey!" came a voice from above her. Her mark had caught her. The brief distraction from the platform had cost her dearly.

The young woman made to run as the man cried, "Thief!"

Many hands grabbed hold of her, forcing her to the ground. She tasted dirt as she was pinned and held face down on the ground. Her hood was pulled back, and she glanced up to see two guards standing over her and watched, with some satisfaction, their faces change from anger to amazement then to fear.

"Lady Selena Morgan?" The man in the crimson robe exclaimed.

Selena groaned and let her head fall back to the ground. *Here we go.*

✳   ✳   ✳   ✳

Selena stared up defiantly at the man seated upon a high dais. He was a tall, thin, middle-aged man, with sharp eyes, and a black goatee that was flecked with gray. He wore fine clothes, a black robe with a large red feather embroidered just below the left shoulder, and a large vibrant red hat with a long red feather sticking out of it. There, upon his white marble throne, sat the formerly infamous thief and mercenary Silas Morgan, her father, and now high lord of Nenholm. His face set in a scowl, and he was breathing hard in barely contained fury. He glared down at his daughter, but his disdain hardly affected Selena anymore.

Attempting to distract herself, Selena glanced around the extravagantly decorated great hall that her father had hung with tapestries. Each one depicted an achievement of one of the many men who'd bore the name Silas Morgan of the centuries. Every time she saw these it made her sick. The efforts her father made trying to rewrite their family history in order to hide his former life drove her crazy. She shook her head and turned back to the dais, still unable to suppress her feelings of revulsion as she gazed upon her father's "throne." Both the throne and the dais itself were made of white marble and were lavishly carved. Her father had shipped in the marble from somewhere else in order to emphasize his power and importance. Why a lord, even a high lord, needed a throne was beyond her. She found herself wondering if the king himself had such a throne.

Eventually, her father broke the silence.

"For generations the Morgan's have sired sons, passing on the name of Silas Morgan to continue the glorious legend. I admit in my youth I cared little for my role in carrying on that name, but now I find myself despairing for the loss of your mother and elder brother. You disappoint me, daughter."

"I know, I know, father," Selena said, rolling her eyes. "I disappoint you."

"Silence!" Silas hissed angrily. "I am at my wits' end, Selena. You were caught stealing in the market place. It would be one thing if you'd been successful, but you've been caught three times pick-pocketing. When I was your age…"

"I know father!" Selena shouted indignantly. She felt a rush of resentment and she fought back angry tears. She turned away so he would not see.

She heard her father descend from the dais and felt him place his hands on her shoulders.

"Daughter, what am I to do with you?" He asked, his voice noticeably softened.

She refused to meet her father's eyes as she fought back the tears. She would not give him the satisfaction of seeing her weep.

At length, her father released her and returned to his seat atop the dais. He snapped his fingers and Selena looked up to see a middle-aged man in chainmail appear from the shadows. He had blond hair and brown, shrewd eyes. He was tall, strong, and his face was stoic. Selena knew this man at once and the mere sight of him sent waves of loathing rippling through her very being.

"You remember Raynor Kesh," Silas said with a gesture at the newcomer.

"You mean your personal bounty hunter?" Selena spat angrily.

"He will now be your constant companion," Silas said with a sly smile, then turned to address the man beside his seat. "Kesh, wherever she goes, you are to be her shadow."

"Yes, my Lord." Kesh replied in a deep voice.

She stared incredulously from her father to Kesh and back.

"Please escort my daughter to her chambers," Silas ordered. "And see that she remains there until the party."

Selena saw Kesh incline his head and descend the steps towards her.

"Oh yes," Selena said, her voice full of resentment. "The famous Silas Morgan's New Years' Eve party. I'm sure you're expecting a great turn out. Tell me, father, how much did you have to pay for people to turn up this year?"

Her father glared at her, but did not respond.

"This way, Lady Selena," Kesh said, with a stern look.

She smirked at him and turned to go. Her father didn't understand his daughter at all if he thought locking her in her chambers and placing a bounty hunter on her around the clock would deter her from doing whatever she wanted. Perhaps she would crash his little party. After all, what's a Morgan without a little mayhem?

❋ ❋ ❋ ❋

As the midnight hour neared, Selena climbed out her bedroom window and descended the makeshift rope she'd made out of her bed sheets onto the stone floor of the courtyard. She glanced up for only a moment, then darted into the shadows cast by the great hall. She cautiously peered up through one of the windows, then her face fell. The hall was empty. Had her father cancelled the party? As she hid in the shadows, still peering through the window into the dark hall, a sudden thought crossed her mind. Her father often left his treasured hat lying on his "throne." She bit her lip in excitement, as a wicked smile crossed her face at the thought of what fun it would be to steal that stupid hat and shred the feather.

She crouched down and moved to the side door, pulling it open just enough to slide inside, then pulled it closed behind her. It was nearly pitch black inside the hall and it took a moment for her eyes to adjust. She cast her gaze about, and saw the vague outline of the dais looming up before her on her right. Moving slowly through the darkness, she had to use her feet and outstretched hands to feel her way forward. Eventually Selena reached the foot of the dais, stubbing her foot against the marble steps. Wincing slightly, she made her way up the marble steps until she stood before the throne.

Her heart was pounding and a smile spread across her face as she stooped and felt around the seat of the throne. Her right hand touched something leathery and she stopped. It was her father's hat. Just as her hands grasped the hat's brim, the great hall's doors burst open and light poured in all the way to the dais. With seconds to hide, she darted across the dais and dove behind one the tapestries. Peering out from behind the tapestry, she saw several servants run ahead and light the chandeliers as a slew of men entered all wearing black robes.

Her eyes narrowed as she recognized the man in front, leading the others as her father. Silas Morgan led the group to the foot of the dais, then ascended to his seat and placed his hat upon his head. Selena glanced around at the others, recognizing many of them.

"I still don't know why we couldn't meet in Farodhold," she heard Peter Astley complain. "It's the midpoint for all of us."

"My Lord Astley," said Lord Alaster Warde, calmly. "We all agreed that meeting in Nenholm would draw the least attention."

"And why have we been summoned in the first place?" Astley asked, irritated.

Selena was intrigued. Though she loathed politics, she did wonder why so many lords would gather here in secret. Astley, Warde, and her father were high lords, members of the Council of Lords who advised the king himself. She watched attentively as her father rose from his seat to address the room, wondering if perhaps the knowledge she gained here would profit her later.

"My fellow lords, I have asked for this meeting to deliver grievous news." He paused for effect, drawing an eye roll from his daughter hidden in the shadows. "You have all no doubt heard that the kingdom of Eddynland was invaded some days ago by some unknown enemy. What you may not have heard is that this enemy has destroyed the capital of Eddynland and that the entire royal family has been massacred."

Selena gasped, as did many of the lords listening.

"Eddynland has fallen, and Alethia is next," continued Silas. "And what has our king done to answer this threat—called a meeting of the Council of Lords to 'discuss things.' Our lands are threatened with war and we are to leave them and travel halfway across the kingdom to 'discuss things.'"

There was a general murmuring of discontent from the crowd below him.

"We need strength in this time of fear and uncertainty," Silas said, with some gusto.

"And who would you have instead of the king, my Lord Morgan? You?" Astley asked, snidely.

"My Lord Astley, I do not aspire to such office," Silas retorted smoothly. "I recommend Lord Warde to replace our weak king."

All eyes, including Selena's, turned to Lord Warde, who looked uncomfortable.

"Lord Morgan speaks out of turn," Warde said, his words coming quick and with some anxiety. "I've known Corin Aranethon since the Second War of Ascension. I chose to support him over the usurper Noliono. He was decisive and strong for several years afterward, but more recently our king has demonstrated indecision and weakness."

"So what are you saying, Lord Warde?" growled Astley

"I am saying that I am reluctant to call for the king's removal."

There was a murmuring of dissent and disapproval, but Lord Warde cut them off.

"However, as Lord Marshal of the South, I have decided that certain preparations must be made. As such, I call for all southern forces to be mustered and brought to Farodhold no later than two weeks from now."

"And if the king objects?" asked Lord Astley.

"We will not allow this dark army to invade our kingdom unchallenged," responded Lord Warde, hotly. "We will defend the south. If the king wants to join us at Farodhold, I will follow him into the battle. If not…" he trailed off, as if unwilling to finish the thought.

"If not," interjected Silas with a smile, "we may need a new king."

"If and when, Lord Morgan," Lord Warde said, with a finality that brought the meeting to an end.

The other lords nodded their assent and began filing out of the hall until it was just her father, Lord Warde, and a tall dashing man with sandy brown hair and eyes whom Selena did not know. When the doors closed, the three began to speak in whispers that Selena could barely hear.

"Lord Warde, may I introduce Kaven Ciles," her father gestured to the stranger. "He leads the Grey Company."

"Mercenaries? What do we need with mercenaries?" Lord Warde asked, rather abruptly.

"I thought it prudent in case we need to create 'options,'" Silas said, slyly.

"My men are already encamped outside of Fairhaven on the south side of the River Waterdale," Kaven interjected. "Lord Morgan has suggested that a night raid against the city might cause its people to support your intervention."

"With Fairhaven threatened, the king will have to support you or lose face with the other lords," Silas added.

"Silas, what is your scheme?" Lord Warde demanded loudly, his voice echoing in the empty hall.

"My Lord Warde," Silas responded, with mock innocence. "My only concern is the security of the kingdom."

"Indeed." Lord Warde said gruffly. It was clear from his tone that he did not believe Silas. "As long as that is true, we act in accord."

Lord Warde left the hall, and Silas turned to Kaven. Her father whispered something in Kaven's ear, who nodded, and they both left.

Selena stood for a moment, considering what she'd just heard, then slid from behind the tapestry and crossed the hall towards the side door. If her father was plotting treachery and war was coming, she wanted no part in it. There was only one option and that was escaping. She'd flee to the north and from there...

Her thought process was broken by a hand grabbing her from behind. She spun around and a looked up, horrified, as the face of Raynor Kesh glared down at her.

# 6

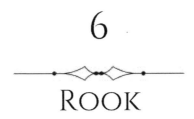

# ROOK

The night was dark and dismal. The cold wind raced across the frozen river Waterdale and howled against the tiny one-roomed cabin nestled on the Eastern Woodlands' western edge. Inside the cabin was a bed in the corner, a small wooden table with two chairs, and scarcely anything else. Dominating the room was a large stone hearth. A tall, grim-faced man with dark brown eyes and hair flecked with gray, sat before the hearth stoking the small fire and tugging his cloak tighter around himself. It was a truly bitter cold night. For the man sitting before the fire, it was a night he would not soon forget.

Jarod Rook, just Rook to those that knew him, had never seen a colder winter in his life. He replaced the fire poker next to the hearth and rubbed his hands together as he held them close to the flames. Staring into the fire, his mind drifted back into other memories from long ago. Consoling memories from a time when his heart was full of pride and ambition, and the winter was not so bleak and bitter. He let out a dark chuckle as his mind reached back to when he was still a member of the Guardians of the Citadel under King Greyfuss Aurelia. It now seemed like a lifetime ago. His face broke into a small grin as he remembered the glory and prestige that came with his posting to Ethriel, the capital of Alethia, but his mood quickly turned sour as he also remembered the murder of King Greyfuss and the disbanding of the Guardians under the new king.

His eyes grew hot and filled with angry tears as the memory of his life in Ethriel came rushing into his mind—a life that included his wife and his future as a privileged member of the king's court. Looking about his meager one-room cabin, his anger burned because he'd been reduced to living like this. Guilt and regret were his constant companions.

For a long time, Rook sat brooding over his losses and regrets. A sharp knock on the door called Rook back from his musings on the past and his attention rushed back to the present. This cabin was remote and there were villages or farms this side of the Waterdale River. His heart was filled with anxiety and his eyes glanced about for something to defend himself. He reached for the closest thing, the fire poker, and moved cautiously to the window beside the door. *Who could be at his door at this hour and in this weather?* He quietly pushed open the shutter and peered through the darkness as the figure of a young man came into view. The young man was wearing simple clothes and a green traveling cloak. Rook knew that garb anywhere. This young man was a member of the Bordermen, defenders of the border between Donia and Alethia, but what was he doing here at this time of night? Rook moved to the door and opened it a crack.

"Who's there?" he growled, peering out at the young man.

The young man started, but quickly moved forward towards the door, a look of desperation on his face.

"Please," the young man gasped. "Please let me in, sir."

"Who are you?" Rook grunted.

"My name is Jonas Astley. I'm a member of the Bordemen," He said, through chattering teeth.

"Peter Astley's son?"

"Y-yes," The young man answered, shivering and looking surprised. "Do you know my father?"

"I've heard of him," Rook lied, with a sudden desire to kick himself. "What are you doing out here?"

"Please, will you let me in, sir," Jonas continued to plead.

Rook eyed him suspiciously for a moment, then opened the door. He watched the young man dart inside and rush over to the fire. Eyeing him suspiciously, Rook closed the door and joined him.

"So, what are you doing here?"

"I was with a company of Bordermen under Captain Flint. We were encamped ten miles from here along the other side of the Eastern Woodlands," Jonas began, rubbing his hands profusely. "We were attacked--"

"Attacked!" Rook exclaimed "By whom? Has Donia invaded?"

"I don't know who it was, but everyone in the company was killed except me."

"How many enemy soldiers attacked."

"One."

"One!"

"Just one. A man dressed in a black hood and cloak," Jonas replied.

Rook watched the young man's gaze fall and a look of horror and shame crossed his face as he related the events leading him to Rook's door. There was no sign of deceit. Throughout the young man's tale, Rook's feeling of anxiety grew. When they reached the point when the captain identified the attacker as XtaKal, Rook's heart began to race and his mouth fell open in shock.

"So, this hooded figure lifted your captain up in the air and choked him to death without ever touching him?"

Jonas nodded, still staring blankly at the flames.

"And the captain called him XtaKal?"

Jonas nodded again.

Rook sat silently for a moment, then stood up quickly.

"Well, then there's only one thing to do." He said, grabbing Jonas by the shirt and hauling him towards the door.

"What are you doing?" Jonas exclaimed.

"I moved out here to escape all the chaos, yet it still manages to find its way to my door," Rook replied, opening the door and tossing the young man out into the cold. "I want no part of it. Take your troubles elsewhere."

"Please," Jonas began, but Rook slammed the door and locked it.

He turned back to the fire, but started as he realized he was not alone. A man in a gray cloak was seated by the fire, his hood pulled up over his head. Rook stood rooted to the spot, his fists clinched and his face contorted with rage as memories from twenty years ago rushed forward into his mind.

"You!"

The man turned and pulled back his hood, revealing a pleasant face. The man had brown hair that fell to his shoulders, a short brown beard, and Rook would have sworn the man's face glowed slightly. His eyes were brown and there was a kindness in them. This though only incensed Rook more.

"Yes, I am here."

"After all these years of silence, you come to me now!" Rook shouted, shaking with anger.

"I've spoken to you many times," the man replied calmly. "You just failed to listen."

"The last time I listened to you, I lost my wife!"

"We both know that is not the whole truth," the man said, looking at Rook sternly. "Your wife was taken from you because of your decisions and your actions. Actions that I warned you not to taken."

Rook stood for a moment, silently fuming before responding.

"What do you want from me?" he demanded, closing his eyes and fighting to contain his anger.

"I want you to help that young man."

"Jonas Astley? Why?" Rook asked.

"He told you that XtaKal had returned."

Rook stared silently at the man.

"You know what that means for the kingdom."

"What does that have to do with Jonas? Or me for that matter?"

"Help him, Rook, and you may learn something new about your wife."

"My wife is dead!" Rook spat, angrily.

"No, she is not."

"What do you mean?" Rook asked, incredulously.

"Help him, Rook, and you will help yourself and others as well."

"No, not without more answers!" Rook shouted, but the man vanished before his eyes. "No!" He yelled, running over to where the man had been seated. Then, turning to the ceiling he yelled, "You are not doing this to me again! I trusted you and look where it led me! It's your fault she's dead! She *is* dead, isn't she? Answer me!"

Rook fell to his knees, unable to hold back the sobs.

"Why do you do this to me?" He asked softly, his face downcast as tears flowed from his eyes. "Answer me, please."

✳ ✳ ✳ ✳

An hour later, a reluctant yet resigned Rook found himself wandering around the dark woods, searching for the young man, Jonas Astley. He'd dressed in haste, only changing into a thicker cloak, grabbing his bow and quiver and hunting knife, and set out into the bitter cold. He'd lit a torch, but the wind had snuffed it out almost at once, leaving him to search the forest in the dark. If he'd not feared the boy might freeze to death or be killed by one of the roving wolf packs, Rook might have waited for daylight. As it was, he trudged through the underbrush with only a glimmer of hope of finding the boy.

He searched for what seemed like hours without any sign of the boy. As he continued his search, he felt his anxiety rising but could not figure out why. Then, without warning, the howling wind fell silent and still. Rook's eyes darted around, unnerved by the sudden change. He made for a nearby grove of trees that were grouped tighter than the surrounding forest. He moved amongst them and peered around. To his right came a soft rustling noise that he would not have heard had the wind not suddenly fallen silent. Rook's eyes moved from tree to tree, searching for the source. Within the gloom, something even darker moved. Like a shadow that detached itself from the blackness, a dark cloaked figure emerged and moved towards Rook, who quickly fitted an arrow to his bow. Fear gripped his heart as his mind reeled. *Was this XtaKal?* He took aim and the figure stopped short some ten yards away. A long anxious moment passed as they stared at one another. Rooks arms began to shake from the strain of holding his aim.

There was a sudden howl to his left. Startled, Rook released his arrow. His aim was perfect, but Rook watched in astonishment as the figure raised its arm and the arrow burst into flames feet from the figure's head. The resulting burst of light blinded him, and he shielded his eyes. When Rook looked back the dark figure had vanished. He looked about frantically, but there was no sign of where the mysterious cloaked figure had gone. There was another howl, followed by another. Then Rook heard a cry for help, that sounded like Jonas. Taking one last look about himself, he then sprinted towards the cry hoping he was not too late.

Rook reached the edge of a glen where the dense foliage of the trees broke, revealing the cloudy sky. Here the dim light broke through the near blackness of the surrounding forest and Rook could see a lone tree in the middle of the glen surrounded by several wolves. Clinging to the branches, just out of reach of the ravenous wolves below, was Jonas.

Rook had only a moment to decide what to do. His only weapons were his bow and his hunting knife. He might be able to shoot two or three wolves before they turned and came at him. Jonas could not be counted on for help, but he might serve as a distraction. The question is how could he communicate with the boy in the tree without shouting. A sudden idea came to him and he pulled an arrow and pencil from his pack. On the arrow shaft he scribbled:

*Drop cloak on wolves after first shot. – Rook.*

He read over his message twice, hoping that Jonas would be able to read and understand the message in the dim light. Fitting the arrow, he took aim, let out a deep breath, and released.

The arrow shot through the darkness and disappeared into the branches. A sharp cry told him his aim was true, but then looked on in horror to see a pair of legs dangling feet from the jaws of the wolves. Jonas, startled by the arrow, had fallen from his perch.

Rook had no choice. He burst from his hiding place, drew back his bow and felled two wolves before the others realized what was happening. The remaining wolves spotted the man on the edge of the glen and let out a howl of rage. Forsaking the easy prey dangling above their heads, they ran at Rook. He had just enough time to shoot one more wolf, then he attempted to climb the nearest tree. As he turned, he felt a large heavy body collide with his own. He tumbled to the ground with a heavy gray mass on top of him. Rolling over onto his back, Rook brandished his knife. The wolf snapped at his head, while Rook kicked it from underneath. Yelping in pain and anger, the wolf retreated and Rook leapt to his feet. The other wolves began circling him, looking for an opening. He crouched into a defensive stance, while calculating his odds, which he knew were not in his favor. Catching a sudden movement out of the corner of his eye, he spun around just in time to see Jonas leap onto one of the wolves, plunging his short sword into the thick gray body. The wolf let out a high-pitched yelp, then slumped over dead. The others hesitated, and then turned on Jonas. The moment's distraction gave Rook enough time to grab his bow. He aimed, fired, and another wolf lay dead. The last remaining wolf, seeing its comrades all lying dead around him, fled the glen at a full sprint.

"Well done," Rook said, breathing heavily.

"Thought I was dead for sure back there," Jonas said, also

breathing hard. "Never expected you, of all people, to rescue me."

Rook grunted, then began walking toward the opposite side of the glen.

"Wait?" Jonas called after him. "Where are you going?"

"I would think that was obvious," Rook answered, gruffly without turning back or slowing his pace. "If we're to make it to your father at Farodhold ahead of XtaKal, we'd better get going."

"You're going to help me?" Jonas asked, jogging up to join him.

Rook didn't answer, but just kept walking. *I'm trusting You, so You'd better come through this time.*

# 7

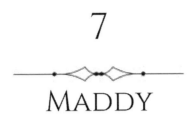

# MADDY

The wind blew hard against Windham Manor. Snow had fallen the night previous. With the temperature well below freezing, the estate lawns were still white and undisturbed save a trail of footprints leading to the eastern wall of the house. There was a loud crack on her window, causing Maddy to wake with a start. She jumped out of bed, threw on her robe and went to the window. Undoing the latch, she pushed the shutters open a crack and peered out into the cold darkness. Jumping back and stifling a scream, she saw hands seize the shutters and pull them open. A young man leapt inside and closed the shutters behind him. Standing back in short, Maddy was about to scream when the young man turned and she recognized the shoulder length brown hair and scruffy face. His brown eyes twinkled in excitement.

"David!" She exclaimed, running forward and throwing her arms around him.

They held each other for a moment, then Maddy pushed him away and punched him in the arm.

"You scared me," she said, trying and failing to look angry.

A playful crooked grin broke across David's face, as he put his arms around her.

"No," She exclaimed, pushing him away again. "You're freezing."

He laughed and pulled her closer against her feigned protestations.

"Did you miss me?" He asked, as she placed her head on his chest.

"Of course I did," she sighed.

"Just making sure," he said, and Maddy noted pain in his voice.

She leaned back to see his face, noting a smile on his lips but a look of pain in his eyes.

"What's wrong, David?"

He smiled, weakly. "I'd heard you and your mother agreed to move in with Baron Windham."

"Yes," she answered stiffened slightly and pulling away from him. "Just until after the New Years' party."

"So what's next? Has he proposed yet?"

"No."

"And if he did, what would you say?" Maddy saw his smile fade and the pain in his eyes worsen. "I see."

"David, you don't understand." Maddy didn't know what else to say.

"Actually, I think I do," he said after an awkward pause. "I should go."

"No, please," Maddy exclaimed, rushing forward and throwing her arms around David.

They held each other for several long moments, just feeling each other's embrace.

Eventually, David whispered in her ear, "Maddy, please don't marry him."

"What?" She pulled away, looking up at him.

"Please don't marry him."

"If he asks, how can I not?" She asked, tears welling up in her eyes.

"Run away with me!"

"But, what about my mother?"

"She will be fine," he said, pulling her close. "I don't want to lose you."

"David, I can't just leave her."

"Then bring her with us. We can leave Windham together. Go to Abenhall or Elengil or anywhere. I don't care as long as we're together."

She stared up at him for a moment, then reached up and gently pulled him into a long passionate kiss.

"Is that a yes?" he asked playfully when they finally broke apart.

She smiled and kissed him again.

✳  ✳  ✳  ✳

David left an hour later after they'd made plans for he, Maddy, and her mother to escape Windham. She'd just lain back in her bed, when she heard a rustling. She sat back up and started. In the far corner of the room stood a man in a dark gray cloak. She would have screamed, but the kind face of the man made her stop.

"Madeline," the man said softly, moving forward to stand by her bedside.

She stared at him, completely bewildered and unable to speak.

"Don't be afraid."

At his words, Maddy felt a strange wave of calm wash over her.

"Who are you?" She asked.

"My name is a strong tower," He answered. "I am a fortress for the weak."

Her eyes narrowed in confusion. "I don't understand."

"Madeline, you will soon be faced with a terrible choice," the man said, his face grave.

"What choice?"

"I've come to encourage you to tell the truth," he answered, calmly.

"Tell the truth? Tell the truth about what?" She asked, becoming frustrated. "I don't understand."

"You will be given a choice: to do what is easy or to choose

- 65 -

the right path which may prove to be the difficult path of sacrifice. I've come to encourage you so that you may know that I am with you."

"Tell me what you mean! What difficult path! I don't—" She exclaimed waking suddenly and sitting bolt upright in bed. She glanced about the room frantically, but there was no sign of anyone else in the room. She shook her head. *Just a dream.*

✳   ✳   ✳   ✳

In the morning, Maddy dressed in a simple dress and descended the stairs to the main floor to join her mother for breakfast. Upon reaching the doors to the small dining hall, she found one of the baron's servants blocking her way.

"Lady Madeline," he said with a bow. "The baron has requested you to join him in the great hall for breakfast."

"The great hall?" She asked, as a feeling of anxiety rose up inside her. "Very well. Please lead the way."

The servant led the way, taking Maddy through the corridor decorated with portraits of the baron's ancestors. At the far end near the door leading to the great hall stood the baron himself. He was gazing up at his father's portrait again, apparently in deep thought.

"My lord," she said, curtsying.

The baron turned towards her and smiled.

"Lady Madeline," he said, bowing and holding out his arm, which she took. "Shall we?"

Maddy looked at him curiously as he led her through the doors into the great hall. As the doors opened, Maddy was shocked to see the entire room filled with people, but then she remembered that the baron was known for holding a New Years' breakfast each year.

"My lords and ladies," the baron said loudly.

The crowd turned toward the door and grew silent. Maddy was very uncomfortable with so many eyes fixed upon her.

"May I introduce Madeline Brice, my guest and hopefully my future betrothed."

The crowd applauded and there was a general murmur of glad greeting.

"That is, if I can keep her from running off," the baron said, garnering laughter from the crowd.

Maddy turned quickly towards the baron, shocked by his sudden announcement of his proposal and noticed that the smile on his face did not reach his eyes. She was immediately filled with fear as the baron led her to the head of the table. *Did he know about her plans to run away with David? No he couldn't. Could he?*

Maddy sat down in the chair to the baron's right and across from her mother, who beamed at her and continued gesturing subtly for Maddy to accept the baron's abrupt proposal. Maddy spent the next half hour miserably contemplating her situation. As she did so, her anxiety only continued to build. She barely touched her meal, even after both her mother and the baron commented on her lack of appetite.

Finally, Baron Windham stood and the crowd around the table grew silent.

"Thank you all for coming," he began with a broad smile. "I would especially like to thank Lord Jon Grehm, who made the trip from Abenhall to Windham to be here upon this New Years'. Please continue to enjoy yourselves as I and my fellow lords excuse ourselves."

The baron turned to Maddy and took her hand.

"Please excuse me, Lady Madeline," Baron Windham said, kissing her hand. "I will see you later."

Maddy watched as he, and several other men whom she didn't recognize, exited the great hall. A vengeful thought suddenly occurred to her. If the baron was going to put her on the spot in front of so many people, she would embarrass him in front of his peers. Without a word to her mother, she stood abruptly and made her way across the hall and entered the hall with all the portraits. The door on the far side was left open a crack. As she neared it, she heard several voices conversing on the other side.

"Everything is in place, Lord Grehm," she heard Baron Windham say.

"Good," said Lord Grehm. "I've received word of a meeting in Nenholm held by Lord Silas Morgan. Apparently, Lord Morgan has manipulated Lord Warde into summoning the southern army and marching to Farodhold. I have sent word to Ethriel and I anticipate the king will summon the Council of Lords to Ethriel as soon as he receives word of Lord Warde's actions."

"Will the king muster the northern army and march south?" she heard the baron ask.

"If he does, this could cause another civil war," said Lord Grehm.

Maddy gasped, and the two men stopped talking. *Had they heard her?* After a brief pause, the two men continued.

"What of King Corin?" asked the baron.

"We both followed him during the Second War of Ascension, but recently many of the other lords have come to regard him as a coward," replied Lord Grehm. He sighed loudly. "We need a strong king to lead us through the coming dark years."

"Are you saying the other lords are planning to move against the king?"

"I suspect something from Morgan. I'm not sure about Warde and Astley."

"And you, my Lord?"

"I reserve judgment," Lord Grehm said after a brief pause. "Most of the northern lords remain loyal to the king, but if things progress as they are, I will require your presence in Abenhall, Gethrin."

"Are you saying you are mustering your forces, my Lord?"

"Consider this your summons, Baron Windham."

"What of my upcoming marriage?" the baron asked, more than a hint of outrage in his measured voice.

"You can wed your bride in Abenhall. We can make all arrangements, then we will journey to Ethriel," said Lord Grehm. "Come, let us make plans."

She heard the sound of footfalls grow fainter as she crouched near the door. Maddy covered her mouth to keep from screaming in fright. These men were conspiring against the king. All thoughts of embarrassing the baron were gone as terror gripped her. This man, who'd fought alongside the king, was now going to betray him. After waiting a few more minutes to make sure the two men were gone, she ran back into the great hall, past a servant who eyed her suspiciously, and sat down at the table across from her mother. She wiped her eyes and refused to look at her mother, who demanded to know where she'd been.

The same servant she'd passed came over to her and leaned down to whisper, the sound in her ear causing her to jump.

The servant straightened up as Maddy stared incredulously at him.

"My lady, I am sorry to have startled you," he said, with some annoyance. "Baron Windham would like to see you in his study."

"Now?"

"Yes, my lady."

Her eyes grew wide, but she nodded and followed the servant out of the great hall and through several corridors until they stood before a set of ornate oak doors. The servant knocked and Maddy heard the baron say "enter." The servant bowed her inside and she tremulously entered the baron's study, her eyes taking in the large room that extended two stories high. Around the perimeter of the room were many bookshelves. To her left was an iron spiral staircase leading to a walkway that ran around the perimeter of the second floor; an ornate wooden balustrade about three feet high ran along the walkway.

On the far side stood a large bay window that took up the entire first floor of the room. Before the window, gazing out into the estate grounds, stood Baron Windham. When she reached the middle of the room, he turned and moved toward a large desk that stood between them. His face bore a smile, but Maddy felt a shiver run down her spine.

"My lady," he said, gesturing to one of the chairs in front of the desk.

Maddy obeyed, looking up at the baron after seating herself.

"It has come to my attention that you have been keeping secrets from me," his voice was calm, but somehow menacing.

Maddy's eyes widened, but she held her tongue.

"My dear Madeline, you must tell me the truth," the baron demanded, calmly. "Do you have anything you wish to tell me?"

Maddy sat dumbstruck, not knowing what to say. The memory of that strange dream she'd had earlier this morning came rushing back; that strange visitor encouraging her to tell the truth. *But how could she?*

"Very well," the baron said clapping his hands.

Maddy glanced to her right to see a side door open and two guards drag a beaten young man inside. The guards threw the young man down at her feet and Maddy gasped as a bloodied and bruised David gazed up at her, his left eye swollen shut.

"David!" She exclaimed, gripping the arms of her chair in fury and fear.

"One of my servants saw this young man climbing in your window and overheard your conversation last night," the baron said, his voice now betraying his anger. "Needless to say, I found the news quite distressing."

Maddy looked horrorstruck, her eyes quickly darting back and forth between the baron and David.

"What are you going to do to him?"

"That depends on you, Madeline."

"What do you mean?"

"I give you a choice," the baron said, moving in front of the desk to stand before her. "You have led me to believe that you love me. Will you pledge yourself to me, forsake your feelings for his young man, and accompany me to Abenhall to marry me? If you do this, I will let David and your mother live."

"And if I refuse?" She asked, already fearing the baron's answer.

He gave her a knowing look, and she buried her face in her hands.

"Take her to her room, and this knave to the cellar," ordered the baron. "Madeline, you have one hour to decide their fate."

As they led her away, Maddy's mind flew back again to the strange visitor's words from earlier that morning. She wiped her eyes as tears poured from them, feeling as though her path had been chosen for her already.

# 8

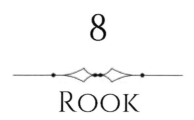

# ROOK

Rook and Jonas were nearing the eastern edge of Elmwood. They'd traveled all day, stopping only once at midday for a meal, but now the sun was setting, its deep red light resting on the tops of the trees.

"Can we please stop for a bit?" came the exhausted voice of Jonas.

"When we reach the shelter of the trees," Rook responded gruffly.

He was more than slightly annoyed with the boy. After all, the young man was supposed to be a member of the Bordermen. They trudged on in silence as the twilight fell upon them. The shadows under the trees lengthened and blended together under their heavy bows. Rook stopped at the edge of the forest as a sudden anxiety came over him. He drew his bow and fitted an arrow, gazing about the tree line. Jonas came to his side, also scanning in amongst trees.

"Why'd you stop?" He whispered at length.

"Shh," Rook hissed, then in a whisper he said, "We are being watched."

They stood silently on the edge of the trees, searching the

darkness for any sign of movement. Rook felt Jonas tap him on the shoulder. He turned, an angry rebuke ready on his tongue, but he stopped short as he saw the look of horror on Jonas's face. Rook followed the young man's gaze towards the plains opening up behind them. There, some fifty yards away, stood alone figure shrouded in a black cloak, a drawn sword in its hand.

"Run!" Rook bellowed, pulling Jonas toward the forest.

They sprinted under the cover of the trees, dodging brambles and wading through brush as they ran. Rook's legs, unaccustomed to such abuse, were exhausted after the day's long journey. His pace slowed, and Jonas flew past him a look of terror etched on his face.

"Jonas," he gasped, but his fatigued legs forced him to stop. He slumped against a nearby tree calling after him. "Jonas!"

It was too late. The young man was gone, enveloped by the darkness. Rook stood panting for several minutes, calling out when he could, but to no avail. When he'd finally caught his breath, Rook set off deeper into the forest in the direction Jonas had run. He moved at a swift walk, saving his energy in case he had to rescue Jonas. Elmwood Forest was less dense than the Eastern Woodlands so it had much thicker undergrowth. Rook had to wade through thick grass and shrubs as he made his way through, knowing that if Jonas had fallen unconscious somewhere to either the left or the right of Rook's path that he would never had known.

Rook wandered the forest for several hours. Every so often he thought he heard movement in the underbrush nearby, but then it would stop. The forest was unusually quiet, which became unnerving after a time. At one point, he paused for a moment to both think and to listen. After several long minutes, he thought he heard a faint cry for help some two hundred yards ahead of him. He hesitated, wondering if his ears were deceiving him. Then he heard it again, louder this time. Rook ran forward, pushing branches and brush out of the way. He skidded to a halt at the edge of a glade, where the trees thinned and light of the stars and moon was able to better penetrate the otherwise thick foliage. In the midst of the glade, illuminated in the half-light, was a dark figure stooped over the body of a young man.

"Jonas!" Rook cried, fitting an arrow and firing. "Get away from him!"

The dark figure turned swiftly and raised a gloved hand. The arrow burst into flames, briefly illuminating a figure shrouded in a black cloak and hood. In his hand was a sword as black as midnight, which seemed to draw in the darkness around it.

"XtaKal!" Rook exclaimed, finally believing Jonas's tale from the previous night. "I said get away from him!"

Rook loosed another arrow. As before, the arrow never reached its mark, but burst into flames. XtaKal then raised a hand and Rook felt himself leave the ground. He stared bewildered as the hand seeming to hold him in midair jerked to the left and Rook felt himself flying through the air and smash into something hard. He crumpled to the ground, his side throbbing in pain.

Slightly dazed, Rook shook his head and got to his feet. He was a dozen yards from where he'd been. XtaKal was still turned towards him. Rook's eyes narrowed, and he fitted another arrow. Before he could take aim though, his bow burst into flames. Rook hurled it away as it scorched his hands. Clenching his teeth and fighting back the pain, he drew his dagger.

"You cannot have him!" He shouted, running forward.

The figure raised its hand and Rook smashed hard into an invisible, but very solid, wall. Falling backwards, Rook braced himself for a killing blow. When it didn't come, he glanced up to see the figure hesitate again. Rook stood up, staring utterly confused. *Why was he still alive?* It was obvious that he was no match for the powerful sorcerer before him. According to Jonas, this same dark figure had massacred an entire company of Bordermen only last night, yet now he hesitated to kill Rook.

Without warning, a brilliant white light erupted between Rook and XtaKal. He heard a high pitched scream like that of a woman in pain, and then the light was gone. Rook blinked frantically, trying to clear his vision. Once his eyes adjusted again, he glanced about searching for the dark figure, who was nowhere to be found. His gaze fell upon Jonas, who was sitting up and an old man was kneeling beside him.

"Declare yourself!" Rook called.

The old man stood, leaning on a staff and turned towards Rook, who recognized the old man at once. He wore a dark gray traveling cloak and hood that was pulled back, revealing a face lined and careworn. His head was covered in thinning gray hair, and he had a long gray beard that fell past his belt. Yet the thing Rook recognized at once was the man's sharp, piercing blue eyes.

"Galanor!" He rushed over and took the old man's hand.

"Rook," Galanor grunted, retrieving his hand and turning back to Jonas. "Help me get Jonas on his feet, won't you."

"I can manage," Jonas said.

"Then let's go," Galanor said, turning away and setting off at a quick pace.

"Where are we going?" Rook heard Jonas ask, but the old man was already out of ear shot.

As they struggled to keep up with him, Rook noticed the trees thinning, and by the time they'd caught up with Galanor, they were standing on the edge of a lake.

"Galanor, where are you taking us?" Rook asked, breathing hard.

Jonas was doubled over, winded and in obvious pain.

"Elmloch Castle of course." Galanor replied pointing at the far side of the lake where the outline of a castle could just be made out. "Quick, before XtaKal returns."

Galanor took off again around the perimeter of the lake.

"So that was XtaKal. Does that mean—" Rook began, but the old man cut across him.

"Not here," he hissed back at Rook. "Not until we are safely inside the castle grounds. Come on."

✳  ✳  ✳  ✳

An hour later, they stood gazing up at the Castle of Elmloch. The old fortress sat on an island on the western edge of Elmloch Lake, a long narrow stone bridge ran from the western shore to the castle gates, which consisted of a gatehouse flanked by two wide towers. Rook looked hard upon the castle, noting the tall towers and battlements, and wondering why such a mighty fortress had been built in the midst of a forest in the first place.

Jonas moved forward to step onto the bridge,

"Stop!" Galanor shouted, but it was too late.

The air in front of Jonas rippled and hissed, forming a barrier that suddenly hurled him backwards over a dozen feet. Jonas landed face up and unconscious. Galanor and Rook rushed over to him.

"Foolish boy," Galanor growled, but Rook noted the look of concern on the old man's face. "Grab his legs."

Rook grabbed Jonas's legs and they carried him across the stone bridge leading to the castle. As they moved forward, Rook felt the air thicken as they passed. It felt as if moving through deep water, yet this time instead of blocking their passage the invisible barrier allowed them through. It was over in an instant and they continued across the long bridge.

Five minutes later, they laid the unconscious Jonas just inside the gatehouse. Galanor stooped down and placed a hand on Jonas's forehead. Uttering something inaudible, Galanor struck him across the face. Jonas's eyes flew open, and he sat bolt up, rubbing his face.

"What happened? Why'd you—" Jonas stammered.

"We just had to carry you across that long bridge because of your foolhardy rush into the barrier protecting this castle," Galanor growled, pointing back across the long stone bridge. "You're lucky to be alive."

"We're both lucky to be alive," Rook said, looking at Galanor. "I thought you'd be in Ethriel."

"Good thing I wasn't," The old man said, gruffly. "You were in over your head as always."

"Same old Galanor," muttered Rook angrily.

"Still the same prideful man, regardless of what you choose to call yourself, Rook." Galanor retorted, with a knowing glance.

"The past should be left where it is, Galanor," Rook said, curtly, noticing Jonas looking at him with new interest.

"Of course," Galanor said, turning towards the great hall. "I think we could use some food and rest. Come along. This way."

Rook helped Jonas to his feet and they followed Galanor. The doors of the great hall opened, and Rook and Jonas beheld the grandeur of the ancient fortress. A single long table ran the length of the hall. In the rafters were hung the banners of the great houses of Alethia. Rook noted that many of the houses represented here no longer existed, such as Noland and Aurelia which had fallen in the aftermath of the Second War of Ascension. The room was lit by several large chandeliers and a roaring fire in a massive stone hearth.

Rook glanced back down and saw Galanor seating himself at the far end of the hall. He and Jonas made their way down the table, and sat down on either side of the old man.

"It's been a long time since we've seen each other," Galanor remarked, clapping his hands.

"Ten years I think," Rook responded as several servants entered the hall bringing dishes and wine.

"Last I knew, you'd decided to leave the kingdom. Did you ever find what you were looking for?"

Rook looked at Galanor, but didn't respond.

"Very well," Galanor said at length. "Less talking more eating."

He waved a hand and the servants filled the table in front of them with foods of all sorts. No one spoke for some time. At length, they pushed away their plates. Galanor clapped his hands again and the servants cleared away the table. They returned with a large bottle of wine and three glasses.

"Tell me Galanor," Rook began, as a servant poured him a glass. "What is going on?"

Galanor's face grew very grave. "It is as before, Rook. I was in Ethriel when I received word that a dark army had invaded Eddynland. The king and his family were captured and murdered.

"What!" Rook and Jonas exclaimed. Whatever Rook had expected to hear, this was not it.

"It is my belief that Methangoth controls this dark army and that he is making another play for the Book of Aduin."

"If it is Methangoth, why has he waited so long?"

"He has waited longer between attempts in the past." Galanor answered, grimly. "He has bided his time, but now his plan has been put in motion. I also believe that this will be his last and greatest attempt."

"Why go after the book again?"

"He hopes it will provide him with the ability to prolong his life."

"Does it contain such knowledge?" Jonas asked, eagerly.

Galanor hesitated for a moment. "No, but that doesn't matter. He will come for it either way."

"What of XtaKal?" Rook asked. "Who is he?"

Galanor's face grew even more grim. The old man hesitated, and Rook's eyes narrowed in suspicion. "XtaKal is a warrior seduced by a great evil, which was bound in the Dark Sword."

Rook and Jonas moved to the edge of their seats, looking expectantly at Galanor, who appeared reluctant to continue. He sighed, looked each of the other two men in the eye, then sighed again. "Very well. More than seventy years ago, during the reign of Edward Aurelia, Methangoth made his first attempt at seizing the Book of Aduin. He built the dark fortress of Ardaband, raised a large army, convinced the kingdom of Nordyke to ally with him, and began a gruesome war with Alethia."

"Seventy years? Wow! How old *are* you Galanor?" Jonas asked, impertinently.

Rook stifled a laugh as Galanor glared at the young man, who looked away sheepishly.

"My age is of little importance, young man," he snapped. "What is important is that it was during this time that Methangoth conjured and forged many dark things, such as the wolves of Ardaband. But he was never powerful enough to forge the Dark Sword."

"But what is the Dark Sword?"

"It is an evil weapon, forged in darkness many centuries ago. It consumes darkness, exudes darkness, and fills the bearer with dark power. The man or woman who grasps the hilt, can never let go. Consumed by the dark power and enslaved to do the will of its maker. Methangoth allied himself with XtaKal long ago, but they were both defeated and the Dark Sword was hidden away."

"By whom?"

"I hid the Dark Sword and protected it with such power as I could muster," the old man replied, his face full of sorrow and regret. "It appears I have failed once again to prevent my former apprentice from his evil schemes and now both Methangoth and XtaKal are united once again against us."

"So that's how XtaKal was able to massacre my entire unit." Rook heard Jonas mumble to himself.

"XtaKal's presence gives further credence to my belief that Methangoth plans to invade Alethia soon."

"We must inform the king, then," Jonas exclaimed, standing as if to leave for Ethriel at that very moment.

"Sit down, young man," Galanor commanded, impatiently. "The king already knows." The old man turned towards Rook. "He asked about you, Rook. As did Queen Riniel."

Rook turned away, unable to speak and his heart was filled with sorrow.

"What does the king plan to do?"

"He remains reluctant to believe such a threat exists and will not summon the army."

"Why?"

"Rook, King Corin has become overly cautious in these latter years. Some may call it cowardice."

"Corin Aranethon is no coward," Rook said, his temper rising.

"Maybe not the Corin you remember, but that was twenty years ago, Rook."

He glared at Galanor, biting back his retort.

"If you would come with me to Ethriel— " Galanor began, but stopped midsentence.

A loud boom echoed through the castle. They all ran to the windows as something hit the barrier protecting the castle, exploding in a burst of red flame.

"What was that!" Jonas cried.

"We must go," Galanor said calmly, turning away from the windows. "XtaKal's true master has come."

# 9

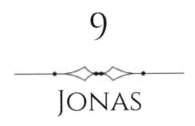

# JONAS

Jonas, Rook and Galanor raced across the courtyard leading to the castle's tallest tower. The ground shook violently as blasts of red flames repeatedly hit the magical barrier protecting the castle. Several times Jonas nearly lost his footing, but he staggered on after the other two men as they made their way as quickly as possible. Upon reaching the base of the tower, Jonas glanced up just as a massive shadow swooped overhead. The other two paused and they all looked up in alarm as a huge flying beast crossed the sky, blocking out the moon and stars. A stream of red flame burst from its mouth and hit the barrier. Jonas glanced at Galanor, who was staring up in horror. The beast let loose another blast, and upon hitting the barrier, sent a massive shockwave rippling through it. The force of the blast knocked all three men off their feet.

"Is that what I think it is?" exclaimed Rook.

"Come on!" cried Galanor, getting to his feet and pulling open the large door. "The barrier won't last much longer."

Jonas and Rook followed Galanor through the door. Just as they were pulling it closed behind them, there was another red flash. The ground shook violently and there was a noise like a thunderclap. Jonas glanced back and saw the barrier give way and vanish in a burst of blue light. Another spout of flame hit the great hall, which exploded in fire and black smoke. The concussive force slammed the door closed, sending Jonas stumbling into Rook and Galanor.

"They've breached the barrier," said Galanor, lighting his staff. "Elmloch Castle has fallen. Come, we must escape."

By the light of his staff, Galanor led them to a small trapdoor in the corner, then down a winding stone staircase that descended down into the core of the island upon which the ancient fortress stood. At the bottom of the stairs lay a long dark corridor. Jonas gazed into the blackness, filled with terror and dread. Never in his life had he experienced such fear. Being sent to the frontier by a father who was ashamed of him, then witnessing the destruction of the entire company of Bordermen by XtaKal, then the threat of being eaten by wolves, and finally being pursued by XtaKal all the way to Elmloch Castle was almost too much to bear.

Galanor led the way down the corridor, Rook following and Jonas bringing up the rear. Suddenly, something rose up in the darkness in front of him. There was a squeak and the flapping of wings. Something hit Jonas in the face, causing him to cry out, cover his head with his hands, stumble over his own feet, and fall to the ground. Galanor and Rook rushed over to find him in the fetal position, whimpering.

"Get up, you cowardly fool!" Galanor hissed.

"It was only a bat," Rook muttered angrily, as he and Galanor grabbed Jonas by the arms and hoisted him to his feet.

Jonas, a bit shell-shocked, stood up shakily. Galanor and Rook moved off, and Jonas scampered forward, trying to remain close to the light of Galanor's staff. They crossed to the other end of the corridor, and found another set of winding stairs leading downward. Galanor led the way, coming out at the bottom into a large store room. Many doors lined the walls, behind which were many smaller store rooms and corridors. He stopped suddenly upon reaching the center of the room. Jonas and Rook bumped into him, then froze listening. The sound of many voices came echoing down the corridor they'd just left.

"Hurry, this way!" Galanor hissed, heading toward the door to his left.

Jonas and Rook ran quickly after. Galanor threw open the door, revealing another dark tunnel. Taking it at a sprint, they all ran down the length of the tunnel and around a corner. The sound of rushing water echoed off the tunnel walls and grew louder with every step. The tunnel ceiling rose up into a vast cavern, and the light of Galanor's staff revealed an underground river, rushing loudly by in the gloom. A simple stone bridge stood over the river. There were no railings and the bridge was very narrow, barely wide enough for one person to cross at a time. Galanor and Rook rushed forward, crossing the bridge with little effort, then turned as Jonas stood on the far back. He was trembling, gazing out over the foaming waters as they rushed passed.

"Come on, Jonas!" cried Rook.

Jonas took a deep breath and placed a trembling foot on the bridge. Jonas's heart was still beating fast. He took another step. The bridge was still solid beneath him.

"Hurry up!" called Galanor. "They're coming!"

Jonas glanced back to see the light of many torches in the corridor behind him. He took a few more steps. He was in the center of the bridge. There was a loud boom, and the entire cavern shook violently. Jonas glanced up in time to see a large stalactite break away from the ceiling and come crashing down on the bridge in front of him. He jumped backwards, but the bridge gave way and he fell into the icy cold waters.

✳   ✳   ✳   ✳

Jonas awoke lying face down on the right bank of the underground river. He pushed himself up into a seated position, and as he did so his head swam and vision blurred. Feeling like he was going to pass out, he reached up to rub his aching forehead and felt a large bump there that was tender to the touch. Cursing his luck, he opened his eyes but could see nothing. The darkness was complete, leaving Jonas to rely on his other senses to guide him. There was no sound save the river, which was flowing much slower than before, and there was no telling how far the river had taken him downstream.

He felt around in the darkness, until his hands found his pack. Hoisting it on his back Jonas tried to stand but his head swam again and he fell back to his hands and knees. Having no other recourse, he began to crawl forward slowly. The sandy bank gave way to cold, rough stone, with the occasional sharp rock that scraped and tore at his bare hands. He reached out and eventually found the wall of the cavern. Feeling his way along, he put the wall on his right side and continued crawling forward. This he did for what seemed like hours. The river continued flowing by and the cavern he was in seemed to go on forever.

He stopped and sat back down against the cold stone wall, beginning to despair, and felt the bump on his forehead again. The merest touch was like hot knives shooting through his skull. He brought his legs up tight against him and fought the pain in his head. A drowsiness fell upon him and he had to fight the urge to sleep. In the hopeless dark, sleep seemed very inviting. He felt his eyelids close. *Just for a minute*, he thought. Then, just as sleep was about to take him, a light erupted in the cavern. Jonas opened his eyes, half-blinded momentarily, he squinted in the direction of the light. As his vision cleared, he saw a fire burning a couple dozen feet away to his right. A man was sitting beside the fire, cloaked and hooded.

"Come, warm yourself by the fire," called the man.

Jonas tried to stand, and found he could do so without his head swimming. He jogged over to the fire and stood uncertainly. The light and heat of the flames was incredibly inviting.

"Who are you?"

"I've come to bring a light to your dark situation," the man said, pulling down his hood to reveal a pleasant face. The man had brown hair that fell to his shoulders, a short brown beard, and there was a kindness in his brown eyes. It may have been a trick of the light, but in the dark gloom of the cavern the man's face seemed to glow slightly.

"Please sit," the man said, gesturing at the floor across from him.

Jonas eyed the stranger suspiciously, but he sat down and drew close to the light and warmth of the flames.

"You are weary. Drink of this," the man said, holding out a bottle of liquid.

Jonas hesitated.

"You can trust me, Jonas."

"How do you know my name?"

"I know much about you, Jonas Astley, son of Peter Astley."

Jonas's eyes widened in amazement.

"Please, drink and be refreshed," the man said, moving over and placing the bottle in Jonas's hands.

The man then retreated back to his former place, sat down, and watched Jonas intently. Jonas uncapped the bottle, and from within a sweet smell issued forth. Jonas felt a calm wash over him, and he glanced between the bottle and the stranger. After another moment's hesitation, he drank deeply. The liquid had no taste, but refreshed him like the water of a mountain stream and warmed him like a strong drink.

"What is this?" Jonas asked, after several wonderful gulps.

"Just water, Jonas," The man answered. "A gift, taken in good faith."

Jonas felt the pain leave his head. He reached up and felt his forehead, but the bump was gone.

"How—" he began, but stopped short.

"I have told you. I am the light in the darkness. I bring healing to those who are sick."

Jonas looked confused.

"You do not remember my name, but you know who I am," the man said, continuing to look intently at Jonas. "I can help you find your way back to Galanor and Rook, and give your life new purpose. Will you trust me?"

Jonas didn't know what to say, but nodded.

"Go place your hand on the wall there," the man said, pointing.

Jonas looked reluctant, but the man nodded encouragingly. He stood and walked over to the wall, his hand hovering over the rough stone. He took a breath and laid his hand on the wall. At once, the wall shimmered and melted away, revealing a large cavern with torches lining the walls. From a large opening in the midst of the ceiling a wide beam of light fell upon a stone pedestal sitting in the center of the room. Upon the pedestal, sat an ancient looking tome.

"You, Jonas Astley, are charged with guarding this book from evil hands," came the man's voice from behind him. "Keep the book safe."

Jonas glanced back, but found both the man and the fire had disappeared. Staring bewildered for a moment at the spot where they'd been only an instant before, he then went over and grabbed his bag. He walked over to the pedestal and placed his hands on the ancient book. The surface was rough and the pages crackled as he opened it. Upon the first page, in a thin script, was written,

"I, Aduin, Protector of the Hall of Records and Loremaster of Alethia, do record herein the histories and secrets of the Kingdom of Alethia."

"*The Book of Aduin!*" Jonas exclaimed.

His voiced echoed loudly off the walls, and Jonas suddenly remembered where he was. He closed the book, and placed it carefully in his bag. Hoisting it on his back, he gazed around the room, his eyes falling on a tunnel entrance across the room. Walking carefully to the tunnel entrance, he grabbed one of the torches close by and peered inside. Taking a last glance at the cavern behind, Jonas took a deep breath and stepped into the dark tunnel.

✳   ✳   ✳   ✳

For the next few hours, Jonas carefully and cautiously made his way through the maze of tunnels. At length, he reached an ancient iron door blocking his way forward. A small barred window set at eye-level showed the forest beyond. He'd finally reached the end of these dark and damp caves. Grabbing the door handle, Jonas pushed and pulled but the door would not budge. He kicked it for good measure, but only succeeded in causing his foot to ache. Hopping on one leg for a moment, he spotted some writing inscribed over the top of the door. Moving closer and holding the torch towards the inscription, Jonas read the faded gilded letters. The language was ancient Alethian, but Jonas easily translated the words since he'd spent time studying the ancient texts held in his father's private libraries in Farodhold. The inscription read:

*Speak my name and the door shall open:*
*I am better than jewels or the finest gold.*
*I am found on the lips of the discerning,*
*And my counsel will never lead to ruin.*
*By me kings reign and rulers decree justice.*
*Blessed is the man who listens to me,*
*For I am the bane of fools.*

He read the inscription several times, until he'd almost memorized them. After staring at the words for several minutes, pondering their meaning, a sudden noise behind him drew his attention. He spun around and heard voices in the tunnel behind him. Jonas's pulse quickened and he blew out his torch, knowing the light would only help whoever or whatever was coming find him. He turned back to the door; the pale light of the moon came in through the barred window. His mind raced, trying to think.

"The bane of fools," he muttered to himself. "Kings reign and rulers decree justice. Discerning and counsel."

The voices were getting louder, and Jonas was beginning to panic. He closed his eyes and focused on calming himself when suddenly the answer came to him. He opened his eyes and said softly,

"Wisdom."

The ancient door shuddered, then creaked open a crack. Jonas pushed and the door swung wide, and he dashed forward out into the dark forest.

\* \* \* \*

After wandering in the forest for several hours, Jonas had to admit that he was indeed lost. The sun had risen, but then dark clouds had rolled in, blocking out his only means of navigating through the forest. He knew he must be deep in the forest of Elmwood, but finding his way out was another matter. What made it worse was that he thought he heard voices from time to time. Sometimes they came from far to his left, and then from far to his right. It was unnerving, and as he could neither see the speakers or hear what they were saying, Jonas grew ever more wary as he moved through the thick underbrush.

Eventually, his wanderings lead him into a dimly lit glade, where there were no trees and Jonas could see the sky. He gazed intently at the edges of the glade, wondering what might be lying in wait. He was about to step out, when two hands grabbed him from behind and pulled him down.

"Get down, you fool!" came the familiar voice of Galanor.

Jonas found himself flat on his back, looking up into the grim face of the old man. He felt a sudden rush of both annoyance and relief.

"Galanor," he said, rising to a sitting position.

"Hush!" the old man hissed. "They are searching for us!"

"Who?"

"No time," The old man said, holding out a hand and helping Jonas to his feet. "We must find the enemy's camp."

"What for?"

"They've taken Rook."

# 10

# SELENA

Selena skidded to a halt facing the cobblestone street leading to the docks of Nenholm. She stole a glance back up the street. Raynor Kesh was sprinting down towards her, hot on her heels. Dashing toward the nearest ship, she pushed past several sailors who were carrying crates up the gangplank, knocking one of them into the waters below.

"Sorry," she called over her shoulder and darted between the sailors milling about the deck.

As she passed them, she saw a look of shock giving way to anger as they reached out to seize her.

"Stop her!" the sailors shouted.

Selena soon had a couple dozen pursuers instead of just the one. Making her way to the forecastle, she seized a hanging rope and pushed off. The sailors shouted at her in dismay as she glided through the air, landing softly on the dock. After gaining a solid footing, Selena ran down the pier to the last ship, which was making ready to set out. The gangplank had been pulled onboard, the sails were unfurling, and the sailors' eyes were all gazing out onto the open sea. Selena glanced back down the pier once more, seeing all her pursuers racing toward her. She had no choice, and dove into the waters below. The shock of the cool water was mild, even refreshing. Selena swam quickly toward the ship, her arms pounding the surface. Abruptly, her outstretched hands hit wood and she seized hold of the hull, and climbed up until she could peer onto the deck. She was hanging on the aft section of the ship. All the sailors were still gazing out onto the open sea. Selena quietly hoisted herself on deck, and quickly made her way below deck.

Selena descended the ladder going down into the hold, darted into a dark corner, and paused to take in her surroundings. She could hear the sailors moving about the deck above her. Then, the noise of stomping feet came from the ladder in front of her. Two sailors descended the ladder, complaining of the heat and work. Selena watched them walk over to a pile of casks.

"This them?" asked the tall, skinny sailor.

"Nah," answered a short, dark bushy-haired sailor. "This lot ain't moving till we make Fairhaven. This way. Come on."

Selena watched the two sailors move further into the hold, then darted forward. She pulled a large, dusty tarp off the pile, found an empty cask, and climbed inside. She pulled the tarp back over herself, and suppressed a smile as she drifted off to sleep. Kesh would never find her now.

※ ※ ※ ※

A sudden noise roused Selena from her sleep. She opened her eyes and looked blearily at her surroundings. For a brief moment, she'd forgotten where she was. She pulled the large, dusty tarp off herself and climbed out of the cask in which she'd fallen asleep. Emerging in the dim light of the sun breaking through the beams of the deck above her, she shook her foggy head and tried to revive herself. Then it all came back, her escape, overhearing her father's plan, her stowing away onboard this ship bound for Fairhaven. She shook her head again, stretched, grabbed her bag, and decided to sneak up on deck to see if they'd made it to port.

"Hey!" someone shout from behind her.

Selena froze, then slowly turned around to see the two sailors from the day before, both of them looking shocked.

"Oh," she said, with a wink. "Hey fellas. Could either one of you direct me to the guest quarters?"

The two sailors' eyes narrowed and Selena sprinted to the ladder and climbed up on deck. The late afternoon sun blinded her for a moment, but as her vision cleared she saw a large city up ahead of the ship. High walls, constructed out of stone with a reddish hue, rose up majestically before her. The ship had apparently made port and was in the middle of docking. The deckhands nearest her shouted and pointed as the muffled shouts from the sailors below also reached her ears. Selena ran for the portside of the ship, skidding to a halt when she reached the forecastle. Her pursuers were right behind her, and she glanced at the dock, which was still some twenty yards away.

"Stop right there, missy!" shouted a stern voice.

Selena turned to see a well-dressed man with a tall, black, wide-brimmed hat, much like her fathers. She smirked as she assumed this boisterous man was the captain of this vessel, then her face fell as she eyed the sword in the man's hand. The sailors behind him leered at her, all carrying clubs and short daggers. She had no choice. Climbing on top of the forecastle, she turned and gave the captain a wink and dove into the waters below.

The shock of the cold water stole her breath, forcing her to gasp as she treaded water for a moment. Shouts from the ship above her and fear of freezing, Selena forced her muscles to move as she swam to shore. Her arms were aching by the time she reached the dock. Climbing onto the nearest pier, she stopped for a moment to catch her breath and collect herself. Then shouts from the nearest ship drew her attention. The disgruntled captain and his crew were running up the pier towards her, and Selena was on the run again.

✳   ✳   ✳   ✳

Later that evening, Selena sat warming herself by the fire. After losing her pursuers, she'd darted down an alleyway and found an out of the way inn. A far shot from the dock, she decided to take refuge there. The owner had eyed her suspiciously, but took her money and showed her to a room on the second floor. After peeling off her wet clothes, which were drying on a line nearby, she'd pulled on her spare change of clothes, which were thankfully still dry despite her unplanned swim to shore.

She had to wait until her things were dry, which gave her plenty of time to think. She gazed into the fire, pondering her next move. If her father was making an ill-advised play for the crown, she wanted no part in it. The last thing she wanted was to get mixed up in her father's ploys and schemes. She wanted adventure. She wanted glory. A smile broke across her face. She wanted fun, away from her overbearing and domineering father.

There was no way she was going to get any sleep tonight. She packed up her things, and was just about to pull open the door when there came a loud knock.

"Who's there?"

The door burst open and Selena backed away quickly, her hand plunging into her bag and drawing out a short dagger. Raynor Kesh glared at her as he entered the small room.

"Did you really think you could escape me?" he asked menacingly.

"A girl can try," Selena answered, scathingly. "What took you so long?"

"I just thought I'd give you a sporting chance, but now I must insist you accompany me to Abenhall. Your father has asked for you to meet him there."

"Why?"

Kesh merely stared warningly at her.

"Very well," Selena said, still brandishing the dagger in front of her. "Thank you for delivering the invitation, but I think I'll pass."

In a flash, Kesh crossed the room, grabbed Selena's hand, and gently but firmly disarmed her.

"I'm afraid I must insist, my Lady," he said, still smiling. He released her and strolled back to the door.

Just then, there was a loud boom from outside and the entire building shook violently. The force caused Kesh to stumble, and Selena grabbed her bag, leapt over Kesh's crouched form, and sprinted out into the hall and around the corner. Several other patrons of the inn staggered out of her way as she pelted through the hall and out into the night. She paused, letting her eyes adjust in the dark alley, then turned to her left. She had only taken a few steps, when the door of the inn burst open behind her. Glancing behind her to see Kesh panting in the doorway, she sprinted up the alley and out onto a wide street filled with people carrying torches. Selena took a moment to glance up and down, finding a large gate to her left, its huge wooden doors were closed and barred, and dozens of soldiers were standing outside as if waiting for something. There was a great swooping noise overhead, causing Selena to duck instinctively. She gazed up into the dark sky in wonder. Then there was a blinding flash and another deafening boom that shook the ground like earthquake. Selena heard the people in the streets cry out in terror. They were pointing at something, but she didn't have time to look. A hand grabbed her shoulder from behind. She shrugged it off, and sprinted away from the gate and the gawking people, turning down another street.

Selena ran and ran. Darting in between people, running in the opposite direction, she soon found herself on a deserted street. She leaned against the wall of a nearby building, gasping for breath. A sudden noise from behind startled her, and she darted down a dark and narrow alleyway, barely wide enough for a single person to pass through. Glancing up and down, she saw the alleyway dead ended into one of the walls of the city, which rose up ominously in the darkness. She leaned back against the exterior of a nearby building and slid to the ground. Selena had no idea where she was, no idea what was happening to this city, and no idea where Kesh might be. Placing her face in her hands, she shook her head slowly fighting back despair.

"Good evening," came a voice to her right.

Selena jumped to her feet and stumbled backwards. Her eyes fell upon a man in a gray cloak, standing a few yards away. The man pulled back his hood, revealing a pleasant face. He had brown hair that fell to his shoulders, a short brown beard, and in the dark gloom of the alley, Selena could have sworn the man's face glowed slightly. Somehow, the man gave her a feeling of peace and apprehension, as if somewhere inside her a battle was waging on how to respond to this man.

"Who are you?" she finally asked.

"You know of me, and I have tried to speak to you many times, but you have never listened."

She stared at the man suspiciously.

"You are on the run, but what are you really running from, Selena?"

"How do you know my name?" she demanded.

"I know much about you, Selena. Would it surprise you to know that I've known you all your life, and that I have loved you since before you were born." His voice was not ominous, but calm and caring.

"What do you want?"

"To help you."

"Help me?"

"Yes. You are headed down a dark path, Selena. I have come to warn you to not follow in your father's footsteps."

"What!" Selena exclaimed, anger boiling up inside her. "I'm nothing like my father!"

He smiled at her patiently. "You are your father's daughter. You may not know it, but you walk his path."

"I don't know who you are or what you really want from me, but I am nothing like my father. Nothing! And I want nothing to do with you!"

She turned and walked to the end of the alleyway. Something

inside her made her turn back, but the man was gone. She stared blankly for a few moments at the spot where he'd stood, then a loud crash to her left drew her attention. Selena turned quickly as a giant fireball streaked overhead, briefly illuminating the city walls before crashing violently into the red stonework. She watched in horror as the walls crumbled, leaving a gaping hole and a giant cloud of dust and debris rising dozens of feet in the air. She crept slowly down the alley, trying to peer through the dust.

In a moment, the dust cleared and Selena saw a host of dark figures standing just beyond the gap in the wall. There was another loud swooping noise overhead, and the figures let out a loud blood-chilling shriek as they began pouring into the city brandishing swords and spears. Selena ran back down the alley away from the walls. She reached a major street where a large number of soldiers were running past her. She turned and moved in the direction of the docks. Blood-curdling screams broke through the din from the direction of the gap in the wall. She shook her head, trying not to think of what might have happened to the soldiers.

Upon reaching the docks, she saw that most of the ships were moving off quickly. Selena sprinted down the nearest pier, and hurled herself at the nearest departing ship, just managing to grab the side. Unlike before, the sailors grabbed her arms and helped pull her on deck. She thanked them, and turned towards the city. Fairhaven was in flames. People near the dock ran here and there with dark figures chasing after them. As she looked on, a tall dark figure emerged from the flames and stood upon the dock, surveying the fleeing ships. She gasped as the figure suddenly held out a hand, seeming to lift a man attempting to run some twenty feet above the ground. The man hung there for a moment, then the figure brought its hand down, and the man hurled into the ground with a sickening crunch.

"XtaKal!" cried one of the sailors.

Selena continued to stare, unable to look away as the dark form turned and lifted a sword as black as night into the air, then brought it down in a giant swipe. From it a great wave of energy erupted into the water, rushing towards one of the ships. Selena followed it until the wave hit a nearby ship causing it to crack in two. Everyone on board leapt into the water as the ship vanished into the dark churning water. Selena glanced back to the dock, but the dark figure was gone.

# 11

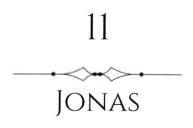

# JONAS

Jonas and Galanor peered out from their hiding place amongst the trees and bushes on the edge of Elmwood. It was night and the plains spread out before them, lit dimly by moon and stars. The wind howled through the trees of Elmwood Forest. It was a bitter, cold wind from the north that pierced through to their very bones. It was as if the thick cloaks they were wearing were not even there.

Upon the plains before them, lay a large camp of men. Banners waved in the cold wind but neither Jonas nor Galanor could not recognize their markings in such darkness. They'd been following the camp as it moved along the edge of the forest for the past few days, trying to learn of Rook's fate. Campfires dotted the landscape. The firelight cast menacing shadows that moved from tent to tent. This was the first time they'd been close enough to possibly identify to whom this army belonged.

"Who are they?" Jonas whispered.

"Mercenaries," answered Galanor. "A lot of them."

"What are they doing here and what do they want with Rook?"

"That's what we need to find out," Galanor said, moving closer to the edge of the brush concealing them. Jonas followed quickly after. After a few moments silence, Galanor spoke again.

"I can't make out the markings on the banners. I have no idea who we are dealing with here." He sighed heavily. "There's no choice. Jonas, you're going to have to infiltrate the camp and learn what you can of Rook and the reason the mercenaries are here."

"What!" Jonas almost yelled in surprise. Then lowering his voice, he said, "I'm not a spy."

"I cannot go," Galanor said simply. "My face is well known. I'd be spotted the instant I drew too close to one of those fires. But you may be able to enter the camp unnoticed."

"But—" Jonas began to protest, but Galanor cut him off.

"Remember," he said, pulling Jonas's hood over his head. "Speak to no one, unless you absolutely must. Try to blend in with the small groups around the fires. Listen and observe, but don't engage with the men. Most importantly, you must return here before dawn."

Jonas stared blankly back at him.

"Jonas," Galanor growled. "You must do this. Find your courage. Trust in the Almighty to see you through."

"Trust in the Almighty?"

Galanor frowned at him. "Surely your father has spoken of the Almighty."

"No," Jonas said, shaking his head. "Father banished the chapel priest when he came to rule Farodhold."

"It is as I feared," Galanor said, sighing and shaking his head. "Alethia has lost its faith in their God."

Jonas stood shifting his feet uncomfortably and not knowing what to say.

"You do know who the Almighty is, correct?" the old man asked gruffly.

"Yes, but how does that help me?"

"He will help guide you if you put your trust in Him."

"Trust in Him?" Jonas said, excitedly. "That's the same thing the stranger said."

"What stranger?" Galanor asked, his eyes narrowing.

"The strange man in the caves below Elmloch Castle."

The next thing he knew, Galanor had seized him by the shoulders.

"Describe him!" He commanded fiercely.

Jonas stared bewildered for a moment, then said, "He had brown hair that fell to his shoulders, a short brown beard, and kind eyes. Could have sworn the man's face glowed slightly."

Galanor's eyes grew wide, but he let go and turned away, clearly troubled. "What did he tell you?"

"He told me to trust him and charged me to keep this safe," Jonas said, pulling out the book.

Galanor turned to look, then stared gaped in amazement.

"*The Book of Aduin*! Where did you get that!"

"I found it in a cavern the stranger showed me."

"Jonas," Galanor began after a long moment's pause. "The man you met is no stranger. There is much we must discuss, but first you must find Rook." He sighed, looking doubtful, then held out his hand. "Leave the book with me."

"I can't," Jonas said, putting the book back in his bag. "The stranger charged me with guarding this book from evil hands."

Galanor looked doubtful, then glanced at the sky. "We don't have time to argue. You have only a few hours before dawn. Learn as much as you can and report back. Keep the book safe."

"But—" Jonas began, but Galanor pushed him forward and he began the anxious trek across the plains toward the camp.

"Be careful, Jonas," he heard Galanor hiss after him.

Jonas walked toward the nearest fire. His heart was pounding in his chest. Nothing in his past could have prepared him for this. He was ten feet from the nearest fire, when he was spotted.

"Hey!" a voice called out.

Jonas froze.

"Who goes there?" called the voice again.

Jonas saw several men rise to their feet, and he panicked. Before realizing what he was doing, he found himself running at a full sprint down the line of tents. There were yells and a horn blew behind him, but it only made him run faster. He passed other fires, but did not stop. Only when his sides were aching did Jonas slow his pace. He skidded to a halt beside a dark tent, gasping for breath. He had at some point crossed into the camp. There were no watch fires here, and tents rose up all around him in the darkness. He stood panting, his heart racing, wondering where he was and how he was going to get out of this. Another horn blast rang out in the darkness, and Jonas jumped. The lights appeared in the tents around him as the men inside awoke. He darted inside one the tents that was still dark and laid down to pretend he was asleep. Yet almost immediately a hand grabbed his arm and hoisted him up. Jonas turned to see the dark outline of a tall man.

"On your feet!" the man ordered. "Get out there and help find the intruder!"

Jonas was marched back out into the cold night, where men were darting to and fro searching for him. It was almost humorous that he was being sent out to search for himself, but Jonas was in no mood for laughter.

"What's going on?" Jonas heard one of the men ask.

"Intruder!" another man answered.

"Be quick!" called a third. "Search the tents."

Jonas joined the nearest group of men, who seemed to be heading deeper into the camp. He allowed them to move on ahead of him when they were far enough away from the other search parties, then he darted down between two rows of tents and ran further into the camp. After passing several more tent rows, he slowed his pace. Eventually he stopped for a rest, breathing hard. The noise of the searchers had grown faint in the distance. His heart was still pounding as his eyes continued to gaze about, looking for a place where he could hide and recover his wits. Based on how long he'd been walking, Jonas estimated he was around the center of the camp. He walked around a corner, but jumped backwards quickly and slid behind the nearest tent. Jonas paused a moment, then peered back around the corner at the largest tent he'd come across thus far.

The tent was illuminated from within, and large banners were flapping in the wind. Two guards stood before the tent entrance. Jonas felt sure that this had to be the commander's tent. He backed away and edged around to the other side of the tent row. The silhouettes of two men were moving toward the entrance. Jonas watched until they'd left the tent, then he darted forward and dove under the canvas.

He found himself in a wide open area, with a large rug covering most of the floor. As he got to his feet, Jonas noticed a cot to his left and a desk to his right filled with parchments. He was about to walk over to the desk, when he caught sight of the body of a man, lying on the floor with his hands and feet bound. He moved cautiously over and peered down at the man's face. Then he gasped as he recognized the battered and bloodied face of Rook, his right eye was swollen shut. Jonas knelt beside him and began to untie the ropes.

"Rook," he whispered. It took several times, but the man finally stirred and opened his good eye.

"Jonas?" he groaned.

"I've come to get you out of here."

He helped Rook push himself into a sitting position with another groan, and rubbed his wrists where the ropes had rubbed him raw.

"Galanor sent you into the camp alone to find me?"

"Not exactly," Jonas whispered, glancing back at the tent entrance. "He sent me to find out what these mercenaries are doing here and learn where they might be holding you."

Rook rubbed his swollen eye gingerly.

"Who are they?"

"Not sure," Rook said, shaking his head slowly. "Didn't seem to be interested in answering questions, just asking."

"Why'd they beat you?"

"I didn't give them the answers they were looking for," Rook answered, holding out his hand. Jonas helped Rook to his feet.

"What'd you tell them?"

"The truth," Rook said, blearily. "For all the good it did me. Didn't believe a word I said."

"How did you get caught?"

"What is this, an interrogation?" Rook snapped.

Jonas hung his head, realizing his insistence on information was poorly timed. Rook had undoubtedly spent the last several days answering questions and suffering at the hands of these mercenaries.

"Sorry," he muttered.

"Don't worry about it," Rook said with a heavy sigh and rubbing his head. "Galanor and I escaped the tunnel. He seemed concerned when we found the door open at the far end."

"Wait," Jonas interrupted. "Was it a large iron door, with a barred window?"

"Yes. How did you know?"

"I had just opened the door and escaped."

"Well, we had just exited the tunnel, when a patrol of these mercenaries attacked us. They must have knocked me out, but I wondered if Galanor had escaped. Didn't know for sure until you told me," Rook said, quickly. "Look, we can spend time rehashing the last few days later. Let's get out of here."

They crept over to where Jonas had entered, and he held the canvas up as Rook crawled under. They were soon back out in the cold early morning. The eastern sky gave only the merest hint of the coming dawn. Their time was running out. Jonas glanced over to find Rook shivering, as he only had on a ragged tunic and pants.

"They took my traveling clothes," Rook whispered, leading off towards the right. "I've got to find some replacements."

"Is this really the time?" Jonas whispered.

"It's either that or freeze to death," Rook hissed back at him.

When they reached a dark tent, Rook turned and whispered, "Hand me your knife."

Jonas did and Rook entered the tent. There was a scuffling noise, a soft yelp, and then silence. A few moments later, Rook reemerged wearing a pair of high traveling boots and a dark gray cloak and hood.

"Did you kill him over some clothes?" Jonas asked, bewildered.

"Just knocked him out and put a blanket on him," grumbled Rook as he adjusted the cloak around himself. "Probably warmer than we are, now lead on."

Jonas stifled a laugh as he turned, then he froze in shock.

Rook also turned and they both beheld a half dozen men standing with their weapons drawn.

One of the men stepped forward.

"I'm afraid you're not going anywhere," he said in a loud ringing voice. "Seize them!"

# 12

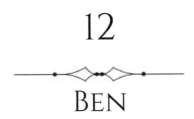

# BEN

The first light of early morning was creeping over the Gray Mountains in the east, yet the peak of Mount Earod still cast its long shadow over the city of Ethriel. The training grounds for the City Watch were silent. Everyone was still asleep except for Ben, who was already up working on his sword techniques. His muscles ached, but he pushed through the pain. It'd been two weeks since his fight with Jacob, which meant that the rematch and his future career in the City Watch would be decided today. He'd worked hard, but in the back of his mind he wondered if his efforts and new skills would be enough. On guard, then head block, then left shoulder block, then right leg block. Thrust, parry, dodge, reverse. Over and over Ben practiced, building his muscle memory while also battling his inner anxiety.

After another hour of training, Ben took a short break. He headed over to the well for a drink, but shouts and cries from the nearby match pit drew his attention. Apparently the other trainees were now awake and quite lively. Walking over, he found a large group of boys assembled along the fence; in the center of the pit was Jacob holding one of the younger boys in a headlock and punching him in the face. The other boys were taunting the young boy and as Ben watched this, something inside him snapped. Before he had time to think, Ben dropped his practice sword, jumped the fence, crossed the pit, grabbed Jacob's arm and twisted it around. Jacob released the boy, who ran for the fence, while Ben swept Jacob's legs out from under him and knocked him to the ground.

Ben jumped back and moved into a defensive stance as Jacob picked himself up, a wild angry look on his face.

"Bad move, Benjie!" He taunted.

"You're done here, Jacob," Ben said, his righteous anger overriding his fear.

"Yeah? And whose gonna stop me? You!" Jacob laughed, garnering the laughter of the boys along the fence. He then pulled out a real knife and brandished it at him. "We've a rematch later today, but looks like you want your final lesson early."

Shock flashed across Ben's face. He should have known better than to fight Jacob. Why had he risked his life helping that kid? He was unarmed and his eyes darted to his discarded practice sword which might have provided some protection. Jacob tossed the knife from hand to hand as he circled Ben, who moved to counter. Jacob thrust at Ben, who dodged and grabbed Jacob's arm.

"Stupid move!" Jacob called, punching Ben in the face and swiping at Ben's exposed left arm. Ben stumbled backwards, grabbing his arm as pain erupted from the gash in his arm. Fighting back the urge to howl in pain and to rage at Jacob, Ben resumed his defensive stance.

Jacob smiled sinisterly but Ben glared back defiantly. His nose was gushing blood as was the gash in his arm, yet Ben remained shakily on his feet and prepared for Jacob's next attack. In a moment, Jacob was on him again, swiping at his chest. Ben had barely managed to dodge the attack when Jacob grabbed his right arm and hurled him to the ground.

This time Ben found it harder to get up.

"You're dead, Greymore!" He heard Jacob shout.

He saw Jacob's shadow move towards him. Ben rolled over and kicked with all his might at Jacob's unguarded legs. A howl from his opponent told him his aim was true.

Suddenly, a booming voice cut through the din of shouts and calls from the boys along the fence. Ben glanced over and saw Captain Saul Gunter and Sir Eric Teague crossing the pit towards them. Anger etched in both of their faces.

"Just couldn't wait to kill each other?" The captain growled, kicking the knife from Jacob's hand and hoisting him up by his shirt.

"Up here, boy," said Sir Eric.

Ben glanced up to see Sir Eric extending his hand to him. He took it, and was hoisted to his feet also.

"Both of you to the infirmary!" The captain shouted. "The rest of you to the barracks!"

"I'll escort this one, captain," Sir Eric said, grabbing Ben by his right arm and dragging him from the pit.

✳  ✳  ✳  ✳

Thirty minutes later, Ben was sitting on a hospital bed watching the physician sow and bandage up his arm under the angry gaze of Sir Eric. Once the physician was finished and had left, Sir Eric rounded on Ben.

"Have you lost your mind, Ben?"

Ben didn't respond nor did he meet Sir Eric's angry gaze.

"Your father has been worried sick. Sent word to the Citadel asking me to look into your disappearance and I find you here of all places." Sir Eric paused. Ben could feel the other man's eyes boring into him. "Have you no remorse for the pain you've caused?"

Ben still didn't answer, but felt all the anger, fear, and frustration of the past several years welling up inside him.

"Answer me, Ben." Sir Eric demanded, almost pleadingly.

"Why did you run away without a word?"

Ben looked up suddenly with defiance in his eyes.

"Because I don't want to be a shopkeeper for the rest of my life!" He burst out suddenly. Both he and Sir Eric seemed shocked at his sudden outburst.

"But why run away?" Sir Eric asked at length.

"I want my own life," Ben said, in a much softer tone. "You've known my father a long time, Sir Eric. You know he thinks me weak and unable to make it as a soldier." Ben noticed Sir Eric's eyes dart towards his wounded shoulder and felt a sudden surge of shame and his gaze fell to the floor. "I just...I had to at least try."

There was a long pause where Sir Eric simply stood looking hard at Ben, who grew very uncomfortable.

"Alright," He said at length, placing a hand on Ben's shoulder. "You want to stay and see if you have what it takes? Captain Gunter told me that you have a match scheduled for this afternoon with another boy."

"Yes."

"The same boy that you were just fighting?"

"Yes."

"He also told me that the winner gets to stay and the loser is sent home."

"Yes."

"Are you sure about this Ben?" Sir Eric asked, with a heavy sigh.

Ben looked up at Sir Eric and, with his eyes narrowed and face contorted with determination, he nodded again.

"Then follow me," Sir Eric said, smiling and leading Ben outside.

They left the infirmary and Sir Eric led the way back to the practice area. Once there, he picked up two practice swords and tossed one to Ben.

"Show me what you know."

Ben immediately assumed a defensive stance, expecting Sir Eric to attack, but the other man simply stood with his sword pointed towards him.

"Attack me."

Ben swung, aiming at Sir Eric's left shoulder, but the other man parried the bow and struck Ben hard on his right thigh. Ben grunted and stumbled away in pain.

"Again!" shouted Sir Eric.

Ben attacked again, this time aiming at Sir Eric's head, but before he could blink, his attack was blocked and Sir Eric was pushing the point of his sword at Ben's neck.

Ben swallowed, blinking in surprise.

"You attack without regard for your opponent's response or the possibility of follow up attacks. Your technique is sloppy, Ben. You must learn to plan your attacks." Sir Eric said, turning his back.

Ben felt anger and resentment rising in his chest. He swung in anger at Sir Eric's exposed back, but Sir Eric had anticipated this. He blocked Ben's blow and brought his blade up hard against Ben's hands, stinging his knuckles. Ben winced, dropped his sword, then felt a sharp blow on his hurt shoulder, sending him to the ground.

"Only a fool attacks in anger, and only a coward attacks when his opponent's back is turned!" Sir Eric shouted down at him. "Pick up your sword and fight honorably or go home now!"

Ben picked up his sword and stood up with an effort; his bandaged shoulder was bleeding slightly and his whole arm was throbbing.

"Shall we continue?" Sir Eric asked tersely.

He glared defiantly up at Sir Eric and nodded.

❊　❊　❊　❊

Ben and Sir Eric sparred for almost three hours. The mental, if not physical, benefit of learning under the tutelage of such an experienced warrior like Sir Eric was that his technique seemed to be improving. At least, Ben wanted to believe he was improving. He spent much of the time either disarmed or on the ground. Sir Eric did not go easy on him and after those three hours his body was protesting the beating he was enduring. At length, Sir Eric held up his hands.

"Enough," Sir Eric said finally. "You've improved, if only slightly."

"Enough to defeat Jacob?"

"I don't know," Sir Eric replied, pointing to the practice pit. "We will both see soon enough."

Ben looked and saw a large crowd gathering there, and felt his heart sink. Sir Eric came over and clapped him on the shoulder, then they slowly made their way over to the pit. With every step Ben's apprehension grew. His stomach was churning and his hands shook. The crowd around the pit was alive with anticipation, and as they neared the perimeter, Ben glanced over and saw several boys betting on the outcome of the match. They glanced at Ben as he walked by and sneered at him. His heart fell further, knowing that he was not the favorite for this match.

They reached the gate, and Sir Eric ushered Ben inside the pit. Captain Gunter and Jacob stood in its center waiting as Ben crossed over toward them. The captain tossed a practice sword at Ben as he approached, and upon picking it up, he noticed that it was much heavier in the hand. Glancing down, Ben saw that it was a steel sword with blunted edges. What little confidence Ben possessed before entering the pit, now instantly evaporated. How could he hope to defeat Jacob now?

"Face each other," The captain ordered.

Ben and Jacob took their positions, facing one another. Jacob leered at him, but Ben stared back determinedly. This was his chance and he wasn't going to show any fear.

"This match will decide who stays and who goes home," The captain said with a knowing smile at Jacob. "First to land a blow on his opponent is the victor."

A long moment of silence followed before he heard the captain yell, "Fight!"

Ben immediately circled to his right as he knew that Jacob would immediately attack his left side. Sure enough, Jacob's blade sliced through empty air as Ben attacked Jacob's exposed left shoulder. Despite being caught off guard, Jacob quickly blocked Ben's initial blow. Jacob turned and lunged at Ben, who parried the blow and turned Jacob's sword. Jacob punched Ben in the chest with his unarmed hand, sending him stumbling backwards. Shaking off the blow, Ben blocked a wild attack on his legs and pushed his opponent backwards.

Ben saw frustration growing on Jacob's face and he smiled. Jacob had expected to win this match easily, but Ben had become more of a challenge now after his training with Sir Eric.

"Wipe that smile off your face, Benjie!" he yelled. "You think you've got any chance in defeating me?"

"You look angry, Jacob," Ben taunted. "What's the matter? Has it finally hit you that you're not going to win this fight?"

"I'll never lose to a weakling like you, Greymore!"

Jacob swung wildly at Ben's legs, but he easily leapt away. Jacob followed up his attack with a wide swing at Ben's head, but he ducked and rolled away. Ben smiled, knowing that he was getting to him. Jacob was becoming angry and an angry opponent was more prone to make mistakes. Ben just had to figure out a way to use Jacob's anger to his advantage.

He glanced to his right and was momentarily blinded by the glare from the setting sun. A sudden idea hit him and he feigned an attack on Jacob's left, forcing his opponent to dodge into the blinding glare. Jacob threw up his left hand to shade his eyes and in that instant, Ben lunged forward striking Jacob in the chest with his sword point. Ben had done it. He'd won.

# 13

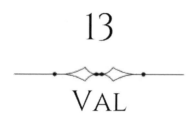

# VAL

The market of Nenholm was alive with activity. It was midday and the merchants were calling to passersby and displaying their wares. Everything from fish allegedly caught this morning, to beautiful jewelry imported from far away. There were eggs, live chickens, pigs and yokes of oxen. The din of the calling merchants and animals was deafening. Plus the plethora of smells and aromas intermixing from the various stalls were enough to numb the nose of anyone used to such assaults on the old factory senses.

Val stood in the midst of the crowded street, her simple brown robes flapping around her ankles thanks to the occasional breeze. Her hood was pulled up over her brown hair, shielding her hazel eyes from the sun as she scanned the crowd, ever searching for her mark.

She moved slowly through the mass of people, still scanning for her target. Suddenly a merchant grabbed her by the arm and she had to suppress the urge to retaliate. He pulled her through the crowd towards his stall, which was more like a small pavilion, that contained many varieties of exotic birds. A snowy white owl caught her attention as its amber eyes gazed appraisingly back at her from its perch. A truly beautiful creature, and there was an intelligence behind those eyes. Recognizing her interest, the merchant quickly moved towards the bird.

"You have an eye for the rare and exotic, young lady." He said smoothly, flashing an unsettling grin. "For this rare bird, I will only ask for ten silver lions."

"No thank you," Val said, moving to leave.

"Uh, five silver lions," the merchant called after her.

She thanked the man, but shook her head, then returned to the crowded street. She could feel him glaring after her, but shrugged it off. As she exited the stall, she caught sight of her target. A man in flowing dark blue robes was standing near another stall some twenty yards down the street. From this distance, Val could see he had a tanned complexion, wore a small purple turban, which was a mark of wealth in his country no doubt, and seemed to be haggling with one of the venders. She had her mark. The man turned away from the vender and moved further down the street. Val moved into the midst of the crowd, edging her way closer to the man. Yet when she'd closed the distance to ten feet, the man turned down a side street where the crowd was less dense. She followed, but had to increase the distance between them to remain unnoticed. Suddenly, the man turned back towards her and Val had to slide over behind a stall that stood against a building in order to avoid detection. She watched from the shadows until her mark turned back around and continued on his way.

With less people, she knew that she would have a harder time getting close enough to her target. She watched and waited until the man was a good twenty yards away again, then Val returned to shadowing him, slowly closing the gap between them. He stopped again at another vender who was selling a variety of cloth. She watched from ten feet away as the man ran his fingers over a length of bright blue cloth, and nodded to the vender as he pulled out his money purse. Val saw her opportunity and moved quickly to close the distance. She was five feet away when someone jostled her from behind. Val spun around to look, then glanced down at her robes to find a bright red circle pinned to her right arm.

Her heart sank as she glanced about for the person responsible, catching sight of Annet's face as she winked at her then turned down an alleyway. She was also wearing simple brown robes with the hood pulled over her head. Feelings of anger and frustration, Val rushed after Annet. She pushed her way across the crowded street and into the vacant alleyway, which was dark. The cobbled street was partially covered with grime, making it slick so that she had to watch her footing. Annet was standing some ten feet into the alley watching as Val approached.

"Val, you are dead," Annet said, simply.

It stunned Val, which only made her all the angrier.

"Why didn't you tell me you'd be hunting me while I was stalking my target?" She shouted.

"An assassin must always be aware of her surroundings. You cannot successfully follow a mark and not take in everything around you."

"This was not a fair test!" Val protested.

"No assignment is fair, Val. When you are stalking your target, you must always be on the watch in case you are someone else's target."

"Give me another chance. This time I won't make the same mistake."

Annet considered Val for a long moment, then beckoned for Val to follow her as she moved to the alley's entrance. She led her to the top of a nearby building and there they surveyed the crowd.

"See that man there?" she asked, pointing.

Val followed her finger to a young man standing in the midst of the crowded street. He had long brown hair, and was wearing a plain tan tunic. She nodded.

"I've been assigned to assassinate him. You will attempt to follow me and if you get the chance, pin your red circle on me."

Annet didn't give Val a chance to object, but leapt from the rooftop into a pile of hay below. "Your second chance begins now!" She called over her shoulder as she got to her feet and disappeared into the crowd.

Val wasted no more time, and leapt into the hay pile also, though less gracefully. Getting quickly to her feet, she moved into the crowd, her eyes darting this way and that in search of her mentor. After several minutes she gave up looking for Annet, deciding that it'd be easier to find the young man. She pushed forward toward the place she'd last seen him, and upon reaching it she saw the young man about a dozen yards away. Then she spotted her mentor, who was quickly closing the distance between her and the young man. Val knew she didn't have enough time to reach her and pin the red circle on her. She'd missed her chance, so she stood there watching Annet, who was feet from her target. Suddenly, she sprang away, disappearing into a vacant stall. Val frowned, her eyes following her mentor completely confused by her actions. Turning back to the young man, she instantly understood Annet's swift abandon of her target. A group of soldiers had just arrested the young man and were dragging him away.

Val moved slowly towards the stall where Annet was hiding, and slipped inside. She found her watching the soldiers from the shadows.

"What now?" Val asked.

"An assassin must always be ready to improvise," she answered, still watching the soldiers as they hauled the young man away. "He will be taken to the castle, no doubt."

"How will you get in there?"

"It would not be my first time to infiltrate the castle in order to complete my mission," Annet said with a grin.

✳   ✳   ✳   ✳

It was night when Annet and Val reached the foot of Nenholm's castle. Its gray walls rose up ominously in the darkness. The two women had changed into black robes to better conceal themselves. Val followed Annet along the castle's perimeter until she stopped in front of a large drain embedded in the wall. She pulled the grate up and led Val into a long, dark tunnel leading steadily downward. The tunnel stank of mold and decay, and the ceiling of the tunnel was short, forcing the two women to crouch as they moved downward. There was no light, so Val had to feel her way along as best as she could. She cringed as her hands were soon covered in some unknown filth as they felt along the tunnel's walls.

"This tunnel was made many years ago by the Guild in case a target was arrested before being dealt with," Annet explained. "Being an assassin is not glamorous work, nor is it for the timid."

Val did not respond and they continued along, eventually reaching another grate at the end of the drain. A dim light was shining through the bars, and Val could not help but be comforted. They emerged from the drain into a corridor, lit only by a few torches standing in brackets along the walls. Cells lined the walls between the torches, yet there were no guards around. Annet stole down the corridor, peering into each cell as she went. At last she stopped, staring through the bars at the young man from the market.

"Kurt?" she whispered.

The young man looked up in surprise, then came to the door. "Who are you?"

"Never mind," Annet hissed, starting to pick the lock. "We've come to get you out."

In a moment, the cell door swung open and the young man, Annet, and Val were running back up the corridor, crawling back up the drain tunnel, and out into the cold night. They stood panting under the shadow of the castle walls.

"How can I ever thank you?" The young man started to say, but Annet, moving as quick as lightning, pulled a dagger from within her robs and plunged it into the young man's chest. Val, horror struck, watched the young man stumble, then fall to the ground.

"Come," Annet hissed, running toward the safety of the dark city streets. Val looked down with pity at the body of the young man for a moment, then followed Annet. They ran on for several minutes, then stopped about half a mile from the castle. They slipped down a dark alley way, and stood panting.

"Why did you kill him?" Val gasped.

"What?" Annet turned towards her with a look of confusion.

"Why did you bother to rescue that young man from the castle dungeons only to kill him?"

"He was a former recruit of the Assassin's Guild," answered Annet, straightening up.

"What!"

"He abandoned his training and the Guild Masters decided that he was a liability. I retrieved him from the dungeons so that our secret passage might remain secret."

"The Guild Masters?"

"They governed the Guild of Assassins," Annet said, quickly glancing up and down the street. "Did you learn anything from observing me?"

"You tell me," Val said, pointing at her mentor's sleeve.

Annet glanced down and saw a red circle pinned to her sleeve.

"When—," she began, utterly perplexed.

"In the tunnel just before you killed the young man."

Annet looked taken aback, then beamed at her student.

"I think you are ready. Follow me." She said, leading down the alley way.

※　※　※　※

About fifteen minutes later, they reached the same building where Val had first met Annet. She led the way inside, down the main corridor, and to the foot of a stairwell. Stooping down, she pulled a threadbare rug aside, revealing a wooden trap door. Swinging the door up, Annet guided the way down a spiral staircase leading down below the building. Val followed behind her down the staircase until it ended in a corridor lit with many torches. At the far end was a large wooden door, which seemed ancient. The wood was cracked in places and the metal bounds and hinges were rusted slightly. Val expected Annet to head straight for it, but instead she turned down a side door and led Val through a maze of corridors. Just as Val was beginning to wonder where her mentor might be leading her, Annet turned a corner and stopped suddenly. Val nearly ran into her, and stumbled back a few steps. When she'd regained her footing, she glanced about the short passage that led to a dead end. Other than a small fountain of water that bubbled and flowed into a basin set to one side, the passage was empty save the two women. Annet turned towards her student and took a deep breath before speaking.

"Are you committed to becoming an assassin?" she asked, looking Val straight in the eye.

Val nodded.

"Then prepare yourself for the trials," she said, turning and placing a hand on the far wall. Val gasped as there was a grinding noise of stone on stone. The wall in front of them opened up onto a roughly hewn tunnel, which was barely lit. Only a dim greenish grow, which seemed to be coming from the walls and ceiling, allowed the first few feet of the tunnel to be visible; beyond that lay a gaping blackness of unknown dangers.

"Behold the Forsaken Labyrinth. This is the final task that all assassins must pass before they are allowed to join the Guild. Most students require years of training before attempting this final trial, but you have shown exceptional aptitude and ability during your training. I have faith in your abilities," Annet said, turning back towards her. "You must leave all your gear."

Val obeyed, taking off her pack and outer robes.

"This will be your only tool," Annet held out a small dagger.

Val took it and held it up. It was of simple design, but the blade was very sharp.

"There is only one way into the maze and one way out. If you enter, you must either survive the trials or perish."

Val gaped at Annet, and saw deep concern in her eyes.

"And if I choose not to enter the maze?"

"You must leave Nenholm, and never return under pain of death."

Val looked at her mentor, her heart beating fast.

"You will face many trials if you enter the maze," Annet said, laying a hand on her shoulder.

"Like what?"

"I cannot say. Only remember this: Endurance, Courage, Discernment, and Mercy." Annet removed her hand and stepped back.

"I don't understand," Val said, looking for some explanation on Annet's face. "What do you mean?"

"I can say no more." Annet removed her hand and stepped back. Pulling a water skin from her robes, she filled it with clear water from the basin and handed it to her student.

Val looked at her, hesitated for a long moment, then turned and stepped inside. The wall grinded back into place, leaving her trapped in the dim greenish light of the corridor beyond. She was in the Forsaken Labyrinth. Her only hope now for survival and vengeance on Silas Morgan was to make it through alive.

# 14

# ROOK

Rook awoke suddenly, finding himself in near complete darkness. He was face down on a thin blanket, his hands tied behind his back and his head throbbed in pain. He rolled onto his back, and regretted it instantly as it caused his head to throb even more. He saw that he was back in the same holding tent. It'd been several days since Jonas had attempted to rescue him. *Poor kid.* In the days following the escape attempt, he'd been interrogated three times. The sessions were long and he never knew the answers to the questions they asked. In between sessions he was returned here to this tent, often battered and bruised. That was two or three days ago, at least as far as he could determine from inside this dark tent. Since his last interrogation, he'd been left in here with his thoughts, wondering how Jonas was fairing.

He mused on this for several minutes before his thoughts were interrupted by the tent entrance opening abruptly. Sunlight poured in blinding Rook as two men entered, hoisted him roughly to his feet, and dragged him outside. Outside the sunlight caused his eyes to smart, and the cold wind cut through his thin clothing as if it wasn't there. Almost instantly frozen to the bone, Rook squinted about in an attempt to try and take in his surroundings. When his vision had almost cleared, the two men turned aside and headed for a large tent in the midst of the camp. Before the tent entrance, a banner stood waving in the wind. Rook recognized the symbol at once: two black swords crossed in an 'X' pattern on a field of gray. His heart sank. Though he'd never been brought to the captain's tent, the thought of further interrogation seemed imminent.

They dragged him inside the tent, forcing Rook's eyes to have to readjust once again. In the dim light, his gaze fell upon a tall, younger-looking man with sandy brown hair and eyes. He was sitting sideways at a small desk littered with papers—here sat the apparent captain of the mercenaries. To the captain's right sat Jonas, who appeared unharmed. Rook stared at him, wondering how the young man had managed to avoid the brutal interrogation the he'd endured. Another chair was brought over and the two men sat Rook down in it forcefully. They cut his bonds and left the tent without a word. Rook sat rubbing his sore wrists and looking at the captain with mixture of anger and curiosity.

"Jarrod Rook," the captain said with mild interest. "Your reputation precedes you."

"Glad to hear it," Rook said, his eyes narrowing as he continued rubbing his wrists. "And you are Kaven Ciles, captain of the Grey Company."

"Guilty as charged," he said, with a smile. "Call me Kaven. I must apologize for your treatment. My lieutenants can be overly zealous at times."

Rook remained silent.

"You're would be savior here, Master Jonas Astley, has been telling me quite a tale."

Rook glanced over at Jonas, who grimaced.

"Don't be too hard on the boy. He may have saved your life." Kaven said, with a meaningful look at Rook.

"What day is it?" Rook asked, with a sigh.

"It's been five days since my men recaptured you. Since my return and my conversation with Jonas here, I've been considering his story and our next move." Kaven retrieved a piece of parchment from the desk and walked over to hand it to Rook.

"What is this?"

"Just read it," Kaven said, returning to his chair.

Rook glanced over the document. It was an agreement between the Grey Company and Lord Silas Morgan. In exchange for sizable fortune, the Grey Company was to stage an attack on Fairhaven. As he read on, Rook's grip on the page tightened in anger.

"So you made an agreement with Silas Morgan. Hope you got payment in advance," Rook said, glancing up at Kaven.

"Of course," Kaven grinned. "His reputation is also well known, both before and after he became a high lord of Alethia."

"So why did Silas want you to stage an attack?"

"You'd have to ask him," Kaven answered.

Rook frowned at Kaven. He suspected the young captain knew the reason behind the attack, but getting the truth out of him wouldn't be easy.

"So why show me this?" Rook asked at length, handing the parchment back.

"Because I know your true name, Rook."

Rook forced his face to remain expressionless. Out of the corner of his eye he saw Jonas glance over at him, but he ignored him.

"I also know you have a past friendship with King Corin. I was hoping you might convince him to grant me an audience."

"Even if I did know the king at one time, to what purpose would you request an audience?"

"Look, Rook," Kaven began, standing and pacing the floor of the tent. "I may not be a loyal citizen of this kingdom, but I do know that a stable Alethia is good for business."

"How so?" Rook asked, in disbelief. "I thought war and chaos was what mercenaries thrive upon."

"Let's just say that there is plenty of chaos out there in the world for me and my men to take advantage of, but we like to know there's a refuge out there waiting for us. A quiet place to relax and recuperate."

"So why stage an attack?" Rook asked, his eyes narrowed in further suspicion. "Why agree to help stir up strife in your vacation spot?"

"Why else?" Kaven shrugged. "The money was too good."

"Of course," Rook said, with a look of disgust. "But something happened didn't it? Something messed up the plan."

They eyed one another for a long moment, then Kaven lowered his gaze and shook his head.

"Alright fine," Kaven said, holding up his hands in sign of surrender. "The truth is that, according to our agreement, we were only supposed to stage an attack on Fairhaven, but before we arrived another army was already laying siege to the city."

"Another army? Who were they? Where were they from?"

"We don't know." Kaven turned and stared off. His eyes were unfocused and his face contorted with angst, as if reliving a traumatic event. "There were thousands and thousands of them. More men than I could count. My men and I were too few to stop them. All we could do was watch. The dark army entered the city and such screams I have never heard. Countless soldiers, all clad in dark mail, slaughtering the people. Then I saw a large shadow cross the moon. A great winged beast that spouted fire from its mouth and towers fell before it. I think you know of what I speak, Rook."

Kaven turned and Rook gaped at him.

"Impossible," Rook said, dismissively. "There's been no dragon in Alethia for hundreds of years."

"Dragon!" Jonas exclaimed. "So that's what destroyed the barrier at Elmloch."

Rook shot him a glance that silenced him. He turned back to see Kaven looking between them.

"Elmloch, eh?" He said, stroking his beard.

"Never mind," Rook growled, waving a hand. "So you don't know where this army comes from?"

"All we've heard are rumors. I fear that Lord Morgan did not account for this dark army's sudden appearance when he planned his scheme."

"If he is even the mastermind of this plot," Rook interjected. He heard Jonas mutter "Methangoth," but Kaven did not seem to hear him.

"They allegedly conquered Eddynland in less than two weeks. After that, they crossed the Waterdale and took Fairhaven in a single day.

"Fairhaven fell in a day?" Rook heard Jonas mumble.

"Since then we've tried to shadow the dark army as it crossed the Elmbrook. That was about six days ago. I tried sending scouting parties, but any that I've sent have never returned. Even still, there's only one place they could be headed, Rook."

"Farodhold," Rook muttered.

"Farodhold!" Jonas exclaimed. "We can't let them destroy Farodhold! We have to do something!"

"What do you suggest?" Kaven asked, obviously annoyed.

"What of Galanor?" Jonas asked. "He can help, right?"

Rook remained silent.

"Galanor the wizard?" Kaven asked, earnestly. "You know where he is?"

"We were traveling together," Jonas said, quickly. "We'd just arrived at Elmloch Castle when we came under attack. He's the one who sent me into your camp to rescue Rook."

"So he's still nearby?"

"I don't know, but I assume so." Jonas replied with a shrug.

"In any case," Rook broke in. "We must get word to Farodhold of this dark army."

"To what end?" Kaven asked, doubtfully. "What possible defenses could they have against a dragon?"

"I don't know," Rook growled, feeling his anger rising. "But we have to do something. They must be warned."

"How will you even get there? The dark army lies between you and the city."

"I might know a way," Jonas interjected.

Kaven turned towards him, looking skeptical, but Rook smiled.

"There you have it," he said, standing with an effort. "Do you have horses we could use?"

Kaven's eyes narrowed as he considered Rook and Jonas, then nodded slowly.

"Good," Rook said, moving towards the door.

They exited the tent and Kaven led the way to a crude paddock where several horses were grazing. He selected two, had them saddled, and Rook and Jonas were astride them in fifteen minutes. Before leaving, Rook turned to Kaven.

"What would you have us do?" Kaven asked, with some uncertainty.

"Shadow the dark army for as long as possible. You may be able to aid in Farodhold's defense."

"For a price," Kaven said, shot him with a meaningful grin. "We do have expenses."

"I'm sure something can be arranged," Rook said, frowning.

"Wait," Kaven said, quickly. He grabbed Rook's hand and forced something round and cold into it. Rook looked down at a small medallion. Upon its gray metal surface was the emblem of the Grey Company—two black swords crossed in an 'X' pattern. "If you meet a member of the Grey Company again this will mark you as a friend. You should find our hospitality much improved."

"Thank you," he said with a nod. Then turning to Jonas, he said, "Lead on."

✳   ✳   ✳   ✳

After a long day of riding without rest, Rook and Jonas checked their horses on a high ridge. A vast expanse of rolling plains ran from the hill upon which they stood to the Bay of Ryst. The sun was dipping lower and the cold wind whipped at their faces as both men gaped. On the plains below them stood a camp stretching out from below the ridge all the way to the bay.

Thousands upon thousands of dark figures moved about the camp in the dim half-light. In the distance stood a large city of many towers—the city of Farodhold. A massive castle stood upon a tall, steep peak in the midst of the city, and the city walls rose high above the dark host. Rook could see the enemy soldiers closest to the city were setting up siege weapons in preparation for a night attack. He glanced over to see Jonas staring open-mouthed at the army besieging his home.

"Jonas," Rook said, reaching over to shake the young man, who started and turned. "Are you alright?"

Jonas didn't turn but nodded, quickly.

"How do we get inside?"

Jonas's jaw set and his eyes narrowed. "Follow me."

Turning his horse northward, he galloped away. Rook followed as they made their way around the dark host, passing within a hundred yards of the enemy camp. Rook glanced to the west to see the last remnants of the sun set behind the horizon. In the distance, barely visible, was an old decrepit looking tower sitting on a low crag near the bay. The enemy forces had chosen to ignore the old ruin, but Jonas made straight for it. Rook wondered why, but decided to give the young man the benefit of the doubt.

When they reached the northern side of the crag, they dismounted.

"We should leave the horses here," Jonas whispered. "We'd never be able to lead them up to the tower and their presence might bring unwanted attention."

"Let's just send them back to Kaven then," Rook said, releasing the reigns and goading the animal off. Jonas did the same, and they both stood watching the horses gallop away until they disappeared into the twilight.

When they were out of sight, Rook turned to Jonas. The young man was still staring off where the horses had disappeared.

"Jonas?" Rook whispered at length. The young man started once again, this time turning towards him. "Where to next?"

Jonas hesitated, shifting his feet awkwardly. When he spoke, his voice was shaky. "Rook, I need to ask you something before I take you any further."

"Oh?" Rook folded his arms.

"Who are you, really?"

Rook looked hard at Jonas for a moment, then placed a hand on Jonas's shoulder. "My name is Jarrod Rook," he said with what he hoped was an amicable finality.

"But what did Kaven Ciles mean when he said that he knew your true name?"

"I have not always gone by the name Jarrod Rook," he answered slowly. "Yet it is my name."

"I don't understand," Jonas said, shaking his head.

Rook sighed, heavily, dropping his gaze.

"Many years ago, I went by another name. I had a wife and was a member of the Guardians of the Citadel and a friend of King Greyfuss Aurelia." Rook turned back and saw Jonas's eyes had grown wide in amazement. "But that was long ago, before the king was murdered, before Noliono usurped the throne, and before the Second War of Ascension. After the war, I left the Guardians and changed my name. I traveled far, searching for something I knew not what. Eventually, I made a life for myself on the frontier."

"So who are you?"

"I already told you," Rook answered sternly. "I am Jarrod Rook, the same man who rescued you from wolves in the Eastern Woodlands. I'm the man who rescued you from XtaKal, and I'm the man who led you to Elmloch Castle. I've risked my life to help you more times than I can count. Do you no longer trust me?"

Jonas looked away. "I suppose I must," his voice was almost bitter. Without another word, he turned and began climbing toward the tower with Rook following close behind.

✳ ✳ ✳ ✳

After an hour of climbing, Jonas and Rook reached the top of the crag, which was a circular crown covered in short grass. In its midst stood the old ruined tower, aged and crumbling. Rook followed Jonas into the ruin, and glanced up to see stars. The tower had been gutted and only the circular stone walls remained. The floor was covered with a thick dust. Jonas walked over and swept away the dust with his hand, revealing a rusted iron handle.

"Here we go," he said, pulling upward on the handle.

There was a loud groan of wood on stone, then Jonas pulled open a small wooden trapdoor. He glanced up at Rook, smiling broadly. Rook joined him, gazing at a stone staircase, leading downward.

"Lead on," Rook said, with some apprehension.

Jonas glanced briefly at him with a look of uneasiness on his face, then descended the stairs. Rook pulled the trap door closed behind them, and they descended into the heart of the crag. There were more steps than Rook could count. Finally, after half an hour Jonas paused and Rook nearly walked into him.

"Sorry," he muttered. "Where are we?"

"We've reached the bottom of the stairs," he heard Jonas say.

"Now what?" Rook asked, trying in vain to pierce the pitch blackness.

"Here, take this," he heard Jonas say as he felt something shoved into his hands. There was a spark of flame, then Rook blinked as the light from the torch in his hand illuminated a long, roughly carved stone tunnel. Jonas lit another and then led the way down the tunnel.

They walked on in silence for a long time, until they reached another set of stairs leading upwards. Rook raised his torch and saw the stairs led to another trapdoor only ten feet above. Jonas led the way and upon reaching the top turned to Rook.

"Blow out your torch," he whispered.

They both did so, and Jonas was about to push on the door when it was jerked open from above. The light of many torches blinded the two men, and hands reached in and pulled them out and onto a hard stone floor.

"Declare yourselves!" A voice demanded.

"My name is Jonas Astley," Rook heard Jonas say.

"Master Jonas?"

Rook's vision cleared and he saw a dozen men were standing over him and Jonas, weapons drawn. They were staring in wonder at the two of them.

"Where are we?" Rook asked.

"You're within the walls of Farodhold," said one of the soldiers. "And who are you?"

"This is Jarrod Rook," said Jonas.

Rook heard a murmur move through the men. Apparently his name was still recognized.

"Master Jonas, there was rumor that the company of Bordermen you were with was massacred."

"The rumor is true," Jonas said, getting to his feet. "Please, take me to my father. There is much we must tell him."

At that moment, there was a loud boom. The ground shook violently, causing them all to stumble and fall.

"It's too late!" yelled Rook over the din. "The dark army attacks!"

# 15

# MADDY

It was night and Maddy found herself wandering aimlessly through the vastness of Windham Manor. It had been two weeks since her confrontation with the baron. Since then, she'd shed many tears and endured many visits from her mother, who'd tried to both console her and convince her that marrying the baron was the best choice. Maddy, finally tiring of her mother's meddling, had taken to exploring the manor and the grounds.

There were many rooms and corridors to explore within the manor. Some were filled with wondrous works of art hanging on the walls. Maddy loved these rooms, one of which contained artwork that actually predated the first Aurelian kings, making the paintings more than two hundred years old.

In another large room she found the walls lined with maps and rows of bookshelves laden with ancient tomes. Deciding that this must be the baron's library, Maddy had spent several nights returning to this room. She loved books and this room did not disappoint. The shelves contained a myriad of books on every subject imaginable. There were books on every topic from battle strategy to gardening techniques. There were books so small that they would fit into the palm of her hand, and others that were half as tall as she was. There were books with faded gold letters and pealing covers, while others seemed to have been printed only yesterday.

Despite her initial excitement in finding the library, Maddy's good mood did not last long and she found herself wandering the halls once again. Eventually, she left the manor and decided to explore the estate grounds. There she found lush gardens, which in spring would have been full of flowers but were now barren. She took to roaming the various trails that wove and twisted in between the gardens and which seemed to have been made specifically for those with no real notion of a destination but only wished to walk. There were paths that led to the hedges on the edge of the grounds, and others that led back to the gardens, and still others that led nowhere. In the bracing cold, Maddy often wandered aimlessly until she could no longer feel her fingers, then she retreated back into the warmth of the manor.

She'd enjoyed her walk through the estate's grounds the first day, taking comfort in her limited freedom. The manor and the grounds had much to offer to someone willing to explore. The second day of her wandering, she became aware of the conspicuous presence of the guards following her every move. After a few days spent out in the grounds with the guards closely following her left little doubt that she was indeed a prisoner rather than a guest at Windham Manor. She gave up her treks through the grounds and remained within the manor itself.

To make matters worse, every night the baron insisted she dine with him. She usually arrived as the servants were laying out the dishes, and she sat waiting for the baron to arrive. He was late every night, arriving disheveled and careworn, and unwilling to talk about his day. It was nearly dinner time now, and Maddy sighed as she reluctantly made her way back to the great hall.

Upon entering the hall, she was greeted by the familiar aroma of the wonderful foods the kitchen so often made for her and the baron. Maddy moved to the other end of the hall and cast her gaze upon the lavishly laden table with food of all sorts. A veritable feast lay upon the polished wood. She often wondered why the baron chose to eat this fine every night, but so far she'd still been unable to discern his reasons. The hot food steamed and the plethora of alluring aromas filling the air was torture. She sat down expectantly and glanced at the door, which stood closed, and she sighed. She wondered if the staff ever got frustrated that all their hard work got cold before it was enjoyed by their master.

In the interim, Maddy gazed about, taking in the stunning décor of the hall. The only sources of light came from the roaring fire in the hearth and the two large ornate chandeliers hanging overhead. The large stone hearth, flanked by stone griffins, always drew her eyes first. She loved the ornate chandeliers with crystal beads dangling from them, which sparkled in the light of the candles. There were several suits of armor lining the walls. Maddy smiled as she imagined them standing sentry over the baron's meal as they glowed red in the light of the fire. Then turning back to the table, she sighed again. It was the same every night. The main doors burst open, drawing Maddy's gaze. The baron entered, looking disheveled and careworn as he had every night for the past two weeks.

"Pardon my tardiness, my lady," he said with a slight bow, then taking his seat he began eating.

They ate in silence for a while, as they always did. Maddy, unable to take the silence any longer, decided that tonight she would break the cycle.

"You've seemed troubled these past few nights, my lord."

He glanced up at her with suspicion, but said nothing and returned to his meal.

"Perhaps if you confided in me, it might relieve some of your stress."

"I'm afraid I cannot confide in you just yet, my lady," he said, glancing up with a smirk. "Forgive my bluntness, but your trustworthiness has yet to be proven."

Their conversation was interrupted by a knock at the door. One of the baron's many servants entered and moved quickly over to the baron.

"My lord," he said with a quick bow. "The captain of the guard wishes to speak to you. He is waiting outside and appears very concerned."

The baron let out a heavy sigh, drained his wine glass, and stormed out of the room. The servant followed in his wake, closing the door behind them. Maddy hesitated for a moment, then she swiftly crossed the room and knelt beside the door listening.

She could hear two men talking heatedly. One was the baron and the other she assumed was the captain of the guard.

"What of the men along the western shore, captain?" came the irritated voice of the baron. "Has word been sent yet?"

"Yes, my lord," replied the captain. "We have over two hundred men who answered the summons."

"That will not be enough," growled the baron. "Lord Grehm has ordered a full mustering of all his lands. We are due in Abenhall in seven days. I want all able-bodied men armed and ready to march in three days, captain. Is that clear?"

"Yes, my lord," said the captain.

"And don't forget to check in on our young friend before you go."

From the hall came the sound of receding footfalls. Maddy opened the door a crack and watched as the two men walked down the hallway to the left and disappeared down a side passage.

She stood up, wondering if the "young friend" meant David, and quickly moved down the hallway to the entrance to the side passage. The door was closed, so she opened it slowly to reveal a set of stone steps leading downward. The faint sound of footfalls echoed back up the stairwell. Again she hesitated for only a moment, then descended the stairs in the hopes that they would lead her to David.

At the bottom of the stairwell, Maddy found herself at the end of a long stone corridor lined with cells. In between each cell hung a lamp that provided only a dim break in the overwhelming darkness. There was also a smell of damp decay permeating the place, which turned her stomach. She had to suppress her gag reflex as she stood there in the entrance to the corridor. Then she was suddenly struck by an overwhelming sense of entrapment. Lingering there for a moment, she debated fleeing back up the stairs to the safety of the dining hall. Yet she couldn't just give up on David. He was down here somewhere, and knowing that gave her resolve and a measure of courage. She pushed the idea of fleeing from her mind and stepped down the corridor.

Upon reaching the first cell, Maddy cautiously looked inside through the small barred window set in the door. Though it was very dark, she could determine that the cell was empty save a bed of stale straw and a wooden bucket. The dank smell grew stronger as she moved further down the corridor to the next cell, which was also empty. On and on she peered into each cell, only to find the same vacancy. When she'd reached the middle of the corridor, she heard the sound of male voices and heavy footfalls coming towards her. Unable to think of any other choice, she pulled open one of the cells and darted inside, pulling the door back in place but not closing it for fear of locking herself inside.

The voices were getting closer. Soon she could tell that they were the voices of the baron and the captain. She heard them pass by her cell and continue on back up the corridor to the stairs. When their voices were mere faint echoes on the stone walls, Maddy left her hiding place and continued on down the corridor in the direction from whence the baron and captain came.

After passing several more empty cells, Maddy thought she heard movement on down the corridor. She paused, listening, but the sound was gone. She moved in the direction she best guessed the sound came from and peered through the cell window.

"David?" she whispered, unable to help herself.

The occupant of the cell came to the window and Maddy saw the beaten and bruised face of her beloved.

"Maddy? Is that you?"

"Oh, David!" She cried, reaching through the bars to touch his face.

"Maddy, you must get out of here!" David hissed. "They will return soon and you cannot be found here with me."

"No!" she shouted. "I have to get you out of here!"

"You can't," he hissed, trying to console her. "The captain has the only key."

"I can't just leave you here!" She cried, bursting into tears.

"That is exactly what you must do, Maddy!" David said, reaching his hand to caress her tearstained face. She looked at him, his brown eyes gazing into her own, pleading with her to leave.

"I can't lose you, David," She whispered.

"It's too late. You don't have a choice, Maddy. You have to go, now." David said, holding her gaze, then whispering, "I love you."

"What is this?" came a familiar voice from down the corridor.

Maddy spun around to find the captain of the guard leering down at her.

"So," he said, moving towards her. "You thought you'd sneak down here and rescue the prisoner?"

"Run Maddy!" David cried.

The captain seized her by the arm and pulled her back up the corridor towards the stairs.

"Let her go!" she heard David cry.

"Shut up, boy," the captain growled. "I'll be back to tend to you soon enough."

✳   ✳   ✳   ✳

Maddy was back in the baron's study. The room was much darker than the last time she'd been here. The large bay window was dark, and the grounds were shrouded in the gloom of night. The tall, two-story room, lined with shelves upon shelves of books, loomed up on all sides. Yet Maddy paid them little mind as she sat, alone, sobbing. Her face in her hands, and her entire body shook with each sob. She had no idea how long she'd sat there. In fact the passage of time seemed immeasurable in her state of heartache and misery, and only served to fill her with further sorrow and dread.

The study door burst open, and Maddy turned to see both the baron and the captain enter, closing the door behind them. The baron crossed the room and stared down at her, fuming with barely controlled anger. He then walked behind his desk, as if assuming a position in order to pronounce judgment.

"Did you really think I wasn't watching you, Madeline?" he asked, hurling aside a stack of papers. "Did you really think you could rescue the young man from one of *my* cells?"

She gazed back at him with tears still welling up in her eyes. The sorrow and misery on her face must have softened the baron's rage, for she watched as the anger on his face transitioned to disappointment and despair. He bowed his head, shaking it slowly from side to side.

"What am I to do?" he asked without looking up. "What will it take for you to choose me?"

"I'm sorry, but I love David," she whispered. "Please, just let us go,"

He looked up at her shocked. She thought she saw him consider letting them go, then his face contorted.

"I guess the only way to convince you to marry me is to get rid of the last obstacle," he said, walking back from behind the desk. "Captain, I believe our guest in the dungeon has overstayed his welcome. Please reconcile this at once."

"With pleasure, my lord," the captain said.

"No!" Maddy cried, lunging at the baron.

He caught her by the arms and held her at bay. "Oh, and send some guards to escort Madeline back to her chambers," he said struggling to hold her. "She's had such a hard evening and needs rest."

"No!" She howled in protest. "Please, no!"

The doors opened and two guards came and wrestled Maddy out of the study as she howled in rage and despair. *How could God let this happen?*

# 16

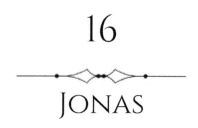

# JONAS

The ground shook violently, as Jonas, Rook, and the guardsmen made for the nearest tower and ascended to the battlements overlooking the plains east of the city. Archers lined the walls, preparing for the enemy advance. They ran along the walls until they reached the captain, who was issuing orders to his men.

"Report, captain!" shouted Jonas, in an uncharacteristically commanding voice.

"Master Jonas!" exclaimed the stunned captain. He stared in wonder for a moment, then shook himself. "Sir, the enemy has the city surrounded."

The man pointed out over the plains. Fires and torches dotted the fields below the walls. As they watched, some of the fires leapt up high into the air and came soaring towards them.

"Ballista!" the men cried, diving for cover.

The fireballs smashed into a nearby tower, scorching the stone and sending shockwaves across the adjoining walls. Getting to his feet, Jonas peered over the walls as another volley was fired.

"Brace!" came the voice of the captain. Jonas gazed skyward as the fiery balls came soaring overhead, yet this time they didn't reach the city. The fiery projectiles smashed against an invisible barrier like fireworks in the night sky. The men all stared up in wonder; all but Jonas and Rook who knew at once what had happened.

"Galanor!" cried Jonas.

"Come on!" Rook shouted. He led the way back towards the tower, with Jonas hot on his heels. When they reached the foot of the stairs, Rook turned towards Jonas. "Where would he be?"

"Follow me," Jonas said, running down the street towards the castle. The din of the continuing bombardment of the besiegers and the crowds of gawking onlookers made their going difficult. Pushing through the crowds, they ran onward. Jonas often glanced from side to side to see the faces of frightened people, looking out from dimly lit windows. Finally, they reached the gates of the castle. A slew of guards stood before the gates, but bowed them inside upon seeing Jonas. They ran on, as Jonas led the way across the courtyard towards the great hall. They entered, but found it empty save the serving staff.

"This way," Jonas called over his shoulder.

Running back out into the courtyard, he headed towards a large tower on the far side. They entered and ran up several flights of stairs, until they reached the highest landing. They skidded to a halt in front of a pair of large iron-bound wooden doors; several guards stood to either side.

"I'm here to see my father!" Jonas gasped, leaning against the cool stone wall.

"He is in council, Master Jonas," one of the guards said, with some uncertainty.

"I must speak to him!" Jonas cried. "I bring urgent news!"

The guards exchanged anxious looks.

"Oh for the love," Rook exclaimed, moving forward and pounding on the doors. "Peter Astley! Open the door and show your ugly face!"

Jonas and the guards stood gaping at Rook, unable to fathom

how this man could insult a high lord of Alethia...unless...

The doors opened and Jonas's father, Lord Peter Astley, stepped out onto the landing. He was an older man with graying hair. His face was lined, but there was fierceness in his eyes and vigor in his bones. He glared for a moment at Rook, then a sudden recognition crossed his face and he broke into a smile. Jonas stared in wonder as his father moved forward and shook hands with Rook, who returned a smile.

"I thought you were dead," Lord Astley said.

"Part of me," Rook said, his smile faltering slightly.

"It's been what, ten years?"

"Longer."

"Strange time for you to reappear," Lord Astley said with a frown.

"The perfect time," said a voice from behind Jonas's father.

Jonas looked and saw Galanor step forward, his face grim.

"It *was* you then," he exclaimed.

"Yes, Jonas," said Galanor, with the hint of a smile crossing his lips. "I made the barrier, and I am glad to see you've made it here unscathed.

"Some of us more than others," he heard Rook mutter as he touched his still swollen eye.

"Jonas?" Lord Astley exclaimed,

Jonas felt a wave of apprehension as his father's eyes fell upon him, but Lord Astley rushed forward and embraced him. Jonas stood, momentarily shocked and relieved at the same time.

"I heard word from the border and feared the worst," he said. Jonas overwhelmed by this uncharacteristic outpouring of affection from his father. "I've never been so happy to see you, son."

He embraced Jonas for a long while, then held him at arm's length, surveying him.

"Galanor tells me you stood up to XtaKal."

Jonas nodded, and he saw in his father's eyes something he'd never seen there before: pride.

"Son, I am so proud of you."

Jonas stared in disbelief at hearing those words. His father looked back at him and they embraced as father and son.

"I'm sorry, Lord Astley, but we have urgent matters," Galanor interrupted, moving between Jonas and his father. He turned to Jonas and whispered, "Is it safe?"

Jonas nodded, knowing at once what the old wizard was talking about. He reached for his bag, but the old man shook his head.

"Yes, of course," Lord Astley said, coming to himself and directing everyone into the council chambers.

Jonas joined the others as they passed through the great wooden doors, which closed quickly behind them. Inside the chambers sat a large rectangular table made of oak. Several chairs sat around the table. On the far side sat the high lord's chair, which was high-backed and ornately carved. Lord Astley took his seat, gesturing for the others to do the same. Only once everyone was seated, did Lord Astley speak.

"We are beset by a great host, which Galanor believes is led by an evil warrior known as XtaKal. This warrior seems to possess great power and lays siege to this city for some unknown purpose."

"His purpose is quite known, Lord Astley, as I have previously stated," said Galanor with some annoyance. "XtaKal is but a servant of the true threat: Methangoth, whose purpose is well known to most in this council chamber."

"So you say, Galanor," retorted Lord Astley. "But where is your proof? Thus far you have no evidence but your word that the evil sorcerer has returned."

"Who else could have enabled this army to take Fairhaven in a single day?" Galanor asked, his voice rising. "Who else could have destroyed the barrier I, Galanor, placed around Elmloch Castle?" Jonas saw the old wizard gaze about the room as if to dare anyone to argue with him. When no one spoke, he continued. "The barrier I have set around Farodhold will hold off the conventional attacks of this dark host, and even the powers of XtaKal."

"But what of the dragon?" Jonas asked, quickly.

Every eye turned towards him and he fell silent.

"Kaven Ciles, leader of the Grey Company, was witness to the fall of Fairhaven," interjected Rook. "He spoke of a great winged beast that spouted fire and broke through the walls and towers of the city."

"What was the Grey Company doing in Alethia?" Lord Astley asked, somewhat aggressively.

"They were contracted by Silas Morgan to feign an attack on Fairhaven." Rook answered. Jonas looked at his father and noted the look of surprise on his face did not reach his eyes.

"Did you know about this, father?" he asked before he could stop himself.

"His father shot him a glance, but for the first time in his life Jonas held his father's gaze, and to his astonishment his father was forced to avert his gaze. "You did, didn't you?"

"No, I did not!" Lord Astley shouted, rising from his seat. "A group of southern lords met in Nenholm some days ago to discuss the defense of our kingdom, since the current king has shown reluctance to deal with the current crisis. Some might even call it cowardice."

Jonas glanced over to see Rook's face contort with rage.

"You would be wise to recant those words, Peter Astley." He said as he rose to his feet.

The two men glared at one another.

"It is of no consequence," Lord Astley said at length. "Lord Warde is mustering an army near Norhold and will soon march south to our aid."

"He is already marching south with over five thousand men," said Galanor, gravely. "But Lord Warde will not save this city."

"Peter, your son and I have seen what XtaKal can do," said Rook. "What's more, if this beast Kaven spoke of is in fact a dragon…"

"It is a dragon," interjected Jonas. "I caught a glimpse of it flying over Elmloch Castle the night we escaped."

"It doesn't matter," Lord Astley said, waving off their concerns. "We will be victorious here at Farodhold. Then we will drive the dark host beyond the Waterdale and back into Eddynland."

"Very well," Galanor said, acquiescing. "Then it comes to my true purpose in coming here." Turning to Jonas he said, "Please bring forth the book."

Jonas nodded, reached inside his bag, and drew out the ancient tome.

"The Book of Aduin!" he heard Rook exclaim.

"Let there be no doubt," Galanor said. "This young man is the new guardian of the book, chosen by God."

Jonas was uncomfortably aware that all eyes were on him.

"Jonas," he heard his father whisper. He turned and saw the joy and pride disappear from his father's eyes, to be replaced with anger and accusation. "You brought this down on us. You brought that book here and doomed us all."

"The dark host arrived here before we did, Peter," interjected Rook. "We didn't bring this doom, but came to help avert it."

"Give the book to Galanor," Lord Astley commanded.

Jonas stood staring at his father, as if seeing him for the first time.

"He cannot, Lord Astley," Galanor said, rising to his feet once more. "He has been chosen as the book's guardian, and as such, he must become my apprentice."

Jonas stared at Galanor for a moment, dumbfounded.

"His place is here!" His father shouted, slamming his fist on the table. "He finally acts like a man and you insist that he abandons his family? He *will* join in the defense of this city."

There was a labored silence, where Galanor and Lord Astley glared at one another. Then the sound of a trumpet blast echoing through the castle drew their attention. They all turned as a man burst into the council chambers.

"My lord," he gasped. "Lord Warde has come."

❊   ❊   ❊   ❊

Lord Astley led the way to the tower battlements. Dawn was approaching and in the dim light Jonas could see a vast host assembling across the plains. The black banners bearing the white wolf of house Warde and the red feather of house Morgan, waved in the wind.

The dark army appeared to be reforming ranks in preparation. Cries and taunts aimed at the dark army came from the men along the city walls below.

"You see," pointed Lord Astley. "Every dawn brings hope, and this dawn has brought us our deliverance. Lord Warde has come, Galanor, and from this vantage point you will bear witness to our victory over this dark army."

Jonas looked out, comparing the two armies. Even caught between the city defenders and the approaching host of Lord Warde, the dark army still outnumbered them significantly. Horns and trumpets sounded from the two opposing sides as they marched towards one another. Jonas felt his heart pounding in his chest as he watched with both hope and dread. The front lines began running towards one another. They were mere yards away. Jonas stared in wonder as Lord Warde's forces reformed into six staggered phalanxes, and drove into the dark army. The phalanxes pierced the front lines of the dark army, forcing wedges between their formations. Jonas then saw Warde's cavalry units ride into the enemies left and right flanks. In a few moments, the enemy's lines crumbled and began running back toward the city. The defenders along the walls rained down arrows upon any that came near.

Jonas was just about to allow himself to smile, turning toward the others. The smile quickly slid off his face as he saw horror etched into the faces of Rook and his father. He followed their gaze skyward, and his jaw fell open in fear and dread. The rays of the rising sun fell upon an immense red dragon as it swooped upon Lord Warde's forces, belching red flames that scattered them and scorched the earth. Jonas watched in growing horror as the dark army rallied and advanced on Lord Warde's terror-stricken army. The dragon made several passes, each time sending scorching blasts of fire into the retreated men. The enemy gave chase and soon overwhelmed Warde's men. The dragon dove and snatched a man on horseback, flying high into the air.

"Lord Warde!" Jonas heard his father cry. Then they all gasped as the great beast let loose of its burden. The man fell more than a hundred feet, disappearing into the midst of the advancing dark army.

Jonas turned to his father, who was staring in disbelief. The sound of rushing wind drew his attention back to the battle as the dragon turned and sent fiery blasts at the city. The blasts hit the magic barrier protecting the city, sending reverberating shockwaves that shook the stones beneath their feet.

"It won't hold!" cried Galanor. "We must flee!"

They all turned and followed the old man back to the stairwell, and down the spiral staircase. Every few steps the tower shook violently, and Jonas nearly lost his footing more than once.

"Galanor," came Rook's voice. "How much longer will the barrier hold?"

There was a deafening explosion and the tower swayed violently as if it might topple over. Jonas glanced out a nearby window just in time to see the barrier give way and shatter into a thousand shooting stars. He stood in shock as he saw several large gaping holes appear in the walls protecting the eastern side of the city. Dark soldiers poured through the gaps as the city defenders abandoned their posts and fled.

"It's too late," Jonas said. "Farodhold has fallen."

# 17

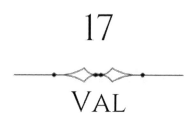

# VAL

A blood-curdling shriek broke the silence. Val awoke and leapt to her feet, brandishing her dagger. Her heart pounded in her chest, and for a brief moment, she was unable to remember where she was. Yet as her eyes adjusted and her breathing slowed to a more normal rate, it all came back to her. She sighed, returning her dagger to its sheath on her belt. She was standing in the middle of a long roughly hewn passageway. Only a dim greenish glow, which seemed to be coming from the walls and ceiling, allowed for a few feet of the tunnel to be visible in either direction; beyond that lay a gaping blackness of unknown dangers. Val closed her eyes, trying to steady herself as her memory came flooding back. She was still in the Forsaken Labyrinth.

Val gazed up and down the tunnel, trying and failing to pierce the darkness. She then knelt down beside the wall of the tunnel near where she'd fallen asleep. There, thinly etched in the hard stone, she found a small arrow she'd carved there prior to falling asleep. This was to prevent her from backtracking and getting further lost in this wearisome maze of tunnels and traps. The small arrow was pointing to her right. She sighed again, got back to her feet, and made her way on through the seemingly endless passageways.

Though she could not be sure as she had no means to measure the passage of time, Val estimated that she'd been in the maze for at least two days and was no nearer to discovering a way out. She had no food and her water skin was empty. On the first day she'd wandered aimlessly through the gloom. On and on she crept as only silence and semidarkness greeted her around every corner and at the end of every tunnel. As she crept along, other tunnels opened up to either side. Dark and foreboding, Val ignored them for now and continued forward. She had no other reason to choose this way except the simplicity of it. In her mind, she was lost already with no other means of finding a direction than to simply stay the course. To second guess at this point was useless.

After what seemed like hours Val stumbled into a large circular room at the end of a particularly long tunnel. The room was lit by a greenish crystal in the ceiling, which provided more light to guide by than the dim passages. On the far wall was a map of the maze, or so it appeared. The room had three exits: the one she'd just come from facing the map, and one leading to the right and the left. According to the map, the tunnel leading to the left was a straight shot to the exit. Hope leapt up inside her, and Val thanked her stars that she'd found this room. She'd sprinted to the left exit and down the tunnel, only to find herself in a room that looked exactly the same as the one from where she'd just come.

She examined the map in this room, which seemed to be exactly the same. Taking a chance, she took the left exit again, this time at a fast walk, but she found another identical room at the end of this tunnel. She scrutinized the map in this room, finding the exact same markings and diagrams as the one previous. Fighting against the growing sense of frustration welling up inside her, Val took the left exit once more, with the same results. She fought the urge to yell in aggravation. What was the point of providing the map, unless...she sighed as she realized the maps were placed there to purposely mislead her. During her training,

Annet had warned her of taking the easiest routes to her desired goal as these often were guarded or deceptions.

Val closed her eyes, took a few deep breaths, then gazed at the map once more. After carefully studying it once more, she decided to take the exit to the right this time. The map showed the right path led to a tunnel that zigzagged many times, often crossing other tunnels, but it appeared to lead to the exit. She turned and walked towards the right exit, hesitated, then reluctantly stepped forward. From there, she trudged on for hours, wondering all the time if she was still going in the correct direction. She'd not come upon another map room, so she tried to take comfort in that fact.

On and on she went, without food and very little rest, for though she met no man or beast, the ominous silence, broken only by horrifying shrieks of some unknown terror, left Val with a sense of foreboding dread. The dim greenish glow seemed to be trying to lull her to give in to sleep, and in the dark gloom she completely lost track of time. She fought her drowsiness as best as she could, but at times almost surrendered to the summons of sleep. Yet this would not last long as the shrieks would awaken her seemingly moments later, and she huddled in fear with her dagger in hand, her eyes trying in vain to pierce through the darkness.

After the first night, she remembered Annet's words: Endurance, Courage, Discernment, and Mercy. She'd realize that her mentor was trying to warn her of how the maze would test her. Taking deep breaths, she steeled herself against the shrieks and the silence. Yet as the endless cycle of attempted sleep and abrupt awakenings continued for days, Val felt her wits becoming raw and her ability to cope diminishing. She jumped at the slightest sound and her nerves were constantly on edge. The one thing that kept her sane was the knowledge that she had to make it through this maze. She had to become an assassin. She had to make Silas Morgan pay.

The next day, Val found a wide underground river blocking her way forward. The far bank was shrouded in darkness so that she could only guess the distance. She was incredibly thirsty, but the greenish glow given off by the walls of the cavern gave the waters a sinister look as they rushed passed noisily. A battle raged up inside her upon finding the river. Her mouth was parched and a deep yearning grew inside her to rush to the river's edge and plunge her face in the promising cool waters. Yet another voice rose up with a warning as she looked out upon green-tinged waters of the rushing river. Nothing in the Forsaken Labyrinth was free. Everything was a test and every reward had to be earned. Yet even with that knowledge, such choices were hard to make. She took a step towards the edge and something cracked under her foot. She bent down and picked up the thing she'd stepped on, then hurled it away in horror. It was the broken jawbone of a man. Her eyes darted around and soon fell upon the scattered remains of many other beings lying up and down the river's edge. She backed away suddenly, breathing hard. Given her thirst and dehydration Val's need for water had blinded her. If not for the chance footfall that trampled on that jawbone, she might have joined these poor souls. Val closed her eyes to steady herself and fight temptation, then began her search for a way across.

It did not take long to find the only means of crossing the river. A rope bridge spanned the river, one rope hung just above the rushing waters, and two ropes hung at waist height to steady the crosser. She inspected the ropes to ensure their stability, not knowing whether the water's ability to kill its victims was limited only to ingestion. She placed a tremulous foot on the rope, testing its tensile strength. The rope gave a little, but not much. It seemed strong enough to support her weight. Val took another deep breath, and began her crossing.

It was slow going as she put one foot in front of the other. The rope was still holding strong, but her anxiety had not diminished. She felt the rope on her left jerk from time to time, but didn't want to risk looking back in case she fell. When she'd made it halfway across, another blood-curdling shriek split the silence. Val's left hand slipped as the rope on which she was leaning gave way. Nearly falling, she immediately grabbed the rope to her right with both hands, trying desperately to steady herself. The greenish waters mere inches from her feet and uncertain doom lying beneath the surface. Suddenly, the rope beneath her feet gave another violent jerk. Val glanced back to the far shore and cried out in terror. There near the anchor points for the rope bridge stood something out of her nightmares. A massive beast covered in thick, matted hair stood upon four muscular legs. She froze, staring in horror as she caught sight of a long snout with long sharp teeth gnawing away at the ropes. She screamed and the creature paused and turned towards her. A pair of glowing red eyes fixed their gaze on her, and she fell silent in terror.

The beast turned back and continued gnawing on the ropes, causing the rope under Val to give a violent jerk. There was no choice. She frantically began making her way across as fast as possible. As she went, the ropes swayed violently beneath her. At one point her water skin was dislodged from her belt and fell into the river with a hiss and splutter. Val glanced down to see it burst into flames, which quickly went out as it sank smoldering into the dark water.

Her fear of the river redoubled now that she knew the fate of anything that touched the water. Knowing that she could not stop, Val forced herself to continue onward. Foot by foot and yard by yard, she moved forward as the ropes constantly threatened to hurl her into the churning waters below. Just as the rope beneath her gave way, her feet hit the far bank. Breathing hard, she looked defiantly at the other bank of the river but the creature was gone. A long shriek echoed off the cavern walls, and Val thought she could hear anger and frustration expressed in it. Not waiting a moment longer, Val ran from the river and her fear prevented her from stopping herself for some time. She fled the cavern and entered a series of tunnels, unable to stop to choose a path as terror gripped her.

As the horror of her recent fright was beginning to fade and there being no sign of pursuit by the beast, Val fell against the side of the tunnel and slid to the floor. There she sat, shaking and exhausted from her narrow escape and panicked flight from the underground river. How long she sat there, she couldn't tell. She may have fallen asleep at one point, but fear forced her to awaken soon after. Drifting from sleep to waking, Val might have just sat there in despair if not for the sudden realization that she was not alone. She looked up suddenly and saw a man sitting across from her. Instinctively she drew out her dagger, but the man did not move. He sat with his hood back, his pleasant face smiling benignly at her. The man had brown hair that fell to his shoulders, a short brown beard, and Val could have sworn the man's face glowed slightly. Not the greenish glow of the maze, but a white wholesome glow. His eyes were brown and there was a kindness in them.

"Who are you?" Val asked, her voice shaking.

"In the past, I have been a mere acquaintance to you, Val, but I am here to become your friend, and to bring you comfort in the midst of your suffering."

"What do you mean? And how can you bring me comfort?" Val asked. "Are you not also trapped in this awful maze as I am?"

"Am I?" The man asked.

"I would assume you are, seeing as we both are wandering around, lost in this godforsaken darkness."

"Not all who wander are lost," said the man. "You are not forsaken, for I am the Light in the darkness."

The man adjusted his cloak, and as he did so it opened. At once the room was filled with a blinding light, as if the sun had suddenly found a way to break through the thick stone walls and bring its light and warmth to this cold dark maze. Val shielded her eyes, and as they struggled to adjust, she saw that the man was wearing a white robe underneath his cloak that shone like the sun. Unable to bear the light any longer, she closed her eyes and heard the man draw his cloak back over his robe. Immediately the darkness returned. When she was finally able to see again, she found the man still seated across from her and looking intently at her.

"Sorry about that," said the man. "Most people can't handle the light. They try to hide from it. In darkness such as this, however, its power is felt more intensely."

Val was confused and so many questions filled her mind. "What's going on here?" she whispered. "Who are you?"

"I have told you, I am here to be your friend and to help guide you through these trials."

"Yes, but..." she began, but the man held up a hand and Val was rendered silent.

"Listen to me, Val," he began, and she saw concern in his eyes. "From much whom is given, much will be required. You are a gifted individual and you will be judged by how you choose to use your gifts. Do not give into hate, but grant mercy to all. Even those who wish you harm."

"Mercy?" Val asked, incredulously. "Mercy to whom? And why do they deserve mercy?"

"Mercy is never deserved, but given freely. Blessed are the merciful, for they shall obtain it for themselves. You must remain steadfast and pure. Strength and courage you will find through faith."

"Faith?" Val asked, finding her voice. "Faith in what?"

"In me, and in my words," He answered, simply. "Remember this: avoid the broad path, which leads to destruction. Choose the narrow path and your way shall lead you home. And never forget this: though you may seem cast out and alone, I am always with you."

"What do you mean?" Val asked, but the man vanished before her eyes.

She blinked, rubbed her eyes, then found herself on the stone floor of the tunnel. She sat up quickly and gazed about the gloom. Dirt covered the right side of her face, and she hastily brushed her face and clothes off. *Had she fallen asleep? Was the man merely a dream?* Val got to her feet, continuing to brush off the dust from her clothes. She shook herself, then drew out her dagger and moved on down the tunnel, pondering what the man said and wondering what lay behind the next bend.

# 18

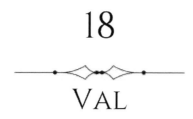

# VAL

Val sat resting along the rough wall of the passage. She may have dozed off several times, but never for long. The random shrieks of the terrifying beast from the river continued to haunt her steps. It had now been three days since she'd entered this seemingly godforsaken maze and she was no nearer to finding a way out.

She stood up, stretched, and moved on down the passage. Darkness gave way before her and closed back in behind her. The solitary nature of the maze, coupled with the seeming pursuit of the unknown beast and the need to escape before she starved, was beginning to take its toll on her. She was becoming desperate. If only she could find a source of clean water, she would feel better, though her stomach had rumbled and groaned for more.

Val came to an abrupt halt, for the tunnel had split between two archways. One was wide and the path seemed to lead upwards, while the other was narrow and seemed to lead downwards. She stood before the two archways, conflicted between the two options. The obvious choice seemed to be the wider path as it seemed to lead towards the surface, yet the dream, or whatever it had been, was still fresh in her mind. The man had said to choose the narrow path and to trust him; easier said than done. Val stood frowning as her eyes glanced between her two choices. After a moment longer, she took the wider path. She wanted out of this maze and had little patience for strangers and their unsolicited advice.

As Val crossed the threshold of the wide archway there was a loud clang. She spun around to see an iron portcullis slam down behind her, barring any chance for her to change her mind. Feeling a sense of foreboding, Val turned and walked forward with her dagger still drawn.

She felt her heart lighten at first as the path continued climbing steadily upward. Yet this was short-lived as the path crested and then turned steadily downward for a long time. In fact, Val suspected the path had actually descended further down than she'd ever been in this infernal maze. There were no side paths or doorways in which to divert from her steady descent down into the depths.

Finally the path leveled out and another, even larger, archway stood before her. Yet her way was barred once again by another portcullis. She stood taking in a strange scene set before the archway and wondering what new task or trap lay before her. In front of the archway was a large stone table. Upon the table were three cups of various sizes and makes, all lined up in a row. Standing on the other side of the table and facing Val were three people: two men and one woman. The two men had their hoods up, shrouding any distinguishing features. The woman wore her black hair over her face, also shrouding her features. Val stared at them for a few moments, then turned to examine the cups upon the table. The cup on Val's left was short and unadorned, made of clay, and one of the men stood directly behind it. The cup in the middle was a tall goblet made of gold, with two handles. The woman stood behind it. The cup to Val's right was a tall, thin chalice made of silver. The second man stood behind it.

Val continued to stand glancing about the scene before the archway, when the three people suddenly began to chant all at once.

*Behind us lies your final task,*
*A way of escape is within your grasp.*
*A simple draft from one of these take,*
*But before, a careful choice you must make.*
*A sip from one will bring you through,*
*But a swift death from the other two.*
*Here we stand, we cannot refrain,*
*To tell what each cup contains.*
*Ask each in turn and we'll reveal,*
*Your fate a sip from which will seal.*
*But be ye warned to trust with care,*
*For two of us are liars. Beware.*

The three people stopped chanting and stood in silence. Val hesitated for a long time, unsure of what to do. Though she was not an avid reader, she'd heard riddles like this before, but in that instance there the prospect of death was not looming over her. In all the riddles she'd heard like this, the unadorned cup was the obvious choice. Yet the stakes were too high for her to jump to conclusions. She pondered the riddle, seeking something in the rhyme that might enlighten her, at length coming to the line "ask each in turn." But what should she ask? The obvious question in her mind was what cup had the poison, but would these people tell her? Then the last line of the riddle came back to her, "Two of us are liars. Beware." If two were liars, it stood to reason that the other must tell the truth. She only had to figure out which was which, then she could figure out which cup held the poison.

She stepped in front of the goblet in the middle and looked up at the woman. The long black hair draped over her face gave her a menacing look, and Val's voice caught in her throat for a moment.

She cleared it and asked, "Is there poison in this cup?"

To her surprise, the man on her left said, "Yes." The woman said, "No." Then the man to her right said, "No."

Val took a step back, considered what had just happened, then stepped in front of the unadorned cup to her left.

"Is the poison in this cup?" She asked, and the man in front of her spoke, then the woman, then the man: "Yes, No, No."

She moved to the silver chalice and did the same. "No, Yes, Yes." She noticed a pattern. The woman and the man to her right always said the same, but the response of the man to her left always seemed in conflict with the other two. She moved through the cups again, asking the same question: "Is the poison in this cup?" She received the same responses.

She had her answer, and made her choice. She reached out a trembling hand toward the tall, thin chalice. As her hand gripped the sides, she found the shining metal was cool to the touch. Upon picking up the chalice, the woman and two men turned slowly and ominously towards her. Val hesitated, as her confidence faltered. *Was this the right cup? Was she absolutely sure? What if she was wrong?*

She stood dithering for a moment longer. Then, taking a deep breath, she brought the chalice to the edge of her lips but did not drink. She tried to take in a whiff of the liquid in the cup, but it had no smell. She closed her eyes, steeled herself for whatever outcome, then drank the contents of the cup.

She swallowed and waited. Nothing happened. She opened her eyes and gasped as the table, cups, and people were gone. Even the cup in her hand had vanished without a trace. Val stood breathing hard, her mind in a whirl. Had that just happened or was she starting to lose her mind? After a few moments of introspection, she turned toward the archway. The portcullis that had barred her way was also gone. Without any apparent obstacles in her way, she stepped forward and on into the darkness beyond.

After several more hours of walking through passages, though she could not be sure exactly how much time had passed, Val found herself on the threshold of a large circular cavern. The ceiling was high above her head and another crystal was hung there, but instead of emitting a greenish glow it shone red, casting its light upon the cavern walls and floor. As her gaze scanned the room, she caught sight of a dark, hooded figure standing on the far side. She hesitated, glancing about the room, but there was no way out save the tunnel she'd just come through. There was but one choice. Stepping into the room, she heard the sound of a portcullis fall into place. Without the need to look, she knew that her way back had been sealed. Whatever test or trap lay in this room, she now had to face. She gazed over at the figure, who stepped towards her. Drawing her dagger, Val prepared to defend herself. The figure seemed unperturbed, and continued advancing towards her. She backed away slowly, but the figure was less than ten feet from her.

Suddenly, the figure drew a long jagged blade from within its robes and came at her. Val screamed and dove out of the way just as the figure swiped at her. Leaping back onto her feet, she assumed one of the defensive stances Annet had taught her. The figure came at her again, swinging the blade wildly. Val blocked the figure's every assault, and she began to wonder why this person was attacking her and also why they were so seemingly inept. Then, Val saw her opening. The figure had overextended her reach. Val brought her dagger up and stripped the sword from the figure's hand. The blade clattered to the floor and the figure rushed backwards, tripping over its robes.

Val watched as the hood fell back, revealing a young woman. Her face was terror-stricken, like that of a wild animal cornered. The young woman's eyes darted everywhere, seeking escape. Val stooped and picked up the woman's sword and stepped towards her fallen foe.

"Please," the young woman said in a high, frantic voice. "Please don't kill me."

Val glared down at her, of the mind to, at the very least, punish this inept woman. For it had been she, not Val, who had attacked first. For that, she deserved just punishment.

The woman bowed her head and began to sob uncontrollably. Val stood over her, a battle waging inside her. For what reason should she withhold punishment? In fact, she should die for what she did. The woman had tried to kill her after all. She had attacked first and Val had defeated her. She was at Val's mercy. Then the memory of her mentor's last words came rushing back: "Remember this: Endurance, Courage, Discernment, and Mercy."

"*Mercy?*" Val said aloud.

The woman's head jerked up and they stared into each other's eyes.

Val shook her head. This woman deserved whatever punishment that she wanted to give her. Why should she be given any less than what she would have done to Val?

Raising the sword over her head, Val prepared to strike and then hesitated. The young woman stared in terror up at her would-be executioner. All at once the words of the stranger came into Val's mind: "Mercy is never deserved, but given freely. Blessed are the merciful, for they shall obtain it for themselves."

Val sighed and then let the sword fall from her hand. The blade clattered against the stone floor, sending echoes through the cavern. The young woman stared up at Val in disbelief as she held out a begrudged hand. The woman took it without hesitation, and as she did so a door opened to Val's left, sending blinding white light into the dim room. She shielded her eyes, then as her vision adjusted she saw Annet was standing in the doorway, waiting with a bemused grin on her face.

✳ ✳ ✳ ✳

"Well done," Annet said, when Val had approached. She handed Val a water skin. "You've passed the trials of the Forsaken Labyrinth."

Val didn't speak, but took several gulps of water, gasping after each swallow. She glanced back at the cavern, but the young woman was gone. The door snapped closed soon after and vanished into the stone wall around it, sealing the maze. As she stood there staring at where the door had been, Val had the feeling that the memory of her time in the Forsaken Labyrinth would haunt her for the rest of her life.

"Come," Annet said, at length. "The Guild Masters are expecting us."

"What?" Val spluttered, but Annet was already moving away.

Val trotted after her, following Annet as she moved down the length of the corridor. She led back into the entrance hall, where the stairs leading to the surface lay on one end and the thick wooden door at the other.

Annet turned and led her straight to the ancient door, opened it and went inside. Val followed her mentor through the door and found herself in a dimly lit room. The air was still and the room was silent save the sound of the nearby torches burning in their wall mounts. Across the room, and hidden in the shadows, sat for hooded figures behind a long stone table—the Masters of the Assassins' Guild.

Val started to step forward, but Annet grabbed her by the arm and pulled her back.

"Wait," she hissed, and bowed slightly. Val followed suit.

"Enter, Annet and Valentine," said a woman's voice. The voice was solemn and ominous. "We've been expecting you."

Annet led the way to the center of the room where a small circular dais stood. She and Val stood upon the dais and they both bowed again, and waited silently.

"Rise," said a man's voice coming from one of the figures on the far right. "You are late in responding to our summons."

"Apologies, master," Annet said, with still another bow. "I had a matter of great concern that I could not leave unfinished."

"Understandable," said the woman who'd spoken earlier. "Our most gifted assassin has now taken an apprentice I see."

"A promising pupil," Annet said. "Her completion of the trials of the Forsaken Labyrinth was the reason for my delay."

"Of this we are aware, but there are more pressing matters than the achievements of a mere apprentice," said the man said, crossly.

"We have an assignment for you, Annet," said the woman. "It may prove to be your greatest challenge yet. You will find all the information you need and your fee on the table to your right."

Annet moved toward the table and Val followed. She watched as her mentor took a large bag of money and weighed it in her hand, then handed it to Val. It was very heavy.

"If you take this assignment, Annett, you and your apprentice will be bound to its completion," came the voice of the woman. "Should you fail, your apprentice must complete the assignment on her own. You both know the penalty of failure."

They both turned towards the Masters, and bowed. Turning back to the table, Annet then took a small roll of parchment and unrolled it. She gasped and dropped the parchment. Val still staring at the money bag, turned and stooped to pick up the dropped parchment. Standing back up, she read the parchment, upon which only two words were written:

*Abenhall*

*Azka*

# 19

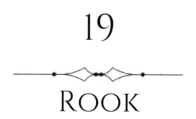

# ROOK

Rook crouched, waiting in the shadows. The night was all about him. The crumbling walls of former dwellings or shops rose up on either side of the alleyway in which he was concealed. He peered out onto the cross-street before him, which appeared empty. Parts of the street and buildings glowed red from the many fires still burning throughout city. Long shadows grew and shrank in the light of the dancing flames. The ruined walls were charred and burned by the looting and ravaging bands of dark soldiers, or from the scorching breath of the dragon. Farodhold, once the greatest city in southern Alethia, was now a smoldering ruin.

Rook took a step out, then hastily retreated as another band of enemy soldiers appeared out of the gloom. There were about a dozen of them, all brandishing weapons that glowed red when they caught the light of the fires. As they drew near, Rook heard them speaking a strange tongue he'd never before heard. It was a guttural speech, which reminded him of the language of Donia. Yet despite its similarity, the speech patterns were distinctly different than any Donian he'd ever heard. Rook waited for the soldiers to pass, then darted across the street and down the adjoining alleyway. Somewhere in the middle, he crouched down and found the hidden trap door. He knocked twice, once, then three times. There was a soft click, and the door opened from within. There in the darkness, Rook could just make out the face of Jonas Astley. They nodded to one another and both descended into a long tunnel, pulling the door closed behind them.

The tunnel was narrow and was barely four feet high from floor to ceiling. It was also pitch dark, but after two days Rook and Jonas knew the way regardless. They followed the tunnel, which ran straight and slightly down for a couple dozen yards or so, feeling their way along until it ended in an ironbound door. Rook knocked again in the same way as he'd done previous, and this time the door opened into a wide, well-lit cavern. Rook and Jonas slipped inside and closed the door behind them, bolting it closed. The cavern was roughly carved out of the bedrock below the city. The ceiling rose some ten feet high and many times that wide and deep. There were several dozen people milling about the cavern. Men, women and children, all huddled together speaking in hushed tones and eyeing Rook and Jonas warily.

They made their way across through the crowds to one of the far corners, where a group of men sat around a long wooden table. The aged Galanor sat facing them, and he looked up with a grim face when they approached. The others also turned and looked as Rook and Jonas took their seats at the table.

"What word?" Lord Astley asked, grimly. "How fairs my city?"

"The roving bands have looted and burned everything from the port to the eastern walls," replied Rook. "I chanced a glimpse at the enemy camp. They are already preparing to march north. I also climbed what's left of the sentry tower at the port and saw several ships still anchored there unscathed."

"Perhaps we could use one of these to make it to Abenhall," said Galanor.

"Even with the army moving on, how can we hope to get all of these people to the port without being seen?" asked Jonas.

"Leave that to me," said Rook, with a sly smirk. "All we need is a diversion and a crew to man the ship."

"You want us to abandon Farodhold?" Lord Astley asked, incredulously.

"Your city is lost, Lord Astley," said Galanor, bluntly. "The army of Lords Warde and Morgan were defeated and slaughtered before your very eyes. You have few defenders and no hope of aid. You and your people will starve if you stay here. We must get to Abenhall and help in the defense of the north."

"I will not leave my city."

"If that is your wish, but will you condemn your subjects to the same fate? Will you condemn your son?"

Rook watched Lord Astley look at Jonas, then bowed his head.

"Father," he heard Jonas say, placing a hand on Lord Astley's shoulder. "I must go with Galanor. The need seems even more pressing than ever with the destruction of our home. If we hide here, this dark army will surely destroy all of Alethia."

"Listen to your son, Lord Astley," Galanor said, rising. "He has grown wiser during the trials of the past few months. God has clearly chosen him as guardian of the Book of Aduin, and as such, he must become my apprentice and the defender of this kingdom."

Lord Astley looked up with wonder and doubt in his eyes, then lowered his gaze and stared at the floor.

"Your mother and brothers are all dead. I can't lose the only family I have left," he said quietly, as if to himself. Then he looked up at Jonas and said, "Very well, my son. Make whatever preparations you need. I will address the survivors. We will evacuate Farodhold when you are ready."

✳   ✳   ✳   ✳

Rook, Jonas and a handful of Lord Astley's men peered out from their hiding places atop the eastern wall. Crouching behind the ruined battlements, they watched in silence as the dark army moved off into the night. Below them, moving about the smoldering remains of the gatehouse, the few lingering bands of soldiers were busy gathering the spoils outside the city and loading into the carts for transport behind the main army. Rook turned and gazed up at the only remaining tower along this part of the wall. Its roof was caved in, but the alarm bell was somehow intact. He turned to the men with him and gave a single nod. They all fitted arrows to their bows, and aimed at the soldiers below. Rook turned back to the tower, gave the signal with his hand, and fitted and loosed an arrow at the nearest soldier. The alarm bell rang out into the night as five arrows found their mark. The enemy soldiers were in disarray, clamoring for weapons and staring up at the tower. Rook and his men shot another five soldiers before the enemy spotted them along the walls.

"Flee! Make for the port!" Rook cried, as he and the others made for the stairs and fled into the dark streets.

He glanced behind him to check if Jonas was still with him. The young man was right on his heels, a look of pride on his face. For several minutes they just ran, not bothering to check for pursuit. At length, unable to ignore the pain in his legs and sides any longer, Rook darted into a dark side street and leaned against a wall, panting hard. Jonas stood beside him, also gasping for breath. A moment later, Rook grabbed Jonas by his tunic and pulled him down to the ground. Jonas began to protest, but he covered his mouth and hissed at him to be silent.

Rook turned back towards the street they'd just left, straining to see if he'd heard right or if his ears had deceived him. It wasn't a few seconds later that a host of enemy soldiers, more than three dozen, came running up the street and back the way Rook and Jonas had just come. Rook could not help but smile. He turned to Jonas, who was also smiling. Their diversion had worked.

Rook and Jonas quickly made their way back to the port, carefully avoiding any more enemy patrols. Fifteen minutes after the diversion began, however they found themselves blocked from the port by a barricade of carts and boxes piled high and guarded by a squad of enemy soldiers. Looking out from their hiding place, Rook could see no other way to the port. He turned to Jonas.

"Is there any way around?" He whispered.

Jonas nodded and motioned for him to follow. Quietly they edged across the street into a side alley that ran parallel to the barricade. For several hundred feet they ran, until they reached the northern wall. Rook felt that this section of the wall was somehow familiar, and smiled broadly when Jonas knelt beside the wall and pulled open a secret trap door. Of course, the way out of the city was the way they came in: the same tunnel leading to the old ruined tower north of the city. The young man held the door open and Rook climbed down. Jonas then followed after and took the lead.

The tunnel was pitch-dark. The last time they'd had torches, but there was no time to look for one now. Rook felt along the rough stone walls, taking care to stay right behind Jonas. After what seemed like ages, they reached the stone steps leading up to the top of the crag, upon which stood the ruined tower. Rook let out a muffled groan as he remembered the numberless stairs that now lay before them. Finally after half an hour, Jonas paused on the steps above him. He heard the young man groaning, then the loud scraping of wood on stone. A gust of fresh air greeted him in the face, then he followed Jonas as they clambered out into the night air. They stood enjoying the wind on their faces, but their revelry was brief for Jonas let out a gasp. Rook spun around and to his horror, a dark figure emerged out of the surrounding night. It was XtaKal.

Rook and Jonas unsheathed their swords, standing ready. XtaKal approached slowly, the dark blade in its gloved hand dragging across the ground, yet making no sound. The figure raised its hand and Jonas was suddenly lifted into the air. Rook rushed forward, bringing his blade low across his enemy's legs. XtaKal dropped its hand and blocked Rook's blow. He prepared for his enemy to parry the attack, but the attack didn't come. Rook spun and brought his blade around at XtaKal's unguarded shoulder, but before his blade could touch his enemy Rook felt himself hurling backward. A sudden, invisible force had grabbed him and threw him hard against one of the walls of the tower. His back hit the wall with a crunch, the sudden impact knocking the breath out of him. His sword fell from his hand as he crumpled to the ground gasping. Glancing up to see Jonas in a defensive crouch as the dark figure once again lifted its hand, Rook rose to his knees and shouted hoarsely into the night.

"No!" Rook cried, as he grabbed his bow and fitted an arrow.

XtaKal glanced around just as Rook's arrow flew from the string. He watched as Jonas fell back to the ground with a crash and the dark figure slashed at the air. From the blade came a shockwave of dark energy that shot out, colliding with the arrow. Rook saw the arrow burst into flames as the shockwave split the air. Then he dove, realizing just in time, that the shockwave was continuing toward him. It flew past him, slamming into the tower wall with a mighty rumbling like a clap of thunder.

Rook rolled over and found his sword underneath him. Grabbing it, he leapt to his feet, but too late. XtaKal had abandoned his attack on Jonas and came at him. Its hand shot out and Rook was lifted into the air.

"Jonas!" Rook cried, as an invisible force began to crush his windpipe. "Go! Run!"

He dropped his sword and clutched at his neck with both hands. XtaKal drew nearer, and though his vision had begun to blur, Rook thought he saw Jonas hurl himself at the dark figure. XtaKal turned quickly to block the young man's blow and Jonas was hurled against the far wall of the tower. XtaKal turned back to Rook and, with a swift motion of its hand, Rook was brought nearer. Black spots began appearing in his field of vision, but he thought he saw XtaKal hesitate. It may have been the lack of air, but Rook thought he saw recognition under that dark hood.

"Kinison?" came a tremulous voice from under the hood; a raspy, hoarse voice that sounded as if it hadn't been used in ages.

Rook felt the force strangling him slacken. They stared at one another for a moment, then the dark figure's hand dropped to its side and Rook fell to the ground hard. Gasping for breath, he looked up just in time to see the dark figure back away, shaking its head as it faded into the surrounding night.

Jonas was at his side in a moment, pulling him to his feet. Staggering and swaying from his battle with XtaKal, Jonas threw Rook's arm over his shoulder and they slowly climbed down the crag towards the port.

✳  ✳  ✳  ✳

Rook and Jonas stood atop a hill overlooking the Bay of Ryst. The sun was beginning to break over the eastern horizon behind them, causing a faint light to reflect off the rolling waves. The ships below were preparing to set sail. A light breeze blew across their faces, creating a cool, calming effect. Yet Rook and Jonas could not rest, for upon the beach, between them and the ships, was a large company of enemy soldiers. To Rook, there appeared no way around them or any means of diverting their attention. It seemed that their only means of escape was now lost.

"What now?" Jonas asked.

Rook didn't answer, but continued to gaze out to sea, while his mind fixated on the battle with XtaKal.

At length, Jonas spoke.

"I think I have an idea," he said, and began to climb down the hill upon which they stood.

Rook, shaken from his thoughts, followed quickly after him. The hill upon which they'd stood was part of several rows of hills, which all ran parallel to the shore. Shallow valleys ran between each row of hills. Upon reaching the valley between the hills, Jonas crouched down and began drawing in the dry soil.

"I think I know a way to get down to the ships without alerting the enemy soldiers," Jonas said, continuing to draw.

"I'm listening," Rook said, looking quizzically at the crude drawing.

"These hills run parallel to the shore," Jonas said, tracing a path between two long curves. "If we follow the hills away from the city, they make a right-angle and run into the shore. The hills will block us from view of the enemy soldiers. Once we reach the shore, we can swim out to the nearest ship."

"What if we run into a patrol or they decide to move north along the shore?" Rook asked. "The hills will obscure their movements as well as ours."

"It's the only plan I've got," Jonas said, somewhat annoyed. "If we don't act now, the ships will have to leave without us."

"I guess we've got to try," Rook said, with a nod.

They headed north, following the shallow valley as it dipped between the rows of hills. They met no patrols and after half an hour, the valley turned sharply to the left and began descending towards the shore. Rook looked and could see the sandy beach some hundred yards off as the waves crashed on the shore.

About halfway to the shore, Rook grabbed Jonas's shoulder and pushed him down into a crouching position. The young man turned to protest, but Rook held a finger to his lips.

There was something or someone moving nearby. He listened intently for several seconds, then pulled Jonas back to his feet and hissed, "Run!"

"Run!" Rook repeated, this time yelling.

All thought of stealth and secrecy was abandoned as arrows fell to their left and right. It was no use, they'd been discovered. More arrows whistled by, landing to either side of them. As they neared the shore, Rook heard harsh yells coming from behind them. Neither Rook nor Jonas bothered to turn and look. They ran on, pushing their exhausted limbs to move faster. The shore was near.

"Look!" called Jonas, pointing south down the beach.

Rook turned and saw two things: a small boat floating near the shore and the entire company of enemy soldiers coming right at them. They sprinted to the boat, pushing it out as fast as possible. When they were twenty yards out, they both clambered in, and Rook reached for the oars. As he did so, an arrow flew past his right ear and stuck in the side. He grabbed up the oars and began rowing as fast as he could against the tide. On the shore, Rook could see the company of enemy soldiers lining the beach and shooting arrows. Most of them fell harmless into the waters, but one or two managed to hit the boat.

"One of the ships is coming towards us!" called Jonas.

Rook made for it, still rowing with all his might. It seemed like an eternity, but eventually they came up alongside the ship. A rope ladder was lowered down to them and they quickly clambered up. Once onboard, Rook leaned against the ship's railing, gasping for breath. Jonas came over to stand beside him. Rook glanced over at him, seeing the look of grief on the young man's face. He clapped Jonas on the shoulder, then slid down to sit on the deck with his back to the railing.

"Rook," Jonas began, tremulously.

"What?" Rook said, gruffly still struggling to catch his breath. He felt the young man's eyes upon him, but he was so exhausted he simply did not care. "What is it, Jonas?"

"I was just wondering, why did XtaKal call you Kinison?"

# 20

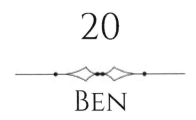

# BEN

"You push the limits of our friendship, Eric!"

It was late evening, over two weeks after Ben's fight with Jacob. He'd undergone two more weeks of training before his induction into the City Watch two days ago. Yet now he and Sir Eric were back in his father's house. Sir Eric sat across the table from him, stroking his short brown beard, while his father stood beside the stone hearth, brooding over the fire. He turned, glaring at Sir Eric, then turned to Ben, who looked away quickly. Once again he was caught between the shame of disappointing his father and the anger of this father's refusal to respect his decisions.

"A month ago my son runs away and joins the City Watch, which is bad enough. Yet now I learn that my best friend helped him do it!" His father exclaimed, brandishing the metal fire poker. "Have you no idea the betrayal I feel now, Eric!"

"Jon, please," began Sir Eric, but Ben's father cut across him.

"Look at him! Wearing *that* uniform!" His father gestured at Ben, then turned his back and slammed his hand against the mantle. "This is not what I wanted for my son! You had no right, Eric! No right!"

Ben looked down at the uniform that he'd been so proud to receive two days ago, and something broke inside him. He rose to his feet as anger surged inside him, and at least for the moment, he didn't care what his father thought.

"Father," he began, His voice sounded bolder than he felt. "I am a member of the City Watch. I chose to do this. I've sworn to protect his city, to protect you, so now I must do this."

The look on his father's face was a mixture of shock and anger. A battle seemed to be going on inside his father, and for a long moment Ben wondered which would win out. In the end, his father's face contorted with rage and he glared at Ben.

"You want to be a man, is that it? You think you're ready to make life and death decisions, is that it?" His father spoke softly, but every word rang with suppressed rage and betrayal. "You believe yourself capable of facing danger and evening killing another human being?"

Ben looked into his father's face. For a fleeting moment, his face softened and Ben saw regret welled up in his dark brown eyes. Yet a moment later, it was gone. His father's face hardened.

"Then get out and neither of you darken my door again." He spoke softly and with such finality that even Sir Eric was hesitant to question.

"Fine!" Ben exclaimed, unable to contain his anger any longer.

He grabbed his gear, and stormed out of his father's house. Bursting out into the dark street, he crossed to the other side of the street. There he stood fuming and pounded his fist against the wall of a nearby building. Ben roared in both anger and pain from hitting his fist, then turned and slid down the wall until he was sitting with his arms draped over his knees. Feeling emotionally exhausted, he bowed his head and stared blankly at the cobblestone street, following the winding edges of the stones. Why could his father not see how important this was to him? Why was he so determined to force Ben to be a merchant rather than a soldier? Why couldn't he just be proud of his accomplishments?

"Benjamin," came a soft voice.

Ben looked up quickly, and saw a kind, familiar face. "I know your face."

"Yes, we have spoken before," the man said, coming to sit beside him.

"Who are you?"

"I have come to bring you a warning, young Benjamin Greymore."

Ben stared in disbelief.

"Yes, I know your name, and perhaps by the end you may know mine." The man said, kindly yet grimly. "You are nearing a great test. You will be sorely tempted by evil. You must resist and listen to my warning."

"Why?" Ben asked, suddenly annoyed.

"Ben, I've come to help guard you, but you must do what I say."

"No!" Ben shouted. He stood and rounded on the man, infuriated that this stranger was treating him just as his father had done. He was not a child, and was about to say so, when he realized that the man was gone.

"Ben?" came a confused voice from behind him.

He spun around to see Sir Eric, looking at him in alarm.

"Did you see—," he began, but trailed off. "Never mind."

"Ben, are you alright?"

"I'm fine." He answered, gruffly.

"Ben," Sir Eric said, after an awkward moment's pause. "You've got to make your own way in life. Your father knows this."

Ben didn't respond.

"Look, I'm leaving on a mission to the Gray Mountains in the morning. I could sure some help, so if you want to join me—"

"Really?" Ben asked in surprise. "You want me to come with you."

"Only if you want, and believe you are ready."

"Of course."

- R.S. GULLETT -

"Then meet me by the Citadel gates at sunrise tomorrow morning."

"I'll be there," Ben said, unable to keep from smiling.

\* \* \* \*

Dawn found Ben standing outside the gates of the Citadel, waiting for Sir Eric. He was still wearing his uniform for the City Watch, excited at the chance to go on a real mission with a member of the Royal Guard. The gates opened and Sir Eric appeared from behind them. A smile broke across Ben's face, but fell almost immediately as he saw Sir Eric was wearing simple winter traveling clothes.

"Ben, why are you wearing your uniform?" He said, looking bemused. "Our mission is somewhat secretive so you can't be seen wearing that."

Ben was embarrassed and looked sheepishly at his mentor.

"Come," Sir Eric said, leading the way down the street. "We'll stop at the barracks and let you change."

Half an hour later, they arrived at the barracks. Ben rushed inside and changed clothes. In his haste, he almost put his pants on inside out and backwards. The other members of the City Watch laughed at him, but he ignored their taunts and jeers. A few minutes later, he ran back out to meet Sir Eric, who was talking with Captain Saul Gunter.

"Where are you off to with this one?" The captain asked, eyeing Ben with disdain and suspicion.

"Never mind that, captain." Sir Eric said, with a meaningful glance. "I'll have your man back in a few days."

"No need to hurry," the captain guffawed, shooting Ben a dark look. "Keep him as long as you want."

Ben scowled at the captain, but Sir Eric merely nodded and led the way out of the gates.

The sun was out and the sky was clear, but as soon as they'd left the city, the wind came rushing at them from the north, bitter and cold.

"You know how to handle a horse?" Sir Eric asked, hopping astride one of them.

Ben nodded, but could not suppress a look of apprehension. He clambered onto the horse, which whinnied in protest. Sir Eric smiled, but didn't say anything. He spurred his horse on, and Ben followed in his wake.

The wind continued to blow from the north and soon Ben was chilled to the bone. He didn't complain, though he felt his fingers go numb from time to time. They rode around the city walls, then took the road as it turned northwest toward the Gray Mountains. The dark peaks loomed up ahead of them like a foreboding barrier. About midday, clouds moved in and snow flurries had begun to fall. It did not stick, but melted upon reaching the ground. All this managed to accomplished was making the dusty roads slick with mud and soak their cloaks and hoods.

As they rode on, the road took them passed several small farms and villages. The inhabitants took little notice of the two travelers, as they strove to complete their outside activities quickly and return to the warmth of their homes. Though he was glad to finally be on his first adventure, Ben lamented that it was winter rather than summer. Sir Eric allowed them to halt only twice to take a meal and feed and water their horses. Ben had hoped to stop at an inn or at least pause long enough in the open country to make a fire, but Sir Eric would not allow it and reminded him of the need for speed and secrecy.

After their second stop in the late afternoon, they left the main road and rode on through wild country full of short trees and tall brush. By the end of the first day, they were entering an area full of rocky hills, where the foothills of the Gray Mountains met the eastern edge of the Forest of Roston. There they stopped and made camp on the southern slope of a large hill and built a small fire. Ben was very grateful for the shelter of the hill and for the warmth from the small fire, though he wished Sir Eric would have made it bigger.

After a light meal, Ben leaned back against a fallen tree and looked across the fire toward Sir Eric, who was glancing about in the dark. It was then that he noticed signs of great anxiety upon his face. In the light of the flames, the lines on his face fell into sharp relief, causing Sir Eric to appear much older and grimmer. He caught Ben watching him, and smiled weakly.

"Ben, I'm sure you've noticed that we left the main road many hours ago."

Ben nodded.

"We are on a mission to inspect a watch post that overlooks a secret pass through the Gray Mountains. There has been no word from the post for nine days."

"So what are we supposed to do?"

"Make contact with the garrison there, inspect the pass, and report back as quickly as possible."

"Why is this pass so important and secret?"

Sir Eric's eyes narrowed as they seemed to stare into Ben, as if to verify his trust in the young man. At length, he dropped his gaze to the fire and spoke with a slow reluctant voice.

"Ben, I'm not supposed to reveal this to anyone outside the Royal Guard. I'm showing a lot of trust in you by simply taking you with me on this journey." He paused and Ben saw Sir Eric shift uncomfortably.

"I am grateful you invited me on this mission," Ben said softly.

Sir Eric smiled. "The pass is known as the Pass of the Knife, and is a narrow path through the Gray Mountains between Nordyke and Alethia. It is only wide enough for one man to pass through at a time, and even then the man might have to squeeze through some areas."

Ben frowned. "If it's so narrow, why is it watched so closely? It's not as if an army could squeeze through."

"It might take awhile, but if unmarked a large host of men could pass through and invade northern Alethia. That is why the watch post was built long ago and remains manned at all times," Sir Eric retorted ardently. "That is also why the absence of any news from the post for more than a few days is worth investigating. It could signal the beginning of an invasion."

They sat in silence for a long time, then Ben asked, "Why are you telling me this and trusting me so much?"

"I'm hoping that one day, years from now of course, you might be inducted into the Royal Guard."

"So this is a test?"

"Most definitely," Sir Eric said with a grin. "Now, get some rest. I'll wake you when it's your watch."

※　※　※　※

At dawn the next day, Ben and Sir Eric prepared to leave. The clouds of the previous day had moved off, leaving a beautiful blue sky. Ben was momentarily grateful for the warmth of the sun, but as they reached the top of the hill they'd spent the night under, the northerly wind returned bitter and cold. About mid-morning, they were nearing a tall mountain in the distance. One of its arms jutted out, blocking their view of the land beyond. All was eerily quiet. No birds or animals broke the silence. The only sound came from their mounts as they moved over the cold ground. Sir Eric brought his horse to a halt, gazing out across the lands before them. Ben turned and saw a look of concern crossing his face. He also gazed out into the distance and immediately saw what made Sir Eric stop. A large plume of black smoke was rising over the mountain's arm.

"Hurry," Sir Eric said, spurring his horse to a racing gallop.

Ben was hard put to keep up with Sir Eric as they raced along the edge of the mountain's arm. When they reached the other side, they turned their horses westward and halted. Both Sir Eric and Ben gaped as a tall tower, encircled by a high stone wall, rose up some hundred yards away. Black smoke billowed from the burned gates and upper windows of the tower.

Sir Eric suddenly spurred his horse to a gallop and raced forward leaving Ben to follow in his wake again. Upon reaching the walls, he dismounted and rushed inside. Ben rode up a moment later, and dismounted just as Sir Eric reemerged.

"All dead," he said, covering his mouth and wheezing.

"Dead!" Ben exclaimed.

"Twenty men slaughtered." He was now studying the grounds about for something. "No sign of a siege or the passage of a host of men large enough to take this watch tower. Those twenty men could have held off a host several times as large for weeks. Something is not right."

At that moment, Ben heard the twang of a bowstring, and his horse suddenly screamed and reared back. He felt himself fall backward, hit his head on something hard, and knew no more.

# 21

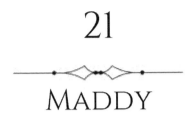

# MADDY

Maddy stood upon the forecastle of the ship, gazing forward toward the grand city rising up ahead of her in the distance. Abenhall, restored after the city was sacked during the Second War of Ascension, its tall towers rose high into the blue sky, built with stone of a reddish hue mined from the Iron Hills. High stone walls of the same color rose thirty feet around the city on every side except the port. A large keep stood on a hill overlooking the city like a guardian. Ships of all sizes moved in and out of the port. As they drew nearer, dark green flags and banners, each bearing a white griffin, waved smartly in the morning breeze.

Under normal circumstances, Maddy would have been amazed by all the sights and grandeur of Abenhall. She'd never traveled outside of Windham until now, and such an experience would have thrilled her. Yet, her heart was full of sadness and despair. With every passing moment, she drew nearer to that fateful pledge; the oath that would forever bind her in marriage to Gethrin Windham. The wedding was later that day. The baron had wasted no time in making preparations. In less than ten days since she'd agreed to marry him, the baron had sent word to Lord Grehm. He'd then made arrangements for a wedding to be held in

Abenhall and invited all the nobles within Lord Grehm's lands. In addition, Maddy had overheard the baron boasting that Lords Cynwic and Reese of the neighboring provinces would also attend. There was also rumor that Lord Silas Morgan of Nenholm would also be attending. She shuddered at the thought of such a despicable man attending her wedding. She'd heard of his miserable deeds even while living a sheltered life in Windham.

The same breeze that carried the flags and banners of the city blew across the forecastle. Maddy stood defiantly as the chill of the wind pierced her thin garments. She fought her body as it attempted to shiver, unwilling to retreat below decks. Unexpectedly, a pair of hands came up behind and placed a heavy coat on her shoulders.

"You will catch cold standing up here without protection," said the baron, coming to stand beside her.

"Thank you," she said, without looking at him.

"You think I'm cold and callus to force you into marrying me?"

Maddy bit back her response, not daring to express her feelings.

"Would it surprise you to hear then that I released the young man just before we set sail?"

Maddy turned quickly and looked at the baron's face, scrutinizing it for any sign of falsehood.

"Yes, I let him go," he said, turning to gaze up at the city. "I wanted to see if you would keep your promise to marry me without the threat of his death hanging over you."

She could not believe it. David wasn't dead, but safe and free. She turned away, fighting back an overwhelming surge of relief and confusion.

"And if I now refuse to marry you?" She asked, finding her composure once more.

"You won't," he answered without turning his gaze. "You will marry me because of your mother, and because you don't really want to be the wife of a blacksmith."

"You presume to know much, and yet you've known me only a short a time, my lord."

"I do, and time will tell, my lady." Then he turned and whispered in her ear, "You know my nature to be a generous one, but you should also be aware that my kindness can turn to cruelty. I desire your love, Madeline, but you should fear my hatred."

He walked away, and Maddy clutched her mouth to keep from gasping. Why had this happened to her? Why would God let this happen?

"Why God?" She whispered, closing her eyes and fighting back the sobs in determined silence. She felt the ship slow as it neared the port. A moment later, she felt someone move beside her. Supposing it to be the baron, she turned away.

"Madeline," said a kind familiar voice.

She opened her eyes and turned. "You?" She gasped.

"You are very brave," he said, with compassion in his kind eyes. "You have chosen to sacrifice yourself for others. No one has greater love than those willing to give everything to save another."

Maddy could not find words to respond.

"I've come to encourage you once more to remain strong. Do not falter now."

"I'm not sure what you mean," Maddy managed to say.

"You may find that traveling the difficult path will enable you to save the lives of many others. Just remember that you are not alone. I will never leave you nor forsake you."

"I don't understand!" Maddy exclaimed. "Are you telling me to marry Gethrin?"

"You already know my answer, Madeline. It remains your choice, but do not delay that choice. If you try to postpone or procrastinate making your choice, you will lose more than you can bear. Just remember that the road that is easiest leads often to destruction, but the narrow path leads to my Father."

"Your father? I still don't understand!" Maddy exclaimed. "Speak plainly. Who are you really?"

"Madeline?" came a voice from behind her.

Maddy turned to find her mother looking at her with concern etched on her face. "Who are you talking to dear?"

Maddy turned quickly back but the strange visitor was gone.

"No one," she said softly. "No one at all."

"Are you alright?" Her mother moved toward her and pulled her into a hug.

"I'm fine," she said.

"Are you sure?" she asked, releasing Maddy and looking at her intently.

Maddy smiled weakly and nodded. "I'm fine, mother."

"Alright," she said. "Just checking."

Her mother left her to gaze up at the looming city as the ship docked. Maddy stared off, wondering what the visitor had meant and whether she could truly go through with the wedding. In a few hours, she would have to make that choice.

❋ ❋ ❋ ❋

It was noon. The clock atop the cathedral struck the hour. Maddy stood before its large doors in her dress and veil. The lace and sashes crisscrossed in a floral design that had brought tears to her mother's eyes. Her hair was braided and inlaid with white and blue flowers. Though the baron may have been cold and calculating, Maddy had to admit he had an eye for fashion. As the clock chimed the stroke of twelve, the doors opened and she stepped into the cathedral. The center aisle was also hung with white and blue flowers. The sun shone in through the stained-glass windows high above, casting brilliant rays of color upon the scene. Up and down the aisle, the lords and ladies stood as she passed and bowed to her. In the midst of the faces, Maddy saw a middle-aged man, tall and thin. The man's sharp eyes were focused on her as he stroked his goatee, which had the appearance of having once been black but was now flecked with gray. He grinned and winked at her, and she turned away quickly in disgust.

At the end of the aisle and in front of the altar, stood the bishop. He was an aged and frail-looking man, with gray hair running along the outside of his balding crown. A thin man, who had the look of someone who might be blown away by the smallest gust of wind, yet as she drew nearer she saw within his pale blue eyes a vitality. He smiled at Maddy, who grinned back in spite of herself.

She turned to the man standing to the bishop's left. Gethrin Windham was rocking back and forth in a plain white robe. He looked at her, and in that moment, Maddy saw in the baron a nervous bridegroom rather than a cold and cruel man who'd manipulated her. She was amazed by the sudden realization, and the feeling of compassion she felt for him.

She reached the foot of the altar and bowed to the baron and the bishop. The baron bowed to her also. She extended her right hand and he took it as they faced the bishop. Maddy's heart was beating so fast. The bishop was praying, but she had other things on her mind. *God, why is this happening? Please help me! Don't make me do this!* The bishop was talking to them now. The moment was quickly approaching when she'd have to make her choice. What was she going to say?

She glanced at the baron, who was looking expectantly at her. She turned to the bishop, who shared the baron's look of expectation. She blinked, realizing that they expected her to say something.

"I'm sorry, I'm just so overwhelmed," she said, garnering a murmur of laughter from the crowd. The bishop smiled benignly at her.

"My dear," he said in a kind, shaky voice. "Do try to pay attention. This is your wedding day after all."

More laughter from the crowd, and Maddy felt her cheeks redden.

"Do you take this man to be your husband for as long as you both shall live?"

"I—" she stammered, looking into the face of Gethrin Windham. In his eyes was a mixture of anxiety and fear. Or was it concern for her?

"Do?" the bishop offered.

"What?"

The bishop sighed as the crowd chuckled once more.

"The word you are searching for, my dear, is 'do'."

Maddy looked at the baron for a moment, but before she could answer the doors of the cathedral burst open. All eyes turned to see a young man sprint the length of the cathedral, stop before Lord Grehm, and whisper something in his ear. Maddy saw the lord's eyes grow wide in shock and fear. He whispered something to the young man, who ran back down the aisle and out the door.

"My good Baron Windham, we must suspend these nuptials at once," Lord Grehm said, soothingly but firmly. "Lords Cynwic and Morgan, Baron Windham, please follow me to the war room. The rest of you please stay in the city as my guests, so that we may resume the ceremony tomorrow."

Maddy watched as Baron Windham crossed the floor to confront Lord Grehm.

"My lord," she heard him hiss in his ear. "You interrupt my wedding for what purpose?"

Lord Grehm turned and looked grave. "News has come. Fairhaven has fallen. The dark army has crossed the river Waterdale. We are at war."

✳   ✳   ✳   ✳

It was late evening. Maddy sat alone at the head of a long oak table in one of the smaller dining halls of Abenhall castle. A small feast was laid out before her, yet she had little appetite and her plate remained empty. The hall was richly decorated with rare paintings and tapestries dating back over a hundred years, yet much of this was cast in shadow as the only light came from a roaring fire in the stone hearth to the right of the table. Maddy stared into the flames, pondering all that had happened to her. Her wedding day had been ruined, yet she was torn between anger and relief. She'd been blackmailed into promising to marry Baron Gethrin Windham, then when the moment had come to say her vows an emergency called both the baron and Lord Grehm away.

Her thoughts led her back to the mysterious visitor whom she'd seen twice now. A stranger to Maddy, but who seemed truly concerned about her. He'd told her to marry the baron, then when the moment came—*was it his doing? Was he somehow testing her?*

The door on the far side of the room banged open, jerking Maddy's attention away from the flames. Baron Windham entered the room and seated himself on the other end of the table. He was clearly angry, and still fuming about, what Maddy assumed, the day's disappointing events.

"Forgive my tardiness," was all he said before drinking the entire contents of his wineglass, then refilling it. He didn't look at Maddy, which told her that some of his anger was directed at her. *Surely he couldn't blame her for the interruption of their wedding.*

"You don't look well, my Lord," she said, breaking the awkward silence. "Are you alright?"

The baron didn't answer, but began filling his plate with food.

"So why did Lord Grehm call you away?"

The baron did not even look at her, but ignored her and began eating. Maddy felt her face burn and contort in anger. She couldn't explain why, but she suddenly wanted to lash out at the baron. Before she could stop herself, she said, "Does it have anything to do with Lord Morgan's conspiracy?" She watched as the baron paused, and glared up at her for a moment. "You know," she continued, pleased with the reaction she'd garnered. "The one where he's attempting to overthrow the king."

The sound of the baron's fork hitting the floor echoed through the silent hall. He stared at Maddy for a long time, but this time she held his gaze.

"Apparently, I misjudged you, Madeline," he said in a soft voice, but hinted with danger. "You have somehow learned of a secret known only to a select few. How did you learn of this?"

"I overheard you and Lord Grehm speaking after our engagement announcement in Windham."

"I see," the baron said, standing and moving down the table towards her. "We have a problem then."

With his approach, Maddy felt her heart racing and fear replaced her previous feelings of anger. "What?" She exclaimed, her voice becoming shrill. "That I know you and the other lords are planning to overthrow the king?"

The baron stopped halfway down the table and stared at her.

"You must think I'm a monster," He said, and Maddy thought she could see pain in his eyes. "Lord Grehm and I are not traitors, Madeline."

"Then what are you plotting?" She demanded. "What was so important that it could stop our wedding ceremony?"

The baron looked at her, as if trying to make up his mind as to whether or not to tell her. At length, he spoke again.

"It is true, Maddy. Lord Grehm and I have learned of a plot to overthrow the king." His voice was slow and cautious, as if struggling to find the right words. "This afternoon, we learned of an even greater threat. An army of unknown origin had attacked and destroyed Fairhaven. We have received reports stating that the city fell within a day, and that the enemy is now marching on Farodhold. If my reckoning is correct, Farodhold may already be under attack or it may have even fallen already to this dark host."

"How can I know this to be true?" Maddy's eyes narrowed in suspicion.

"I know you have little reason to trust me, but it matters not. Lord Grehm and I must leave for Ethriel in the morning and warn the king."

"What of the wedding?" She asked, somewhat hopeful.

He shook his head, pain in his eyes. "I would ask you to accompany me to Ethriel."

Maddy looked and saw that the baron was not demanding this of her, but making a request. Her heart was softened, and before she could stop herself she said, "I will accompany you."

The baron's face broke into a smile. He knelt down beside her, took her hand, and kissed it.

"You honor me, my lady."

As he moved back to his seat, Maddy was mentally kicking herself. She'd missed her chance to return to Windham, and now she was accompanying the baron across the kingdom to the capital. What lay in store for her there, she could not even guess.

# 22

# SELENA

Selena stood alone upon the forecastle of the ship. Night had fallen and a dense fog lay all about the ship. It seemed as though she stood upon an island and the world about her was shrouded and silent. She felt trapped and alone, as the ship continued to drift through the dark waters with barely a sound. Then without warning, a brilliant red light pierced through the fog. Selena gasped as the fog instantly drew back and Fairhaven rose up before her. Fires dotted the city and great plumes of black smoke billowed up from the city's many towers. Her eyes fell upon the castle high above the rest of the city, burning with fire and its walls crumbling in several places. Terror gripped her heart as she beheld the once great stronghold of the south now lying in ruins.

Suddenly, the ship collided with the shore, sending her flying forward over the ship's railing and down on the sandy beach below. Rising to her feet and rubbing her head, she stared out in horror as a dark figure appeared on the shore. In its right hand was a sword as black as midnight, which seemed to devour any light that came near. The figure raised its left hand and Selena felt her feet leave the ground. Her heart pounding in her chest, she rose into the air and flew towards the dark figure. She tried crying out, but she found her voice caught in her throat.

When she was a mere ten feet away, the figure dropped its hand and Selena fell hard upon the beach below. She got to her feet and looked at the figure, who stood motionless before her. A sudden gust of wind blew in from the west and the dark figure's hood flew back. The face she saw was familiar, then Selena heard herself screaming in terror as the face transformed and her own piercing blue eyes stared back at her.

\* \* \* \*

Selena started awake and raised up, her eyes darting around frantically in the dim light. As her eyes adjusted, she found herself in the hold of a ship and a blanket wrapped around her body. All around her lay other refugees from Fairhaven. She laid her head against the nearby wall, breathing hard. *It was just a dream.* She closed her eyes and slowly shook her head from side to side. *Just a dream.* How could she be the dark figure she'd seen in Fairhaven? It was absurd.

They'd been sailing for over a two weeks. The ship had made immediately for Nenholm. When the city officials refused to let the ship dock, the captain had turned the ship northwest and came around the Island of Nen, then turned eastward and made for Abenhall. It had been a long and difficult voyage. The cramped space and smell of so many people was nauseating, but she was not alone in her feelings. The limited food, water, and space on board had left the passengers tense and unsettled. They'd run into a storm on the north side of the island, which put everyone even more on edge. There was a lot of anxious talk amongst the other refugees that the officials in Abenhall might turn them away, leaving them to starve to death onboard the ship.

Despite their predicament, Selena refused to complain. She'd watched the destruction of Fairhaven and survived. The memory of that dark figure on the shores of Fairhaven had given her nightmares off and on for the past few weeks, leaving her startled awake and breathing hard in the middle of the night. Even now, the fear and dread of that dark figure left her heart racing and sweat on her forehead. *It was just a dream.*

The sound of hurried footfalls above her head drew her attention. Seldom being allowed on deck, Selena often had to wait for any news, but not this time. The trap door was flung open and one of the sailors called down to those in the ships hold. The other refugees stirred and Selena leapt to her feet, gathered her things, and ran up the stairs. The sailor tried to stop her, but she pushed passed. Sprinting the length of the ship, she ascended to the forecastle and stared in wonder at the city of Abenhall. Tall towers rose high into the blue sky, built with stone of a reddish hue mined from the Iron Hills. High stone walls of the same color rose thirty feet around the city on every side except the port. A large keep stood on a hill overlooking the city like a guardian. As they drew nearer, Selena saw dark green flags and banners, each bearing a white griffin, waved smartly in the morning breeze.

There were many more ships attempting to dock. Selena glanced back over her shoulder as the captain bellowed orders to his men. Drawing close to one of the long piers, they cut off another ship also trying to dock. The sailors cursed at one another and shook their fists. Selena looked along the pier to see many soldiers moving about, all wearing dark green tunics, emblazed with the white griffin of house Grehm. Fear suddenly gripped her. She could not risk being caught by the soldiers. Waiting until they were within a few feet of the pier, Selena leapt over the side and rolled onto the wooden platform. She then jumped to her feet and skulked behind two other refugees until they joined a larger group moving down the pier towards the shore.

As they drew nearer, Selena saw a large contingent of soldiers barring the way forward. The crowd of refugees was forced into single file lines, moving slowly forward as each refugee was individually searched by a soldier. Although the likelihood of one of these soldiers knowing her face was slim, she couldn't take the chance. She doubted the destruction of Fairhaven would stop a man like Raynor Kesh from tracking her down. Taking a step backwards and allowing several other refugees to move in front of her, she sidled her way toward the side of the pier and was about to dive into the water below when a hand grabbed her shoulder and spun her around.

She gaped up at the face of Raynor Kesh, his brown eyes narrowed and flashed with anger. His face was covered in dirt and grime, and his blond hair was disheveled and matted.

"Lady Selena," he said through gritted teeth.

"Kesh," she said, with a fake smile. "Survived after all then?"

Kesh's face contorted and his voice betrayed his inner struggle to remain calm. "Takes more than that to stop me, my lady. Now, I would thank you to accompany me to the castle where your father is waiting."

"Thank you for the invitation, but I am really busy at the moment," she answered, snidely.

Kesh's grip on her shoulder grew tighter and almost painful. She looked up into his eyes as they flashed with renewed anger.

"I'm afraid that I must insist, my lady," he said. "You can accompany me or I can carry your unconscious body. Your choice."

*　　*　　*　　*

Raynor Kesh shoved Selena through a pair of ironbound doors and into a large council chamber. She stumbled forward and nearly fell. Standing just behind the threshold, she gazed about the richly decorated room. The room was long with large marble columns. Thin windows rose upward into the high ceiling high above their heads, ending in a rounded half-circle. Light of the rising sun poured into the room. Shelves, laden with of books, line the wall. Staircases on the far side led up to a walkway where more shelves stood. In the center of the room was a long wooden table, where several men sat. They all turned gazing at her as she entered. Selena recognized several of them, including lords Grehm,

Cynwic, and Reese. There was also a man she didn't know, with dark brown hair and a long scar running across the left side of his face. Then Selena saw her father, Silas Morgan, his sharp eyes glared at her. She was pleased to see his prized hat was covered in dust and the red feather was torn and bent.

He caught her glance at his damaged headwear and as she stepped towards them, she saw her father get to his feet and hurl his hat at her.

"So, here you are!" he cried. "Kesh, you finally found my daughter and bring her all the way to Abenhall, looking like this? What do you have to say for yourself?"

Selena began to speak, but Kesh cut across her.

"My lord," he said, and Selena caught a hint of anxiety in his voice. "I tracked her to Fairhaven just before the city was attacked. After the walls were compromised, I saw her board a ship and I just managed to escape myself. My ship arrived in Abenhall first and I've been watching the port for her ever since."

"You disappoint me, Kesh," Morgan growled, as he crossed the room towards them, stopping a few feet away. "Yet, I do know my daughter possesses many of my own skills. You also failed to capture me several times before the Second War of Ascension and my rise to Lord of Nenholm."

Selena stole a look at Kesh. His face remained stoic but his eyes betrayed his anger and resentment.

"Lord Morgan!" shouted Lord Grehm, rising to his feet. "May we return to the matter at hand?"

Selena saw her father turn and glare at the other men around the table. "As a matter of fact, Lord Grehm, there is little more we can hope to do. Lord Warde is dead and both our armies were slaughtered. Farodhold has also fallen to the dark army and the dragon."

"We still have the army of the north!" shouted Lord Grehm.

"Of which I have nothing to do with. I wish you luck mustering your forces in time to face the enemy." Lord Morgan retorted snidely.

"Lord Morgan," Grehm said, almost pleadingly. "Your knowledge of this threat is essential if we have any hope to defend the north."

"Very well," Lord Morgan sighed. "If it is not too much trouble, Kesh, please take my daughter to my chambers. I will join you when I have finished."

Kesh placed a hand on her shoulder, but she shrugged it off and stepped forward.

"Don't play coy, father dearest! Admit the reason you don't want to help is that you're the cause of all this!" she shouted.

All eyes turned towards her as she pointed accusingly at her father, who turned to glare warningly at her. She ignored his unspoken threat though and continued.

"I overheard your meeting in Nenholm. You planned all of this with lords Warde and Astley. Both the fall of Fairhaven and Farodhold were you doing."

She glanced around the room to see everyone else's eyes widen in fear and outrage at her words.

"My lords," Lord Morgan said, his voice measured but full of malice. "My daughter is obviously exhausted and confused by her long journey. Please excuse her outburst and mine as well, Lord Grehm. Let us return to preparations for the north's defense. Kesh, please escort Selena to my quarters and make sure she is fed and gets some rest."

Kesh seized Selena by the shoulders. She yelled and protested, but she was unable to break the man's grip on her. He marched her out of the council chambers. Though she knew the truth, there was nothing she could do.

✳   ✳   ✳   ✳

Night had fallen over Abenhall. The port was closed and the streets cleared by Lord Grehm's men. All was quiet and Selena couldn't stand it. The room she was in was sparsely lit, save the light coming from the fire burning in the hearth. She paced the floor of her father's chambers, located high up in one of Abenhall Castle's many towers. The only ways out of the room was a fifty foot drop out the window or through the door, which was guarded by six of Lord Morgan's men and Raynor Kesh. Selena was furious, angry at being caught again, and fuming over her father's evil plot and her inability to convince the other lords of his duplicity and betrayal. She continued to pace the room, pausing at the window every once in a while to stare out into the night.

At one point, as she was gazing out towards the port again, there was a rustling noise behind her. Her eyes darted to the far corning of the room, which was shrouded in darkness. A tall man in a long black cloak emerged from the darkness, causing Selena to gasp and nearly fall out of the open window. She caught herself just in time and stared in shock and fear at the man.

His black eyes flashed in the firelight. Selena was frozen in place, and could only stand silently gaping at the menacing figure. The man's face showed signs of age and his long black hair was mingled with gray. Yet upon his face was a grim smile as he stared at her. The man's mere presence sent chills down her spine and his dark gaze made her reconsider leaping out the window behind her.

"Selena Morgan," the man said in a deep voice. "You have the same rebellious spirit as your father."

Selena wanted to object to the comparison, but the words caught in her throat. Instead she simply squeaked, "Who are you?"

"My name is Methangoth, and I have come to make you an offer," he replied, his eyes surveying her. "I need you to retrieve something for me. If you can get it, I will make sure you get what you most desire."

"And what do I desire?" Selena asked, finding her voice. "She'd heard this man's name before, but could not remember where.

"Like everyone else, you desire power," he answered her. "Power and freedom to do what you want to do." He paused, waiting for her to respond.

"And what do you want in return?" she asked at length.

"There is a young man coming to Abenhall. He carries with him a book of great importance. I need you to get that book and bring it to me."

"A book?"

"Yes," the man growled. "If you could obtain it for me, I care not how, I will pay you handsomely."

"Gold?"

"If that is what you wish?"

"And who is this young man?"

"His name is Jonas Astley."

# 23

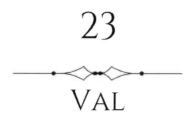

## VAL

It was mid-morning when Val and Annet stepped off the gangplank onto one of the long piers extending out from the port of Abenhall. The cold wind whipped at their gray traveling cloaks, forcing the women to pull them tighter around themselves. While Annet continued walking towards the city, Val could not help but stop and gaze at her surroundings. The city rose up before her and her eyes darted here and there, looking at the numerous buildings, which were surrounded by high stone walls and towers. Everything seemed to have been constructed out of stone with a reddish hue. The walls ran around the city on all sides except the port, which was teeming with ships of all sizes. The city reminded her of Nenholm, but Abenhall was larger and its port much busier. She was so overwhelmed by the grandeur of the city that she didn't notice Annet's approach until the other woman seized her by the arm.

"Wake up," Annet said grumpily, pulling her down the pier. "There will be plenty of time for sight-seeing later."

They continued down the pier, but Val couldn't help but gaze all about the city. As they drew nearer, Val saw a large castle standing on a hill overlooking the city. Many towers rose from within the castle as it stood sentinel over the city below. Dark green flags and banners, each bearing a white griffin, waved smartly in the morning breeze. As she looked up at the keep, she felt a sudden sense of foreboding and she immediately lowered her gaze. There at the end of the pier Val saw a large contingent of soldiers barring the way into the city. The area was full of people being forced into single-file lines, and the soldiers were searching each one in turn.

Val felt Annet grab her by the arm, and pull her aside.

"Here's your chance to prove you're ready," she said with a meaningful look toward the soldiers. "We need to split up to get past the checkpoint. Once through, meet me at a local tavern known as The Griff Inn."

Val nodded, suddenly filled with anxiety.

"You'll be fine," Annet said, seeming to read her emotional state. "Just remember your training."

Annet darted away, and was soon lost in the crowd of people. Val took a deep breath, then made for the opposite side of the crowd. It was a slow process. She pulled her hood down over her hazel eyes and drew her gray traveling cloak tighter around her. After what seemed like hours, she made it to the front of the line. In a small area, surrounded by a hastily constructed wooden palisade, stood a row of four small wooden tables some ten feet apart. Behind each table sat a soldier with a sheet of parchment and quill. Two or three soldiers were standing on either side of each table. Another two dozen soldiers were standing on either side of the rows to corral the people coming in for inspection.

"Next," came a harsh voice from her right.

Val turned and saw the man behind the rightmost table beckoning her over. She was suddenly seized by the arm by one of the soldiers and dragged over to the table. The soldier seized her hood and yanked it back, her long brown hair falling over her face.

"Name?" asked the man, gruffly.

"Uh…" Her mind froze as she straightened her hair.

"Your name, girl!" The man said, looking up to glare at her. "Tell me your name!"

"A-Alice," Val lied. "No surname."

"Fine," the man said, turning back to his parchment. "Where are you coming from?"

"Nenholm."

"You're not a refugee from Farodhold or Fairhaven?" he asked, without looking up.

"What?" She asked, slightly confused. "Oh, no."

The man behind the table eyed her suspiciously and said, "Search her."

Val's arms were seized and pinned to her sides by one guard, while another carelessly patted her down. Then he pulled open her bag and rummaged through it, dropping her few belongings on the ground. She wanted to struggle, but fought the urge. At length the soldier dropped her empty bag next to the pile of her belongings and shook his head at the man behind the table.

"Fine. Take this." He held out a slip of parchment, which she took. Then he shouted, "Next!"

Val stooped and gathered her things.

"Move," came the voice of the soldier nearest, grabbing hold of her shoulder.

"I'm moving," Val said, shrugging him off, but as she did so, her dagger, which had been tucked safely inside her belt, fell to the ground with a clatter. For a brief moment they both looked at the dagger, then at each other.

"She had a weapon! Arrest her!" the soldier shouted, moving to seize her.

Val ducked beneath the man's reach, but several other soldiers were now after her. She seized the dagger and pelted across the make-shift corral, then melted into the crowd moving into the city. The shouts of the soldiers could be heard close behind. Her heart was beating fast as she moved with the crowd as it slowly made its way into a wide street running north. Her eyes danced around, glancing here and there in an effort to take in her surroundings.

Yet, Val had no knowledge of this city, leaving her no option but to run. She pushed her way through the crowded street and darted into a narrow alleyway. Her eyes fell upon a row of crates, stacked haphazardly beside a door. She quickly hid behind them, peering back down the alleyway just in time to see two soldiers glanced towards her and then continue on down the street. Panting slightly, she leaned back again the wall behind her. She'd made it passed the checkpoint, but now she'd have to find her way to the inn with half the city looking for her. All she could think was, *Annet is going to kill me.*

It was near nightfall before Val found her way to the Griff Inn. It was located near the northern wall of the city, nestled in a quiet alleyway just off the main road. It had taken longer to find it due to her lack of knowledge of Abenhall and the presence of so many soldiers patrolling the streets for her. Val was forced to call on all her skills of evasion to make it here, but was now worried Annet had left her because of her delay.

The inn was large and had a rundown look to it. The wooden posts holding up the porch were rotted and warped so that the roof sagged just to the left of the entrance. The windows were grimy and only allowed a faint hint of the light and warmth inside to escape. Most of the windows were sagging and in bad need of repair. Val approached the inn's entrance with caution, standing before the door and glancing from left to right. There was no one coming from either direction. She paused, took a deep breath, and pushed open the door.

The smell of alcohol, smoke, and sweat greeted her immediately upon setting foot inside the inn. Standing upon the threshold, she found herself gazing into a large and dimly lit room. A fire burned in a large stone hearth to her far right, and a long wooden bar stood before her. Several unsavory types sat along the bar and a few more were seated around the randomly placed tables. Several of them glanced at her when she entered, but then returned to their drinks and conversations.

"In or out!" shouted the man behind the bar, in a deep voice. He had a wide, muscular build and a look of irritation on his lined face. "We don't need to heat the rest of the alley too!"

"Sorry," Val stammered, closing the door and continuing to gaze about.

She eventually meandered over to the bar and sat down. The barman came over and stared at her for a long moment.

"I'm looking for someone," Val said, softly.

"Speak up, lass," the man said, gruffly.

"I am looking for someone," she repeated.

"Ain't we all," guffawed the man. He smiled at her as several of the patrons at the other end of the bar laughed at the barman's joke. When Val didn't join in, his smile fell and he scowled at her.

"Look, lass, lots of people comin' and goin' all the time," he whispered, leaning over the bar. "I can't keep tabs on all of 'em."

"I was supposed to meet a woman here," Val said, quickly. "She may have paid for a room."

"Ah, then why didn't you say so in the first place?" the barman said, raising up. "Follow me."

The barman moved out from behind the bar and walked over to a door that was slightly hidden behind one of the tables. Val felt uneasy, but could think of no other option but to follow the man. He held open the door for her, but Val refused. Grumbling about wasted chivalry on women these days, he moved through the door into a dark hallway lined with doors. He then led her to the far end, and knocked on the door.

"Enter," came a familiar female voice.

The man pushed open the door, and beckoned Val inside.

"Annet!" Val cried, as she entered the shabby room.

Her mentor was sitting before a small fire, still in her traveling cloak. Val glanced at the tiny stone hearth, which was leaning slightly to the right, then glanced around at the shabby room. The whole thing looked like it was on the verge of collapsing in on itself, but Val said nothing.

"Enjoy your stay," the barman said, closing the door. His heavy footfalls could be heard as he made his way back up the hallway.

"Took you long enough," Annet said, stoking the fire.

"I had some trouble," Val admitted.

"I heard," Annet said, turning towards her. "In fact, the whole city is talking about the young woman who managed to break through the checkpoint and evade capture. You're infamous, Val; the least desirable status for someone trying to remain anonymous."

Val wanted to respond, but knew better. She dropped her gaze, but felt Annet's eyes upon her for several long seconds before her mentor turned back to the fire.

"What gave you away?"

"This," Val said sheepishly, holding up the dagger.

"That's the dagger I gave you just before you entered the Forsaken Labyrinth. The dagger I told you not to bring." Annet said, with a sigh. Val felt Annet's eyes burning into her again. "You knew we'd most likely be searched upon arriving here. Why did you bring it?"

"I tried to leave it, but somehow I just couldn't," Val murmured. "Even in the labyrinth I at least had this dagger."

She lifted her gaze and saw Annet studying her face and expression. At length she spoke.

"Attachment is a weakness you cannot afford, Val. Even your attachment to me," Annet scolded. "You may have passed the trials of the Forsaken Labyrinth, but perhaps you weren't ready to come with me on this mission after all."

"I am ready," Val said, defiantly. "I made it here, didn't I?"

"Val," Annet said, standing and placing her hands on Val's shoulders. "This is not training nor is it a simple test. This is a real assignment. You and I are bound to its completion. Should I fail, you must complete the assignment on your own. You understand the penalty of failure?"

Val looked into the other woman's eyes and saw concern and anxiety.

"I won't fail," Val said, maintaining her gaze.

"I hope not," Annet said, releasing her and sitting back down. "I spotted our target this morning."

"Why didn't you finish the assignment then?" Val asked, incredulously.

"Azka is not someone who can be dealt with easily. We must ensure we are completely prepared," Annet said, patiently.

"Who is this Azka?" Val asked, moving over to sit in a chair next to Annet.

Annet did not respond immediately, but sat staring into the fire, as though her mind had become lost somewhere in the past. At length, she spoke again.

"He is a dark-skinned man from the distant land of Kusini. He was once a member of the Guild; one the greatest assassins ever trained. He should have been one of the Masters, himself, but he refused to join them more than once. I met him just before the Second War of Ascension. We were both summoned before the Masters and we were both given crucial assignments. I completed mine, but he chose to forsake the Guild and protect his target."

"What!" Val exclaimed. "Who were your targets?"

"It's not important who my target was. What is important is that Azka was sent to kill Corin Stone, an orphan boy living in the city of Stonewall. This should have been an easy target for one with such extraordinary talents like Azka, but he chose to forsake his task. Following the war, he left Alethia to return to his own land. Several assassins were sent after him, but none of them ever returned. There was a fear that Azka would return and seek vengeance on the Guild, but as the years passed the Masters chose to let the matter rest, at least until a new opportunity presented itself. Then word came that Azka had returned to Alethia and the Guild decided the time had come to deal with him."

"Why?"

"The Guild believes that he has returned for some purpose," Annet answered, continuing to stare into the flames. "A purpose so dangerous that the Guild decided to try killing him once more."

They were silent for a long time. At length, Val broke the silence.

"So if Azka is so dangerous, what's your plan for dealing with him?"

Annet smiled at Val, her eyes twinkling. "Sit down and I'll tell you."

The following morning, Val sat perched upon a rooftop, overlooking the main road. The building was near the north gate, which was the only gate still opened for public use. All other gates had been closed and barred shut by order of Lord Grehm due to the danger of the invading army to the south. Though the enemy was still hundreds of miles away, there was a tension in the air. As she gazed down, trying to spot the dark-skinned man, she could not help but notice the change in the people moving through the streets. The venders and traders had a hard time drawing shoppers to their stalls. Instead of taking their time, the people moved deliberately down the street, often not looking up as the venders called to them as they went.

She looked up at the rooftop across the street. There she saw Annet perched, also gazing down at the street. Val watched as Annet moved swiftly over to a ladder mounted on the side of the building, then scanned the crowd below. There in the midst of the crowd walked a tall, dark-skinned man. He wore a dark brown cloak, and his hood was pulled back, revealing a baldhead. Val blanched as the man turned to look straight up at her. He nodded at her, seeming to know her intent, then pulled his hood over his head and ducked into the crowd of people. Val stood up, scanning the street below for any sign of Annet or the target. At last, she saw two figures disappear into an alleyway some thirty yards away.

One was wearing a dark-brown cloak and the other a gray cloak.

Val leapt down from her perch, landing on top of a canvas awning, and slid to the ground. Pushing her way through the crowd, she darted into the alleyway and on down to where she thought the other two had gone. It was not far into the alley that Val came to an abrupt halt. Standing before her, Annet crouched with her sword drawn as her target also stood with blade in hand. The man spoke, and his voice was deep and calm.

"It has been some time, Annet."

"Yes, it has."

"The Guild sent you to kill me, then?"

"Yes."

"Then what are you waiting for?" he said, crouching down and bringing his blade up in a defensive posture.

Val saw Annet hesitate, and a smile played across Azka's face.

"You and I were trained to be assassins by the Guild, but since leaving I have further trained as a warrior," he said, his voice still calm. Val could not help but feel the confidence exuded by the man. "You would do well to forget your assignment, and instead serve as a messenger. Tell the Guild that I have no ill will towards them. If they will forget me, I will forget them."

"You know I can't do that, Azka," Annet said, her voice shaking slightly. "I have but one choice: to kill you or die trying."

"I think you are wrong about that," the man said, dropping his guard entirely so that the blade scraped the ground.

"Val," Annet said, without turning from her target. "Remember your promise."

Annet took one step, then a dozen soldiers emerge from their hiding places. They came from all around them, cutting all avenues of escape but one. Annet shoved Val into a small gap between the buildings, then stepped in front of it to hide her.

"Run Val!" She exclaimed. "And remember your promise!"

Val stared in horror through the gap as soldiers seized her mentor. Then, as one of them peered through the gap at her, Val turned and ran. She didn't stop running until she was several streets away. Leaning against the wall and panting, she swore between gasps and hung her head as the shame of abandoning her mentor washed over her. She slid to the ground, her face in her hands, and she wept bitterly. *Now what do I do?*

# 24

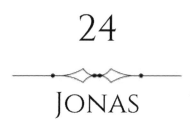

# JONAS

Jonas stood upon the forecastle with Rook, gazing out toward the grand city rising up ahead in the distance. Abenhall was the site of a gruesome siege during the Second War of Ascension; yet now the city stood proud in the light of the rising sun. Tall towers, built with stone of a reddish hue mined from the Iron Hills, rose high into the pale blue sky. Stone walls of the same color rose thirty feet around the city on all sides except the port, which was teeming with ships of all sizes. As they drew nearer, Jonas could make out a large castle standing on a hill overlooking the city. Many towers rose from within the keep as it stood sentinel over the city below. Dark green flags and banners, each bearing a white griffin, waved smartly in the morning breeze.

Despite the grandeur before him, Jonas's mind was elsewhere. In the span of a month, he'd lost his home and his family. His father had expressed pride in him for the first time in his life. Yet on the voyage from Farodhold to Abenhall, the captain had informed him that his father, Lord Peter Astley, was slain while helping his people escape the enemy soldiers. Somewhere on the streets of Farodhold, his father lay unburied. The thought filled Jonas with rage and regret. What if he'd stayed to help his father instead of going to help Rook at the wall? What if he'd led Rook back to the port another way? What if he'd been more like the son his father had wanted? What if he'd followed in his father's footsteps as a warrior and knight of Alethia rather than pursuing knowledge and book-learning?

Jonas's eyes burned with angry tears of regret and loss. So engrossed was he in his own misery that Jonas didn't notice the other man standing upon the forecastle with him. He started slightly when he finally did notice, then looked away ashamed. Rook didn't speak nor call attention to Jonas's tearstained face. There was no need. Somehow, Jonas knew that Rook understood his pain and that thought brought a wave of questions to his mind. He wiped his eyes and turned towards the man whom Jonas thought he knew. This was the man who'd rescued him from wolves in the Eastern Woodlands. The same man who'd also rescued him from XtaKal, and who'd helped lead him to Elmloch Castle. Now it seemed that the man with whom Jonas had shared so many adventures was not who he seemed.

Rook turned to look at him and Jonas realized he'd been staring and turned away quickly.

"Ask me," he said.

"What?" Jonas turned quickly back with feigned confusion.

"Ask me."

Jonas hesitated, but then sighed. "Fine. Who are you really?"

Rook smiled, but Jonas saw it didn't reach his eyes. "I was once known as Kinison Ravenloch."

Jonas's eyes grew wide.

"I see you've heard that name," Rook continued. "I was once the Lord Commander of the Guardians of the Citadel, and served King Greyfuss Aurelia. When the king was murdered, I was framed and sent away in exile. The usurper, Noliono Noland, held my wife captive believing that doing so would ensure my cooperation. Soon after, I was recruited into the Shadow Garrison."

"What's the Shadow Garrison?"

"It was a group of loyal men who sought to protect the line of Aranethons, the true heirs to the crown of Alethia. They hoped to one day help the true heir ascend to the throne," Rook said, with a long sigh. "I met Galanor at a tavern some distance from Ethriel and he inducted me into the Garrison. I agreed to find and bring back the heir, Corin Aranethon, in exchange for Galanor rescuing my wife, Sarah."

Jonas's heart was racing in excitement. He'd always wanted to know more about the heroes of the Second War of Ascension, but his father had not been forthcoming nor could he find many writings of the events.

"Yet after bringing Corin to Elengil, I learned that Galanor had not been able to rescue her," Rook continued, as he gazed at the approaching city. "I took it upon myself to enter Ethriel and rescue my wife, but I was betrayed by an old friend. I sat in the dungeons of Ethriel for months, sinking into despair. Then, I was visited by God in a dream or something and He told me that I had to surrender my will and obey Him if I wanted to rescue Sarah."

"And did you?" Jonas asked, unable to contain his excitement.

"No," Rook said. Jonas felt sympathy for Rook as the man's eyes filled with tears. Rook turned away for a moment, struggling to collect himself. Jonas looked away, feeling for the man and trying to wait patiently for him to continue.

"I was afforded a chance to save her, but I chose to do things my way. During the battle before the gates of Elengil, I rode off with a friend to the enemy camp. There, I found Methangoth holding Sarah and my friend's sister hostage. The evil sorcerer had planned a trap for us, and my friend was presented a choice of which one of us would lose the most important person in our lives: my wife Sarah or his sister Aylen. Before he could choose, King Corin rode up with a host of men and Methangoth sent a fireball at my friend's sister. But in an act of courage and selflessness, my sweet Sarah dove in front of it."

Rook quickly wiped his eyes and refused to speak for a long while. Jonas could tell that even though it had been years, Rook had never processed the pain of losing his wife.

"She gave her life to save your friend's sister?" Jonas offered at length.

"Yes," Rook answered, struggling to regain his composure. "And I failed her."

"You did what you thought was right," insisted Jonas.

Rook smiled. "There is a way which seemeth right unto a man, but the end thereof are the ways of death."

Jonas looked quizzically at him.

"If you are to be Galanor's apprentice, you will need to learn the difference between what you think is right and what truly is right."

"Indeed he does," said a voice from behind. "And he will."

Jonas and Rook turned to see Galanor climbing up to the forecastle to stand with them.

"You have much to learn, Jonas Astley," the old man said sternly.

Ignoring the old man's chiding remark, Jonas asked, "What will happen now?" "Southern Alethia has all but fallen. The Island of Nenlad may resist for a time if it is invaded, but the dark army is reported to be marching north towards Norhold. With Fairhaven and Farodhold fallen, the only major fortresses left in the south are Norhold, located in the southern arm of the Iron Hills, and Noland, located on the plains east of the Iron Hills."

"I know where those fortresses lie," said Jonas, impatiently. "And if Farodhold could not hold back the dark army, neither of those can hope to hold out for long."

"Perhaps," admitted the old man.

"In any case, the sieges of those two cities may buy the north some time to prepare," Galanor said, stroking his long gray beard.

"Perhaps, but what lies in the north that can hope to defeat the dragon?" Rook asked, incredulously.

Galanor shook his head. "We have but one hope. We must place our faith and fate in God's hands."

"What do you mean?"

"I relied too much on my own power at both Elmloch and Farodhold," Galanor said, his face bent in shame. "I thought I alone could protect this kingdom. I have grown too proud in my old age."

"You defended us for a time," Jonas offered.

"Yet I forgot where my power truly comes from," Galanor said, turning to look sternly at him. "A lesson you should learn and never forget."

"What do you mean?"

"You are the guardian of the Book of Aduin and protector of the kingdom. As such, you will be imparted with power from the Almighty as I am," Galanor answered gazing intently. "I will teach you all I know, but you must never forget that your power comes from Him and not from yourself." He turned and stared off toward the western horizon. "Perhaps if I had called upon His name, Farodhold would not have fallen."

They were silent from some time after that. The city drew nearer, and soon the ship was docked. Jonas, Rook, and Galanor disembarked, and before long were walking along the pier towards the shore. As they drew nearer, Jonas noticed that a large contingent of soldiers were barring the way into the city. The area was full of refugees from Farodhold, forced into single-file lines, and searched by the soldiers.

They entered the crowd of people and gradually made their way forward. Upon reaching the front of the line, two soldiers, each wearing dark green tunics bearing the white griffin of house Grehm, seized Jonas and confiscated his bag.

"Unhand that young man's property," Galanor shouted.

"Be quiet, old man," one said, brandishing his sword threateningly at them as the other rummaged through the bag's contents.

Galanor drew himself up and extended his staff. There was a flash of blue light, and Jonas watched in amazement as both men were lifted into the air, their arms flailing about frantically.

"Since you're just hanging there, listen to my words carefully," the old man said, gruffly. "I am Galanor, loremaster and defender of Alethia. You will return the young man's bag at once, and then take us to Lord Jon Grehm post haste."

"Help! Let us down!" the two men cried out, while more soldiers came running toward the commotion. Jonas watched as the newcomers gawked at their comrades floating in midair. Then one of them turned towards the old man.

"Galanor!" he exclaimed, coming over.

Rook and Jonas prepared to defend themselves, but the man raised his hands in sign of peace. "Lord Grehm has been expecting you," the man said. "I am Sir Thomas and I was ordered to bring you to the castle at once."

There was another flash of blue light and the two soldiers fell to the ground with a loud crunch.

"Very well," Galanor said, with a small grin. "Lead on."

The castle of Abenhall was one of the few structures to survive the Second War of Ascension. Though the city itself was built long ages ago, the old fortress was more than two hundred years old. It was built by Jarod Eddon when his family was granted the lands around the Bay of Ryst by house Myr. Though both great houses fell during the last war, King Corin Aranethon granted Jon Grehm lordship over these lands. Lord Grehm had worked diligently to restore the castle and city to their former glory over the last twenty years. Jonas, who'd never been beyond southern Alethia, was amazed by the city. Larger than both Fairhaven and Farodhold combined, Abenhall was the major port city for the entire kingdom. Standing before the castle's main gates, Jonas stared up in awe at the walls and towers. He only realized his companions had left him when he finally dropped his gaze and saw them crossing the castle courtyard.

"I will let Lord Grehm know you have arrived," Sir Thomas said, when they'd entered the great hall.

Galanor seated himself at one of the long tables, as Jonas and Rook milled about the hall. At the far end was a dais, upon which sat another table perpendicular to the others. A high-backed chair sat in the middle, with two other chairs on either side. Jonas moved down the nearest wall, gazing up at the tapestries hanging upon the walls. As he moved down the row of tapestries, he paused at an aged one that hung down to the floor and stared confused at it. He sat his bag down against the wall and studied the images depicting an embattled city, surrounded by a wooden palisade, and a large forest that did not resemble any of the lands about Abenhall that Jonas had seen.

Glancing over, he then did a double take, as he beheld the most beautiful young woman he'd ever seen gazing back at him. She was tall and slender, with long, dark brown hair that perfectly framed her face. Her narrow nose flowed into her full lips, which were parted slightly. Yet the most captivating thing about this woman was her eyes, piercing blue. The young woman was also wearing dark eye-shadow, which made her eyes even more striking. Realizing that he was staring, seemingly spellbound by this young woman's eyes, Jonas quickly turned back to the tapestry. After a long moment, he stole a glance at her, only to find her standing close beside him and looking at him out of the corner of her eye.

"These tapestries depict events from Jon Grehm's past," she said, at length. "His family is from a small village called Castel, nestled near Oakwood Forest."

"Oakwood?" Jonas asked, turning towards her with sudden interest. He'd heard many tales and heard many stories about that infamous forest. "That's a dangerous forest."

"So I've heard," the young woman said, pointed at the tapestry. "Castel is a small town, so every male child born in the town was trained from a young age as a defender on the wall, and Jon

Grehm was their captain."

"How do you know so much about Lord Grehm?" Jonas asked, take aback.

"My father spent time in the north before the war. I've heard so many of his stories its too many to even count. But I'm being rude. My name is Selena Morgan," she said, extending a hand.

Slightly taken a back once again, but not wanting to offend, Jonas took the young woman's hand. He released it almost immediately, and turned away to hide his embarrassment.

"I'm Jonas," he muttered, awkwardly.

"Lord Astley's son?"

"Yeah," he answered, turning back towards those captivating blue eyes.

"I'm so sorry about Farodhold," she said, and her face became downcast.

"It's fine," Jonas said, instantly shaking his head. He felt her face was too beautiful to wear any expression other than a shining smile.

"So I guess you're here to escape the war."

"Among other things."

"What other things?"

"Well," Jonas said, hesitating.

"You're here with that wizard, Galanor, aren't you?" She said, turning towards the table where the old man sat.

"Yes," Jonas said, hastily. He secretly wanted those eyes back on himself.

"They say he has the Book of Aduin and that's why the dark army keeps attacking," Selena said, turning back towards him. Jonas felt a thrill as he gazed stupidly into them. "They also say that everywhere he goes, the dragon follows him."

Jonas looked at her and sudden suspicion gripped his heart. Yet those eyes seemed to be telling him to trust her.

"He doesn't have the book though," he said, feeling the sudden need to impress her. "I do."

"You!" She squealed.

"Shhh," he hissed, then pointed at the bag he'd dropped.

"In there?" she whispered, her voice full of excitement.

He nodded, and watched her beautiful eyes suddenly grow hungry as they gazed down at his bag. Feeling unsettled, he was about to ask her why she was so interested in the book, but his thoughts were interrupted by the presence of someone else.

"Hello Jonas," came a voice from behind him.

Both Selena and he spun around and saw Rook standing there. Jonas was filled with sudden embarrassment and shame.

"Who is your friend?" Rook asked, smiling and giving a slight bow.

"I am Selena Morgan."

"Morgan?" Rook stopped short and the smile fell from his face. "As in the daughter of Silas Morgan?"

Jonas turned to see a flash of anger cross Selena's face, but then it was gone and she smiled up at Rook, politely.

"Yes, he is my father," she said then turning to Jonas she bowed. "I'm sorry but I must go. It was nice to have met you Jonas."

Jonas watched her walk away, then felt Rook's eyes on him and he rounded on him.

"What's the big idea, sneaking up on me like that?" He said, angrily.

"I didn't mean to sneak up on you, Jonas," Rook answered with a suppressed chuckle. Then his face turned grim. "Be careful, though. The Morgans cannot be trusted."

"You're one to talk, Rook," Jonas retorted. "The longer I've known you, Rook or Kinison or whatever your name really is, the more I realize I don't know you."

"You begin to realize a truth about people," Rook replied, frowning slightly. "You think you know someone, but even basing that on what they say and do is still only wading in the shallow end of who they really are inside."

Jonas turned back to the tapestry, noticing the bottom rustling slightly near where his bag sat. Yet before he could investigate, the door to the great hall burst open and Sir Thomas entered with several other soldiers. Galanor stood, and Jonas and Rook moved over to join the older man.

"My lord, Galanor," said Sir Thomas. "I apologize, but while I was at the port, Lord Grehm left the city with his entire host. I was not informed until just now."

"What? Where is he bound?"

"For Ethriel, my lord," Sir Thomas answered.

"Then perhaps our coming is not in vane," Galanor said, turning to Rook and Jonas. "If Lord Grehm has mustered his forces, perhaps the king is already aware of the danger from the south."

"So what now?" asked Jonas.

"We must catch up with Lord Grehm," Rook replied, turning to Sir Thomas. "Are there any horses left in Abenhall?"

"There are a few."

"Take us to the stables," Galanor commanded. "We must make haste and reach Lord Grehm."

Jonas ran over to grab his bag. Picking it up, the bag fell open and he stared in horror.

"The book is gone!" Jonas cried out in alarm.

There was a loud bang. Jonas turned in the direction of the noise, and saw the side door to the great hall fly open and a mane of long dark brown hair disappear through it.

# 25

# SELENA

The sky grew dark as a chilled wind blew down from the north. A lone rider, shrouded in a dark traveling cloak, paused on the plains running north of the Iron Hills. The rider pulled down her hood, revealing her long dark brown hair and piercing blue eyes. Selena paused, reigning in her horse, and dismounted in the gathering twilight. She glanced behind her as the sun slipped beneath the horizon. In the far distance, she thought she could see the faint shapes of riders on horseback.

Selena sighed. Since her decision to obtain the Book of Aduin for the sorcerer, everything had gone wrong. She'd managed to steal the book from that stupid boy, but had also been seen while fleeing from the great hall. Then she'd spent half a day ducking the patrols and escaping the castle. After that, she was spotted stealing a horse, and was almost caught riding through the north gate.

After escaping Abenhall, she rode hard east along the Iron Hills. Stopping about half a day's journey to rest, it was then she realized she was still being pursued. Riders were on her trail, not more than a few hours behind her. Realizing the earnestness of her pursuers, she'd left the shelter of the foothills and ridden hard and fast out across the plains. Mile after mile had passed beneath her feet, but still her pursuers remained close behind. Now three days out from Abenhall, her pursuers were still hot on her trail. Two maybe three riders were on the plains in the far distance; still several hours away, but if they rode through the night...

Selena knew she could not run forever, nor could her horse continue at such a pace. She stood wondering what to do when the wind changed directions. Blowing in now from the east, Selena nearly doubled over from gagging and heaving. The most disgusting stench she'd ever smelled came rushing towards her. The smell was not comforting, but it did inform her that she was nearing her goal. The stench was coming from the Deadwood Marshes, and her destination was on the near side of the dreaded swamplands. She jumped back on her horse and turned southeast, back towards the foothills.

After riding for another hour, Selena stopped short. Before her and wearing a gray cloak, stood a lone man blocking her way. His right hand was extended, signaling her to halt. She considered merely riding to one side or the other, but something about the man made her pause. Then she recognized the man, and a sudden yet familiar feeling of both peace and apprehension washed over her.

"I know you," she said, gazing down at him. "You're that stranger I saw in Fairhaven."

"Yes, I am he," the man said, calmly. "You may consider me a stranger, Selena, but I remind you that I know you very well. Come and sit with me."

He turned and began walking away into the darkness toward an old tree, apparently dead for it was bereft of foliage. Selena dismounted, and turned to follow the man. To her amazement, she saw him already seated comfortably beside a campfire under the tree. She wandered over, leading her horse, wondering how she had not noticed the fire.

She tied the reigns to the tree, and sat down across from the man.

After a few moments of silence, she spoke. "Who are you?"

"Have you not guessed yet?" The man asked, bemused. "I am the same one who came before, and I've come again to remind you of the warning I gave, which you have ignored."

"What warning?"

"That you are headed down a dark path, Selena. The same path that your father has chosen."

"I am nothing like him!" Selena protested.

"You have made an agreement with the same dark sorcerer, and chosen to begin your young life with stealing. The same path that your father chose many years ago."

"I am nothing like him!" Selena cried, jumping to her feet in anger.

"Peace," the man said. It was not a request, but a command. His voice was steady, but there was a power behind it. A power Selena had never before experienced. "You have a choice before you, Selena. You may choose to give the book to Methangoth, binding yourself to him, or you can choose to return the book to those from whom you stole."

"How can you ask me to do either?" Selena said, beginning to pace. "If I don't give Methangoth the book, he will kill me. If I return the book, they will certainly lock me up or worse. Besides, what's in it for me if I give it back?"

"You wish for a reward for simply doing the right thing?" The man asked, his voice calm but stern.

She wanted to retort, but something in the man's eyes stopped her. She turned away, unable to handle the piercing gaze. There was compassion in those eyes, but also a sense of expectancy and resolution.

"Your path diverges, Selena," he said, breaking an extended and uncomfortable silence. "Choose carefully. I will reveal to you that your decision today will have lasting consequences for years to come. If you give the book to Methangoth, you will doom the kingdom to many years of suffering. If you return the book, you will help save the kingdom from a great evil. Heed what I have said, and know that I love you."

Selena turned back to demand more information, but the fire and the man was gone. She glanced up at the tree, then stared in wonder to see a few green leaves on the lower branches.

Selena stood below the tree for a long time, while a great battle raged between her mind and her conscience. In the end, however, she chose to continue eastward. Yet even while she rode, her mind provided a continuous stream of reasons to justify her choice. *How could I simply return the book? And just what would happen to me if I double-cross Methangoth? And who is this irritating stranger who keeps appearing and chastising me? What right did this man have to tell me what was right? Like my father, indeed! And how could he love me? He doesn't really even know me!*

As she rode on, a long arm of a mountain stretched out across the foothills, as if it was reaching to block her path. Unabated, she rode around the mountain's arm, then she stopped and gaped as an ancient fortress rose up on her right, seemingly embedded in the side of a large mountain. Made of dark stone, apparently mined from the nearby Iron Hills, the fortress had a menacing exterior, which was obviously meant to strike fear in all who set eyes upon it. A massive keep rose high into the air, and extended back into the mountain behind it. A high wall encircled the keep, starting from within the steep slopes in the east and terminating into the sheer cliff-face overlooking a vast chasm in the west.

"This must be the Deadwood Fortress," Selena said to herself. "I'm finally here."

From her father's stories, she knew that the Deadwood Fortress was originally built to guard the road between Abenhall and Elengil over four hundred years ago by King Henry II. She also knew that it had once served as the political prison for King Kelbrandt Aurelia, following the First War of Ascension. It was an unpleasant place to be at anytime, let alone twilight. Yet somehow, she understood why a man like Methangoth might want to meet here of all places.

She turned her mount towards the fortress and rode forward, turning from the left to the right in growing anxiety as the darkness grew around her. All was silent, save her horse's footfalls echoing off the cold stone. As they drew nearer her horse seemed to grow more reluctant to continue on toward the foreboding place, but Selena urged her mount onward and patted the horse's neck. Yet despite her efforts to comfort the frightened animal, Selena felt her own anxiety growing with each step. She gazed up at the crumbling towers that loomed forebodingly over her head, and she felt the hairs on the back of her head stand on end. A shiver ran down her spine, and she shuddered involuntarily. Her eyes darted across the face of the keep and towers, where hundreds of windows lie. She somehow sensed a growing watchfulness within the crumbling ruin, and though it may have been her ever increasing fear, Selena could not shake the feeling that her proximity to the ancient ruin was prompting a wakefulness. As if her drawing near was causing the old fortress to wake from its long deep slumber.

She reigned in her mount when they reached the gatehouse, and dismounted. Tying the horse to a nearby post, Selena crept through the gatehouse, stopping when she reached the courtyard. Rising several stories high, the ancient decaying keep loomed up in the darkness. She started and gasped, backing away into the darkness of the gatehouse as a light appeared in one of the windows high above her. Fear gripped her heart, but she was determined to see this through. Looking back, Selena could not decide whether curiosity or madness drove her to ascend the main stairs and cross the dark corridor to stand before the very door of the lit room. She stood for a long while, breathing hard and staring as the light fell upon the floor just before door. Steeling herself, she stepped forward and pushed the door open.

Standing upon the threshold, Selena gazed about the room, which was lit by a large fire in the hearth. Ancient tomes filled the dusty shelves that ran along the perimeter of three-quarters of the room. A large window dominated the far wall, with a large desk sitting before it, littered with more books and parchments. In the corner nearest the door, a small table sat with two chairs facing one another.

Selena walked over towards the table and saw an ornate chessboard sitting upon it. Being unable to muster the patience required to master the game, she frowned at it for a moment as she took note of the placement of the pieces. From what she could tell, it appeared to be nearing the middle of the game, with the black player having an obvious advantage. The white player seemed to be attempting to maneuver a pawn into a promotion position while also moving a knight within striking position of the black player's queen. Yet, being at best a novice chess player, Selena observed little more from the board save that the black player had several pieces capable of placing the white king in check. She picked up a black bishop and examined it. It was beautiful and ornately carved. A robed figure, and to her surprise she saw that the piece was carved in the likeness of a woman with long hair.

"You are late," came a low growl from behind her.

Selena spun around and gasped as she saw a tall man, shrouded in black robes, standing beside the hearth. Unnoticed when she'd entered the room, the man was turned away from her, silhouetted against the flames. Slowly he turned and Selena beheld his face. Methangoth's black eyes flashed in the firelight.

"Do you like the chess set?"

Selena stood silently gaping at the menacing figure. He stepped towards the chessboard, and Selena flinched involuntarily, backing away and instantly regretted coming here.

"I enjoy playing with new pieces each time I play," he continued, picking up the very bishop Selena had previously held and examined it in his hand. "Yet I find there is only one opponent I enjoy playing against."

Selena remained silent, unable to think for fear.

"It's been days since I tasked you with finding the book," Methangoth said, turning towards her with a dark scowl. "I trust you have not come here empty handed."

This was it, the moment of decision.

As if reading her thoughts and hesitation, Methangoth stepped towards her. "I warn you, girl, don't test my patience. Give me the book."

Her heart was pounding, and she began to perspire.

"Give me the book!" he shouted.

"No!" Selena screamed, and fled from the room.

She sprinted down the corridor towards the stairwell on the far side. Never in her life had she ran this hard or this fast. Not even with the city of Fairhaven burning around her did she feel this amount of terror. Not daring to stop or turn to the side, she sprinted as fast as she could as the sound of pursuit echoed in her ears. She reached the stairs leading back down to the courtyard, but before her foot reached the first step, her feet leave the ground. Dazed and confused for a moment, she felt her body slam hard into the stone wall, then she crumpled to the floor in pain.

Barely aware of her surroundings, she felt rather than saw Methangoth step in front of her.

"Get up!" she heard him shout. Then she felt her body rise up off the floor. She shook her head to clear it, and gasped as she found herself floating in midair, her feet dangling a foot off the stone floor.

"Young fool," the man laughed darkly. "You cannot escape me!"

He stepped towards her so that his face was inches from hers. She flinched involuntarily as she felt his hot breath on her cheeks.

"You are just as duplicitous as your father," he growled, and despite her fear and anxiety, Selena had to suppress the urge to disagree. Her face contorted though, making Methangoth smile darkly.

"Give me the book, and you may still live."

Selena remained silent.

"Very well," he said, the smile fading from his face.

He stepped back and she heard him speak in an unfamiliar language, then she felt her body slam backwards into the stone wall behind her. Her arms and legs were forced to extend outward, her feet still feet off the ground. Then, she felt dozens of invisible fingers searching her from head to toe. In spite of her predicament, she actually giggled a few times as the fingers tickled her. Methangoth stood watching, his face set in anticipation. After a few minutes, she felt searching fingers cease, and Methangoth's face contort in rage.

"You don't have it!"

Selena didn't answer.

"Where is the book!" he roared.

She still didn't answer, but watched him roar in a fit of rage. Then the wall behind her crumbled and fell outward. The cold night air rushed in, subduing what little warmth remained in the ruined fortress. Selena felt herself float out through the gaping hole in the wall, and she gasped as she looked down to the courtyard far below.

"You have but one choice," Methangoth roared. "Tell me where the book is, or die. Choose!"

# 26

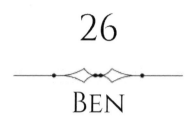

## BEN

Ben sat upon his horse gazing up at the watch tower. Suddenly, red flames erupted from its peak and black smoke billowed from its upper windows. He sat gaping in horror, then he saw Sir Eric rush past. He and his horse galloped towards the burning tower. Ben called to him, but Sir Eric did not seem to hear him. He spurred his horse to follow and watched Sir Eric as he reached the walls, leaped from his horse, and rushed inside. Ben reigned in his horse and was about to run after his mentor, when Sir Eric reemerged, a look of shock and disbelief on his face. There was a noise behind him. Ben turned to see several black figures emerge from the brush. He turned back to see more black figures emerging from within the walls.

"It's a trap!" he shouted.

He turned back to Sir Eric, who was still standing before the gates, oblivious to his danger. Ben was about to call out to him, when he heard the twang of a bowstring. His horse suddenly reared back. Ben felt himself falling backwards. The world was fading out. Darkness closed over him.

Then the scene changed. The day had gone, and darkness was all around them. He was lying on the ground, the dirt and stones embedding themselves into his skin.

"Ben," he heard someone whisper.

He tried to raise up, then realized his hands were still bound behind his back. He turned over and pushed himself to a sitting position, then turned to gaze about for the source of the voice. Sir Eric was sitting a few feet away, though his face was barely recognizable.

"Where are we?" Ben asked.

"We're in one of the enemy tents. We've been taken prisoner," Sir Eric began, his speech was slurred and hard to understand from all the swelling in his face and lips.

"Who are they?"

"I don't know," continued Sir Eric with an effort. "The symbol they bear, a red dragon on a black field, I've never before seen. The one thing I do know is that you have to escape and warn Ethriel."

"You mean *we* have to escape?"

"No," Sir Eric said, his eyes boring into Ben. "They are going to kill me soon, since I won't tell them anything. Before they do, take this."

Ben watched in amazement as Sir Eric wriggled his right hand free from bounds and pulled off his badge, marking him a member of the Royal Guard. He reached over and pinned the badge under the sleeve of Ben's left shoulder.

"Find a way to escape and warn the city. If they don't believe you, show them my badge."

Ben began to protest, but the scene changed again. The darkness once more surrounded them, save the large fire that blazed before him. Ben was on his knees and his hands were tied behind his back. He turned and saw Sir Eric beside him, also kneeling and bound, his face covered in blood and bruises. There was a strange taste in Ben's mouth. He spat on the ground and saw blood mixed with his spit. A shadow passed between Ben and the fire. He looked up to see a big, muscular man, all in black gazing down at them. A large wooden club was in his right hand, and upon his left shoulder was a badge bearing a red dragon, wings extended, on a black field. Ben glanced into the man's face to see he was missing his left eye. The right one glared down at him.

"Answer me!" The man yelled in a deep bellowing roar, hitting Sir Eric in the face with his empty hand. "How many more of you are there?"

Ben turned to see Sir Eric fall to the ground, then turned back to see the man looking down at him.

"Perhaps you will be more willing to answer me," the man growled, leering at him and brandishing his club.

"Leave him alone," he heard Sir Eric say.

Ben watched the big man turn and walk over to Sir Eric.

"What did you say?" he demanded, a bemused smile on his face.

"I said, leave him alone."

The big man turned to his men and let out a loud laugh, which his men echoed heartily. Then in a flash, the big man withdrew a knife from his belt and slashed across Sir Eric's throat.

Ben, unable to believe what just happened, stared dumbfounded as the life drained from his mentor's face. He wanted to shout. To lash out at the big man, but all he could do was stare in disbelief. The big man came over to Ben, and stooped until his face was inches from his.

"Unless you want to end up like him," he said, pointing with his knife at Sir Eric's body. "Tell me what I want to know."

Ben couldn't speak. He just continued to stare in disbelief. The man's expression changed from bemusement to rage. Ben closed his eyes, knowing his death was near and that there was nothing he could do. Sudden pain erupted from the side of his head as he felt the club hit him. The shock of the blow forced his eyes open and stars flashed before them. His head swam, his vision faded, and darkness took him again.

✳   ✳   ✳   ✳

Ben woke with a start. His heart was racing, his mind still reeling from the horrible dream. *Only it wasn't just a dream. Everything he'd dreamt had really happened.* He found that he was lying on his left side, the dirt and stones embedding themselves in his face. He tried to get to his feet, but the bindings on his wrists and ankles held fast and he fell back to the ground. Coughing and wincing in pain, Ben rolled over onto his back and gazed about. He was alone in a small tent, which was dark and empty. His head was throbbing and his body pulsated with pain. As the nightmare faded, the events of the past several days came back, and more clearly than the terrible dream he'd just endured. He closed his eyes, trying to push the horror from his mind and failing.

There was a noise from outside the tent, prompting Ben to quickly struggle into a sitting position. The entrance to the tent opened and the light of the early morning sun temporarily blinded Ben. His eyes quickly adjusted and he saw two men, bearing the familiar badge of a red dragon on their left shoulder, enter the tent. They guffawed as they grabbed Ben under his arms and dragged him out into the cold morning.

The light and warmth of the sun on his face brought him a little comfort as the men carried him across the camp. Yet his reassurance would be short-lived, for a cold wind blew in from the north and threatened to steal all the heat from his body.

"Another trip to the captain's tent, eh boy?" he heard one of the men ask, continuing to laugh at him.

"Maybe this time you'll answer his questions and we can get rid of you proper," the other snickered.

Ben ignored their taunts, already used to this daily routine. He turned from side to side, taking in the familiar path they'd brought him. Ahead of him stood the watch tower, its high stone walls now crumbling in ruin. Half the tower's upper floors had fallen in and black smoke still rose from within.

All about the ruined tower, a large camp of men was assembled. Every day, the two men had come and dragged him to the captain's tent for interrogation, and each day Ben noticed the camp seemed to be growing larger. He could only guess at their number now, but he was sure that there were hundreds of men encamped between the mountain's arms. Within a few more days, he knew their numbers would swell even larger. He also knew that there was only one reason to sneak such a large army through the pass: to destroy the city of Ethriel.

The two men dragged him inside the captain's tent and threw him onto the floor.

"What's this?" he heard someone say in a deep growl.

Ben looked up to see the big man stepping towards them, an angry scowl on his face.

"We brought the prisoner, captain," said one of the men cowering slightly.

"Get him out of here," the captain ordered, hitting the two men over the head. "I'll tell you when I want him."

"Yes, captain," they said together.

Ben felt himself hoisted up once again, dragged outside and across the camp, then hurled back inside his dark tent. The two men left muttering to themselves, and Ben was left alone once more. He pushed himself back up into a sitting position, then gasped to see someone sitting across the tent from him.

"Hello again, Ben," said a familiar voice.

"You!" Ben said, his eyes adjusting better to the darkness.

He could make out the kind eyes and face of the stranger who'd appeared to him just before he'd ran away to join the City Watch. It seemed like a lifetime ago, but in fact was only a little over a month ago.

"I see you remember me," the man said with a smile. "I hope you also remember our previous conversation?"

"You told me that I always have a choice, and that my choices have consequences," Ben answered.

"For you and for your father," the man added.

"Why are you here? Are you a prisoner too?"

"I am here to help you and to offer you guidance."

"Can you help me escape?"

"You will have a chance at escaping, yes, but you must heed my words, Ben," he said, shifting his robes. "A great danger is approaching."

"I know," Ben said, impatiently. "I have to escape and warn Ethriel."

"Not from this army from Donia," the man said calmly. "Your very soul is in danger, Ben."

Ben looked at the man, unable to hide his confusion.

"Remember these words: 'For what shall it profit a man if he shall gain the whole world, and lose his own soul?'"

"The choice will be yours, now hurry. Your chance for escape is nigh. Wake up!"

✳   ✳   ✳   ✳

Ben sat up blinking in the darkness. He was in the same tent, but it was night and though he could not remember why, his head was throbbing in pain.

He heard movement outside, so he laid very still. Two men entered the tent, carrying another man.

"Drunk again," one of them said as they lowered the unconscious man to the ground rather roughly. "This is the third time since we came out of the pass.

"Jimmy's never been able to handle his liquor," snickered the other.

"Let him sleep it off in here, otherwise the captain may kill him just to make an example," replied the first man.

"What about the prisoner?"

Ben closed his eyes and felt one of the men nudge him with his boot.

"Nah, he's out cold," he heard the man say. "Probably had too much fun during his interrogation."

"Well, come on," said the other man. "Let's get back to the fire before all the food and drink is gone."

Ben waited until he was sure the two men had left, then he turned towards the drunk man, lying on the far side of the tent.

"Uh, hello?"

There was no answer, and Ben scooted over to investigate. Ben was pleased to find that the man was still unconscious. When he drew closer, he could hear the man snoring softly. The smell of alcohol was strong on the man's breath and clothes. Ben prodded the man with his foot, but the man did not stir. In fact his snoring did not change or falter. Seeing his chance, Ben searched the man for something to cut his bonds. Finding a small dagger on the man's belt, he drew it out and cut his hands and legs free. He sat rubbing his wrists and ankles for a few moments, trying to help waken his sore limbs. Returning to the man, he took his long black cloak and buckled the man's sword and belt around his own waist. Ben then took the red dragon badge and pinned it to the cloak, and crawled to the tent entrance to peer out.

The immediate area around the tent was clear. Taking one more furtive look back at the sleeping drunk, Ben stole out of the tent and skirted down the adjoining tent row until he reached its end. The night was cold and dark. Dense clouds covered both moon and stars. A light breeze blew through the camp occasionally, chilling Ben to the bone as most of his winter gear had been confiscated by his captors. Ben stole from cover to cover as his teeth chattered and his body shivered. The light of a nearby fire caught his attention and the warm inviting glow was very tempting. Yet he knew the cost of that warmth might be his life.

Veering wide of the inviting flames, Ben ran down another tent row trying to think of how he was going to escape this camp. He glanced up into the darkness, trying to gain his bearings. In the distance, he thought he saw the faint outline of mountains on his left. He breathed a sigh of relief, knowing at the very least that he was moving in the correct direction.

Near a small cluster of tents, he paused to listen. Away to his right came the neighing of horses. Hope leapt up in his heart as he made for the noise and found a small paddock erected just inside the boundary of the camp. The silhouettes of several armed men moved about the paddock. Ben watched the men and patiently waited for an opportunity. After several minutes of shivering in the dark, the sound of a horn could be heard some distance away behind Ben. All but one of the soldiers around the paddock ran off in the direction of the horn blast, and he saw his opportunity.

Rushing forward through the darkness, he hurtled the paddock and leapt astride the nearest horse. The horse reared and let out a loud whinny, which drew the attention of the last remaining guard. Ben heard the man shout, but ignored him and urged to horse forward. Leaping over the paddock they galloped toward the camp perimeter, making for a gap between two watch fires. The men sitting around the fires leapt to their feet. Ben heard the twang of several bows, but the arrows did not find their mark. They passed the outer perimeter of the camp and off into the night.

\* \* \* \*

Ben rode on through the night, until the sun began rising above the mountains to his left. He ignored the cold and the numbing of his extremities, making his way across country to avoid recapture. Knowing search parties would be on his trail soon if not already, he urged his horse onward in spite of the cold and semi-darkness surrounding them. Though the warming of the morning sun was welcome, in the light of day there was no hope of continuing unmarked upon the road or otherwise. He needed a place to hide both himself and his horse, but question was: where could he hope to find such a place in this unfamiliar region?

Ben turned quickly, gazing across the hills behind him. The sound of pounding hoofs and the voices of many men came from over the hills he'd ridden over. His heart racing, he urged his horse on and galloped over the hard ground. The hill began to give way to open ground and small farms. He recognized this area as the same that he and Sir Eric had passed on their way up to the watch tower. It seemed like ages ago instead of just days.

Soon he reached the village where they'd left the road for the open country. The woodlands ran up along both sides of the town. At points the trees grew amongst the houses and shops so that the town seemed to be enveloped by the woods. Instead of going straight through town, he wandered through an adjoining field to stop behind a large barn near the road. He dismounted, tied the horse to a nearby post, and crept forward toward an open window near the front of the barn which faced the road. What he saw made his heart sink.

The several small houses made up the village, running along either side of the road. Near the center of town was a two-story inn. Looking down the road, Ben could see twenty or thirty men, moving on either side of the road, apparently searching the villagers' homes as they went. They were all wearing the black uniforms of the invading army. He watched them for several minutes, then he saw two men emerge from the nearest house. One of them, a burly-looking man wearing a long black cape, cast a look toward the barn where he was hiding. He ducked, unsure if he'd been seen. Crawling forward until he reached the far side of the barn, he leapt to his feet and ran to the back where his horse was tied. Ben stopped short, gaping open-mouthed at the place where his horse had been tied. The animal had pulled up the post and was gone.

Ben's mind was racing as panic began to overwhelm him. *What was he to do? Where could he go? Was there any point in trying to flee any longer?* Hearing voices from the far side of the barn, brought Ben out of his terror-driven thoughts and he ran to a small hillock behind the barn and dove behind it. Crouching down and peering up over the crest of the hillock, Ben watched a dozen men moving about the perimeter of the barn. One of them noted the hole where the post had been and called to his companions. They converged and began following the trail left by the post as it was dragged across the ground. Ben could barely make out what the men were saying.

"Fetch the horses now!" said the man in the black cape. "Our quarry is near!"

"Yes, captain," said the others, most of which ran off in the direction of the town, leaving only the captain and one other behind.

"What's to be done once we find him, captain?" the other man said softly and moving over closer. "Do we bring him back?"

"Orders are to kill on sight," replied the captain, crouching down to study the ground. "No need to bother with capture."

There was a long moment of silence, then the captain glanced up suddenly, and for a moment he appeared to be looking straight at Ben, who froze in terror. The man stood, his eyes locked on the place where Ben was hiding and he looked like he was about to move towards Ben when the others rode up. The captain tore his eyes away and hopped astride his horse. Calling to his men, the captain rode off with the others close behind. They galloped away over the hills, and Ben watched them until they'd disappeared from sight.

Waiting for several minutes to collect his wits, Ben slowly crept back from the hillock and away from the barn into the surrounding woodlands. He soon found shelter in a dense patch of trees several hundred feet north of the town. There he decided to wait for dark, then he planned to steal a horse and continue on his way to Ethriel. He wondered if the captain and his men had found the horse. If they had, they would know that he was somewhere nearby and would return to the village, thus making any attempt to escape nearly impossible. Yet a voice in his heart urged him onward. He closed his eyes and summoned all his remaining courage, knowing that if he could not get through to Ethriel, the city would have no warning of this invading army until it was too late. He had to get through. He was the city, and maybe even the kingdom's only hope.

City's

# 27

# MADDY

Maddy stood upon the battlements of the Citadel, gazing out upon the city of Ethriel below. It was midmorning and the white towers and walls of the city gleamed brightly in the light of the morning sun. She was wearing a simple blue gown. A light blue cloak wrapped around her, the hood pulled over her light brown hair. The northern winds were still blowing and whipping the cloak around her, but the sun felt warm on her face. After admiring the city's splendor for a while, Maddy descended back down to the courtyard. She saw the baron and Lord Grehm conversing outside the great hall, and moved away, trying to avoid them.

"Lady Madeline," she heard the baron call.

She paused, closing her eyes for a moment. Then she turned and forced a smile, moving towards them.

"Good morning, my lady," the baron said when Maddy had reached them.

He took her hand and she bowed to him and Lord Grehm.

"My lady," Lord Grehm said, nodding to her as he turned to walk into the hall.

She frowned, wondering why he'd left so abruptly.

"I am pleased to see you, Madeline," said the baron.

His voice was tired and there were dark circles under his eyes. She'd hardly seen him since they'd arrived in Ethriel two days ago. He took her hand again and kissed it gently, looking expectantly at her. "I will be at dinner tonight, I promise."

She smiled and nodded.

"I apologize for my absence, and for the events of the past few weeks," he continued, and Maddy noticed the sincerity in his eyes.

Her smile faltered, but she said nothing.

"Barron Windham," came the voice of Lord Grehm from behind him. "Your presence is required."

"I must go," the baron said.

He kissed her hand again, then turned and entered the hall, the great ironbound doors closing behind him with a muffled boom. Maddy stood for a moment, took a deep breath, and walked towards the gates, which were closed. Several men were standing nearby, all wearing white tunics and cloaks with the hoods pulled over their heads and swords on their belts. On each of their tunics was pinned a badge, upon which was a golden sword pointed down in the center of a crimson field bordered in gold, marking all of them as members of the Royal Guard.

"Open the gates, please," Maddy said, addressing them and fighting her anxiety. "I wish to explore the city."

The guards looked unsure.

"My lady," said one of them, as he stepped forward and pulled back his hood to reveal sandy brown hair and kind gray eyes. "My name is Liam. I am a lieutenant in the king's Royal Guard. I am under strict orders from the king to allow no one to wander about the city without protection."

"Very well," she said, resolutely. "None of the baron's men are about, so which one of you would like to accompany me?"

They all glanced awkwardly at one another for a moment, then Liam spoke again. "I and two others will accompany you, my Lady. Only please stay close to us. This city is not as safe as the village of Windham."

Maddy smiled and nodded, and Liam and his men led the way through the gatehouse, the great ironbound doors swinging wide to allow them through.

Maddy walked through the busy streets of Ethriel, overwhelmed by the greatness of the kingdom's capital city. At first she stayed on Citadel Way, which was the main street that ran from the gates of the Citadel straight to the city gates. All along this main thoroughfare stood shops and stalls of every kind. The shops closest to the Citadel were mostly well-established venders, while the traders and merchants who'd just arrived in the city from foreign parts lined the streets closest to the gates. Most of the shops close to the Citadel were apothecaries, cobblers, tailors, and other more tame vendors.

Seeking to see more, Maddy turned down a main avenue off the Citadel Way, and found it lined with several taverns, both large and small, with intricate signs hanging above the doors. Some of the signs bore animals, both real and mythical, and others bore funny-looking men holding flagons of some foaming beverage. Looking further down the avenue, she saw some shabbier buildings off down an alleyway. Before she could take a step, she felt a light hand on her shoulder that was quickly withdrawn. She turned and saw Liam looking at her.

"I apologize, my Lady," he said, quickly and looking around. "We should probably keep to the main streets."

"Very well, Liam," Maddy sighed. "Lead on."

She waited for the soldiers to turn to go, then she sprinted down the alleyway. She soon heard Liam and the others calling out for her, but she continued down the dark alley. About halfway down the alleyway, she paused to look at a shabby-looking inn with a sign bearing a lion on its hind-legs as if it was dancing. Above the lion, in peeling letters, the sign read: *The Dancing Lion*. She smiled and was about to open the door when two hands grabbed her from behind. A rough hand covered her mouth as she tried to scream. She was dragged into the small gap between the buildings, then the rough hands spun her around and she beheld her captor.

"David!" She exclaimed.

His once shoulder length brown hair had been cut short, and his face was covered with a beard, but his brown eyes still twinkled in excitement. She threw her arms around him and they held each other for a long moment, then Maddy pushed him away and punched him in the arm.

"You scared me," she said, trying and failing to look angry. "You're always scaring me!"

"I can't help it," he said, a playful crooked grin breaking across his face. He put his arms around her again, and they stared into one another's eyes. "You're just so cute when you're scared."

"Hardly," she said, ducking under his arms as he leaned in to kiss her. "What are you doing here?"

"I heard the wedding was interrupted in Abenhall," he said, still smiling playfully. "I came to see if I could still win you back."

Maddy's smile faded, and she turned away. She felt him come and lightly place his hands on her shoulders. She longed to turn around, to kiss him, to tell him of her undying love for him, but she couldn't.

"What's wrong, Madeline?" he whispered in her ear. "Aren't you happy to see me?"

"Of course," she said, turning to face him. "But it's too dangerous for you to be here, David. If the baron found out..."

"He won't," David said, and his face contorted with anger and resolve for a moment, then it faded. He looked intently at Maddy and said, "Just tell me that you still love me and I will fight for you. I will take you away from this place."

"I..." she began. She wanted to tell him so badly, but what if she did and he risked his life in a fight with the baron, a professional soldier. What if David was killed? How could she live with herself if that happened? "I can't."

"You can't tell me that you still love me?" David asked.

Maddy saw a smirk on his face, but pain in his eyes.

"If anything happened to you..." she trailed off and turned away.

"Maddy," David said, soothingly. "We can't live in fear of the future. We have to live in the moment, and if this moment is all we have left then I want to spend it with you."

He gently turned her around, cupped her face in his hands, and kissed her. Their lips locked, and they pulled each other into a tight embrace. Maddy was overwhelmed with feelings, both physical and emotional. For a moment she lost herself in the kiss, wanting desperately for the world and time to fall away, leaving her and David together in this moment forever. Eventually their lips broke apart and David smiled his crooked smile down at her.

"Seems I already have my answer," he said.

"David, I will always love you," Maddy said, pulling away and taking a few steps back. "But I can't abandon my family, I have to keep my promises."

"What about what you want, Maddy?" David asked taking a step towards her, his voice becoming pained.

"It's not that simple," she whispered, tears forming in her eyes.

"It *is* that simple," David said, gently taking her shoulders in his hands. "Maddy, what do you want?"

"I..." she began, but a sound from behind caused them both to turn. Three members of the Royal Guard were running towards them.

"Go! Go before they see you!" Maddy hissed.

"I won't leave without you, Maddy," David said as he took her hand and kissed it.

"David..." she began, but could not think of what to say.

He darted into the gap between the buildings and was gone.

"My lady, are you alright?" said Liam, when he and the others reached her. "We have been looking everywhere for you."

"I'm fine, Lieutenant," Maddy said, still gazing at the place where David had disappeared. "I'm ready to return to the Citadel. Please lead the way."

* * * *

A few hours later, Maddy sat in her room in the Citadel, once again gazing out upon the city below. The sun was beginning to set and the cold night was approaching. Her mind was full of confusion. Her choices, which made perfect sense yesterday, she now questioned with uncertainty. In fact, everything about her life seemed out of focus. Her past decisions were called into question, her present situation was significantly more complicated, and her future was cast into a mist of doubt.

If she remained with the baron, her mother would be safe and she believed that she would be following the guidance of the mysterious visitor. Yet, if she went with David, she'd be free of all this responsibility. Who cares if her actions had consequences for others? As long as she and David were together, what else mattered?

A knock at the door brought her out of her musings.

"Enter," she said, and the door opened to reveal two members of the Royal Guard. They entered and stood to either side of the door. Then a woman in her late thirties entered, wearing a simple, light blue gown embroidered with silver flowers. She had deep brown eyes, and long, light brown hair that was braided into a loose tress that hung down to her lower back. A beautiful silver tiara, studded with sapphire and amethyst, sat upon her head.

"Queen Riniel," Maddy gasped.

"You are Madeline Brice?"

"Yes, Your Majesty," remembering her place, and bowing low. "Please, call me Maddy."

"Thank you, Maddy," the queen said in a kind voice. "Am I disturbing you?"

"No, Your Majesty," Maddy stammered, still bowing. "Please come in."

Maddy glanced up to see the queen enter and nod at her guards. They exited the room and shut the door behind them.

"There is no need for all that," the queen said, crossing the room to the window.

The queen stood gazing out upon the city for several minutes. Maddy stared in wonder for a moment, but then looked away as she realized her rudeness.

"Are you enjoying your time in Ethriel?" the queen asked, turning away from the window and sitting down in a nearby chair.

"Yes, Your Majesty," Maddy said, also taking a seat facing the queen.

"Please, call me Riniel," the queen said, smiling.

"Yes, Your Majesty. I mean, Riniel," Maddy stammered.

"May I ask how old you are, Maddy?"

"I am eighteen."

"So young," the queen said, after a pause.

She was looking at Maddy with a mixture of concern and pity.

"Your Majesty," Maddy began then corrected herself again. "I mean Riniel, why have you come to see me?"

"I wanted to speak with you," the queen answered, simply. "You are the betrothed of Baron Windham, are you not?"

"Yes," Maddy answered, a bit more curtly than she intended.

"Are you happy with this arrangement?"

Maddy saw that the queen was looking hard at her, patiently awaiting her response.

"I think so," she said, but then suddenly fear sprang up in her and she said quickly, "I mean, yes I am."

"You don't seem sure, Maddy. May I ask how you two became betrothed?"

Maddy sat looking at the queen for a long moment. In the queen's eyes there was comfort and concern. A look she'd never seen in her own mother's eyes. Before she could stop herself, she had recounted the events of the past several weeks in detail. While she spoke, the sun had continued to sink low in the sky. When she finally finished, twilight had covered the Citadel grounds. During the majority of her entire story, the queen had sat patiently with a look of polite interest. Yet when Maddy had mentioned the mysterious visitor, she noticed the queen shifted slightly as if suddenly uncomfortable. There was a long pause after Maddy finished. At length the queen spoke.

"This visitor in your tale," the queen began, shifting again in her chair. "I too have spoken to him, both in person long ago and in prayer every day since."

"You mean," Maddy began, but trailed off in wonder.

"Yes, this visitor also visited me and counseled me during a very difficult time in my life."

"What did you do?"

"Maddy, I did not always listen or take His words seriously. It is something that still grieves my heart to this today," the queen said, and her eyes shifted to the floor.

Maddy watched in wonder as tears began to trickle down the queen's cheeks.

"Your Majesty?"

"I told you to call me Riniel," the queen said, wiping her tears and smiling.

"Sorry, Riniel," Maddy corrected. "So what should I do?"

"Maddy," the queen answered, with a meaningful look. "If this is the same visitor that came to me, my advice would be to do what He says no matter what."

"But what about David?" Maddy asked, her voice catching as she was unable to mask her emotions.

"Maddy," the queen answered kindly. "I understand your feelings and confusion, but if you choose a different path you are opening yourself up for great sorrow."

"So what should I do?"

"You must trust His words," the queen answered, gravely. "The choice, ultimately, is yours Maddy. Only you can decide what you will do.

# 28

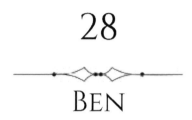

## BEN

It was early morning. The first light of the rising sun fell upon Ben as he sat astride his stolen horse. He was gazing out across the plains toward Mt. Earod and the city of Ethriel. The lower city extended out from the lower slopes and in a wide band along the plains below. His eyes fell upon the wide road leading from the lower city up along the mountain slopes into the upper city. The Citadel Way, as the main thoroughfare through the city was known, was where most of the merchants and venders lived and worked. His father's shop sat just off this main road, which Ben continued following with his eyes until it terminated at the massive gate sitting at the edge of a wide plateau high above the upper city. The Citadel of Ethriel stood upon this high plateau. It was magnificent to behold.

The night had been cold, while the northern winds seemed to cut right through his clothing and freeze his very bones. Yet as he gazed out across the plains toward his home and felt the warm sunlight on his face, Ben felt instantly assured his mission would succeed. A deep sigh escaped his lips. He'd made it. It had taken four days and many narrow escapes, but he'd finally made it through. He urged his tired horse onward toward the city gates, with a sense of pride and accomplishment billowing up inside him. The ground rushed passed as the gates drew nearer. To the side of the gates stood the training grounds where he'd fought Jacob and been recruited by Sir Eric. Those events felt like a lifetime ago instead of just weeks previous.

The gates were now before him, and Ben would have continued riding on through if a group of men, wearing the simple blue garb of the City Watch and brandishing spears, had not moved in front of him and blocked his way. He checked his horse a dozen yards from the line of defenders and called to them.

"Stand aside!" he shouted. "I bring news from the north!"

"Benjie?" came a familiar voice. Ben turned and saw Jacob standing amongst the mass of defenders. "And where do you think you're going?"

"Jacob," Ben said, glaring at his foe. "I thought you were sent home after our fight."

"The captain decided to reconsider the outcome in light of your lucky break," Jacob sneered.

"Well, stand aside. I have to get to the Citadel."

"Can't do it, Benjie," Jacob said, with mock-remorse. "I've got orders you see."

"If you don't stand aside, I will ride you down," Ben said, maneuvering his horse to make good on his threat.

The men before him brandished their spears in warning, and they stared at one another for a handful of heartbeats. Ben was about to spur his horse onward, when a loud voice called to them.

"What's all this?" came the familiar voice of the captain.

All turned to see Captain Saul Gunter walking towards them, his long bushy brown beard and mustache, and stocky figure unmistakable.

"Jacob, what's going on here?" The captain's eyes fell on Ben and a sneer broke across his face. "Ben, what are you doing here? Where is our dear Sir Eric?"

"Dead, sir," Ben answered.

A look of shock flashed on the captain's face, to be quickly replaced with disbelief and anger.

"Don't lie to me, boy," the captain growled. He was now standing between Ben and the assembled members of the City Watch. "Tell the truth. You just couldn't hack it and Sir Eric sent you back here in disgrace."

"I'm not lying," Ben insisted. "Sir Eric and I were captured by a massive army from Donia."

"Donia?" the captain exclaimed, as he and the others laughed. "You and Sir Eric rode north almost two weeks ago, and now you return alone with news of some imaginary army? Where's your proof, boy?"

"Right here!" exclaimed Ben, pulling out Sir Eric's badge and holding out for all of them to see.

Several of the others gasped, and Ben saw Jacob eyeing him with wonder and amazement. Yet when Ben looked at Captain Gunter, his face was set and his eyes narrowed.

"Sir Eric gave me this before he was killed," Ben said, his voice shaking slightly with grief.

"Say nothing more, boy," the captain hissed, then turning to Jacob he said, "Bring me a horse, now!"

Jacob hesitated, looking from the captain to Ben and back, then he ran off towards the stables. The captain walked over to Ben, and whispered, "If you are lying about any of this, boy, I'll have you locked in the stockade for a year."

Ben nodded, and the captain turned back just as Jacob came running up with a horse.

"You will follow me to the Citadel," the captain said to Ben, then turning back to the rest of the men, he said, "The rest of you will resume your duties."

The men parted, and the captain led the way through the gates with Ben close behind. They made their way up the Citadel Way as quickly as they could, maneuvering through the crowded street and sending the people scurrying out of the way as they rode past. Half an hour later, they reached the gates of the Citadel and the captain and Ben dismounted. The great ironbound doors were closed and several men in white tunics and cloaks stood before the gates, their hoods pulled over their heads and drawn swords in their hands.

"Declare yourself!" one of them shouted.

"Saul Gunter, captain of the City Watch, here to speak with the king and the Council of Lords."

"And who is with you, captain?"

"Benjamin Greymore, one of my men who brings important news from the north."

"I am Liam, lieutenant in the Royal Guard and charged with securing this gate," the man said, stepping forward and pulling back his hood to reveal sandy brown hair and kind gray eyes. "You may deliver your message to me and I shall deliver it to the king."

"I cannot," Ben said. "I have ridden far and through many perils to deliver my news. It is for the king's ears and his counselors only."

"Where is Sir Eric Teague? Wasn't he with you when you departed?"

"He is dead," Ben said, closing his eyes and bowing.

"Dead!" exclaimed Liam. "This is grievous news. Do you have any proof?"

"This," Ben held out Sir Eric's badge again.

The lieutenant and all his men stared in wonder. At length, Captain Gunter broke the silence.

"May we pass now, lieutenant?" the captain asked, impatiently.

Ben watched as Liam seemed to consider both he and the captain for a moment, then he turned and nodded to his men.

"You must leave both your horses and weapons here at the gates," he ordered, as the massive gates creaked and groaned as they opened.

Both Ben and the captain relinquished their weapons and their horses were led away. Only then did Liam lead the way into the Citadel. Ben stared in awe at the ancient fortress, amazed at where his fortunes had taken him. Then, seeing the anger on the captain's face, Ben followed after them as Liam led the way into the old fortress. They climbed several staircases, and crossed many corridors, until they stood before the doors leading into the chamber of the Council of Lords. Ben could not help but stare in awe and wonder.

"Wait here," Liam said when they'd reached the doors to the hall. "I will request an audience for you and the boy."

He opened one of the doors and closed it behind him, leaving Ben and the captain to wait outside.

"Remember my warning to you, boy," the captain hissed. "And you'd better not embarrass me in front of the king and the Council of Lords."

Ben nodded, without looking at the captain. After several long minutes, both doors of the chamber swung open and Liam beckoned them inside. Upon entering the chamber, Ben first noticed the large and intricately drawn map displayed on the wall to his right—a map of the kingdom of Alethia, perfectly represented except that this map had been drawn before the annexation of the island of Nendyn. Ben's eyes then fell upon the large, ornately carved circular table made of oak, around which sat eleven chairs. These men comprised the Council of Lords, whose purpose was to elect and advise the king as he ruled the kingdom. Although the election of a king for life was the initial and primary purpose of the Council of Lords, several centuries ago the Council adopted an advisory mandate to the king. The king, once elected, held the absolute final decision; however, since the Council of Lords was made up by the leaders of the most powerful houses in the kingdom, the kings of Alethia have been forced to listen to the lords' counsel.

Ben and the captain came to a halt just before the table, and it was then that he noted that only nine of the chairs were occupied. He immediately recognized the man sitting straight across from him as King Corin Aranethon. All of Ethriel knew him by sight, though Ben had only seen him from afar, but had no need to glance at the simple golden crown that sat upon his head. Ben also knew the crown was not the real crown of Alethia, which was held in the king's treasury. This crown had been made for him for his first coronation which occurred during the Second War of Ascension. It had been made from gold donated by the people of the city of Elengil. Ben thought it said a lot about the king's heart that he would still choose to wear the donated crown rather than the real one. The king had brown hair, flecked with some gray, and sharp brown eyes. He smiled at Ben and the captain as they entered.

"Welcome, Captain Gunter and Benjamin Greymore," he said, with arms held wide. "Lieutenant Liam tells us you have important news."

Ben hesitated, looked over at the captain who glared at him and nodded impatiently. He closed his eyes, took a deep breath, and told of how he and Sir Eric had arrived at the watch tower to find it burning. He then proceeded to tell of his and Sir Eric's capture, Sir Eric's execution, and his eventual escape and arrival in Ethriel this morning. During his recounting, Ben noticed that one of the lords, sitting on Ben's right, was eyeing him with disdain and suspicion. He was a middle-aged man, with sharp eyes and a black goatee, flecked with gray. He wore a black robe with a large red feather embroidered just below the left shoulder. Hanging on the man's chair was a large vibrant red hat with a long red feather sticking out of it. The man was leaning back in his chair with his fingers steeple in front of his face. When Ben had finished, this lord leaned forward and turned towards the king.

"Your Majesty, if I may," he said smoothly.

"Proceed, Lord Morgan," the king said with a gesture.

*Lord Morgan? Silas Morgan? The Silas Morgan?* Ben stared in amazement as the sharp eyes of the once infamous thief and mercenary and now high lord of the island of Nendyn, turned back towards him.

"Young man," Lord Morgan began, with a masked sneer. "What proof do you possess of your interesting and fantastic tale?"

"Sir Eric gave me his Royal Guard badge, just in case you doubted my story." Ben brought forth the badge for the third time that day, but this time it did not garner the same shocking response as it had previously.

"I see a badge of the Royal Guard, but how do we know it belonged to Sir Eric?" Lord Morgan asked, skeptically.

Ben was ready for this question. Prior to giving him the badge, Sir Eric had called attention to the crest of house Teague that he'd pressed on the back of the badge. Ben turned over the badge and held it up so all could see. A general murmur broke out, and he was pleased to see that Lord Morgan was no longer sneering but eyeing him with uncertainty.

"Your Majesty," Ben said, with growing confidence. "I have seen the army that is coming through the Pass of the Knife. Their numbers grow every day. Sir Eric believed their purpose was to lay siege to Ethriel itself."

The king looked at him hard for a long time, but did not speak.

"Your Majesty," said the man to the king's right.

"You have something to say, Baron Windham?" the king said turning towards the speaker.

Ben also turned towards the baron. The first thing he noticed was the long scar running down the left side of the baron's otherwise handsome face. He was middle-aged and wore his light brown hair short like most military men Ben knew.

"You have heard reports of the dark army from the south," Baron Windham said, gravely. "I grant the death of Sir Eric is a grievous one. From what I knew of him, he was a valiant man. Yet long ago, I ventured to the Pass of the Knife and say now that no such army that this young man describes could pass though it in such a short amount of time. It is more likely that a raiding party from Donia took the watch tower by surprise, then caught this young man and Sir Eric the same way. Even a skilled warrior can be caught unawares by new strategies and techniques. If you diverted troops to investigate, I would wager that they would find the tower deserted and these raiders retreating back into Donia. If you would heed my advice, Sire, focus our forces on defending the Pass of Stenc."

There was some murmured agreement from several other lords. Ben scanned the faces of the others, falling upon one lord with red hair, mutton chops, and a kind face. The lord had friendly blue eyes and had the continence of one to be trusted.

"My lord," Ben said, as if pleading with the man.

"Sire," the man said at length.

"Lord Brandyman?" the king asked.

"I also have been to this pass, and I believe this young man speaks the truth," Lord Brandyman said, with a nod towards Ben. "I have always feared that Donia might try and use this pass and now I fear this army out of the Pass of the Knife comes not to raid, but to conquer. We could be caught between these two armies, like prey between a set of giant pincers readying to snap closed."

Lord Morgan and Baron Windham got to their feet to argue, but the king held up a hand.

"Return to your seats. I will hear all viewpoints," he ordered, glaring at the two men until they sat down. Then he turned back towards Lord Brandyman and asked, "What action would you advise?"

"I would send the forces of Lord Grehm, Reese, and Cynwic on to the Pass of Stenc. You can hold mine and Lord Moore's forces here to reinforce the city's defenses."

"Sire," protested Lord Morgan. Ben watched as the man leaned forward again and looked at each of his fellow lords in turn. "My forces were destroyed at the battle before Farodhold. I have seen the power of this dark army and the beast that accompanies it. Mark my words, we will need every last man to defend the Pass of Stenc."

Another wave of murmuring rose up, but the king held up both of his hands for silence.

"Thank you, Ben, for bringing this news to us," the king said, looking at Ben. He could clearly see doubt in the king's eyes. "Your bravery will not be forgotten."

"In the meantime," the king continued, turning back to the members of the council. "We need to discuss this further." The king clapped his hands and the doors behind them opened. "Please stay within the Citadel for the moment, in case we need to speak to you further."

"Your Majesty," Ben and the captain said, bowing and turning to go.

"Captain Gunter," Ben heard the king call after them. They both turned back. "I think this young man merits a recommendation to join the Royal Guard."

"Yes, Your Majesty," he heard the captain say, with more than a hint of reluctance in his voice.

Ben and the captain were led from the chambers and back out into the courtyard. When their escorts were out of earshot, the captain suddenly grabbed Ben by the tunic.

"You think you're something special now, don't you?"

Ben looked into the angry face of the captain, inches from his own. The captain's bad breath filled his nostrils, nearly causing him to pass out. "I will be dead before I see you join the Royal Guard."

"Let go of me, captain!" Ben shouted, as anger burned inside him.

He seized the captain's arm and twisted himself loose. The captain, the better fighter, grabbed hold of Ben again and hurled him to the ground.

"You are nothing, Greymore," the captain growled. "After the king gives leave, you are to report to the stables. Consider yourself on permanent horse dung duty for the rest of your life."

Ben leapt to his feet, glaring at the captain, who leered back at Ben as if begging him to try striking him. Having learned enough not to attack in anger, he fought the urge to strike the captain. He instead saluted the captain, then stormed off.

✳   ✳   ✳   ✳

It was mid-afternoon. Ben had wandered through the Citadel grounds, ultimately finding himself lingering in the beautiful gardens where some of the flowers were still in bloom even in the midst of this harsh winter. His mood had softened during his wanderings, despite the knowledge that the captain would never recommend him for the Royal Guard now, and that his career had a very bleak outlook.

His musings were interrupted by a soft noise from around the corner. He stopped to listen. It sounded like a woman's voice and it sounded like she was in trouble. Ben rounded the corner and stopped short, staring in wonder. Sitting on a stone bench, sat a young woman more beautiful than any he'd ever seen. She wore a simple blue gown, with a light blue cloak wrapped around her, the hood pulled down, revealing her light brown hair. Upon his sudden appearance, she'd risen to her feet and stood watching him suspiciously with her light brown eyes. Ben noticed her cheeks were tearstained.

"Who are you?" the young woman asked, her voice shaking.

Ben stood dumbfounded, unable to speak. Her melodious voice was like music to his ears.

"If you don't tell me who you are and what you want, I'll call for the guards," she said, pulling her cloak tighter around her and backing away a step.

"Sorry," Ben finally managed, holding up his hands. "I'm Benjamin Greymore."

Her eyes narrowed, looking hard at him before saying, "I'm Madeline Brice, companion of Baron Windham."

"Baron Windham!" Ben said, incredulously.

"Do you know him?"

"Yes," Ben grimaced. Then he mumbled, "He's a bit too old for you isn't he?"

Ben regretted his words instantly, for the young woman's face contorted in rage.

"Just who do you think you are!" She nearly shouted. "You don't know anything about me!"

"Sorry. I'm sorry." Ben said, quickly. "I just, I met Baron Windham today and he just seemed..."

Ben trailed off awkwardly, not wanting to offend the young woman further.

"Uh huh," she said, her rage replaced with annoyance. "What are you even doing in the Citadel, Benjamin Greymore?"

"My captain and I were summoned before the Council this morning," Ben answered, fighting to suppress his anger. "I just returned from a mission north of the city and we had to make our report."

"Your captain?" she asked, her eyes narrowed.

"Yes, I'm a member of the City Watch."

"You," the young woman said, with a laugh. Ben thought it would have been a sweet, charming laugh, if it had not been so derisive. "But, you're too short and thin to be a soldier, aren't you?"

Ben's face fell. This young woman was like everyone else.

"I'm sorry," the young woman said, hastily. "I didn't mean to offend you."

Ben saw sincerity in her eyes, but it didn't matter. Her words stung all the more. He shook his head, realizing his stature would always mask his ability and fortitude.

"Forgive me, but I should be going," he said with a bow.

Before she could say anything, he spun on his heal and stormed away without another word.

# 29

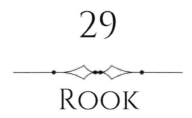

# ROOK

The cold winds blew across the plain north of the Iron Hills. The night was dark and foreboding. Great menacing clouds were rolling in overhead, and the sound of distant thunder could be heard over the howling winds. Rook brought his horse to a halt on the plains running north of the Iron Hills. Jonas and Galanor followed suit. They'd pursued the young thief for the past five days, following close behind across the open plains. Four days ago, the trail moved into the foothills and became harder to follow; then the trail had disappeared all together. They'd ridden on hoping to find some trace of the thief, but upon reaching the western edges of the Deadwood Marshes they'd doubled-back, fleeing the stench and entrapment in the dreaded swamplands.

After two more days of riding, they'd finally returned to the point where the trail had disappeared. Rook dismounted and studied the ground, trying to discern the path the thief had taken. He led his horse on foot while his companions rode slowly behind. Before him lay a long arm of a mountain stretched out across the foothills. Rook stopped, looking to his left and then stood gaping. The others also paused to stare. An ancient fortress loomed up before them, seemingly embedded in the side of a large mountain. Made of dark stone, the mere sight of it filled Rook with fear as the memory of a previous visit to this fortress came rushing back into his mind.

He dropped his horse's reigns and fell to his knees, clutching the sides of his head as if to force the memories back into the depths of his mind. *No! Not here! Not again!* He shut his eyes tight against the visions swirling before him.

"Please not again!" He shouted into the darkness.

"Peace!" came a loud voice from in front of him.

Rook's eyes popped open. His expression quickly turned to anger as he beheld a man in a gray cloak standing before him with his hood pulled back, revealing a familiar face. The man had brown hair that fell to his shoulders, a short brown beard, and kindness shown out of his brown eyes. Rook rose to his feet and his fists clinched as his face contorted in anger.

"No," he said, as he shook with suppressed rage. "Not again."

The man did not speak immediately, but surveyed Rook.

"What do *you* want?" He demanded.

He turned toward Galanor and Jonas for assistance, but found them both frozen in place and staring forward with unseeing eyes.

"What is happening?"

"I have come to speak to you, Kinison," the man said, calmly and consolingly.

"That is not my name!"

"I have come to warn you," the man continued, ignoring Rook's outburst.

"Warn me of what?"

"A great trial lies before you, Kinison. One that you have never experienced before," the man said, and Rook noticed great pain had filled the man's eyes. "I have come to warn you of this. I've come to offer you peace and comfort, and to remind you that I am with you always."

"Always!" Rook spat. "You mean like you were with me twenty years ago when Sarah was killed? Like you were with me during all those horrible years without her?"

Rook fell back to his knees, and sobbed into his hands. A long moment passed, then he felt a hand on his shoulder. He looked up angrily to see the man standing over him with a pained smile.

"Yes, Kinison," he said calmly. "I was there when Sarah was taken from you. I was there every moment during the last twenty years. I am with you now as you are about to endure a horrendous trial. And I will be with you always."

"What trial?" Rook demanded. "What could possibly be worse than watching helplessly as your wife is engulfed in flames?"

He got to his feet and was about to shout more at the man, but he found the man had vanished.

"No!" Rook shouted. "Not again! You claim you're always with me, but then you vanish! Why are you doing this to me?"

"For your good, Kinison," came a voice. "Trust in Me and you will persevere. Have faith and you will see your wife again."

*   *   *   *

The massive keep rose high into the air, and extended back into the mountain behind it. A high wall encircled the keep, starting from within the steep slopes in the east and terminating into the sheer cliff-face overlooking a vast chasm in the west. The very air that had seemed frozen in time around him, moved suddenly as if released by some unseen power or force. Rook, as if coming out of a dream, turned toward Galanor and Jonas who were looking at him with a mixture of concern and bewilderment. He shook his head and turned back toward the dark fortress before them.

"Are you alright?" he heard Jonas ask.

"I'm fine," he answered, bluntly.

"Behold, Deadwood Fortress," Rook heard Galanor say. "Long ago, this was the prison of King Kelbrandt Aurelia, following the First War of Ascension."

Not waiting for the history lesson, Rook hopped astride his mount and rode forward.

"Rook?" Jonas called after him.

Rook didn't answer. Somehow he knew this was where the thief had fled, and that he was being led here all along. Galanor and Jonas quickly rode up beside.

"Rook, where are you going?"

"I can't explain it, but I know our thief is in there."

"Wait," Galanor said, riding in front of Rook so he had to veer away.

"What are you doing?" Rook asked, infuriated.

"We cannot go into that old fortress," Galanor said.

"Why?" Rook demanded.

Galanor did not answer, but turned toward the fortress and waved his staff out in front of him. The tip of the staff glowed white for a moment, then there was a rumbled deep in the mountains in front of them. The fortress shook and loose rubble fell from the towers and battlements. The rumbling ceased as quickly as it had begun, and Galanor turned to Rook and Jonas with a look of anxiety.

"There is a powerful spell of concealment over this place," he said, breathing heavily. "I just attempted to penetrate it without revealing our presence, but I think it is too powerful. To break through, I would have to call upon power that would certainly reveal us to our enemy."

"So what do you propose we do?" Rook asked, impatiently.

Galanor stood thinking for a moment, then rode forward slowly motioning Rook and Jonas to follow. As they moved forward, his staff was still glowing softly.

"What are you doing?" he heard Jonas ask.

"I am attempting to conceal our movements," Galanor answered in a whisper. "If I am successful, the very spell of concealment protecting this fortress will also hide us."

Rook gazed up as they neared the ruined fortress. Made of the same dark stone as the nearby Iron Hills, the dark stone gave the fortress a menacing look. Though the fortress appeared abandoned, Rook now felt a watchfulness in the shadows within; unseen by the three men now riding through the gates, but scrutinizing their every move. They were now nearing the threshold of the gatehouse, which provided the only way through the high stone walls. They paused and dismounted within the gatehouse, tying their horses to posts embedded in the walls. The ancient doors lay fallen from their rusted hinges, decaying on the ground before the threshold. Galanor motioned for them to follow and Rook and Jonas fell in behind the older man.

"We must continue on foot," Galanor said softly, leading the way. "Do not speak, for I fear what may be watching us lies concealed the shadows within."

Just as they stepped toward the gates, Rook noticed the air in front of him seeming to grow warm and almost tangible. He held out his hand and for an instant the air before him grew solid as if to bar his way. The others also paused, feeling the air's seeming reluctance to allow them to pass. Galanor held out his hand and just as suddenly as it had began, it ceased. Somewhat shaken, three men moved forward unimpeded through the gatehouse and out into the courtyard beyond.

As they moved silently across the courtyard toward the keep, Rook's eyes darted all along the walls, seeking among the many windows the source of his unease. There was an oppressive presence here, unseen but much felt by the three men. Yet there was nothing but the occasional howl of the wind and the sporadic falling of rubble from the crumbling ruins.

Without warning, Galanor stopped, causing Jonas and Rook to run into one another. He held up his hand for silence. Rook followed his gaze up along the side of the keep and on to a high tower above the upper ramparts. From one of windows in the highest room, there appeared a light.

Galanor held out his staff once more, its tip glowing white. For an instant, the walls of the fortress rumbled and shook, then fell still. Galanor turned to Rook and Jonas, shaking his head.

"The spell is too strong. I cannot risk revealing our presence."

"Galanor," Rook began. "We must know if the thief is here. Either use your power or allow us to climb up and investigate."

Galanor sighed, then nodded.

Rook led the way inside, but hesitated at the near complete darkness beyond. Galanor shoved him aside, lighting his staff, and proceeded into the keep.

After climbing countless stairs and navigating a labyrinth of corridors, the three men stood before the door leading to the highest room in the tallest tower. Panting and wheezing, they paused a moment to catch their breath. A faint light came from beneath the door, giving the corridor outside an eerie glow. After pausing a moment, Rook stepped towards the door, but Jonas darted in front and attempted to throw it open. The door was locked.

Jonas made several vain attempts to force the door open, but to no avail. Rook seized the young man, and pulled him aside as Galanor moved toward the door. He held out his hand and the door swung slowly open.

The room was bare, save a small cot in the corner. The stone walls stood naked and the windows were open to the elements. The room was noticeably colder than the corridor outside. Jonas tried to push his way forward, but stopped suddenly when they noticed the young woman lying unconscious on the floor. Jonas stood gaping, but Rook stepped forward and stooped next to her to check if she was alive. Her long dark brown hair covered her face, and as he brushed it aside he and Jonas audibly gasped. Rook's initial reaction was to her beauty. Even he, who was twenty years her senior, could not help but admire the young woman's full lips and sharp chin. Yet as he gazed upon her, his eyes narrowed and his face grew grim. There was something familiar about this face. He searched his mind, trying to trace the feeling of sudden apprehension he felt toward this young woman upon first glance. Then without warning, Jonas rushed forward and shook her roughly.

"This is her!" He shouted, as the young woman stirred, blinking uncertainly up at them.

Then, seemingly instinctively, she smacked Jonas hard across the face, leapt to her feet, and backed away from them until her back was pressed against the stone wall.

"Who are you?" she demanded, her eyes darting to each man in turn.

"You stole something from me," Jonas said through gritted teeth, gingerly rubbing his face. "I'd like it back."

Rook saw sudden recognition in the young woman's eyes. A look of terror crossed her face, to be quickly replaced with a mask of anger and resentment.

"I've stolen nothing," she said, heatedly. "And even if I did, that person should have been more careful with his things."

Anticipating Jonas's angry response, Rook held out an arm to stop the young man as he lunged forward. He held Jonas fast as the young man thrashed about, trying to get at the young woman.

"Jonas Astley," he shouted. "Is this any way for a man of your high station to behave?"

Jonas shook himself loose, but Rook's reprove seemed to have sunk in and he relaxed.

"You wouldn't ask that, Rook, if you knew this young woman," said Galanor.

"You know this young woman?"

"Her name is Selena Morgan," Galanor replied.

"Morgan? As in Silas Morgan?" Rook asked, thoughtfully.

"Yes," Jonas sighed, glaring at Selena. "As in the daughter of a thief, posing as a high lord. As in the spawn of dirt!"

"I'm no thief!" Rook heard the young woman shout.

"Liar!" Jonas spat, angrily.

"That is enough, Jonas!" Galanor said, rebuking him. Then he turned toward the young woman. "In case you hadn't realized,

Selena Morgan, you're a prisoner here and we've come to rescue you. For most people, this would garner some gratitude."

"Don't lecture me," said the young woman, defiantly. "I don't need anyone to rescue me."

"Our mistake," Galanor said, diplomatically. "Then if you would just return the young man's book, we'll be on our way."

"I don't have any book."

"I know it was you, Selena!" shouted Jonas.

"I didn't steal anything!"

"Very well," Galanor said, his voice rising in exasperation. "If you are not a prisoner and you do not have the book we are looking for, we will leave you as we found you." He turned towards the door, motioning Rook and Jonas to follow. "We will reseal this door and be on our way."

"Wait, what!" Selena exclaimed. "You're going to leave me here like this!"

Rook suppressed a smile as Galanor turned to address the young woman.

"Of course," he said with a smile. "You have everything under control, yes?"

"But..." she stammered. "Can't you just leave the door open?"

"Then you do need rescuing after all?"

Rook saw the battle raging across her face between her pride and desperation.

"Fine!" she answered, exasperatedly. "I guess I could use some help."

"Very well," said the older man. "We can get you out of here, but only if you agree to return what you stole."

"I didn't..." she began, but then cowered under the piercing glance of Galanor. Rook smiled, seeing the young woman's resolve break. "Fine, I'll take you to the book."

"Excellent," said Galanor. "Please, lead on."

❋   ❋   ❋   ❋

Selena led them back down through the labyrinth of corridors, and descending countless stairs. The brightening eastern sky hinted at the approaching sunrise as they stepped out into the courtyard. The wind had not abated, but nipped at any exposed skin. They followed her out through the gatehouse, then she turned to the left and followed the outer wall for several paces. Near a small cluster of stones, Selena stooped and began pulling the stones away. They waited in anticipation for a few moments, then she held aloft the Book of Aduin.

"At last!" came a deep voice from behind them.

Rook was filled with a sense of dread as he recognized the voice. They all turned and saw two dark figures standing just outside the gate. The figure to Rook's left held a dark sword, while the taller figure on the right stepped closer and pulled back his hood and removed all doubt to his identity.

The man was tall, with long black hair streaked with gray. An evil grin was spreading across his face, and both Rook and Galanor spoke the man's name in unison: "Methangoth."

"You have something I need, Selena," Methangoth growled.

"No!" She cried.

Rook glanced around just in time to see the young woman turn and flee.

"The book!" he heard Jonas exclaim, as the young man took off after her.

Galanor stepped forward, extending his staff. A blue light flashed and a wall of energy appeared between them and the dark figures.

"Do you honestly think you can stop me?" Methangoth said, sneering. He waved his hand and a blazing red beam shot forth, rending the wall in two. The wall vanished, leaving Galanor and Rook stunned. "You are weak old man."

Recovering, Galanor ran forward and a shining white sword, seemingly made of pure light, appeared in his hand. Rook drew his sword also and followed after the old man. Methangoth followed suit, conjuring a blazing red sword and moving forward, with

XtaKal on his heels. A few silent steps and the battle was joined.

Rook lost track of Galanor, as the old wizard fought against his former apprentice. Rook's focus was solely on XtaKal, who advanced and brought the evil blade down at his shoulder. He rolled away, pondering the odd attack made by his opponent. A shoulder attack was a foolish opening blow. Rook blocked another wide attack at his feet, following up by bringing his sword in a short stab at XtaKal's exposed chest. The dark figure jumped back and brought the dark blade up in a defensive stance. They circled one another for several minutes. Rook could hear explosions going off around him, but did not turn to look. As they circled one another, he wondered why he was still alive. He knew XtaKal could have ended this fight long ago. His enemy could have lifted Rook into the air and strangled him like he almost did outside of Farodhold...so why hadn't he?

"Who are you?" Rook shouted. "How do you know me?"

The dark figure did not answer, but Rook thought he saw the hood turn slightly. XtaKal hesitated, and his sword dropped slightly. Rook seized his chance and swung at the dark figure's head, but the attack was blocked. Rook felt himself lifted and hurled backwards. He felt his body slam into the nearby stone wall of the fortress and he crumpled to the ground, gasping. The dark figure stepped near, and Rook realized his sword had been knocked from his grasp. He felt an invisible force begin strangling him again, but he stared up defiantly.

"End it then," he gasped.

Once again, Rook saw the dark figure hesitate. Then a sudden gust of wind caused the dark figure's hood to fall back, uncovering a familiar face. Rook gaped in joy and horror as he beheld the face of his *wife*.

"Sarah!" Rook gasped.

The woman blanched and backed away, her face full of shame and rage. Her once dark brown hair and eyes were now replaced with long white hair and burning red eyes. Her once lovely face was now gaunt, but it was her. Rook saw recognition in those red eyes. Her face changed from rage to sorrow. Tears poured from her eyes. Rook felt the force strangling him slacken, and he fell to the ground hard. He got to his knees, gasping and looked up into the strange face of his wife.

"Sarah!" He said, but she shook her head uncertainly.

She backed away, holding out her hand defensively.

"No, don't go," Rook said, getting unsteadily to his feet.

A sudden blast of red fire hit nearby, and Rook turned briefly to see Galanor run up beside him. Another blast came flying toward them, but Galanor threw up a shield. Rook felt the heat from the blast as it hit the shield and dissipated. Then he saw Methangoth vanish in a burst of black smoke. To his horror, he then saw Galanor hurl a blast of blue flame at Sarah.

"No!" Rook cried, grabbing the old man's arm. He turned and saw Sarah quickly reach inside her robes. Just as the fireball was about to reach her, a column of black smoke erupted around her. An instant later, she was gone. The fireball flew past, hitting the wall with a resounding boom.

Rook fell to his knees, and bowed to the ground. His eyes full of burning tears. Galanor grabbed his shoulder, but he shook the old man's hand off. The overwhelming rage and loss of the past twenty years rushed to the surface and Rook looked up suddenly, unable to contain it any longer. A howl of rage and loss erupted from deep within Rook, echoing off the ancient fortress and the lands about, as if the mountains were filled with men in the throes of utter agony. Yet as his voice fell silent and he fell back to the ground, a small voice within him whispered comfort. *Sarah is alive.*

# 30

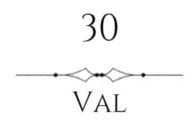

## VAL

The sun was setting behind Val as she rode east. The reddish-orange light fell upon the plains running north of the Iron Hills, casting long shadows across her path. It had been almost a week since she'd left Abenhall to search the wilderness for signs of Azka. She'd spent several days searching the city, and even considered breaking into the castle to rescue Annet, but with little knowledge of the castle's layout or the garrison strength, she'd been forced to give up any attempt to rescue her mentor. She was on her own.

After using her limited investigative skills, she eventually discovered that Azka had left the city. She stole a horse and rode out east in hopes of catching up to her target. The long ride had given her time to consider her situation and the question of whether or not she could complete this task was always on her mind. As she crossed the plains, she found signs of travelers but no definitive sign that Azka was among them. With little recourse, she continued east in the hope that she was gaining on her target.

When night eventually fell, Val was forced to make camp. She lit no fire, hoping to conceal herself from unwanted attention. Yet during the night Val saw out in the distance ahead and to her right among the Iron Hills, flashes of blue and red light followed by the sounds of thunder. She considered making for the lights immediately, but the darkness prevented her from doing so. She was forced to sit and wonder what could be causing the flashes of light and what they could mean.

A sudden rustling noise from nearby brought Val's attention back to her little camp. Val rose to her feet, as sudden fear gripped her. The rustling was coming from just north of her, but the air was still and the wind silent. She stared out trying to pierce the darkness beyond, but to no avail.

"Peace, child," said a voice from the darkness. "You have nothing to fear."

A calm seemed to wash over her, but Val fought against it.

"Who are you?" She demanded.

"Why do you sit in the dark?"

There was a burst of light and a small fire appeared on the ground before her, the warm light illuminating a man sitting on the other side of it. She instinctively drew out her dagger, but the man did not move but simply gazed benignly up at her. The man had brown hair that fell to his shoulders, a short brown beard, simple robes and a traveling cloak. As she looked at him closer, sudden recognition swept over her.

"You're the man I met in the labyrinth!" she exclaimed, gazing at the man in wonder. "How did you find me?"

"As I told you before, 'Not all who wander are lost,'" said the man. "I've come to you now, to remind you of my words in the maze."

"I already heeded your words," she insisted. "I spared that young woman."

"But you did not heed all my words," the man continued, his face growing stern. "Your choice to go up the wide path led to your confrontation with the young woman."

"How did--?" she began, but cut herself off. "So what would have happened if I had chosen the narrow path?"

"No one is told what might have happened," the man said. "Yet the mercy you showed that young woman has granted you mercy in return, as I said it would."

"What do you mean?"

"You are pursuing a man called Azka."

"You know Azka?" she asked, watching a smile play on the man's face.

"I do, indeed," he answered. "You must spare his life as he will spare yours."

"But if I don't kill him, the Guild will never stop hunting me. And what about Annet?"

"You are not responsible for Annet any more than she is responsible for you. You both must make your own choices…and live with the consequences of those choices."

"Can you not save her too?"

The man's eyes filled with tears, and Val was taken aback.

"Everyone is given the same choice," He said, his voice measured, but full of sadness. "But only those who accept Me can be saved."

"Saved? Saved from what?" Val asked, totally confused.

"From yourselves. From evil and sin," He answered, rising to his feet. "Spare Azka and you too will be spared by him. Choose mercy, Valentine, and you will receive mercy. Choose to kill him and only death will you reap. It is your decision."

Val watched in amazement as the man vanished before her eyes. She rushed over and searched the ground where he'd been, but there was no sign of him. Only the fire, still burning before her, gave her assurance that the man's appearance had not been some dream or hallucination. She sat beside the fire, warming herself and contemplating the man's words and what her next move should be.

✳ ✳ ✳ ✳

In the morning, Val awoke and gazed eastward. A bitter wind blew in from the north and she shivered from the cold. Standing there, she debated with herself on her next move, eventually deciding to continue her pursuit of Azka and tabling the question of whether to kill him or not.

She left the plains for the foothills and made for where she believed the flashes of light had appeared. After riding for most of the day, she came around a long arm of the Iron Hills and stopped in her tracks. Mouth hanging open, Val gazed in wonder and dread at an ancient ruined fortress, seemingly embedded in the side of the mountain behind it. The fortress was apparently made from the same dark stone as the mountain itself. A massive keep rose high into the air, and extended back into the mountain behind it. A high wall encircled the keep, though it was broken in several places. She felt a shudder creep up her spine as she beheld the foreboding exterior. Then she saw thin wisps of smoke rising from several places along the wall.

Scarcely believing her own eyes, she rode forward cautiously as her curiosity overcame her fear. When she was a dozen yards away, she paused, and stared curiously at the craters in the broken walls. They were still smoldering. Val turned and inspected the grounds before the walls. There was no evidence of any siege weapons in the vicinity of the walls, and the aged fortress was so decrepit-looking that Val was certain that no one had lived here for a long time. The damage, though appearing to have occurred in the past few days, was not due to a recent siege or major battle.

Along one part of the wall, she found the footprints of both men and horses. They appeared fresh. She glanced at the tracks then at the smoldering craters in the walls and shuddered. The flashes of light and thunder of the previous night came into her mind, and a renewed terror gripped her heart as she wondered what kind of people could wield such power and inflict such damage to these thick stone walls with no evidence of siege devices. Yet another thought entered her mind. *What if these people had encountered Azka?* It was a slim chance, but currently her only lead. She had no choice but to find them, whomever they were. Val returned to her horse and rode off, following the trail of the horses leading eastward.

When night fell once more, Val found a suitable place to make camp. Dismounting and leading her horse on foot, she found cover under a small outcrop and tied her horse to a nearby tree. She ventured far to find firewood, which was scarce. As she was on her way back, she happened to glance eastward and saw a light spring up somewhere in the distance. She paused, excitement building inside her. The light had a warm reddish glow, like the light of a campfire. It was near the edge of a large arm of one the mountains, looming up from the Iron Hills. Val guessed it was at least two hundred yards away. She dropped the firewood and made her way carefully and quietly towards the light.

As she drew nearer, she saw three men sitting around a modest camp fire. She pulled up her hood to hide her features and moved in closer, until she was within twenty yards of the camp. She could hear them talking, but could not make out what was said. Finding a place from which to both conceal herself and observe, she strained intently trying to hear.

Two of the men were debating something, while the other tended the fire. She caught phrases like: "what of the book," and "are you certain she took it," and "how could you let her escape." Val frowned, trying to discern what these men might be talking about. Unable to help herself, she crawled closer in order to better observe the three men. When she was less than ten yards away, she found an old rotted tree she could hide behind. Peering out from behind it, she studied the three men warily, for they were as different as three men could be.

A young man, about her age, was seated facing Val and staring blankly into the fire. He was garbed in simple clothes and a green traveling cloak. She supposed he was a commoner, or deserter of the Bordermen. One of them, older than the first as far as Val could tell, was sitting with his back to Val and facing the younger man. All she could tell was that he was tall and that he wore a large dark traveling cloak.

Then there was an elderly man sitting next to the younger man. He was wearing a dark gray traveling cloak and hood that was pulled back, revealing a face lined and careworn. His head was covered in thinning gray hair, and he had a long gray beard that fell past his belt. Yet the thing that struck Val the most was the man's deep piercing blue eyes…which were looking right at her.

She crouched lower, but the older man stood up and moved towards her while the other two men followed after. Val turned to run for her horse, but they were too fast. One of them came at her from behind. She grasped his cloak and hurled him to her left. Recognizing she could no longer hope to flee, she turned and drew her dagger. Taking in her surroundings, she noted that the young man was on the ground and that the other two were standing before her. The middle-aged man was standing with bow drawn, and the older man was wielding a staff; its tip glowing in the darkness. Val was caught. Facing a wizard and a bowman, she had no choice but to surrender. The young man was back on his feet, and drawing his own sword. She dropped the dagger, and they moved in quickly to secure her.

They sat her down beside the fire, and bound her hands and legs. The middle-aged man yanked back her hood, revealing her features.

"It's not her," he muttered moving over and sitting down.

The older man then spoke to her, his eyes staring intently at her. She got the feeling that those eyes could see right through her. It was very unnerving and she quickly found that she couldn't hold his gaze for long.

"This is Jarod Rook and Jonas Astley," he said at length, gesturing at the middle-aged and younger man, respectively. "And

I am Galanor. Does that name mean anything to you?"

"Yes, I know that name," she said, looking away. "Galanor was a wizard. He helped King Corin during the Second War of Ascension. Many believe him to be dead."

She glanced back up and saw a frown cross the older man's face.

"Who are you and why were you spying on our camp?"

"My name is not important and my business is my own," she snapped, glaring at all three of them in turn.

"When your business includes spying on our camp, it becomes our business," said Rook, sternly.

"Peace!" Galanor nearly shouted.

She watched as the two men glared at one another, then surprisingly, the younger of the two stood and walked away into the darkness.

"Please pardon Rook, he's had a rough day." The old man's tone was placating, but it wouldn't work on Val. "We've all had rough days recently. What with the invasion in the south and the harsh winter…these are difficult times to be sure."

Val remained silent.

"Tell us your name and what you want from us, and we may let you go," he said.

"If you are really Galanor," she began, doubtfully. "Then you must be responsible for the lights I saw two nights ago."

"Lights?"

"They came from a ruined fortress," Val answered, glaring at him as if to dare him to lie to her. "I saw the scorch marks and craters in the walls. They were still smoking. It looked like a great battle had taken place, but the fortress appeared abandoned and there were no signs of siege weapons. Curious as to who or what could cause such devastation and why, I followed the hoof-prints to your camp."

"Why are you out here in the wild anyway?" Jonas asked, suspiciously. "If you are making for either Elengil or Ethriel, there are easier paths."

Val said nothing.

"There are other ways of making her talk," she heard Rook say, ominously as he returned to the fire.

She couldn't help but glance over at him, and saw rage in his eyes. Her heart began to race.

"If there is no other way," Galanor sighed. "Proceed, but keep her screams to a minimum won't you?"

Val tried to stand, but fell over. Rook stooped down, but she landed both feet in his gut. Suddenly, she was lifted into the air. She thrashed about for a moment, then went still as she looked down at the three men. Galanor held his left hand outstretched towards her, while Rook and the young man gazed up in anger.

"I trust this confirms my identity and our sincerity," he said, his calm voice barely masking his anger. "In a moment I will let you down. Then you *will* tell us everything. Am I understood?"

Val found herself nodding, and she felt herself slowly lowered back to the ground.

"I am on the trail of a man," she began, pondering how much information she could divulge without giving away her assignment. "He has dark skin and a bald head."

The other two men looked at Galanor, who eyed Val all the more suspiciously.

"Why do you pursue this man?"

"I was sent to find him," she said, racking her brain for ways to phrase her responses so that her true motive remained hidden.

"By whom?"

"People I work for."

"And who are they?"

She hesitated.

"Isn't it obvious?" Jonas cut in. "She's an assassin, Galanor! She's been sent by the Guild to kill Azka!"

Val tried to mask her shock, but knew Galanor saw right through it. *So they knew Azka and he'd visited their camp recently.*

"Thank you, Jonas," he said condescendingly. "I think we all know what her true purpose is now."

Val glanced over to see the young man look down sheepishly. *Perhaps she could get more out of this boy.* She decided to turn the tables on them.

"Who is this woman *you* are after?" She asked, looking at Jonas, who looked up at once. "I heard you speaking earlier of a book and a woman."

"Selena," she heard Jonas mutter, then a look of panic and anxiety crossed his face.

"Be silent, Jonas," Rook warned. "Any knowledge she gains may be used against Azka or us." He turned to Galanor. "So what do we do with her? We can't just let her go."

She glanced back to see the old man staring at her once more with those piercing blue eyes. After a few more uncomfortable moments, he spoke again.

"The sun will rise soon. Send Jonas to find her horse," he said as he gripped his staff and stood with an effort. "Bind her hands behind her back, and give Jonas the reigns. She will accompany us on our journey to Ethriel. Once there, we will allow the king to deal out judgment."

Jonas left and by the time he returned with her horse, the eastern sky was already growing lighter. They helped her astride her horse, then they rode slowly off eastward.

All in all, her first assignment was not going well.

# 31

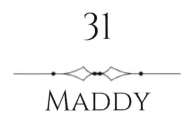

# MADDY

The early-morning sun rose over the bustling city of Ethriel. The merchants and traders were setting up their stalls for another day. The shop owners were setting out their signs and calling to passersby to stop in for their latest merchandise. It was a familiar sight to Maddy as she came walking down the Citadel Way with Lieutenant Liam at her side. It had been two weeks since she'd seen David and had her heart to heart with Queen Riniel. Ever since then, she agonized about what to do…until last night, when she made up her mind to at least see David one more time. She would heed the queen's advice and follow the visitor's words, but she just couldn't end things so abruptly. She had to speak with him one last time.

Lt. Liam had agreed to come with her and she had come to trust him, especially after he divulged to her his negative opinion of the baron. As per her request, he was wearing a simple brown cloak over his Royal Guard uniform, and she was wearing her light blue cloak again, with the hood pulled over her light brown hair. They appeared to be nothing more than two shoppers taking an early morning stroll.

The northern winds were howling, heralding a winter storm brewing to the north of the city. Maddy quickened her pace, knowing the onset of the storm would draw attention to her absence in the Citadel. They turned down the alleyway, leading to the inn where Maddy had last seen David. She paused, gazing at the gap between the buildings where David had disappeared.

"Are you sure about this, my lady?" Came Liam's voice in her ear.

She did not turn towards him, but nodded.

"Very well. I will be nearby if you need me," he said with a slight inclination of his head.

While he moved down the alleyway to stand behind a stack of crates, she turned and gazed at the shabby-looking inn. Her eyes darted to the sign bearing a lion on its hind-legs, as if it was dancing. Her eyes read, once again, the peeling letters that read: *The Dancing Lion*. Steeling herself, she reached to open the door when two hands grabbed her from behind again. This time, she withdrew her hand and spun on the spot, bringing her hand across her would-be assailants face. A smile broke over her face as her hand struck the familiar cheek. David grunted and staggered back.

"Ouch!" he exclaimed. "Geez! What was that for?"

"For every time you've scared me, plus interest!" She laughed.

With him still rubbing his face, she rushed over and hugged him. He laughed, and hugged her back.

"I guess I deserve it then," he said, holding her close.

"I guess this means you've chosen me?"

Maddy pulled away and looked up into David's face, his brown eyes expectantly awaiting her answer. In her heart, she longed to say yes, to kiss him, to tell him of her undying love for him...but she couldn't. This was it. She had to end things.

"I can't," she managed.

"You can't what?" he asked, a look of hurt rising on his face.

"I can't go with you David."

"Why not?"

She turned away, not wanting him to see the tears forming in her eyes. She felt him come and lightly place his hands on her shoulders again, and fought the urge to turn around and kiss him. She wanted to go with him, to pledge her undying love for him, but she couldn't.

She shrugged his arms off and walked a few paces away.

"I am marrying the baron, David," she said, her voice betraying her emotional state.

"No."

"What?" she asked, turning to face him.

"No, Maddy." His jaw was set and his eyes full of determination. "I won't let you marry that monster."

"How can you stop it?" she asked.

"I would kill him before I let you marry him."

"I think that's enough," came Liam's voice.

The lieutenant stepped out from his hiding place, looking stern. David stepped in front of Maddy as if to protect her.

"Who are you?" he demanded and Maddy saw his right hand reach for something inside his cloak.

Liam smiled and pulled away his cloak to reveal his uniform and his badge, his right hand resting on the hilt of his sword. Maddy was relieved to see David's hand reappear from his cloak empty.

"Wise decision, young man," Liam said, nodding to Maddy. "I have no love for the baron, but I cannot allow you to make threats against his life...at least, not until he leaves the safety of the Citadel. Until then, I am charged with his and Lady Madeline's protection."

"You trust this man?" David asked, turning to Maddy.

She nodded and she saw hesitation cross his face.

"My Lady, if we are to return before we are missed, we should leave now," Liam said, gesturing back up the alley.

She turned to David, pulled his face down and kissed his cheek, then walked over and took Liam's arm. They walked several paces up the alley, then she paused and turned back. David was staring at her, his face stricken in disbelief.

"Goodbye, David," she whispered, as tears ran down her face.

She turned and, wrenching her arm from Liam's grasp, she ran up the alleyway and out into the crowded street beyond.

*   *   *   *

Maddy ran until she couldn't run any longer, dismissing the looks and calls of the onlookers as she passed them. Her heart felt like it had been ripped apart. Tears were flowing from her face, partially blinding her. Wiping her eyes as she ran, she hit something solid, bounced backward, and fell onto the street.

"Hey!" came a somewhat familiar voice. "Look where you're going!"

She wiped her face, and saw she'd knocked someone over. She watched as he got to his feet and she saw it was the young man she'd met in the Citadel.

"Oh, Lady Brice," he stammered, coming over and offering his hand. "Let me help you."

"It was my fault," she said, as he helped her up.

"Are you alright?"

"I'm fine, thank you uh—"

"Ben Greymore."

"Right," she said, dusting herself off. "I am sorry for barreling you over."

"I'm used to it," the young man said, sulkily.

"Ben!" came a rancorous voice from the other side of the street.

Maddy turned to see a stocky man, with a long, bushy brown beard and mustache. His face was contorted in rage as he came towards them, then, seeing Maddy, his attitude was subdued somewhat.

"Captain Saul Gunter of the City Watch, my Lady," he said with a quick bow. "Is this young man bothering you?"

"Not at all," Maddy answered quickly. "In fact, I nearly barreled over him."

"Well, if he was any skinnier he'd be mistaken for a short lamppost," the captain snickered.

Maddy saw Ben's face fall. She suddenly felt the urge to defend him, but could think of nothing to say.

"If you will excuse us, my lady," the captain said, bowing again. Then turning on Ben, he grabbed the young man by the arm and hurled him down the street.

"Get back to your duties and stop bothering your betters!" she heard the captain bellow.

Maddy stood watching them leave, then made her way back to the Citadel.

※　※　※　※

When she arrived at the Citadel gates, she found Lt. Liam standing on a small platform and addressing several other members of the Royal Guard. When he saw her, he jumped down and ran over to her.

"My Lady," he said, bowing to her.

"I'm fine, Liam," Maddy said, consolingly reading his face.

"Please never do that again," he whispered. "When you fled, I feared for your safety. I was preparing to send out search parties to comb the city."

"As well you should have," came an angry voice from behind them.

Both Maddy and Liam turned as the other members of the Royal Guard parted and Baron Windham came marching towards them.

The look on his face made Maddy want to run, but she stood her ground.

"The Lady Brice's safety should be of gravest concern, lieutenant," the baron growled as he reached them. "I demand to know how she left the Citadel unescorted. The king's decree--"

"Do not hold these fine men accountable for my resourcefulness, my Lord," Maddy said, soothingly. "I, and I alone, am accountable for my actions."

"Please return to our chambers, my Lady," he said, scowling at her. His voice was dangerous and scarcely hid his fury. "I have some business to discuss with the lieutenant, then I will join you there."

Maddy wanted to protest, but the look on the baron's face left no room for negotiation. She bowed, cast a meaningful glance at Liam, then walked through the gates and into the courtyard of the Citadel.

＊　＊　＊　＊

Maddy was reading in her chambers when the baron burst through the door. He was fuming, hands clinched into fists. He didn't say a word, but went straight to the bottle of wine sitting on the table. She remained seated as she watched the baron pour a goblet of wine, drink it in one draft, and pour himself another. He turned towards her, his face contorted with rage and his free hand still clenched and shaking as he fought to contain his anger.

"May I ask where you've been sneaking off to, my Lady?" he asked through clenched teeth.

Maddy's heart was beating fast, but she maintained her composure. She had the choice to tell the baron where she'd been, lie, or simply remain silent. Before she could answer, the baron hurled the goblet at her. She dove out of the way, but the baron was upon her in a moment. He seized her and pulled her up, and pinned her to the wall. The smell of wine was heavy on the baron's breath.

"Do you think I'm a fool?" The baron's voice was full of barely restrained rage. "Do you think that for even a moment, your movements are hidden from me?"

"Please," she sobbed, trying to free herself, but his grip held fast. A feeling of complete helplessness and fear overwhelmed her as she whispered, "You're hurting me."

The baron hesitated, then his grip relaxed. He released her and she fell to the floor, and continued to sob.

"I'm sorry I hurt you," he said, taking a few steps back. She looked up and saw he was still seething. "Just tell me, were you sneaking off to see David?"

Maddy hesitated, the baron's angry face blurred in her tear-filled eyes, then she nodded.

The baron turned away, his fists still clenched and his whole body shaking. Maddy felt terror seize her heart. Would he beat her or even kill her?

A loud knock at the door interrupted her thoughts.

"Who is it?" the baron yelled.

The door opened and a young page entered, shaking slightly.

"Well?" the baron demanded when the page did not speak.

"The king requires your presence in the Council Chambers, my Lord," the page squeaked.

"I will be there shortly," the baron growled, gesturing at the door.

The page left quickly, then the baron turned back to Maddy. She'd managed to compose herself, but her heart was still racing. He stepped towards her and held out a hand, which she took with some trepidation.

He seized her arms and pulled her close so that her face was mere inches from his.

"You will accompany me to the Council Chambers," he said, with imminent threat in his voice. "You will stand behind my seat. You will not speak and you will not move. You will not leave my side for the remainder of our stay here in the Citadel. Am I understood?"

Maddy nodded.

"Compose yourself," he growled, seizing her hand and pulling her towards the door. "Come on, we don't want to keep the king waiting."

\* \* \* \*

The doors to the council chambers opened, and the atmosphere of the room rushed at Maddy like a tidal wave. The room was silent, but the air was so tense that it seemed to pulsate with apprehension and fear. She glanced around as they entered the room, taking in her surroundings. She'd never been allowed inside the chambers of the Council of Lords. She first noticed the large and intricately drawn map displayed on the wall to his right—a map of the kingdom of Alethia. Then her eyes fell upon the large, ornately carved circular table made of oak, around which sat eleven chairs, one for each member off the Council. Of the eleven chairs, only five were occupied. These men comprised what was left of the Council of Lords. A mass of parchments and maps littered the top of the table, and upon every face was a look of despair and hopelessness. Large bags were under every set of eyes as the long sleepless hours took their toll. The baron took his seat and Maddy stood behind him, as instructed.

"Welcome Baron Windham," said the king in a melancholy voice. His sharp brown eyes were glaring at him. "Glad you could join us. We have just received news from the battle at the Pass of Stenc." He turned and gestured towards a man sitting to his far left. "Lord Morgan, please read the report again."

Maddy glanced over and recognized the man at once as the man who'd leered at her during her interrupted wedding ceremony. There was a smile upon his face, which was unsettling in a room full of frowns and despair. He twirled his black goatee, which flecked with gray, and began to read from a parchment in his left hand.

"Your Majesty," he began in a smarmy voice. "This comes from Baron Samuel Brandyman. According to this report our northern forces met the enemy at the Pass of Stenc some four days ago. The enemy seemed routed, and fled into the pass. Our forces pursued the enemy, but then a great winged beast came upon them. Our forces fled in terror, and the enemy attacked again in force. The rider that brought the report stated that the beast belched fire and burned any who crossed its path. He also reported that the lords Rnal Cynwic and Jordan Reese were slain during the fray."

Maddy gasped audibly, drawing attention to herself.

"Perhaps this news is too much for your delicate ears, my Lady," Lord Morgan said, with a condescending smile towards her.

The baron shot a meaningful glance up at her, and she gave a slight cough.

"No, my Lord," she said, after clearing her throat. "Please continue."

"As you wish," Lord Morgan with a slight bow. He then cleared his throat and continued. "Baron Brandyman has retreated north of the Belwash, while the enemy has crossed into the plains north of the pass. They also report that the dragon has attacked their camp each night, and many of his men have deserted."

"How many men does Brandyman still have?" the king asked, his face bowed in sorrow.

"He estimates five hundred at most," Lord Morgan stated.

There was a general murmur of dread from everyone.

"What of reports regarding the army mustering in the north?" the king asked, turning to Lord Grehm.

Lord Grehm sighed, then got to his feet to address the room. "It seems that an army has indeed come through the Pass of the Knife and entered northern Alethia. Our scouts estimate the army numbers in the thousands."

This time the murmuring was louder and even Maddy felt a sense of approaching doom.

The man to the king's right stood up, and everyone, including Maddy, glanced towards him. He was taller than most, had blond hair and brown eyes, and seemed resistant to the dread felt by everyone else.

"Your Majesty," he said with a slight bow.

"Lord Thayn," the king said, turning towards him.

"It would seem the report of young Ben Greymore, which was

so eagerly dismissed by Lord Morgan and Baron Windham, has been proven true after all." Maddy saw the baron's fists clench at this remark, then saw Lord Grehm giving the king a meaningful look. "I believe that it is time to implement the Shadow Initiative,"

Maddy glanced around at the other lords, but even Lord Morgan seemed confused. She, as well as everyone else, turned back to the king, who was looking at Lord Thayn with deep concern and consideration.

"Do it," the king said after a long moment's pause. "I'll have the prince report to you immediately."

Lord Thayn bowed and left the room in haste.

"Would you care to enlighten us about this secret initiative, Your Majesty?" Lord Morgan asked, irritably.

"No," the king replied, bluntly. He stood, with some effort, and gazed at each member of the council in turn. "We have little time, my Lords, and must see to the city's defense. Each of you has men in the city, plus the members of the Royal Guard and City Watch." He turned to Lord Morgan. "When does Brandyman think the army in the south will cross the Belwash?"

※　※　※　※

After the meeting, the baron escorted Maddy back to their chambers. On the way there, she went over what had been said during their deliberations. Not having any military experience, she wondered if all their preparations would be enough to protect the city. She also wondered what this Shadow Initiative was and why Lord Thayn had left so quickly.

Once they'd reached their chambers, the baron ushered her inside and closed the door behind him. The distraction of the council meeting fell away and sudden anxiety returned as she looked at the baron's angry face.

"You are very intelligent, my Lady," he said through gritted teeth. "But not more so than myself."

He took a step towards her, forcing her to take another step backwards to maintain distance.

"You will make a fine Lady of Windham, Madeline Brice," he said, his voice barely a whisper but potent enough to echo in her mind. "But know that if I ever catch you sneaking off to see that stupid young blacksmith again, I will kill him and your mother."

He turned and left the room, slamming the door behind him. Maddy stood, shaking in fright, hoping that her conversation with David had hurt him enough to keep him away. She moved over to the bed, sank down to her knees and muttered, "I did what you asked. Please keep him safe."

# 32

# SELENA

Night had fallen as Selena reached the village of Greywater, which sat on the west side of the Rockwicke River. It was a tiny town just a few miles north of where the river emptied into the Deadwood Marshes. The sky was clouded over and the mist from the marshes had condensed into a foul-smelling fog. Selena could think of no reason for building a town so near the marshes, but she was glad of it nonetheless. Though she had wanted to continue on through the night, both she and her horse were exhausted and in need of food and rest.

Upon entering town, she dismounted and held tightly to the reigns of her horse. Gazing about, she saw that the town consisted of a smattering of houses and a decrepit-looking inn. With little recourse, she made for the inn and stood gazing unsure at the building's sad exterior. The roof on one side seemed to sag inward slightly and the windows were so fouled with grime that barely any light could escape through them. Selena actually wondered if the inn was even open.

She tied her horse to a post standing just outside the inn, and pulled her dark traveling cloak tight around her. Her hand reached for the handle, but then she withdrew suddenly and glanced behind her. She could feel a presence hidden somewhere in the gloom, but her eyes could not pierce the fog. She reached and pulled open the door, cast another worried glance behind her, then entered the inn.

The smell of smoke, mold and sweat hit Selena immediately upon entering the inn and nearly knocked her backwards. There was a smattering of tables, each occupied by one or two patrons, all with disreputable appearances. From their grimy faces, shabby clothing, and leering gazes, Selena felt the overwhelming need to flee. While considering whether she dared try to endure sleeping outside in the foul air coming from the marshes or suffer the leering gazes and smell of smoke and body odor wafting about the inn, her eyes fell on the man sitting at the bar. She did a double-take as she took in the man's dark complexion and shaved head. She'd heard of people from Kusini from her father, but had never before met one. He wore a dark-brown cloak, and wore a stoic expression as he ate his soup. Realizing that she was staring, she moved toward the bar and pulled back her hood to free her long dark brown hair. She heard a few muttered catcalls coming from the tables behind her, but she ignored them.

"Help ya?" The old barman said, coming over to squint at her. He had gray wispy hair and a large nose. His eyesight must have been bad for the man stared at Selena loutishly.

"If you can't do anything about the smell," Selena muttered, snidely.

The man glared at her, his mouth twitching angrily.

"Fine," she said, glancing down the bar again at the dark-skinned man. "I'd like a clean room, or if that's not possible, the least filthy room you have."

"Got a mouth on ya, no mistake," the barman said, still glaring. "Keep talking like that and you'll be sleepin' in the street."

"You're really willing to turn away a paying customer?"

"Room's five silver lions," the barman spat.

"That's outrageous!" She exclaimed.

"Been a bit more polite and I might have been more accommodating," the barman retorted.

"I'll give you two lions," she growled, pulling out the two silver coins. "And not a bronze shield more."

The barman considered her for a moment. She hoped he would not turn away good silver.

"Give 'em here, and I'll show you to your room," the barman muttered, holding out his hand.

Selena handed over the money, and he moved from behind the bar and led her out into a dimly lit hallway. Three rooms ran along the right side of the hall, and two along the left. The barman led her to the nearest room on the right, and held the door open with a sneer. Selena stepped into the doorway, and beheld the most shabby-looking room she'd ever seen. It was dark and bare. There was no bed, but merely a small pile of hay in the corner with a worn, threadbare blanket lying on top of it full of holes. Beside the hay sat a small candle, unlit. The rest of the room was bare and there was no fireplace or other means of warmth than the blanket. Selena wrinkled her nose as the smelled of mold and excrement hit her nostrils.

"Enjoy your stay," the barman sneered, as he pushed her inside and pulled the door closed behind her.

Selena pulled her cloak around her even tighter, knelt down in the corner, and closed her eyes. She had left her father's castle in Nenholm, for this?

✳   ✳   ✳   ✳

Selena awoke in the middle of the night, with the sudden feeling that she was not alone. The foul smell of the room instantly reminded her of where she was and of the events of the night previous. A sudden fear hit her, and she wondered if one of those stinking vagabonds from the bar had managed to break into her room. She got to her feet, and glared at the surrounding darkness.

"Who's there? Show yourself!"

A faint light appeared from the far corner, and the form of a man sat silhouetted against the light. As her eyes adjusted, she realized that the light was actually emanating from the man.

Selena backed away as far into her corner as possible, her eyes darting towards the door.

"Peace be with you," the man said, and the light grew bright enough for her to make out his features.

Selena gaped as recognition finally hit her.

"You!" she gasped. "

"Me," he said adjusting his robes and gazing up at her. "Would you care to sit with me?"

"Sit with you?" She stared at the man in disbelief. "How did you find me?"

"I merely followed the path you have chosen, Selena. The path I warned you not to take."

"What path?"

"The path once chosen by your father," he said gravely. "Why do you still tread the path that leads to destruction?"

"What do you mean?" She demanded. "I chose right. I didn't give Methangoth the book!"

"But neither did you return it to its rightful owner," the man answered, calmly. "You, like so many before you, desire to obey the letter of the law but fail to obey the spirit."

"What is that supposed to mean?"

"It means, you only obey so far as you think you must, but your heart remains committed to your own desires," the man said with a sigh. "You have not trusted in me and my will for your life."

"Why should I trust you?" Selena demanded, her voice going shrill. "I don't even know you!"

"But you do, Selena. And I know you better than you know yourself. I have never guided you down a wrong path, and I have shielded you from great harm, though you may not have noticed. Even now, I will give you the chance to escape if you will but trust my word and do as I instruct you."

Selena considered the man for a moment, then nodded.

"You must do exactly as I instructed or the consequences will be severe. There is a great darkness rising that threatens this kingdom and all of its people. If you would do more than save your own life, do as I say."

He waited until she nodded, then continued. "Do you recall the dark-skinned man at the bar?"

She nodded again.

"You must go to him and tell him who you are, about the book, and from whom you are fleeing."

"But I don't know him either," she protested.

"But I do," the man said, simply. "Trust me and you can trust him. He will protect you and take you to Ethriel."

"Why there?"

"You will take the book and give it to King Corin. Once that is done, the king will protect you from Methangoth and from the coming darkness."

"But how do I know I can trust him?" She asked, almost pleadingly. "What sign do you offer that I can trust either of you?"

"Why do you ask for a sign, when you lack any faith in him who supplies the sign?" the man asked simply. Selena stared in wonder at the man's wisdom and patience with her. "If you ask for his help, the dark-skinned man will provide it. That is the only sign you need."

"But—" Selena began, but both the man and the light faded and vanished.

"Trust in my words, Selena," came the man's voice. "Obey my instructions and you will be saved. Finally, know that you are of great worth to me, and that you are loved."

Then there was silence.

✳   ✳   ✳   ✳

Selena awoke sometime later, and found herself still wrapped in her cloak in the corner. She stood and felt her way to the door, pulling it open so that the dim light from the hall came into the room. She glanced back toward the corner where the strange visitor had sat, silently wondering if she was slowly losing her mind. She shook her head and walked down the hall and into the bar.

Despite the thick grime on the windows, the morning sun still managed to penetrate through to provide a little light in the dingy, smoke-filled room. Initially the room appeared empty, but as Selena glanced down the bar she saw the same dark-skinned man exactly where he'd been sitting the previous night. He was quietly eating breakfast and did not acknowledge her presence. She hesitated, remembering her conversation with the visitor, then she took a step towards the dark-skinned stranger. Suddenly the door behind her opened, sending undiluted sunlight into the dark bar. Before she could react, a hand grabbed her from behind and spun her around. Selena's pulse quickened as she looked up into the face of Raynor Kesh. His blond hair was matted and there were bags under his brown eyes. His chainmail was rusting in places, and he was noticeably thinner. A look of utter rage was etched on his lean face.

Selena took a step back, but Kesh seized her by the arm and pulled her in close to hiss in her ear, "Did you really think you could escape me?"

"Let go of me!" she shouted, struggling.

He hurled her against the bar, and the impact knocked the wind out of her. She fell to the floor, doubled over and gasping for breath. As she lay there, a deep voice echoed in her ears.

"You should not have done that, Raynor."

Selena stole a glance up at the speaker, to find the dark-skinned man standing between her and Kesh.

"Azka," Kesh growled, but Selena heard apprehension in his voice. "This doesn't concern you!"

"On the contrary, this young woman is under my protection."

"Why?"

"It doesn't matter," Azka said, in a matter-of-fact sort of way.

"What matters is that if you try to touch her again, I will be forced to hurt you."

Selena got to her feet slowly.

Kesh threw drew his sword.

"Kindly stay behind me, Selena," Azka said, drawing his own sword.

She didn't bother to ask how he knew her name, but simply obeyed his word.

The two men eyed one another for a moment longer, then Kesh lunged at Azka, who parried the blow and knocked Kesh back and over a nearby table. Kesh quickly got back on to his feet, bringing his blade up in a defensive posture.

"I'm giving you one last chance, Raynor," Azka said, a smile spreading on his face. "Walk away."

"You know I can't do that Azka," Kesh said, and Selena was surprised to see a look of fear on his face.

Kesh quickly seized a nearby flagon and hurled it at Azka's head. He ducked, giving Kesh an opening. He hurled his entire body at Azka's, the impact sending Azka flying into the bar and onto the floor. In a moment, Kesh was standing over him, his bladed lifted to deliver a killing blow. Not quite understanding why, Selena instinctively seized a nearby flagon and hurled it at Kesh. Her aim was true and Kesh had just enough time to turn and see the flagon flying at him, before it smashed hard against his head.

Kesh crumpled to the floor and Selena ran over to Azka, who was now in a sitting position on the floor. She offered him a hand up, but he shook his head.

"Thank you, Selena," he said, rising effortlessly from the floor and sheathing his sword in one fluid motion.

Unable to think of what to say, she simply gaped at him.

"I couldn't be sure you'd help me, so I asked for a sign," he said, with a knowing smile. "Thankfully, you delivered."

He moved towards the door, then stopped and pitched a couple of silver coins at the barman, whom Selena had not initially seen cowering in the corner behind the bar. Then Azka stepped outside.

"Wait," she called after him, crossing the bar at a run and emerging out into the morning sunlight.

She found Azka holding the reigns of two horses, one of which was hers.

"How did you know I would help you?"

"I didn't, but a mutual acquaintance said I could trust you," he said, offering her the reigns. "Come, we must go."

"Go?" she asked, as he hopped astride his horse.

"To Ethriel," Azka said, smiling down at her. "I believe you have a certain something to deliver to King Corin, and I have promised to protect you along the way."

Selena gaped at him again as he turned his horse and trotted down the street. She mounted her own horse and hurried to catch up with him. All the while, thinking that perhaps this stranger...this visitor might have well earned her trust after all.

# 33

# SELENA

The bleak day was fading to twilight when Selena and Azka reached the river Rockwicke. It had been two days since they'd left Greymore, the tiny village on the edge of the Deadwood Marshes. Standing upon the western bank, they gazed up and down the stream as the loud waters rushed by them. They'd discovered that all the bridges had been burned or broken down, so they'd spent the last few hours trying to find a good place to ford the river. Finally, Azka discovered a place where the river was shallow and slow enough to cross, but as they began to cross, the water rose up past Selena's knees. Their crossing was unimpeded, and they quickly reached the far bank. Yet on the other side, Azka paused and gazed southward for several long minutes. At length and without a word, he turned and led the way down to a broad road leading eastward. After several minutes, Selena had attempted to engage him in conversation, but each time he'd held up a hand for silence.

So they rode in silence for a few hours, until the sun began to dip below the horizon. With twilight falling all about them and the shadows lengthening, Azka stopped abruptly and gazed northward. Selena followed his gaze to what appeared to be a very shallow and wide dip in the lands running north and upward into the forestlands beyond. Then it struck her that she was looking at what remained of a wide track, but now the grass had covered it once again. A greenway, of sorts, that long ago must have been a major road but was now reclaimed by the grasslands around it.

Azka turned and headed up the greenway, and Selena watched him for a moment. This was her chance, if any, to escape Azka and flee. She hesitated, her mind reeling from the various options set before her. After another moment, she urged her horse forward and followed quickly after Azka. The road ran fairly straight for a few miles, then turned eastward and ran up a tall hill, upon which lay a large pile of rubble. When they drew closer, Selena realized that the rubble was in fact the ruins of a modest castle.

"All that remains of the fortress of Rockhold," Azka said, and she heard sadness in his voice. "For me, this place holds a deep significance as it was here that I was forced to make a hard choice."

"What choice?"

He did not answer, but stared at the ruined fortress for several long moments. Selena wanted to know more. What was so important about these ruins that he'd waste so much time bringing her here? Instead, she decided not to push the issue and remained silent. At length, he turned to her.

"I am sorry for this detour, but it has been many years and I needed to see this place one last time," he said at length.

"One last time?" She asked when he continued to stare.

"Ask me no more," he said, curtly turning and proceeded back down the hill.

She shook her head in frustration, then followed Azka back down the greenway towards the main road east.

As they rode, Selena still sensed that Azka was on edge. Even after visiting the ruins, her traveling companion remained silent and wary, constantly casting a glance to their right and left. She sensed that something was causing him great anxiety. They'd reached the main road at nightfall, and continued on through the darkness. After about an hour, he'd paused once again to listen to the night and then left the road and rode north into the nearby forestlands. Tying their horses further in, she and Azka crept back to the forest edge. Selena was just about to ask what they were doing, when a slew of men came riding by on horseback from the east. She gaped at the men as fear rose in her heart, for they were all wearing black and bearing the unnerving symbol of a red dragon. She'd turned towards Azka, but he held out a hand shook his head. They'd waited until the men rode over the next hill and vanished from sight, then Azka had turned towards her.

"Are they--?" but she couldn't finish.

"Indeed," Azka whispered. She was surprised to see fear on his face. "A scouting party or patrol of some sort, which means Alethia must have lost the battle at the pass."

"What pass?"

"The Pass of Stenc, which divides the kingdom," he answered, gravely. "The scouting party's presence means that the dark army has indeed invaded the north."

"How far is the pass from here?"

"Many days journey," he answered. "Yet if they are sending scouting parties up this far north, the army cannot be far behind. We must take more care, and travel only by night or we may never reach the city."

"But if the enemy has reached the north, will we be safe in Ethriel or anywhere?" Selena asked, but Azka did not reply.

He rose to his feet and crept quickly and noiselessly back to the horses. Surprisingly, Selena struggled to keep up with Azka. A sudden fear crossed her mind of being left in the forestlands, lost and alone. She'd been alone and in worse situations before, but for some reason, she didn't know why, something inside her would not let her abandon Azka. Perhaps it was the fearful presence of this dark army that brought back memories of Fairhaven, or maybe just that the visitor had told her to go with him. She shook her head. In any case, Azka was her traveling companion and she could not leave him now.

Following quickly after, she caught up with Azka where they'd left their horses. Swiftly and quietly, they crept deeper into the forest, Azka picking his way through the thicker patches of trees. They traveled this way for several days, stopping only during the middle of the day to rest. They ate and drank little, and never lit a fire. Selena was always cold, but grateful that the trees grew in thicker patches that kept out the bitter northern winds.

Finally a day came when Selena awoke to find Azka stooping over her. A week ago, the sight of this large dark-skinned man looming over her would have terrified her, but he'd woken her this way so often that it was now more annoying than anything.

"What is it?" she asked, stretching.

"We must go," he answered, helping her up onto her feet. "I've scouted ahead, and we will soon reach the eastern edge of the forest. We can no longer rely upon the cover of the forestlands to hide us."

He brought over their horses, and they led them on foot to the very edge of the forest. Anxiety welled up inside Selena again with every step, until, standing just within the tree line, she beheld the plains beyond. It was mid-morning, and the sun was shining brightly down upon the grasslands. There was a soft breeze coming from the east, and Selena pulled her hood down to let her long brown hair blow freely in the wind. It was the first sunny day since they'd left Greymore, and, closing her eyes, she took great pleasure in the sun's bright and warm rays on her face.

"What are you doing!" she heard Azka hiss.

Selena's eyes popped open and she realized that while she'd been enjoying the sunshine, she'd inadvertently walked several paces out from under the trees. She raced back to Azka's side, as he glared at her.

"Here," he shoved her horse's reigns back into her hands, jumped astride his horse, and galloped off.

It was all Selena could do to keep up. They rode on like this for a few hours. A few times Azka stopped abruptly to listen. In the far distance in the south and west, Selena thought she could hear the faint sound of galloping horses. Finally they came up over a hill and it was Selena's turn to stop abruptly as she stared at the grand vision before her.

Following the road leading eastward, a great city rose up in the distance. Built into the side of a mountain, the upper sections seemed to be carved out of the mountain slope itself. Selena's gaze rose up the slope until her eyes fell upon a shining white castle on a wide outcropping that overlooked the city and plains below.

"Behold, the city of Ethriel," Azka said, coming back to join her. He pointed up at the castle high above them and said, "There, upon Mt. ⌐⌐⌐⌐⌐Earod, sits the Citadel, fortress of the king of Alethia."

"Amazing," muttered Selena, who'd never seen anything like it.

Azka's rich deep laugh brought her out of her revelry, and she immediately felt embarrassed.

"It's all right," he said, catching her eye, then turning to gaze up at the city before them. "I may not have said it when I first saw this city, but it is amazing."

After another brief moment, Azka said, "Come, we must hurry on."

He spurred his mount, and galloped down the hill towards the city with Selena right behind him.

✳    ✳    ✳    ✳

They reached the city around mid-afternoon. They were stopped momentarily at the city gates by the City Watch. A stout man with a long, bushy brown beard and mustache came out to meet them. Azka dismounted and spoke quickly with him. Soon they were allowed to pass through the gates.

They had to leave their horses in the stables, which meant they would have to make their way to the Citadel on foot. The city was bustling with activity. Selena was overwhelmed, for everywhere she looked, hundreds of men of the City Watch were moving about the walls and streets. As they made their way up the streets, there was an obvious absence of street vendors. She turned to mention this, but couldn't catch Azka's gaze. He was focused on reaching the Citadel, and his long strides made it difficult for Selena to keep up.

After what seemed like hours of walking, they reached the gates to the Citadel. The great ironbound doors were closed and several men in white cloaks stood before the gates, their hoods pulled back and drawn swords in their hands.

"Declare yourself, stranger!" the foremost man shouted.

"My name is Azka. This is Selena, daughter of Lord Silas Morgan," he said, his voice deep and confident. "We are here to see the king."

"I am Liam, a lieutenant in the Royal Guard and charged with securing this gate. I apologize for any discourtesy, Master Azka," the foremost man said, sheathing his weapon. "The city will soon be besieged and duties of the Royal Guard are now doubly felt."

"No need to apologize," Azka answered with a wave of his hand. "Just take us at once to the king."

With that, Liam bowed and the gates opened to welcome them inside. Selena did not have time to enjoy the grandeur of the Citadel, for Liam and Azka hastened forward and it was all she could do to keep up. He made for the throne room, where more members of the Royal Guard stood watch. Liam signaled to them and they opened the oaken front doors.

The hall was massive and decorated with many tapestries, each depicting events from Alethia's recent history. The light from the setting sun poured in through the beautiful stained-glass windows. The torches were ensconced, lining the hall, which left small gaps of darkness between each of them. The hall must have been a merrier place at other times, but Selena sensed a feeling of dread and hopelessness coming from within.

At the far end of the hall stood a high dais with steps leading up to the kings' throne. Above the throne was hung a white canopy bearing a red rose. The king sat with several others standing to either side of him. Selena could see a smile spreading on his face as he watched them draw nearer to the foot of the dais. Selena glanced to the others standing beside the king and cringed as she recognized one of them as her father. He was glaring at her with an expression she heartily returned in kind.

"Your Majesty," Azka said with a low bow.

Selena did the same, but as she raised up she saw the king get to his feet and gaped for it was only now that she realized his left leg was missing. She watched in wonder as the king made his way down the steps and embraced Azka as a brother.

"It's been far too long, my old friend," the king said, a smile upon his careworn face.

"Indeed," Azka said, with a slight incline of his head. "Though I wish it were under better circumstances."

"Yes, of course," the king said, stepping back to address Selena. "Lady Morgan. Your father said you'd disappeared from Nenholm. What brings you all the way to Ethriel?"

"Your Highness," Azka said and the king turned. They exchanged a meaningful look, and the king nodded. "We should continue this in private."

He turned towards the others present, who bowed and excused themselves. Her father looked like he wanted to say something, but bit back his words and left with the others.

When they were alone, the king turned back towards them.

"So, Azka," he said, gravely. "What's this all about? Why have you come?"

"It is a long story," he said, grimly. "But one that must be told by Lady Morgan."

Selena froze. This was it. The moment had come at last. Her heart leapt in her throat. She swallowed hard, trying to calm herself before speaking.

"Selena," came Azka's deep voice, sounding as thought it was coming from a great distance. "The book?"

She reached in her bag and withdrew the book. She saw a look of astonishment cross the king's face as he slowly reached out to take it from her.

"How?" the king stammered, looking from her to Azka and back.

"It is a long story," Azka answered for her, casting her a sidelong glance to remain silent.

"I wish to hear it."

"I only know a part of the tale, Your Highness," Azka admitted. "As I previously stated, the Lady Morgan should be the one to tell the story."

"For goodness sake, Azka," the king growled, moving over to sit in one of the chairs below the dais. "I told you long ago to call me Corin."

"Yes, Your Highness," Azka said with another inclination of his head.

Selena saw a smile play across his lips, and had to suppress her own when she saw the same smile on the king's face.

"Very well," the king said, with a wave of his hand. "Lady Morgan, if you please."

Selena took a deep breath, then plunged into her tale.

✳   ✳   ✳   ✳

Selena walked slowly and aimlessly through the Citadel gardens. After over an hour spent recounting her tale from Nenholm to Ethriel, the king had agreed to retain custody of the Book of Aduin and excused her to the Citadel grounds. Expecting her father to be lingering near the front door, she ducked out the side door. Wandering through the courtyard, she found the entrance to the gardens and hoped she might escape searching eyes among the tall hedges.

The sun was sinking low in the west and the gardens fell into twilight. Selena found a stone bench to rest and think. It was quiet and peaceful, something Selena found unsettling and actually caused her more anxiety than anything. She was used to being on the go and constantly pursuing some goal or target. Now that she'd reached the end of her journey, she felt uneasy and anxious about her future.

A rustling sound came from behind a nearby hedge, and Selena jumped to her feet. Her heart was pounding in her chest as she prepared to flee from whoever came around the corner. A few heartbeats later a young woman, wearing a light blue cloak with the hood pulled over her head, came around the corner. She froze in her tracks, and they both stood staring warily at one another.

"Hello," the young woman said. "Are you Lady Morgan?"

"If my father sent you," Selena began, glaring at her suspiciously.

"No no," the young woman said soothingly. "My name is Madeline Brice, and I was sent to find you by the king."

The young woman stepped towards Selena and removed her hood, revealing long, light brown hair and eyes. She smiled warmly at Selena, and some of her suspicion faded.

"Call me Selena," she said, irritably. "Does the king want me to return?"

"No, he just wanted to make sure you were safe," she answered, pleasantly. "And please, call me Maddy."

"So the king sent you?" Selena scoffed.

"Well, yes," Maddy answered. "Within the Citadel, we are safe for the moment. Besides, the king believed you might receive me better than a slew of Royal Guards."

Selena said nothing, but merely returned to her seat.

"Are you all right?" Maddy asked her at length.

Selena let out a long sigh, but said nothing.

"May I sit with you?"

Selena shrugged and Maddy joined her on the bench. After another long moment of silence, she spoke again.

"It is beautiful here."

"What do you want exactly?" Selena asked, standing up and rounding on her.

She was pleased to see Maddy's smile had vanished and been replaced by a look of shock.

"I was sent to check on you, Selena. I thought you might want someone to talk to after your long journey."

"Well I don't need to talk," she shouted, beginning to pace. "I just need to be left alone."

"Look, I don't know you, Selena, but I can recognize when someone is troubled."

"Troubled!" Selena said, her voice going shrill. "I was dangled out of the side of Deadwood Fortress by Methangoth. I've been pursued by a bounty hunter halfway across the kingdom, my father wants me locked away in some dungeon, and some stranger keeps appearing to me and demanding that I trust him."

She turned and saw that Maddy was staring at her open-mouthed.

"What!" Selena demanded. "Why are you staring at me like that?"

"You said you'd had dreams about a stranger?"

"Yeah, so?"

"So have I."

# 34

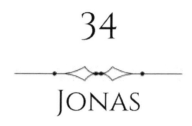

# JONAS

Never in his life had Jonas Astley seen such a vision of grandeur and strength as the city of Ethriel. He could not help but gaze in wonder at the tall white walls and towers shining in the mid-afternoon Sun, not to mention the gleaming Citadel seated high upon the mountain side. He felt a hand grip his shoulder and shake him slightly. Starting, he turned to see Rook smirking at him.

"There's more to see inside if you're ready," he said, with a chuckle.

Following Galanor, they were stopped at the gates by no less than a dozen members of the City Watch. While Galanor and Rook spoke to them, Jonas continued to gaze up and down the walls to see other members of the Watch busily preparing the city's defenses. He paused to wonder if even this great city could withstand the power of the dark army and the dragon. Turning back, he saw Rook beckon him forward and he ran up to join them. They moved quickly through the city towards the Citadel. As they went, Jonas felt overwhelmed by the splendor of the city and felt his two eyes were not sufficient to see it all. He did note the obvious absence of street vendors, but assumed that this was due to efforts to secure the city before the enemy arrived. The only people on the streets were the hundreds of soldiers, in various uniforms, patrolling the streets and preparing for the coming battle.

They were stopped again briefly at the gates of the Citadel by two dozen members of the Royal Guard, but Galanor identified himself and they were promptly ushered inside. One of the guards was assigned to lead them into the Citadel and to the great hall. The hall was massive and decorated with many tapestries, each depicting events from Alethia's recent history. At the far end of the hall stood a high dais, with steps leading up to the kings' throne. Above the throne was hung a white canopy upon which was embroidered a single red rose. The king sat alone and Jonas noticed a smile spreading on his face as he watched them draw nearer to the foot of the dais. The king rose and descended the steps to meet them at the foot of the dais.

"Galanor," the king said, embracing the old man, then turned to embrace Rook. "Kinison, my old friend."

Jonas glanced over to see Rook's smile falter.

"Forgive me," the king said quickly. "I know you prefer your new name."

"There is nothing to forgive, your Majesty," Rook answered, with a bow.

"And this is Jonas Astley," the king said moving over to shake his hand.

"Your Majesty," Jonas said, bowing low.

"Well, I don't need to ask what brings you to Ethriel."

"Your Majesty knows why we are here," Galanor said, grimly. "The situation is graver than you know."

"Not as grave as you might think, Galanor," the king said with a knowing smile.

Jonas watched in interest as the king reached behind his throne, then he gasped in amazement as the king pulled out the *Book of Aduin*. He glanced at Galanor and Rook to find his astonishment mirrored on their faces.

"How?" Galanor asked.

"This was brought to me by two unlikely companions," he said, handing him the book. "Would you like to meet them?"

They nodded, and the king gestured to the guard at the side door.

"No way!" Jonas exclaimed, as Azka and Selena entered the room.

They came over to stand on the king's right. Jonas's face quickly went from shock to anger. The look on Selena's face was one of sorrow and regret, but it had no effect on him. He knew she was a very capable liar, and wondered how the king of Alethia could be so easily manipulated.

"You!" he exclaimed, his hands clenching into fists as he fought to contain his outrage. "Your Majesty, this young woman stole that book from me!"

"Calm yourself, Jonas Astley," the king commanded. "Selena has told me her story, and she regrets her decision to steal the book from you."

"It is more than that, Corin!" said Rook. "She was going to give it to Methangoth!"

Jonas glanced over at Rook to see his own outrage reflected on his face.

"You forget yourself, Rook," the king said sternly. "As I said, I have heard her story, and the evidence of the return of the book is sufficient to prove her sincerity. Azka has spent time with her and tells me that he gave her multiple chances to escape. She never tried even once, but actually saved his life and then accompanied him to Ethriel, where she handed over the book to me without demand or subterfuge."

"Azka," Jonas heard Rook say as he moved to shake the other's hand. "I bring news of a plot against you."

"I am aware of the assassin's sent to kill me, my friend." Azka said with a smile.

"We caught one of them, a young woman, while on the road to Ethriel," Rook said, solemnly. "She escaped our custody when we crossed the river Rockwicke."

"I would not worry, my friend," Azka said, with a bow. "I know where my trust and hope lies."

"The whereabouts and motives of these two young women are now irrelevant," Galanor interjected. "What is important is to reveal to the king that Jonas is now the new guardian of the Book of Aduin."

It was now the king's turn to look amazed.

"This boy is the new guardian," the king said in disbelief. "But what of you, Galanor?"

"The proverbial torch has been passed, Your Majesty," Galanor replied, coming to place a hand on Jonas's shoulder. "The book must be returned to Jonas immediately."

"You always had a way of telling me what to do, without it seeming like a command, my old friend," the king said with a smirk. "Yet, I am reluctant to give such a dangerous object back to a guardian from whom it was so easily stolen."

Jonas felt his heart sink, and felt a wave of shame wash over him.

"You need not look far, Your Majesty, to be reminded of your own mistakes," Galanor said, patting Jonas's shoulder. "Much is in motion. Within the week the kingdom may no longer be yours, and you may yet live to regret your decisions here. Choose wisely upon whom you will entrust the kingdom's greatest and most dangerous asset."

"Your words seem grim to me, Galanor," the king said after a lengthy pause. "We will speak more on this. The Council of Lords meets in two hours. I want all of you there. Until then, the book will remain in my custody."

"What about her?" Jonas couldn't help asking, gesturing at Selena.

"She is tied to the book somehow," Galanor interjected. "I think she should attend also, Your Majesty."

The king glanced between Galanor, Jonas, and Selena.

"Very well," he said at length. "Meet in the Council Chambers in two hours."

\* \* \* \*

They all left the throne room, exiting into the courtyard. Jonas glared in silence as he watched Selena sprint off towards the nearby gardens. After a moment's pause, he ran after her. He heard both Rook and Galanor calling after him, but he ignored them. Breaking into a full sprint, he crossed the courtyard as Selena disappeared past the hedged opening, which led into the gardens.

Upon entering, Jonas found himself in a hedge maze with the wide passage leading to the left and to the right. He turned left at a brisk walk, taking little note of the odd tree and flower bed placement. He did notice the benches staggered along the passages where visitors to the gardens could pause and enjoy the pleasant surroundings. Jonas's eyes darted around, looking for any sign of Selena's trail. Coming around a corner at nearly a run, he skidded to a halt as Selena stood before him in the middle of the passage. She was staring at him, crouched in a defensive posture.

"Leave me alone, Jonas," she said her voice shaking.

"Like hell I will," Jonas shouted, instinctively dropping into a combat stance himself. At the subconscious level, he detected a reluctance and uncertainty in her voice, but chose to ignore it. "You stole the book from me. You made us chase you all the way to Deadwood Fortress. You lured us into a trap set by Methangoth. You nearly got us killed. Then you abandoned us after promising to return the book. And you expect me to just forget all that!"

"I...I was scared," she stammered, her face falling.

Jonas was again struck by Selena's beauty, but he shook his head as if to remove the thought from his mind and glared at her.

"You were scared!" He exclaimed. "You think you were scared!

I was given guardianship of the most dangerous book in the whole kingdom, then had it stolen from me by some stupid girl duped by an evil sorcerer."

Jonas saw Selena's eyes narrow and anger fell on her beautiful face. He had a brief moment to prepare before she attacked. Her right fist flew at his head, which he parried and sent her flying into the hedge behind him. He spun around, just as she righted herself and kicked him in the gut. Jonas stumbled backwards and doubled over, as Selena followed up her attack by plunging her right elbow into his exposed back. Jonas fell to the ground, winded and struggling to keep conscious. He attempted to get up, but as he did so felt Selena's foot impact his stomach. The blow sent him rolling into the nearby hedge, coming to rest on his back.

Aching all over, he turned towards her and held up his hands. He was relieved to see her hands lower. Then in a surprising act of mercy, she came over to offer her hand. Reluctantly, he took her hand and she helped him over to a nearby bench.

"You done?" she asked, mockingly.

Still catching his breath, he merely nodded.

"Look, Jonas," she began, sitting down beside him. "I'm sorry. I made a mistake. Several mistakes. I'm trying to right my wrongs, but it's not easy."

"You could've destroyed us all." Jonas managed.

"I know that now," she said, staring at the far hedge. "I just. I don't know. I wanted to outshine my father, but after talking to Azka and the king, I know now that merely being a good person puts my father's entire life to shame."

Jonas turned and looked at her, as if seeing her for the first time.

"The kingdom is falling apart and all I could think about is my own selfish ambition." Tears were forming in Selena's eyes and Jonas's brow furrowed as he tried to discern if she was being sincere or if she was just that good at acting. "I'm different now."

"Why?"

"I met someone, a strange visitor."

Jonas's eyes narrowed in suspicion, but she didn't seem to notice.

"Somehow, in the midst of all this madness, he offered something that I've never found anywhere else."

"What?" Jonas asked when she didn't continue.

"Love," She answered, turning to look him straight in the eye. "He said he loved me and wanted what was best for me. Never in my life has anyone cared a rat's tail about me. I didn't believe him at first, but after months of encountering him at the most unexpected times I finally do."

There was a loud trumpet blast which drew their attention. Selena stood up and offered her hand.

"That's the signal that the Council of Lords is convening. We should go."

Jonas took her hand and walked out of the garden, his mind trying to make sense of everything she'd said…and comparing her story to his own.

❇    ❇    ❇    ❇

"What is she doing here?" came the angry voice of Lord Morgan.

Jonas and Selena were standing behind Galanor, who was seated in one of the several empty chairs around the large oak table. The king sat to their left and Lord Morgan stood across from them. They both felt a strong hand grip their shoulders, and they glanced up to see Azka towering over them with a scowl on his face. Jonas opened his mouth, but saw the dark-skinned man shake his head once to either side. He quickly turned back to glared with Selena at her father.

"They are here at my request, Lord Morgan," the king answered irritably. "Please sit down."

Jonas watched Lord Morgan reluctantly take his seat, casting a dark look on both him and his daughter.

"This bickering is pointless," the king said, irritably. "The enemy is approaching quickly from the north and from the south. We are preparing our defenses as best as we can, but it may not be enough."

"Your Majesty," Galanor began gravely. "I am not speaking as a prophet, but as one who has seen the might of this army and the dragon who controls it."

"Controls it?" the king exclaimed.

Everyone in the room, including Jonas, gaped at Galanor. In all their travels together, he could not recall Galanor ever sharing such a theory with him or Rook.

"What do you mean?" Lord Morgan asked with sudden interest.

"Your Majesty," Galanor said with a meaningful glance. "Please bring forth the *Book of Aduin*."

The king looked reluctant and a little outraged that Galanor had divulged his possession of the historic and legendary book to the rest of the Council. At length, he nodded to one of the pages who scurried away. A moment later, the page came in with the book and was about to lay it in front of the king, before he pointed at Galanor. The page brought the book over and laid it before the old man. Jonas, looking over the old wizard's shoulder, gazed open-mouthed as the wizened hands pulled open the aged leather bindings. The soft cracking of old paper could be heard clearly in the silent room. Finally after turning several pages, Galanor cleared his throat and read from the ancient tome.

*Herein lies the history of the Great Uprising in Alethia and the fall of the Atolnum Empire. Upon his defeat, the evil emperor, whose name shall not be written here, was defeated. Yet even in death, the people feared the emperor's power and his promise to bring death and destruction upon his return. The last remaining of the twelve loremasters ordered the emperor's remains be buried in a tomb high in the Southron Mountains. The loremaster then magically sealed the tomb, cursing any who would dare attempt to open the tomb.*

Galanor closed the book, and turned to address the room. "I believe that Methangoth has opened the tomb and released the ancient evil within. The dragon we've seen at Fairhaven, Farodhold, and the Pass of Stenc, is in fact the evil emperor reborn."

There was a general murmuring and Jonas felt fear seize his heart, as if ghostly hands had reached inside his chest and squeezed the vital organ and disrupted its crucial rhythms.

"How is this possible?" the king asked, and Jonas was shocked to see horror etched on his face.

"The Book of Aduin states that the emperor ruled for countless years, and somehow possessed immortality. How this is possible, the book does not share, but I know that Methangoth sought this power more than any other. While he was my apprentice, he often asked to study the Book of Aduin. I forbade it until I felt he was ready. I know now he managed to get his hands on it at some point and learned of the emperor's tomb. He must have believed the knowledge of immortality was ensconced there with the evil tyrant's remains."

"But how can one return from death?"

"It is a power beyond my understanding, Your Majesty," Galanor admitted. "Moreover, I know that the power to vanquish this new evil is also beyond my own."

The room was silent for a moment, then the snide voice of Lord Morgan broke the heavy silence.

"What fairytale is this?" he said waving his hand as if to ward off an annoying fly. "What utter nonsense. No one can return from the grave."

"Your lack of wisdom concerning the realms beyond the material world reveals itself once again, Lord Morgan," Galanor retorted.

"Your Highness, the old wizard has admitted that he cannot kill this beast," Lord Morgan said with a sneer at Galanor. "Yet if this beast is indeed a dragon, fear not. Legends tell us that many warriors have faced and slain such beasts. We shall carry on the proud tradition."

"Such thoughts are folly," Galanor shouted, rising to his feet. "This is no mere beast, but a dragon in body only. The power and mind of a being so evil that the realm beyond could not keep back its return now besets our kingdom. Would you slay a ghost with a sword?"

"No, but I would silence you with a mere stroke," Lord Morgan said, rising in his turn.

"Enough!" shouted the king. "Lord Morgan—"

But the king fell silent as trumpets sounded and bells rang in alarm.

"To the battlements!" Galanor shouted.

The occupants of the room clambered over one another in a mad rush for the doors. Jonas and Selena ran on ahead, descending the stairs to the courtyard and sprinting across to the stairs leading to the battlements. They stopped and gazed out across the city to the hills beyond the outer walls. The last light of the setting sun cast long shadows across the plains before the city. Jonas felt his mouth fall open as countless dark figures came marching over the hill, silhouetted against the failing light and descended into the plains below. So great was their number that their black forms covered all the hills and plains surrounding the city. He glanced to his right to find terror etched on Selena's strikingly beautiful face, then he glanced to his left to see Rook and Galanor jogging over to join them. They also were gazing out at the fearful sight drawing near to the city.

"What now?" Jonas heard himself ask.

"We fight or die," Rook said solemnly.

"This fight cannot be won," Galanor added, gravely. "But there is still the Shadow Initiative."

# 35

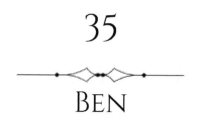

# BEN

A month. It had been over a month since Ben made his daring escape from the Pass of the Knife and returned to the city of Ethriel. Over a month since he'd stood before the Council of Lords and reported of Sir Eric's death and the massive army coming through the pass. Yet in the weeks since his return, the king and his council had done little to prepare the city. Then four days ago, the order had come down from Captain Gunter that the king had commanded the full mustering of the City Watch and Royal Guard. That the entire city was to make ready for a long siege and the Watch began retrofitting the city walls with augmented defenses.

This sudden shift in the king's attitude towards the approaching enemy should have brought Ben some hope. That he should find reassurance that Sir Eric's sacrifice and Ben's efforts to warn the city in time would not be in vain. In his own mind, he had demonstrated great bravery and courage in escaping the enemy camp. Then his daring and evasion of every attempt by the enemy to recapture him should have afforded him at least praise from his captain. Then his determination to reach Ethriel and warn the king and the Council before the army arrived demonstrated his unyielding loyalty and devotion to the kingdom.

Yet instead of praise and commendation, Ben had been punished. The captain had been true to his word. Following their meeting with the king, the captain sent Ben to the stables and for the past month he'd shoveled horse dung from dawn until dusk. For the first few days, the smell had been overwhelming. He'd even retched a few times, but now his nose had gone numb to the filth. He knew that the smell had even penetrated his clothes, and accompanied him everywhere else he went.

This was his life now. Toiling in the mire and filth: this was his reward for all his trouble escaping the enemy and reaching Ethriel to warn the city of the approaching danger. Even now as the sun was just beginning to set, Ben was still clearing out a particularly filthy stall and fuming all the while at the injustice of it all. He'd refused to even go see his father, unwilling to face the man who'd refused to support his dreams or celebrate his accomplishments. No, he would toil here in horse excrement rather than stomach the 'I told you so' even one more time.

"Benjamin Greymore," came a deep and unsettling voice.

Ben started, spinning on the spot and glancing around. The stable was dimly lit, save for the lamp he'd hung in the stall he was clearing. From the entrance of the very stall he was cleaning stood a tall figure, seeming to emerge from the shadows as a great foreboding specter. Ben backed away until his back was against the far wall, bringing his pitchfork up in a defensive posture.

"Who's there?"

"My name is Methangoth," the man said, shifting so that the lamplight caught his features.

The stranger wore a black cloak and hood, so Ben knew he was not the visitor he'd met previously. He had long black hair and black eyes that gleamed menacingly in the dim light of the lamp. Aside from the stranger's abrupt appearance, Ben could not fathom why the man's presence filled his heart with sudden fear and threatened to steal the last of his failing courage.

"I've come to offer you a very lucrative opportunity, Ben," Methangoth said, with a grin. "An opportunity for you to achieve your goals and punish those who have persecuted you."

There was a relish in the man's voice when he said the word *punish* that made Ben cringe, but at the same time he was tempted by the man's idea.

"Okay," he finally said, dropping his guard slightly. "Tell me about this *opportunity*."

Methangoth's smile grew wider.

"This city is lost, its king will perish. Yet, you might save yourself if you aid in its capture?"

"You want me to betray my oath? My friends?" Ben's anger rose.

"What friends?" Methangoth chuckled darkly. "You have no friends. The other members of the City Watch have no respect or concern for you. Your captain hates you. If you were to go missing, who would even volunteer to search for you?"

The truth of these words rang loudly in his ears. Ben felt a wave of despair and humiliation wash over him as he tried to fight back against these emotions.

"I may not have friends or respect, but I won't betray my oath," he said, as firmly as he could.

Methangoth's smile faltered, replaced with thinly veiled anger. He looked more intently at Ben and spoke in a measured tone.

"I admire your loyalty, Ben, but are you sure that you don't misplace that loyalty."

"What do you mean?"

"If you remain loyal to those who do not honor such loyalty, should you still be bound by such an oath? Didn't the king say, 'this young man merits a recommendation to join the Royal Guard?'"

"How do you know what the king said to me?" Ben stared in disbelief as the king's very words were quoted to him.

Methangoth's smile returned. "It's been over a month. Has the king acted on this? Has the captain made a recommendation or honored you at all for your bravery?"

Ben opened his mouth to speak, and then closed it again. He stared bewildered, wondering how this man could know so much about him.

"You are undervalued and unappreciated, Ben. Yet I believe you are capable of much more. You simply must reach out your hand and grasp it."

Methangoth paused and looked intently at Ben, who dropped his gaze. He knew he was playing right into the other man's hands, but he didn't care. Everything he'd said thus far was completely true. He was undervalued and unappreciated by everyone. Even his own father continued to underestimate him. Here was his chance to seize an opportunity to prove them all wrong and seize the honor and respect owed to him.

He looked up into the grim man's face, his eyes narrowed. For a long moment, they studied one another for a long moment, then Ben nodded.

"Tell me what you want me to do."

"There is only one thing I want you to do," Methangoth said, his smile widened to reveal his yellow teeth.

Ben instantly felt regret for asking, but pushed the feeling aside.

"When the fighting starts, open the city gates."

Ben blanched. *Was he serious?*

"Do this, and you will have proven yourself loyal and worthy to me," Methangoth said. Then his smile faded to be replaced with a scowl that would haunt Ben for the rest of his life. "Fail me, and you will find a new definition of the word 'pain.'"

At these words, Methangoth disappeared in a puff of black smoke that left him coughing and wheezing. *What had he gotten himself into?*

\* \* \* \*

As the sun was sinking ever lower and leaving the world in an ever darkening twilight, Ben left the stables, gazing about as if he expected to see the dark sorcerer lurking nearby. He paused, watching the other members of the Watch moving about in preparation for the coming onslaught. There were hundreds of men moving along the walls, setting up additional defenses, and preparing archer slits and the barbicans. He glanced over at the armory where even more men were receiving their armor and weapons. He recognized several faces and fought back the feeling of indignation that he was not allowed to fight.

He walked a bit further towards the Citadel Way, and saw more members of the Watch busily constructing palisades across the main streets and avenues in case the outer walls were breached. He turned and looked down the Citadel Way as it dead-ended into the gatehouse, a structure more than sixty feet tall and thirty feet thick. It had three portcullises that could be lowered into place if the main gates were breached. Spread out over the width of the gatehouse were at least a dozen murder holes, where the defenders could pour boiling water or burning oil onto the attackers from above and inside the gatehouse. In two hundred years, no army had ever managed to breach the city walls, and yet the city had never faced such an army as the one Ben knew was drawing near from the north. And if the reports were accurate, there was a second larger army marching from the south as well.

"Greymore!" came the familiar angry roar of the captain.

Ben took a deep breath and turned to see the unmistakable stocky figure of Captain Saul Gunter walking towards him from the armory. His mouth was thin under his long bushy brown beard and mustache, and his brow was furrowed in anger.

"What are you doing out here?" the captain bellowed as he came near. "I told you to finish cleaning the stables!"

"I've finished, captain," Ben said, in a defeated tone. "I came out to see if you need any help with the defenses."

"We don't need any help from the likes of you." The captain grabbed Ben by the shirt and hurled him backwards. Ben staggered and fell back hard against the stone street, scraping his arms and tearing his clothes. Several other members of the Watch paused to glance over and laugh at him.

"Saul," came another familiar voice.

Ben turned and his heart dropped. Striding up the street was his father.

"Been looking for you everywhere," his father said when he'd reached the captain. Ben saw him glance down at him with disdain in his eyes. "Heard the Watch could use some extra hands. I see my son is making a worth while contribution."

"Yes well, not everyone is cut out to be a soldier," the captain answered with a smile. "We can always use more men like you, Jon. Please, go to the armory and get outfitted, then report to the north wall for assignment."

His father walked away without another word to Ben.

"Now get back to your 'duties,'" The captain called over his shoulder to Ben as he strolled back towards the city gates. "I'm sure your 'customers' have left something new for you to clean up."

Ben got to his feet, and dusted himself off, glaring angrily after them as the laughter of the others continued to echo in his ears. If he'd been on the fence about betraying his father, the captain and this ungrateful city, he wasn't any longer.

*   *   *   *

The sun had nearly set. Ben kept to the ever darkening shadows as he crept along the city walls. He made for the side entrance to the gatehouse, which was hidden in a nook along its right side. There was no guard as the rest of the Watch was still busy with preparations. Ben darted into the nook, and pressed against the side door. It didn't budge. The old wood was rough to the touch, as Ben ran his hands along the door's surface. His left hand fell upon the large iron ring. He seized it and pulled hard. The old door swung open with a loud groan, as the ancient hinges seemed to protest against their sudden arousal from long sleep. His heart thumping hard in his chest, Ben stole inside, and pulled the door closed with another long, earsplitting groan.

The room was pitch black and had the musty smell of disuse. Ben knew he was in a seldom used storeroom on the bottom floor of the gatehouse. On the far side of the room, he knew there was a door leading to the stairwell and the upper floors. He just had to find it. Feeling around with both his hands and his feet, Ben made his way slowly across the room.

Eventually, after much stumbling and cursing, Ben found the far wall, its smooth stone surface cool to the touch. He felt his way along the wall until his hand found the rougher surface of the large wooden door. His pulse quickened as his hand grasped the door handle. He was about to pull it open, when he heard the sound of footfalls on the other side of the door. Panic seized him and Ben scampered blindly in the dark, trying to locate somewhere to hide. He found a pile of barrels and scurried behind them just as the door opened and the light of a torch burst into the room sending the darkness fleeing into the corners.

Ben watched as two men entered the room and immediately recognized them as members of the Watch. They both were armed and stood just inside the door, gazing about intently. The one closest to Ben held the torch, and he was constantly moving it around so that the shadows danced around the room. At one point, the man seemed to be looking straight at him. He ducked further behind the barrels, his heart beating fast. As he was crouching down and trying to calm himself, Ben heard the two men talking.

"The captain said it was down here," said the one holding the torch.

"Well, go find it already," the other said, impatiently. "We've got to get back to the defenses."

"I know that," said the first. "But the captain gave us both orders to find it."

Not really caring what "it" might be, Ben watched as the two men slowly crossed the room. As they did so, he edged out from behind the barrels and crept slowly towards the open door. They had their backs to him and the one with the torch turned and walked behind a stack of crates. With the light of the torch temporarily blocked, the rest of the room fell into darkness and Ben, seizing his chance, ran for it. Not waiting to see if they'd spotted him, Ben sprinted up the spiral stairs until he reached the upper landing at the top of the gatehouse. There his way was blocked by another door, but he seized the handle and pulled hard. This time the door opened smoothly and he leapt inside.

This room was better lit and had several archer slits looking out on the plains before the city. The room was empty. Ben glanced through the archer slit and gaped in astonishment. Thousands of torches covered the hills and plains before the city. He glanced to his left and saw the locking mechanism for the gates and portcullis. He froze, his heart racing in his chest as he pondered the simplicity of sabotaging the gears and prevent the portcullis from lowering or the gates from locking. This was it. He'd reached that pivotal moment in his life when his next decision would determine every decision and every day after.

His hand reached out and grasped the lever, the surface of the ancient wood felt rough on his hands. There was a deafening boom in the distance. An instant later the entire room shook violently, causing Ben to fall backwards and lose his grip on the lever. He slammed into the hard stone wall and fell to the ground. The impact knocked the wind out of him, and he struggled back onto his hands and feet while gasping for air.

The door burst open and Captain Gunter and Lord Silas Morgan entered the room. They were in full armor, a helm on each of their heads and swords and shields in their hands. He watched as the captain scanned the room, but Ben had fallen behind a crate so that he could see the captain but the captain could not see him. Seeming satisfied they were alone, the captain strolled across the room and grabbed hold of the lever. Ben watched unable to believe his eyes as the captain pulled down on the lever. There were several loud clicks, indicating that the locks on the gate were released. The captain turned and Ben watched the two men exchange a smile, then they left the room, Ben stared in disbelief. The door closed just as the gatehouse shook violently once again.

Crouching there in the dark, Ben fought a difficult battle in his mind where he considered whether or not to reactivate the locks or leave them. He wondered why the captain would betray the city. He also considered reactivating the locks since it was primarily because of the captain that he was willing to betray Ethriel. He got to his feet and walked over to the gate lever, grasping it in both hands. This was it. This was one of his moments. He closed his eyes, took a deep breath, and pushed the lever back into place. Several clicks told him the locks had reactivated, securing the city. Ben had made his choice.

He ran to the door and out onto the walls. The men standing along the walls suddenly ducked, and Ben instinctively did the same as the dragon swooped down over the walls. Ben straightened up, following the beast's path away from the city. The beast then turned and flew back towards the city at a different point further down. Twenty yards from the walls, a massive ball of red fire burst from his mouth. The fiery ball hit the walls and sent shockwaves that knocked men off their feet. Ben gaped in horror as the dragon circled back around again to assault another point in the wall, and all hope evaporated. His decision to aid or betray the city was irrelevant. *What strength did men possess to oppose such power?*

# 36

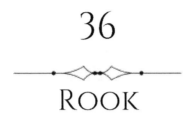

# ROOK

It was night. Dense clouds covered the sky, blocking out all light of moon or stars. Rook stood upon the walls, gazing out at the thousands of torches and watch fires dotting the plains beyond. As he stood there, the dragon flew high over the city spouting fire from its mouth. A fireball smashed against the wall to his far right. He glanced over to see hundreds of men running and crouching along the walls trying to escape the beast's assaults.

After several passes, the dragon flew back to hover over the dark army, which had yet to move. Rook turned to gaze out at the plains again, knowing that it would not be long. He'd stood at this proverbial precipice before, waiting for the plunge into an epic battle to save the kingdom. Yet it was different this time. Not only did it appear that there was little hope for victory, but his stake in the outcome of this battle seemed so much higher than last time. He scanned the sea of dark figures, wondering if XtaKal was lurking among them...wondering if the woman who'd been his wife was still even in there somewhere. He shook his head. Here he stood on the brink of the greatest battle since the Second War of Ascension, but all he could think about was if there was a way to save Sarah.

"Galanor is looking for you," came a voice on his left.

Rook turned to see Jonas walking up the battlements towards him.

"The old wizard should have known I'd be here," he answered, turning away as Jonas came to stand beside him.

"He did," Jonas replied, his voice anxious. "Told me right where you'd be."

There was a long silence. At length Rook spoke again.

"It's funny," he began, somewhat pained and awkward. "Ever since you turned up on my doorstep, my life has been caught up in this great upheaval. I thought I'd left this all behind. I wanted to escape into exile so as to die in peace."

There was another long pause.

"What was it like?" Jonas asked at length.

"What was what like?" Rook asked, still staring out into the plains before the city.

"The final battle of the Second War of Ascension. What was it like?"

"Oh, that," Rook said, turning away once more. "Unlike anything you've experienced. Though you've experienced much battle and bloodshed, the battle before the gates of Elengil and the battle of Tordin Plains, which took place south of the city, were the worst moments of my life."

"That's when you thought you'd lost Sarah?"

"Yes," Rook replied, after a long pause. He fought back the tears and pushed the overwhelming loss he'd felt back down. "This is not the time to speak of this."

"What other time is there?"

Rook glanced over and saw with sudden realization that Jonas had matured greatly over the past few months. The boy that had stood on his porch that cold night was still there, but so was this young man who'd stood by him throughout their journey. He'd even braved a mercenary camp and certain death to come rescue him. The young man seemed to now possess a new hidden strength. Perhaps he was ready to be the guardian of the *Book of Aduin*. Rook gazed at Jonas for a moment, smiled in spite of their current situation, then turned away again.

"Somewhere, out there, is my wife. The woman I married and thought was dead. I thought I'd lost her forever. For twenty years I lived with the reality that she was gone and would never come back." Rook paused to regain his composure. "Now I've learned that she was never gone, but twisted into this dark warrior by an even more evil being. Here we stand, Jonas, on the edge of the greatest battle of our lives and all I can think about is saving her."

"Rook," Jonas began with some hesitation in his voice. "You've lived longer and seen much more of the world than me. Can you be sure that your wife is still in there? I saw her face at Deadwood..."

Rook shot an angry look at Jonas and the young man trailed off. The look of fear on his face caused Rook to soften and he turned quickly away. He sighed, knowing he wasn't really angry with Jonas, but that the young man was merely voicing the very thing he feared most. *Was Sarah truly gone? Had he really lost her so long ago, or was she still in there somewhere in need of rescue?*

They stood in silence for a while. There seemed to be nothing left to say. The cold wind blew in, whipping their cloaks and stinging their faces. Rook stood resolute with Jonas by his side. After what seemed like an hour, Rook noticed the night grow silent and still. A long moment of utter stillness stole over the city and its inhabitants. Soldiers along the wall stopped what they were doing to gaze out at the source of the change, as if they expected the enemy to have vanished. Then, the silence was broken with the beat of many drums; sounding off first on Rook's right, then on his left. Horns sounded from all along the enemy lines and the army cried out into the night. The clashing of metal mingled with dark taunts and harsh shouts coming up over the plains. Rook knew the moment was near and he turned to Jonas.

"Find Galanor," he said, grasping the young man by the shoulders. "Tell him it has begun. It's now or never."

He released Jonas, who nodded and quickly left in search of the old wizard. Rook turned back to see the enemy marching towards the city. Siege towers were looming closer. He could see the light of the enemy torches as they glinted off spear and helm. Rook drew his bow fitted an arrow.

"Make ready!" Rook shouted at the archers along the walls.

Light sprang forth from arrows being igniting like the lighting of hundreds of candles all along the walls.

"Take aim!"

The sound of dozens of bows being bent came to his ears. They held for only a moment, but what seemed like an eternity. The blood beat hard in Rook's ears. His eyes ran along the arrow shaft. He closed his eyes, wondering again if Sarah was out there somewhere.

"Fire!" he shouted.

Hundreds of arrows were loosed. Rook was already fitting another arrow, but others near him were staring at the fiery arrows as they fell among the enemy.

"Make ready and take aim!" he shouted, trying to shake the men out of their stupor.

They scrambled to catch up with Rook. The enemy lines were even closer now, and though many had fallen dead from the defenders first volley, the enemy seemed unfazed.

"Fire!"

The arrows flew and fell among the enemy. Rook saw many dark figures drop to the ground, but there were always more to take their place.

"Fire at will!" He cried, fitting another arrow and loosing it.

While he was firing, the enemy's front line reached the walls. Rook glanced to his right to see ladders being hoisted up and enemy soldiers beginning to scale the walls.

"Swords!" He cried, dropping his bow and drawing his own sword.

The first of the soldiers reached the top of the walls before most of the men had responded to Rook's command. He watched in dismay as several of his men were killed, a look of shock and horror etched on their faces as they fell dead. Rook's anger burst and he ran with disregard for his own safety, sword swinging hard in all directions. Several fell under his broad strokes as he ran passed. More enemy soldiers were climbing onto the wall, and Rook soon found himself cut off on both sides. His men were dying all around him, and he knew his turn was coming soon. He dropped into a defensive posture as the enemy came at him from both sides.

He dispatched several more, but more ran up to replace them. Rook was growing tired and began to wonder when he would feel death's sting. A sudden noise from behind him pierced the din of battle. He glanced back to see Jonas and Lord Ardyn Thayn leading several others down the wall towards him, killing any who stood in their way. Rook's heart leapt and renewed vigor flowed to his arms and legs. Turning, he fought his way towards his friends.

"Rook!" Lord Ardyn gasped when they'd slain all the enemy soldiers between them. "The battle does not go well. All along the wall, the enemy has broken through."

There was a loud creaking noise. They all turned towards the gatehouse and Rook's heart fell as his mind raced to the worst scenario.

"To the gate!" he cried, racing through and slaying any of the enemy left between him and the gatehouse.

He knew the others were close behind, and burst through the door leading to the upper floors. Upon reaching the landing on the top floor, Rook threw open the door to the room that contained the locking mechanism and froze in shock. A short and skinny young man was facing off against a man with a red hat and a long red feather sticking out of it. Rook's eyes narrowed in anger as he recognized the man at once.

"Morgan!" Ardyn called, his voice betraying his shock.

"Help me, Lord Thayn," Morgan cried, glaring at the young man. "I caught this young traitor trying to unlock the gates."

Rook's eyes narrowed as his eyes found a small badge on Morgan's right shoulder...the emblem of a red dragon. Fury instantly rose up inside him.

"You have betrayed us all!" Rook cried, coming to the young man's aid. "Morgan, you traitor!"

Ardyn was quickly by his side, along with Jonas. They hemmed Morgan in, but Rook knew he would not be so easily beaten. Rook feigned to Morgan's right, but Jonas didn't pick up on it. He attacked also, but Morgan disarmed and seized him from behind. Holding a knife to Jonas's throat, Morgan leered at Rook and the others.

"Drop your weapons!" He shouted.

Rook glared at him, but reluctantly dropped his sword. He heard the other's weapons fall clattering on the stone floor as well.

"You're too late, Kinison!" Morgan taunted. "You may have stopped me from opening the gate, but the dragon will breach the walls and this city will fall."

Morgan hurled Jonas at the others, sending them all crashing to the floor. As Rook leapt back onto his feet, he saw Morgan turn and flee through the open door and out on to the walls. Heedless of the others, Rook grabbed his sword and ran after him. Rage welled up inside him, threatening to overwhelm him. He saw red, channeling the strength and rage of a berserker. Some dozen feet ahead of him, Morgan was dodging between enemy soldiers. Rook, in hot pursuit, smashed his way through the enemy, swinging his sword wildly and dispatching the black-clad soldiers right and left.

Morgan reached the next tower and disappeared. Two large soldiers moved to bar Rook's way, each wielding long swords and shields bearing the red dragon. Undeterred, he increased his speed. The soldiers held out their shields and thrust their swords out like spears, but just before reaching them Rook kicked off the side of the battlement to his left and flipped behind them. Before they could turn, Rook sprinted through the tower door and slammed it closed behind him.

Finding himself on a dimly lit landing, he paused only for a moment to decide between up, down, or through the room before him. He grabbed hold of the door in front of him and ran through into the dark room. Finding it empty, he cross the room in a flash and threw open the far door. Leaping back out onto the battlements, Rook found fewer black-clad soldiers here as the members of the City Watch fought veraciously to hold them off. He spotted Morgan's red hat further down the wall and sprinted after him.

Suddenly from overhead came a deafening roar. Rook glanced up to see the dragon circle and dive at the defenders along the wall. He dove out of the way just as the beast belched forth red flames which smashed hard against the wall. The reverberation knocked many of the defenders off their feet and gave the attackers a chance to scale the wall. Rook had a sudden idea. He steadied himself and grabbed a bow from a nearby fallen soldier. He fitted an arrow and aimed at the passing dragon. Taking a deep breath then releasing, he fired. The arrow shot forth into the night, sailing true towards the beast's belly. Rook looked up in hope, then his heart fell as the arrow bounced harmlessly off the dragon's thick hide. He watched the dragon turn to look at him, then its eyes flashed red in anger and defiance. Rook suppressed a smile, then raced down the wall back towards Morgan.

He could feel the beast's eyes following him as it circled high above. Morgan was a dozen yards ahead of him now, which was close enough. Rook glanced up to see the dragon diving at him, and he skidded to a halt. Just in time, for the dragon belched forth a massive fireball which smote the wall with such force that even the upper stonework began to give way. He watched Morgan stagger and plunge from the wall onto the city street some forty feet below. The dragon flew off, obviously thinking its prey destroyed. Rook gazed down below, looking for his enemy's stupid red hat and feather.

All of the sudden, the wall beneath Rook's feet began to shake. He glanced about to find this entire section of the wall was shaking and crumbling. He turned to run, but the stones beneath his feet gave way and he fell backwards into the air and down onto the street below.

*　*　*　*

Rook opened his eyes and immediately shut them again, as he felt a wave of pain shoot through his head. After a brief moment and remembering his purpose, he forced his eyes open and found he was lying in a pile of rubble. He glanced up to see a large section of the wall had collapsed in on itself. Some of the wall remained and was still high enough to prevent the enemy from pouring inside and members of the City Watch were fighting both atop the wall and below, struggling to hold the enemy at bay.

Rook had miraculously not broken any bones, and only suffered some minor cuts and bruises. Struggling to his feet, he sensed the approach of someone. He glanced up just in time to see Morgan coming at him with a large stone held over his head. Rook leapt aside as the rock flew at him. He looked around for his sword, but could not find it. Morgan came at him again, this time with a long staff. Rook had no weapon, so he prepared to defend himself unarmed.

From his left came a holler. Both he and Morgan turned to see Ardyn and Jonas running towards them. Morgan let out a howl of rage as he hurled the stone, which barely missed Rook, and attempted to flee.

"Oh no you don't!" cried Rook as he staggered to his feet and ran off after him.

Both he and Morgan were injured, so it was Ardyn and Jonas who caught up with Morgan first. Ardyn cut him off and Jonas came up behind. Rook was a few yards away when Morgan leapt backwards and caught Jonas by surprise again. The young man was disarmed in a moment. Rook staggered up, but Morgan was ready and held Jonas's sword out in a defensive posture.

"I should've never made a bargain with you, knave!" Rook spat.

"There are many things you should've never done," Morgan laughed. "Now the end of the Aranethon's is near and I will be rewarded with my own crown."

Rook stared in surprise at the maniacal look in Morgan's eyes.

"You think that by destroying this kingdom that you will assume the throne?"

"Not this throne, but a throne yes, my dear Kinison," Morgan laughed again. "You see, the dragon intends to burn Alethia to ashes. He wants this land to burn and be left barren for all time. But I will be rewarded with land and a crown elsewhere."

"You are insane," Ardyn said, his eyes narrowed in anger and disgust.

"Am I?" he laughed again, this time even higher and more maniacal. "Even now much of the kingdom burns and smolders. What power can resist the dragon?"

"I know of one," Rook said through gritted his teeth. "The Almighty."

"You think God will save you?" Morgan droned. "You think God cares about you and this pitiful little kingdom?"

"Yes." And for the first time in a long time, Rook believed it.

"Now who's insane?"

With that, Morgan slashed at Ardyn. Rook took advantage of Morgan's momentary weakness and tackled him from behind. They crashed to the ground and began struggling over the sword. Morgan wrestled it away and Rook cried out in pain as the cold bite of steel cut into his chest. Morgan turned and parried Ardyn's attack as Rook's head momentarily swam. He glanced down to see his tunic turning red with blood. He looking up once again, his vision cleared and he saw the forgotten dagger on Morgan's belt.

Rook dove forward and tackled Morgan again, withdrawing the dagger. Morgan flipped over and raised up to attack Rook, but instead impaled himself on the dagger. They both stared at one another in shock. Morgan gasped, his breath shallow and rattling. Rook released the dagger and fell back as his vision blurred and grew dark. As if through a long tunnel, he thought he heard Morgan cry out in anger and shock. Then, he knew no more.

# 37

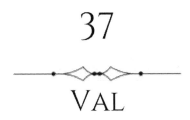

# VAL

It was twilight. Val stood gazing up at the gates of the Citadel, carefully hiding herself in the shadows of a nearby building. The sun had barely set and darkness lay all about her. For over a week after she'd escaped, she'd pursued her target. Exhausting all her skills at tracking and deduction, finally finding herself standing before one of the greatest fortresses in all Alethia. She knew Azka was within the Citadel, but he might as well be on the other side of the world.

Annet had told her how to infiltrate the legendary fortress, but Val had nearly been caught attempting to enter the same way. For days she'd searched for a way inside, but to no avail. Now she could only stand gazing up at the only thing impeding her accomplishing her objective. She watched as members of the Royal Guard moved about in front of the gates. There were dozens of them. Some were visible and some were concealed in recesses and in hidden passages all along the walls. They were also in constant motion and Val could never keep track of more than a handful at a time. Yet despite all of this, she could not give up. There was too much at stake. If she failed, both she and Annett would pay for it with their lives. She had no choice but to keep trying, waiting for an opportune moment. It had now been several days, yet still Val remained by the gates day and night.

She glanced overhead when the dragon had flown over, but she didn't concern herself with such distractions. The entire city could fall, but she had to complete her assignment. The sounds of battle came faint from the city walls below, yet still Val waited close to the gates. Then, the opportunity came. She could scarcely believe her eyes as the gates opened and a man with dark skin and bald head exited the Citadel. Val shook off her shock and gazed intently at her target. There was no doubt in her mind that this was Azka.

He paused to speak with a few members of the Royal Guard, then pulled his hood over his head and trudged down the Citadel Way towards the lower part of the city. Val waited, concealed in her hiding place until he turned the corner, then she moved swiftly to shadow him.

The streets were deserted. Every able-bodied male had been conscripted into the City Watch. Those unable to fight were hiding in their homes, praying for deliverance. So the only sounds that crept up the streets were their own footfalls and the occasional echo of battle from the walls below. Val carefully kept within sight of her quarry as he made his way down the street. Her heart was racing. Though the city was mostly dark, she could not risk her target spotting her.

She had pursued her target across the kingdom and now he was within her grasp. Yet she had no idea how to dispatch him. All of her attention for the past few days had been focused on gaining entry to the Citadel, but now she was trailing Azka through the streets of Ethriel. As she followed him, various tactics came into her mind but none of them seemed remotely likely to succeed. Yet she couldn't lose her target again. Even if she had to follow him across the kingdom again, Val would be there when the opportune moment arrived.

Azka suddenly stopped in the middle of the street up ahead of her. Val dove behind a large pile of crates and peered out at him. Azka still had his hood pulled over his head, hiding his face and features, but it seemed to her that he had glanced over his shoulder. He turned around and glanced this way and that, pausing for a moment on the place in which she hid. For a brief moment, she wondered if he'd seen her. Then without a sound, Azka moved further down the street.

Val was about to follow after him, but the sound of many men came echoing up the street. She glanced over her shoulder as several dozen men in white cloaks came racing by her, all of them members of the Royal Guard. They ran past her hiding place and on towards the city walls below. She paused to wonder if the battle was going so poorly that the king would send his body guards to aid in the city's defense. She also knew that this would be the perfect time to infiltrate the Citadel if her target had remained there instead of wandering the empty streets for some unknown reason. Waiting until the last of the Royal Guard members had past, she then peered out to acquire her target...but he was gone.

Val had searched frantically all along the street where she'd last seen Azka, but there was no sign of him. She'd darted up the side streets and alleyways, but found nothing. She was on the verge of tears and hysterics. How could she have lost him? He'd been within her grasp. The sound of more men coming down the street came to her ears and she darted down a nearby alleyway to watch them pass.

More members of the Royal Guard came racing by, all in white cloaks that whipped wildly behind them as they ran. Val glared at them, as if to blame them for her losing her mark. To her surprise, a man in a dark brown cloak came down the street just after the members of the Royal Guard.

It was Azka. He still had his hood pulled over his head, hiding his face and features, but there was no mistaking him. How had she gotten so lucky? He stopped short, glancing here and there along the street. At one point, he looked down the alleyway in which she was concealed. She peered out at him, and for a brief moment, she wondered if he'd seen her. Then without a sound, Azka moved further down the street.

Val followed after him, taking care to remain in the shadows. She watched as he paused again for a moment, then turned down an alleyway off the main road. Silently, she sprinted down the street and peered around the corner. To her dismay, the alley was deserted. She glanced around, seeking a sign of her mark but to no avail. Taking a deep breath, she moved down the alley determined to find him. Azka was here somewhere, she just had to find him.

Night had fallen completely and the sound of the battle raging on the walls and before the city echoed loudly up the empty streets. Even here, in this forgotten alleyway, the noise was unnerving in Val's ears. Yet her battle did not lie upon the walls or before the city, but here in the city streets. Her pursuit had led her to this dark and dingy alleyway, and now she stood gazing at a shabby-looking inn, with a sign bearing a lion on its hind-legs, as if it was dancing. She glanced above the lion at the peeling letters, which read: *The Dancing Lion*. She frowned at this for the name sounded vaguely familiar. She shook her head and moved towards the door and pushed it open.

She prepared herself for the typical greeting such establishments often gave and she was not disappointed. The smell of alcohol, smoke, and sweat rushed to greet her immediately upon setting foot inside the inn. Standing upon the threshold, she found herself gazing into a dimly lit room, smaller than most inns she'd visited. A small fire burned in the stone hearth away on her right, and a long wooden bar stood before her. There were several tables set randomly about the room, yet they all stood empty. The only occupants of the room were the barman and a single patron seated at the bar. He was wrapped in a long dark gray cloak and hood. He and the barman were hunched over in quiet conversation. The barman paused and glanced up when Val entered.

"In or out!" shouted the barman, irritably, then he and the other man continued their hushed conversation.

"Sorry," Val muttered, closing the door behind her.

She moved over and took a seat at the other end of the bar. The barman cast a suspicious glance at her, then came over and offered her a mug.

"No thank you," Val said, softly. "I'm looking for someone."

"Nobody else her except me and this gentleman here," he said, gabbing a thumb towards the stranger.

She glanced over towards the man, but he took the opportunity to turn away and move over to one of the tables.

"I'm looking for a dark-skinned man, with a bald head. I was told he'd been here." Val asked, unabashed.

She turned back just in time to see the barman's eyes dart towards the side door.

"You've seen him then?" She asked, standing. "Is he still here?"

The barman's eyes narrowed.

"What do you want with him?" He asked, quickly. "He wasn't much for talk and he seemed dangerous."

"Just tell me what room," Val insisted, leaning over and placing four silver lions on the bar.

The barman gaped at the money for a moment, then reached his hand out to take it. Val's hand shot out and seized the man's wrist. Her strong grip shocked the barman and it was evident in his eyes.

"His room?" She asked again, her gaze intent on the barman.

He glanced back down at the money, then back at her.

"Room three," he whispered at length.

"Thank you," she said, releasing the barman's wrist and stepping back from the bar.

She moved towards the side door and into a dimly lit hallway beyond. Off the hall were five rooms, two on the left and three on the right. Above each door was a number etched into the wood frame. Val quietly moved towards the room marked with a "3" and eased her hand onto the door knob. She turned it and pushed the door open slowly and silently. A small fire burned in the grate, which was the only light in the near empty room. Save a small lumpy bed in the corner, the room was bereft of furnishings. The room's only occupant was a man seated on a threadbare rug in the midst of the room. He wore a dark brown cloak with the hood pulled back to reveal a bald head. Even in the dim firelight, Val noticed the man's dark skin. His back was to her and he appeared to be in a deep state of meditation.

This was her chance. Val moved quietly across the room. The man's head moved slightly with her first step. She froze, but he did not stir. She took another step inside, watching for any response, but he appeared unaware of her intrusion into his room. She took another step, then another. As she moved across the room, she unsheathed her dagger without making a sound. Her time and training had led to this moment. She soon stood over the man, her dagger at her side. This was her moment of glory. She would succeed where her mentor had failed. She'd traveled across the length and width of the kingdom to find this man. Now her target sat before her seemingly aware of his impending doom. She raised the dagger to deliver the killing blow. Still Azka, the feared former assassin who had bested her mentor, remained still and unmoved.

This wasn't right. Her hand slowly fell back to her side. This couldn't be the same man who'd bested Annet. She suddenly became uneasy. None of this was right. Val was filled with sudden fear and her hand rose once again to prepare to kill this man. If she didn't, the Guild would find and kill Annet. After that, they'd send someone to find and kill her. She couldn't let Annet be killed. No, she had to complete her assignment. She had to kill him.

Her eyes were filling with tears as she stood there and her hand began to shake. She had to kill him. There was no other choice. Even now, her chance was slipping away. He might stir at any moment and she would lose her only opportunity to kill him. Azka had to die or both she and Annet would die. She closed her eyes, steeling herself to commit the act. It had to be done. She took a deep breath and dagger slowly fell back down. Val, tears streaming down her face, backed away from the man. She just couldn't do it.

A deep voice spoke, rending the silence of the room. Val started and she instinctively dropped into a defensive posture.

"If I truly thought you were capable of my murder, I would not have let you get so close," the voice said.

Val took several steps backward towards the door and stared open-mouthed as Azka got to his feet and turned towards her. She prepared to defend herself, yet to her surprise, he smiled and bowed to her. She could only stare in amazement as the tall, dark-skinned man seemed to beam with pride at her.

"I was told by a mutual friend that I would meet you again. He told me that should you be given the chance to kill me, that you would choose not to," Azka said, raising his hands in a sign of peace. "I was to spare your life, in turn."

Val suddenly remembered the words of the mysterious visitor: "You must spare his life as he will spare yours."

"Annet trained you well," Azka continued as he stooped and rolled up the rug upon which he'd been sitting. "Yet even so, I was aware of you from your first step into this room."

"Annet," Val muttered, her gaze falling. "What am I going to do?"

"Fear not," Azka said placing a hand on her shoulder. "You are not responsible for Annet. She made her choice long ago. But you still have a choice."

"What choice?" Val asked, incredulously. "I have no choice. I can't abandon my mentor."

"You have chosen not to be an assassin."

"What? When did I decide that?"

"Just now, when you decided not to kill me."

Val dropped her gaze as the truth of that statement hit her hard.

"But there is one man I must kill!" She exclaimed.

"Vengeance is not yours to simply take, young one," Azka said. "You must let go of such things and move on."

"Move on!" Val nearly shrieked in anger. "My brother was murdered right in front of me. I will not rest until—"

"Silas Morgan is dead."

"What?" Val stammered as the shock of his words hit her like a tidal wave.

"He was killed earlier this night during an attack on the outer walls," Azka said, calmly. "Your brother has been avenged by God."

Azka came over and placed a hand on her shoulder. She glanced up and saw in his dark eyes a look of kindness and concern. It was unnerving and she couldn't hold his gaze for even a moment longer.

"You have gleaned much knowledge and honed many skills, young Val," Azka said in a consoling voice. "The question remains what will you now do with your abilities?"

"I don't know," she admitted with a sigh. Her entire existence for months had been to train in order to avenge her brother's murder. Now she had no purpose.

"If you will renounce your loyalty to the Guild, I can offer you a chance to use your skills for good rather than evil."

"What are you talking about? What chance?"

"A chance to join a cause for good in this world. A chance for you to use your abilities to help others rather than just yourself."

This was all too much. She'd come to kill this man, but now he was offering to give her a way out of the Guild. She stared wide eyed, and shaking her head.

"It is your choice," he said calmly. "Just like it was your choice to spare me or kill me. What will you choose?"

There was a long silence, then Val looked up into Azka's waiting gaze.

"I choose to help others," she answered.

"Hold out your hand."

She did so and he placed something in her hand. She glanced down to see a large black coin with a shield in the middle of it barring no sign or crest. Val turned the coin over to find the other side covered in an ancient script.

"What is this?" she asked.

"Illumina. Tueri. Inducas." Azka said in a strange tongue. "It means: Enlighten. Defend. Lead. Welcome to the Shadow Garrison."

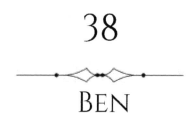

# 38

## BEN

"Are you alright?"

Ben lifted his head as the world swam in and out of focus. Standing over him was a kind-faced young man with sandy hair and green eyes. Ben attempted to nod, but the motion made his head ache.

"I think so," he moaned, closing his eyes and rubbing his forehead.

"All of you, get up!" came the voice of another. "Morgan is escaping!"

Ben glanced up to see the speaker was the man who'd come to his rescue; a tall and grim-faced man with dark brown hair flecked with gray.

"Ardyn, Jonas, he's getting away!" he called and disappeared through the open door.

"Let's go, Jonas," came the voice of Lord Ardyn. Ben glanced up to see him staring after the other man. "Help the young man to his feet and come on! We have to help Rook!"

Ben watched Lord Ardyn also disappear through the door as he accepted Jonas's outstretched arm, and got to his feet.

"I'm Jonas by the way," the young man said, with a weak smile. "Come on!"

Jonas turned and sprinted the length of the room and disappeared after the others. Ben attempted to take a few steps, but his head began to spin. He made it to the wall and leaned his head against the cold stone. He had little awareness of time as he stood there, and was only vaguely aware of the din of the battle coming from outside. Eventually, his headache subsided and he could move without fear of falling or passing out.

He shook the fog from his groggy head and moved toward the doorway of the gatehouse, reaching it just as a familiar face appeared there. Ben stepped backwards in shock as the face of Captain Saul came into focus. He was still wearing his armor, but he seemed to have lost his helm and his face was covered in dirt and grime. There was no mistaking his stocking figure and long bushy brown beard and mustache. The captain was glaring at him, his brow furrowed in anger. He glanced down to see the captain held a drawn sword in his hand, then glanced back up to find a glimmer of satisfaction and even glee in the captain's eyes. Ben took a few steps backwards in fear.

"So you thought you'd play the hero, eh, Greymore?" the captain leered.

Ben took another step backwards, and drew his sword as the captain entered the room.

"Tell you what," the captain said, with a sense of palatable satisfaction in his voice. "Drop your weapon and stand aside, and maybe I'll let you live."

Ben hesitated. The memory of his previous fight with the captain, and its unfavorable outcome, came rushing to the forefront of his mind. Yet, he couldn't surrender now that he knew the captain was a traitor. His eyes narrowed and he made up his mind.

"No," he said, gritting his teeth.

"Ever since you showed up for training that day, you've been a thorn in my side, Greymore," said the captain with some relish. "Now I finally get my chance to be rid of you once and for all."

Ben dropped into a defensive stance, but the captain just laughed.

"You honestly think you can defeat me?"

"I guess we'll see, won't we," Ben mumbled.

The captain's face contorted in rage. He flew at Ben, bringing his sword down hard against Ben's. The force of the blow knocked Ben back a few steps, and he staggered. The captain followed up with a swipe at Ben's exposed head. Ben ducked just in time, the sword so close that the sound of the steel slicing through the air above him rang in his ears. Ben rolled to the side as the captain hurled himself forward, hitting the stone wall. The captain turned quickly and Ben glanced behind him towards the open door.

"Thinking of running away?" the captain taunted. "I always knew you were a coward."

Ben glared back as anger welled up inside him.

"Better a coward than a traitor!" he found himself shouting.

"Traitor!" The captain roared. "I've given decades of my life to the defense of this city. Even remaining loyal to the true ruler of Alethia during the Second War of Ascension."

"The true ruler?"

"Princess Riniel, you fool!" the captain exclaimed, his face deranged. "The Aurelian line of kings may have failed, but she remained in the city when her cousin ran. I, Saul Gunter, was a member of the Guardians of the Citadel. By the end of the war, I was a lieutenant with rank and privilege. Yet, my loyalty never wavered. Even under Noliono, my allegiance was only to the princess. I would have served her, died for her, but then she betrayed us and married Corin Stone, the whelp from house Aranethon, a fallen and disreputable family. Then the usurper came to Ethriel and destroyed traditions that were centuries old. He disbanded the Guardians in favor of a new order, the Royal

Guard. I was dismissed in disgrace like some worthless peasant, barely able to reenlist as a member of the City Watch."

Ben stood gaping at the captain, unable to find the words. He'd never known any of this.

"But I thought King Corin saved Alethia?" he said, half in shock at the captain's revelation.

"One man's hero is another man's villain, boy!" the captain spat, his face contorted in fury. "I worked hard, reapplied to the Royal Guard, even had Sir Eric write a recommendation letter to the king, but all for naught. The king refused to promote me and I was left to captain the Watch until death or dismissal."

Ben simply stared at Captain Gunter, and in the depths of his heart he found sympathy and compassion for him.

"I'm sorry that happened to you," he found himself saying.

"You're sorry!" the captain roared in anger. "I don't want pity from a worthless worm like you! I want revenge! I want this city to burn!"

As if he was unable to contain his wroth any longer, the captain rushed at Ben, who was taken off guard slightly. He parried the attack and kicked the captain hard in the back. The captain went reeling into a stack of barrels, which collapsed under his large weight. There was a moment's pause, then the captain let out a howl of fury. Ben took a step backwards as the captain turned and flew at him. His and the captain's swords rang as blow after blow was delivered and answered. The crash of steel and the hard footfalls caused the ever mounting din of the battle outside to fade as this moment, this fight, dominated each man's mind.

Ben was barely able to defend himself against the captain's furious attacks. The heavy blows came swiftly with little time between them, which gave Ben only time to defend and no chance to attack back. At length, Ben noticed the captain's attacks growing weaker and there was more time between each one, which was good because he felt his arms growing heavier with each blow. After several minutes, they broke apart and Ben was pleased to see a hint of shock on the captain's face. They both were heaving and gasping for breath, which also made Ben smile in spite of the situation.

"Not as helpless as you thought," Ben said, continuing to gasp.

"You're dead, boy!" wheezed the captain.

They circled each other while catching their breath, each looking for a drop in the other's guard. All at once, there was a deafening roar from outside. The whole room shook violently and both he and the captain were knocked off their feet.

"Drat that dragon!" Ben heard the captain exclaim as they both got to their feet.

Another loud rumbling noise came from the door behind Ben. The floor shook beneath their feet and he chanced a glance behind him, but a cloud of dust had risen up obscuring his view. He turned back just as the captain was swinging at his right side. Ben jumped to his left, but the captain punched him in the gut with his left hand. He staggered backwards, dropping his sword and gasping. Looking up, he saw the captain bring his sword up to deliver a killing blow. In that brief moment, Ben dove forward and hit the captain in his chest, sending them both crashing to the floor. He heard the captain's sword clatter as it fell from his hand. Now they were both unarmed, but Ben still didn't like his odds.

The captain roared with rage, hurling Ben at the wall to his left. He hit the wall hard and fell to the ground as all the remaining air was driven from his lungs. *He was going to die.* Lying there, doubled over and gasping for breath, Ben knew he'd been beaten. He waited, still gasping and expecting the killing blow at any second. After several long seconds, Ben looked up to see the captain running for the door. The sound of the captain's laughter came to his ears and Ben gaped, wondering what could have distracted him from killing Ben. His eyes fell on the lever to the gates lying on the floor broken off from its mechanism, and then he realized that the captain had won.

Ben got unsteadily to his feet, his own anger burning inside him because of his failure. All feelings of sympathy or compassion were driven out, filled by the desire to hurt and even kill the traitorous captain. He grabbed his sword and staggered to the door.

The battle was raging outside, and he noticed the enemy greatly outnumbered the defenders. The captain was running across the battlements towards the next tower. Unable to stop himself, Ben ran blindly out into the fray, dodging any attacks aimed at him. The captain disappeared into the far tower and Ben sped up in pursuit.

He reached the tower door and slammed it shut behind him. Then, he felt someone hit him from behind, sending him crashing onto the hard wood floor. Ben rolled over to find the captain towering over him. Kicking at the captain's exposed legs, he succeeded in knocking him backwards. The captain hit the nearby wall, but was quick to right himself. He spun his sword in his hand, plunging it down at Ben's exposed chest. Ben rolled to his right and drew his sword in quick succession. He was just in time to block the captain's next attack aimed at his back. The captain grabbed Ben by the shirt and hurled him backwards. Ben staggered and fell back hard against the far door, which sprang open. With nothing to catch him, he fell backwards onto the hard stone floor, scraping his arms and tearing his clothes.

There was another deafening roar, and Ben glanced up in time to see the dragon swoop over the walls. All of the sudden, the section of the wall some thirty feet away began to shake and crumble. Ben stood up and turned to run, but the captain was there. He punched Ben in the face sending him flying backwards again. Stars flew before Ben's vision as he lay dazed for a moment. He felt himself lifted from the ground and held aloft. Shaking his aching head, he gasped as he realized the captain was dangling him over the side of a gaping hole in the wall. The enemy was massing on the other side of the hole, and members of the City Watch were fighting atop the rubble to keep the enemy at bay.

"This is the end, boy!" the captain yelled, a wicked smile on his face. "The simple pleasure of being the one to kill you is sweetened by the fact that you can see for yourself that none of your actions could've prevented this. The city will fall and burn despite the pathetic efforts of Ben Greymore, the fool who believed he could change things."

Ben grabbed the captain's hands, but could not break his grasp. He clung to his foe's arms in the desperate struggle to save himself from falling onto the stone streets far below.

"Goodbye, young fool!" the captain roared in delight, releasing his grasp and slinging Ben into the abyss below.

Yet at the last moment, Ben managed to catch himself on a small outcropping some four feet below where the captain stood. He heard a howl of anger from overhead, then the whole wall shook violently again. Ben only just managed to keep his hold on the wall, but heard a scream of shock and fear. Glancing up, he saw the captain fall forward into the hole and pass where Ben clung to the wall. The captain disappeared into the darkness below, and his howling came to an abrupt halt. Ben clambered up to the top of the wall and then gazed back down, his heart full of vindictive pleasure at the captain's demise. Finally, he'd achieved a favorable end to one of his enemies. He didn't even fight to suppress the smile spreading on his face at the thought of the captain's lifeless body sprawled somewhere below.

A sudden trumpet blast rang out into the night. It came from high above and echoed down into the city below. The trumpet called all the remaining defenders to retreat to the Citadel. Ben stood there, vowing to himself to find a way to make every one of his enemies pay the same price for the pain they'd inflicted on him. All he needed were the tools and the opportunity. Eventually Ben heeded the call, but he walked away from that moment in time changed forever.

# 39

# MADDY

Maddy stood gazing out upon the battlefield below. She was still wearing her light blue cloak, with the hood pulled over her light brown hair. Beside her stood King Corin and Queen Riniel, all with anguish etched on their faces. The dragon swooped down upon the defenders from on high, then dove for the northwestern wall. They all gasped as the dragon belched forth a fiery ball that smote the wall, and to their horror the great stones gave way and crumbled beneath the beast's attack. The wall crumbled inward and left a gaping smoldering hole, through which the enemy began to pour into the city.

"Almighty, save us," Maddy heard the queen whisper.

She turned to see the queen covering her mouth with both hands as the king signaled to nearby members of the Royal Guard. Maddy recognized one of them as Lieutenant Liam.

"Lieutenant, signal the defenders to retreat to the second line of defense," she heard the king say.

"Yes, Sire."

Maddy turned back then gasped audibly.

"Sire, look!" she exclaimed.

They all turned to see the enemy torches had withdrawn to beyond the city wall. Something or someone was holding them at bay.

"Who holds that section of the wall?" the king asked.

"Kinison, I mean Rook, was stationed near there," the queen answered.

Maddy couldn't help but notice grief in her voice.

"They can't hold out for long and look," the king pointed towards another section of the wall. "The dragon continues to undermine our defenses at every turn."

There was a long pause, then the king spoke again.

"Lieutenant, signal the retreat."

Another moment's pause, then the trumpets rang out into the darkness. Maddy cast her gaze back onto the battlefield and saw one of the nearby gates forced open. Enemy soldiers poured inside the city.

"It's too late," she cried.

The others looked and dismay fell upon them all.

"Forget the second defensive line!" the king exclaimed. "Call all forces back to the Citadel. We will have to make our last stand here."

Maddy watched as more and more enemy soldiers poured into the city, chasing after the retreating defenders. Her eyes fell upon a nearby section of the city and she gasped as she realized that it was where *The Dancing Lion* was located. The shabby-looking inn where she'd met David would soon be overrun. She cast a look behind her, but the others were busy with preparations to defend the Citadel. The enemy would be there soon. David could die if she didn't warn him. She'd made her decision to marry the baron, but she couldn't just let David die.

While the others were busy, Maddy made her way down to the Citadel gates, which were open and receiving the retreating defenders. It was chaos, which she used to her advantage. She slipped past the members of the Royal Guard who were trying to maintain order, forced her way through the waves of frightened people pushing their way towards the gates, and ran out into the dark city.

The streets below the Citadel were flooded with people fleeing the battle from every walk of life. Everyone from poor farmers to wealthy merchants were running for their lives, all seeking refuge in the fortress high above. Following her previous route, Maddy quickly forced her way through the crowds headed in the opposite direction. Eventually, the flood of people lessened and she found herself on a deserted street. Having some difficulty discerning the correct way as the battle and frantic flight of so many people had laid waste to any familiar landmarks, Maddy eventually found herself facing the dark and deserted alley where the inn lay. The streets were deserted and the sounds of battle were still far enough off in the distance. She ran down the dark alley until she reached the inn, but found the windows dark and the door broken open.

"David," she whispered, starting for the door.

A hand caught her arm and pulled her behind a stack of nearby crates. Maddy struggled and attempted to scream, but her assailant was too strong and covered her mouth. The person's hands were rough, like those of a blacksmith. Recognition suddenly dawned on her, and Maddy stopped struggling and turned towards her attacker.

"David!" she exclaimed.

"Shh!" he hissed, pulling her into an embrace.

She held onto him for a moment, then pushed him away. David's brown eyes were looking at her with happiness and longing, which she wished she could return.

"Why have you come?" he demanded.

"I came to warn you," she began, but he cut her off.

"I know," he said, glancing about. "The walls have been breached. The trumpets signaled a full retreat. But why did you come?"

"I," she began, awkwardly. "I don't know."

"I see," David answered, looking at her hard once again. "Well, I think you do know, and you just won't admit it."

There was a long silence as they looked at one another. Maddy felt the same conflicting feelings of elation upon seeing him and depression at knowing she could never be his again.

"We need to get back to the Citadel," David said at length. "The streets will soon be overrun."

She nodded. David took her hand in his and pulled her back up the alley towards the streets beyond. Just before they reached the street, several things happened at once. David pulled Maddy back into the alley and forced her down as the dragon swooped overhead. There was silence for the measure of a heartbeat, then a loud boom in the distance. The ground shook slightly then all went silent again. It was at that moment that Maddy realized that David was holding her tightly to himself, covering her with his own body. She suppressed a grin as he helped her back onto her feet. Then he released her hand and drew his sword as several figures came running down the dark street, each with their weapons drawn and a strange symbol of a red dragon on their black cloaks.

They waited until they had passed, then David led Maddy back out onto the street. Her heart was racing as they made their way back toward the Citadel. All was in darkness and the sounds of battle seemed far away. David led the way as they skirted the along the side streets and tried to avoid the main roads. Eventually they neared the edge of the upper city and had to follow the Citadel Way. When she caught sight of the gates, Maddy felt a sense of relief. There was still a large crowd outside trying to get into the Citadel. David held tight to her hand as he guided her out onto the main street.

Out of the corner of her eye, Maddy thought she saw a shadow separate itself from the surrounding darkness and move behind them. She glanced back and gasped. David spun in place, drawing his sword as they both saw the baron coming up the Citadel Way, weapon in hand.

"My Lady, you continue to disappoint me," the baron said, his scarred face thrown into sharp relief in the light of the torches.

Like so many times before, the look of fury on his face made Maddy want to run yet she stood her ground.

"Stay behind me, Maddy," David said, bringing his sword up.

The baron laughed as he continued towards them.

"Come with me, Madeline, and I may let this young fool live."

"You shall never touch her again, beast!" David shouted.

Maddy's heart was beating fast as she fought to maintain her composure. There were many members of the Royal Guard about, but none seemed to notice their plight.

"This is your last chance," the baron said, imminent threat in his voice. "Come with me or watch David die by my hand."

"It is not her choice any longer!" David exclaimed, rushing forward.

Maddy watched in horror as David wildly swung at the baron, who effortlessly parried the blow and knocked the young man to the ground. David rolled away as the baron drove his sword down into the very spot he'd just been laying. He righted himself just in time to block the baron's next attack. Maddy saw a look of satisfaction on David's face, but she knew the baron was only toying with him.

She gasped aloud as David swung wide and actually nicked the baron's arm, forcing him to stumble back. David glanced over his shoulder towards Maddy, his crooked smile appearing on his young face. Then just as suddenly, the smile was replaced with shock and horror. They both looked down to see the baron's sword embedded in David's chest.

"David!" Maddy cried as the baron withdrew his sword and the young man staggered back, barely able to stand.

He turned back towards her, tried to say something, then fell forward and didn't move again. She rushed forward, but the baron caught her by the arm and hurled her back. Falling backwards into a nearby building, Maddy crumpled to the street gasping.

"You would have made a fine wife, Madeline Brice," she heard him shout over the din of the crowd. "I warned you that if I ever caught you sneaking off to see this stupid blacksmith again, I would kill him. Now to deal with you and your mother."

"No!" she exclaimed, turning and running back towards the city.

✳ ✳ ✳ ✳

There was no thought, only instinct as she ran through the dark streets. There were voices and sounds of battle, but in her panicked state nothing registered. Her mind was set on one thing, escape. Dimly she thought she heard the baron shouting at her to stop, but she continued to run, heedless of anything but the need to get away. She could hear footfalls close behind echoing in her ears. Her legs grew weak and her sides ached from breathing in the cold air, but still she ran as the ever-present sound of pursuit goaded her onward.

She turned a corner too quickly bounced off something solid, and stumbled back onto the rough pavement. She shook her head and glanced up to see a slew of enemy soldiers looking down on her. Several of them bore wicked smiles and licked their lips. She screamed trying to get to her feet, but as she did so one of the soldiers hurled a spear at her.

Time seemed to slow as she watched the spear flying through the air towards her. She knew it was over. Her death was nigh and there was nothing she could do. The air beside her stirred, and she opened her eyes to see the baron diving in front of her. She gasped as time seemed to resume its normal movement forward and the spear embedded itself in the baron's chest.

"Gethrin!" she exclaimed as she crawled towards him.

One of the soldiers grabbed her by the shoulder and flung her away, then he pulled the spear from the baron's body and turned towards her.

"Now it's your turn," he said in a raspy voice.

There came the sound of many footfalls from behind her. She turned just in time to see Lieutenant Liam and two dozen members of the Royal Guard come running up the street and attack the enemy soldiers. The one closest to Maddy fell first with several arrows buried in his chest.

Taking no more heed to the battle, Maddy crawled back over to the baron and turned him over. His face was already pale and his tunic covered in blood. The baron's eyes were closed and his breathing labored.

"Gethrin," she whispered, kneeling beside him.

He opened his eyes and looked up.

"Why did you do that?"

"I couldn't just let them kill you."

"But I thought..."

"I never really wanted to hurt you," he began, then a fit of coughing cut him short.

"I only wanted you, your love, your devotion," he finally managed, a weak smile on his face.

He reached up to stroke her cheek, but she recoiled. The smile disappeared from the baron's face. The light faded from his eyes and his outstretched hand fell lifeless to the ground. Maddy looked down to see his eyes staring blankly at the starless sky above. She began to sob, though she didn't understand why. Reaching over, she closed the baron's eyes and crossed his arms. The grief overwhelmed her and she knelt sobbing uncontrollably. The world seemed to have shattered all around her. David and the baron were both dead. The enemy army was destroying the city. What hope was there for the future?

A hand gently gripped her shoulder and she glanced up to see Lieutenant Liam standing over her.

"My Lady," he said, panting slightly. "Are you all right?"

She stared at him blankly.

"My Lady," he urged. "We must return to the Citadel."

Maddy was confused by his urgency. She wondered why this man was so pushy. There was no need to rush anymore. The world was coming to an end.

"Lady Brice," he shouted, shaking her gently. "We must leave here."

She heard the urgency in his voice, but it didn't matter. Nothing would matter ever again.

# 40

## SELENA

"Maddy! Maddy!"

Selena grabbed hold of the young woman's shoulders and shook her. Maddy stirred, looking up at her as if waking from deep sleep.

"Selena? What are you doing here?"

"No time," Selena answered, pulling on Maddy's arm. "We must get out of here before more of them arrive."

"They're dead," Maddy murmured.

"Who?"

"The baron and David are dead."

"Who's David?"

Selena watched as Maddy's eyes filled with tears.

"Nope!" she shouted, hoisting her onto her feet. "There's no more time for tears, Maddy. We have to go!"

She released her grasp on Maddy's arm, but upon letting go the young woman collapsed onto the ground again in a fit of sobs. Selena grabbed her arms again and pulled her back onto her feet, then slapped her across the face.

"Lady Morgan?" came the shocked voice of Lieutenant Liam.

"Not another word, lieutenant," she said, glaring at him momentarily then she turned back to Maddy. "Snap out of this! You're stronger than this!"

Maddy's eyes finally fixed on Selena, and she saw recognition in those piercing blue eyes.

"Selena," she said, shaking her head.

"Come on, Maddy!" she shouted, pulling her back up the street.

A few minutes later, Lieutenant Liam and his cohort of the Royal Guard led the two women back into the safety behind the high walls of the Citadel. There were many people now inside, cowering in fear of the impending attack on the ancient fortress. Once inside, Selena led Maddy to the Great Hall, which was also full of people, and sat her down at one of the long tables. Selena ran off to the kitchen and returned with a clean rag and a small bowl of hot water. She bent down and examined the bewildered young woman, dabbing her forehead gently as Maddy stared off blankly. She was clearly in shock over something that had happened in that alleyway.

"Sorry for slapping you back there," she said.

The sound of a familiar voice, even in the midst of so many in the Great Hall, seemed to wake Maddy from her inattentive state. She turned and looked at Selena, then shook her head.

"No, thank you for helping to rescue me."

Selena shrugged. There was an uproar near the main doors to the hall. Over the din came a familiar loud booming voice that Selena recognized at once as Azka.

"Where is Selena Morgan and Madeline Brice?" he cried, his eyes searching the crowd of people.

Selena leapt up onto the table and waved her hands. Azka and several others moved quickly towards them. When they'd drawn near, Selena jumped down and checked on Maddy. She was still staring off with a stricken look on her face.

"Lady Morgan," Azka said in his deep voice. "You found Lady Brice I see."

Selena nodded, with a glance toward Maddy.

"The king wishes to speak with both of you," Azka said, taking Maddy gently by the arm.

He led them out of the great hall and down several corridors until they stood before the chamber of the Council of Lords. Selena found it strange that there were no guards posted, but then realized that all the members of the Royal Guard must be out on the battlements defending the Citadel. Azka pushed open the heavy doors to reveal several people seated around a large and ornately carved circular table made of oak. She recognized the king at once, but there were two people she also recognized. First was the middle-aged man with dark brown eyes and hair flecked with gray. He was the same grim-faced man who'd helped free her from the dungeons within the Deadwood Fortress. To his right sat the sandy brown haired young man she'd stolen the *Book of Aduin* from back in Abenhall. His green eyes were looking at her with mild suspicion. The old man from Deadwood Fortress was there too. She purposely avoided his eyes as his gaze seemed to pierce right through her.

"Lady Morgan and Lady Brice, welcome," said the king, gesturing at two of the chairs across from him. "Please be seated. We have much to discuss and little time."

There was something in his voice that made Selena feel on edge. She slid into a seat next to Maddy and looked expectantly.

"I believe you remember Jonas and Rook from your travels," the king said with a slight smile, then he turned to the middle-aged man. "Rook, please tell them what you told me," the king said.

All eyes turned to Rook, who stood and looked only at Selena.

"Lady Morgan, your father is dead by my hand."

He paused and Selena gaped at him in shock, then regained her composure and gave a little shrug as she internalized the whirlwind of thoughts. She turned to the map of Alethia hanging on the wall, her gaze falling on the area of the map where the Island of Nendyn lay. She heard very little of what the middle-aged man said after that, for a sudden thought had entered her mind. *Who would ascend to her father's seat in Nenholm?*

"Lady Morgan?" came the king's voice from what seemed far off.

She started and looked back to find all eyes on her.

"I'm sorry, Your Highness," she said, with a slight bow.

"No need to apologize," the king said, inclining his head. "I was just saying that there is a man outside that claims to have served your father. I was wondering if you knew him."

"What's his name?"

"He says his name is Raynor Kesh."

"Kesh?" Selena said in shock. Two thoughts raced into her mind. She could either claim no knowledge of Kesh, hoping the stupid bounty hunter died in the attack on the Citadel, or she could claim him and use him to help claim her father's seat. She had only a moment to decide.

"Yes," she answered, hastily. "I know this man."

The king turned and gestured to a servant standing nearby, who immediately ran out the side door of the chamber. The servant returned with a much disheveled Raynor Kesh. She was pleased to see his blond hair was matted and there were deep bags under his brown eyes. He'd lost his chainmail, and his face was gaunt with a look of stoic expectancy etched upon it. She smiled at him, knowing such a man was ripe for manipulation.

"Your Highness," the old wizard cut in. "The kingdom is in disarray. We've no more time for this."

"Of course, Galanor," the king said with a nod. "Those of you left in this room are the last remaining lords and ladies of Alethia, save Ardyn Thayn, whom I've sent on an important mission." He looked at each of them in turn. "Lord Jonas Astley, Lady Brice, and Lady Morgan, you represent our hope for the future. This city is doomed, but I've made arrangements for your escape."

"Escape where?" Selena said, forgetting herself for a moment. "My apologies, Your Highness."

"To Stonewall," the king said, with some irritation. "There is a secret tunnel located here in the Citadel that leads out of the city. From there, you will all travel to Castel and then to Stonewall."

"But what of Nendyn?" Selena could not help herself.

"As far as we know," cut in Galanor irritably. "The island has either been conquered or destroyed by the dragon and the dark army. Our only hope lies to the north."

Somehow Selena couldn't believe this.

"May I have a moment," she said, standing and gesturing at Kesh.

"Only a moment, my lady," the king answered, kindly but firmly. "We have precious little time."

She led Kesh out into the hall and once the doors were closed, rounded on him.

"You still wish to serve House Morgan?"

Kesh glared at her.

"Why should I serve you?"

"If you help me, I will be in a position to pay you handsomely," Selena said, with a knowing smile.

His eyes narrowed, but there was interest in them.

"I know my father never paid you," Selena replied savoring this turn of events. "You were never able to collect your bounty for me. Now the one who set the price on my head is dead instead of me. If you help me claim my father's seat, I will reward you substantially. So, will you serve me, Raynor Kesh?"

He looked at her long and hard.

"Choose quickly," she hissed, glancing back at the door.

At length he gave her a single nod.

"I need further assurance than that, Raynor," she said, somewhat forcefully. "Pledge your fealty right now, and I will take you into my service as a knight of Nenholm."

"I pledge my life and fealty to you, Lady Selena Morgan, until death." He said, dropping to one knee and kissing her hand.

"Rise, Sir Raynor Kesh," Selena said with some relish. It felt so good to hold so much power.

Suddenly the visitor's voice echoed in her mind and his words from days ago came rushing back to her. *You've chosen the path once chosen by your father...that leads to destruction. You only obey so far as you think you must, but your heart remains committed to your own desires.* She paused for a moment, then shook her head as she pushed the words from her mind.

"Travel to Nendyn and tell those that remain that Lady Morgan will return soon."

He saluted her, then hastened away at a surprising speed for one so gaunt. Selena returned to the council chambers with a smile she could not suppress on her face.

Suddenly there was a deafening roar from overhead, then a mighty boom and crash. "The dragon attacks!" cried Galanor.

"We've no more time!" the king shouted. "Get yourselves to the escape tunnel."

"What of you?" cried Rook.

"I will stay with my people," the king yelled over the din. "Now go!"

"Corin--," Rook began to argue.

"I've made my decision, Rook!" the king yelled. "Now go!"

Selena glanced between them, then saw Jonas and Galanor headed for the doors. She grabbed Maddy by the arm and pulled her along after them. Rook followed soon after with the queen in tow. She was protesting and screaming that she could not leave the king. They soon made their way out into the grounds of the Citadel. Smoke rose from most of the towers and there were noticeable cracks in the walls. The people found shelter where they could, but little protection could be found from the dragon's assaults. She knew that even this fortress would soon be overrun.

Galanor led them across the smoky courtyard towards the south wall. It was here that a lone door stood that was originally made to serve as a servant entrance to the lower city. Several onlookers followed them and begged to be allowed to come with them.

"Galanor," she heard Rook say. "We can't just leave these people here."

The old wizard looked hard at him, then nodded his assent.

"We must hurry, but even so there is no reason that these people can't use the same way out that we are," he said gruffly.

Rook came over to Selena and placed the queen's hand in hers.

"Selena, take the queen and Maddy through the tunnel to safety," he said earnestly.

She frowned at him, but nodded. Rook ran off towards a crowd of people as Selena pushed the other two women through the door. She couldn't help but cast another glance back behind her before she too entered the tunnel.

\* \* \* \*

After what seemed like hours, Galanor finally led them out of the dank, musty tunnel into the smoky night air. They emerged into one of the side streets in the lower city. There appeared to be no one else there as they all gathered around the old wizard.

"The north gate is near. If we are careful, our departure may go unmarked."

They moved as silently as possible through the ruined city towards the north gate. They found the gatehouse was burning and black smoke rose high into the night sky. The massive doors had been thrown down and scorched. There seemed to be no enemies at hand. Selena's heart was pounding in her chest as they went. Her fears subsided a little as they passed through the gate unscathed, and she saw the open country ahead was devoid of enemy soldiers.

Her revelry was short-lived because the moment they all emerged beyond the walls, two pillars of black smoke erupted in front of them. As the smoke dissipated, two figures emerged that froze Selena's blood: XtaKal and Methangoth.

# 41

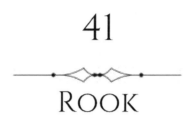

# ROOK

Rook emerged from the tunnel just as the two pillars of black smoke appeared. Drawing his sword, he moved quickly forward as the smoke began to dissipate and the two dark figures emerged. He ran up and forced his way to the front of the crowd and placed himself in front of Selena and Maddy. Galanor and Jonas also moved forward to protect the people.

As the smoke dissipated, Rook immediately recognized the tall man, shrouded in black robes on the right. An evil, satisfied grin was spreading across his face, and both Rook and Galanor spoke the man's name in unison: "Methangoth."

"At last!" Methangoth growled. "I must thank you Galanor. You've conveniently gathered all the people involved in the recovering of the *Book of Aduin* here for me. Now I can take custody of the book and dispatch these loose ends in a single move."

"You will never lay a hand on the book," Galanor growled in turn. "You and your minion cannot win."

The dark sorcerer's black eyes flashed dangerously in the light of the fires burning around them. Rook's gaze shifted to the figure beside Methangoth and his heart felt like it had been squeezed.

"Sarah," he whispered.

Still shrouded in black robes, but now with her hood pulled back to reveal her face and features. The same woman with the burning red eyes that he'd seen outside the Deadwood Fortress now stood before him. Her long white hair whipped around her head in the swirling wind. Rook saw recognition in those red eyes, but this time her face remained etched in anger.

"Give me the book," Methangoth growled, turning to Selena and Jonas.

"No!" Selena cried. Rook glanced around just in time to see the young woman turn and flee.

Galanor stepped forward, extending his staff. A blue light flashed and a blast of blue lightning shot at Methangoth.

The dark sorcerer was only just in time to deflect Galanor's attack, but he sneered at them menacingly.

"Do you honestly think you can stop me this time?" Methangoth said.

He waved his hand and a blazing red lasso shot forward and seized Selena. She screamed and fell backwards. Galanor's hand extended and the lasso vanished in a puff of smoke. Methangoth knelt and raised both hands over his head. A hundred blazing red swords appeared spinning in a wide circle over him. Suddenly, they turned and shot at the group.

"No!" Galanor cried, as he raised both arms and a blue shield bubble encased them all.

The swords hit the shield and burst into harmless smoke. Rook glanced over and saw Galanor staggering under the strain of sustaining the shield under such bombardment.

"You are weak old man." Methangoth cried as the last of the swords hit the shield and vanished. Rook looked back to see him spinning his opened hands in front of him. As he did so the ground began to shake and cracks formed all around the group.

"Enough!" Galanor cried, slamming his staff into the shaking ground. A burst of white and blue light shot outward in all directions, and Rook saw Methangoth knocked off his feet and sent flying backwards over a dozen feet.

Rook stared in wonder to see XtaKal still standing there, unfazed by Galanor's attack. He glanced over at the old man, who gave him a meaningful nod. Rook nodded back. Galanor was making XtaKal his responsibility to deal with.

Rook turned and stared at his wife, or rather the woman who'd been his wife. He'd thought of this meeting every moment since their last encounter outside the ruins of the Deadwood Fortress. His only goal was determining how to save her. He'd quizzed Galanor on the ancient lore regarding the XtaKal. Yet even though he was a Loremaster, Galanor could offer only limited knowledge regarding this foe. Yet Rook knew. Over the past twenty years, he'd traveled beyond Alethia and learned much of ancient lore. He had but one chance to save her.

His eyes fell upon the sword in his wife's right hand. There was his foe's namesake. The sword, which was as black as midnight and pulsating with raw and unlimited power, seemed to draw in the darkness around it. No light could escape it. He made his decision and chose his target.

Rook rushed forward, raising his sword to attack. He saw XtaKal drop into a defensive stance. To his right, he caught a glimpse of a Jonas also rushing forward.

"No!" he cried.

He was too late, for XtaKal raised her free hand and caught him midstride. Jonas was hurled high into the air and flung against the ruined wall.

"No!" Rook cried again, rushing forward at XtaKal again. "Sarah stop!"

She reached out her hand and an invisible hand caught Rook, lifting him up into the air. He felt the same invisible force begin to crush his windpipe. He dropped his sword and clutched at his neck with both hands.

"Fight me fairly!" He gasped, as his vision began to blur.

His only hope to defeat her was to shame her into not using her powers. As he gazed down and watched the face of his wife go in and out of focus, he thought he saw hesitation cross her face.

"If you're going to kill me," he managed to say. "Then at least defeat me fairly. Please, you owe me that much."

Rook felt the force strangling him slacken. They stared at one another for a moment, then XtaKal's hand dropped to its side and he fell to the ground hard. Gasping for breath, he got to his feet and picked up his sword. Still seeing hesitation on her face, he took the initiative and aimed a blow at her exposed shoulder. She was quicker than him, parrying the attack and bringing the evil blade down at his own exposed shoulder. Rook dodged the attack, then blocked another wide attack at his feet. She was not trying to kill him. In the back of his mind, Rook somehow just knew this and used it to his advantage.

There was a brief pause, then without a word she advanced on him once again. They exchanged several blows, each one faster than the other. She was quicker than he was, and at length she defeated his defenses, cutting Rook on his left shoulder. He stumbled backwards from the blow. XtaKal followed up her attack with a quick punch to Rook's chest, forcing him further backwards. He tripped over his own feet and fell. XtaKal was on him in a moment, plunging her evil blade into his already damaged shoulder. Rook cried out in pain.

"Sarah!" He cried, looking deep into her red eyes. "You are not this. You are not XtaKal!"

The same hesitation crossed her face once again. She withdrew the sword from his shoulder, and took several steps backwards as if in disbelief at her own actions. Gasping, Rook rolled away and staggered to his feet. He turned to see XtaKal watching him and they stared at one another for a moment. A sudden thunderclap and shockwave knocked them both off their feet. Rook realized that he'd lost track of Galanor, as the old wizard fought against his former apprentice. His focus had been solely on XtaKal. He mentally kicked himself for his failure to mind his surroundings as he slammed into the ground on his hurt shoulder. He lay there for a moment gasping in pain, then got back onto his feet once again and located his foe. She was also getting to her feet and watching him closely.

"Sarah," Rook said. "What happened to you?"

She looked away, the tip of her evil blade dipping to the ground. Rook realized he still held his own sword. Her defenses were down. Rook could attack and, if he was fast enough, kill XtaKal.

"I know you don't want to kill me," he said, wincing from the pain in his shoulder.

She glanced back at him and Rook noticed the redness of her eyes had dimmed.

"Kinison," he heard her whisper in the same raspy, hoarse voice he'd heard on that hill top overlooking the Bay of Ryst.

"What happened to you?" he asked.

Her face was downcast and Rook saw tears falling from her eyes.

"Kill me," she pleaded.

"What?"

"Kill me. I don't deserve to live."

"Don't say that." Rook insisted stepping towards her.

"You don't know," she said, shaking her head violently. "You don't know what I've done."

"It's not your fault," Rook insisted. "It's the sword. The XtaKal made you do those things."

"I've hurt so many," she said, beginning to weep. "I've killed so many."

Rook could almost feel the shame and regret felt by his wife.

"It's not your fault, Sarah."

Rook could hear explosions going off around him, but did not turn to look. The only thing that matter at this moment was his wife.

"I deserve to die," she whispered.

"That's not true," Rook whispered, taking a few steps towards her. "The fact that you're able to feel remorse and shame means your heart can still be redeemed."

She looked up at him, and he saw a glimmer of hope in her eyes.

"How can I be forgiven?"

"Let go of the sword, Sarah," he answered, preparing for what would come next.

Sure enough, the fire in her eyes returned and her face contorted in anger.

"You will not take this vessel from me!" she hissed.

His wife's mouth was moving and her voice spoke, but Rook knew that this was the XtaKal speaking.

"You have held this woman hostage too long!" Rook shouted. "Sarah, fight it! Fight the evil! It does not have your heart! Fight it!"

XtaKal's hand rose as if to reach out and strangle Rook, but then her hand began to shake violently. Heartened by this, Rook took a few more steps forward. He watched as her hand fell back to her side and heard her cry out.

"No!" she cried. "No, I won't kill him!"

This was it. This was his chance. Rook rushed forward, bringing his blade up. She gazed at him in shock, bringing her own sword up in defense.

He swung low, then high, then wide. Feigning a stabbing attack at her exposed chest, he brought is sword up and down in a swift slicing motion. Sarah glanced down at her right arm and saw her hand was missing. She fell to her knees, clutching her severed limb and let out a bloodcurdling scream. Rook dropped his sword and rushed to his wife's side. Her eyes rolled back as she cried in agony, and he caught her just as she began falling forward. Holding her tightly, he watched her writhe and twist as if in incredible agony and pain. Tears were pouring from her eyes. Then all at once, she went limp in his arms. He quickly bandaged her arm to stem the flow of blood, then gazed down at her.

"Sarah?" he whispered, but she did not stir. "Sarah!"

Rook began to weep, hugging Sarah tightly.

"Sarah!" he shouted, fearing the worst.

She remained limp in his arms. Rook felt on her neck for a pulse, but found none, so he bent down over her face, but there was no breath. The Dark Sword pulsated nearby, drawing Rook's gaze. His wife's hand, which he'd severed from her, vanished also in a puff of black smoke, leaving the evil blade sticking hilt up in the ground. He saw a young man standing behind the sword, but paid him no notice.

"Sarah?" He whispered again.

Suddenly, he felt his wife stir, and gasped in wonder as a dark mist rose up from his wife's body. Two blood red eyes seemed to gaze down at them both. He saw within those eyes pure hatred and evil. They stared down at them for a moment, then the mist and eyes vanished into nothing.

"Sarah?" he whispered again.

At this, she opened her eyes and gazed up at Rook. They were no longer red, but the dark brown he remembered. The same eyes that he'd spent many hours happily gazing into when they were courting so long ago.

"Kinison," she said, and it was the same sweet and kind voice.

"Sarah."

She closed her eyes and a shudder went through her entire body.

"XtaKal?"

"It's over," Rook answered, soothingly. "The nightmare is over. I feel that I too have wakened from a terrible dream. I've lived for so long without you…" he trailed off, unable to speak.

She opened her eyes and gazed at his shoulder.

"You're hurt."

"I'll live," he said with a smile.

He would have picked her up and carried her from this place, but his shoulder prevented such a gallant act. He could only cradle her in his arms.

She reached up to wrap her arms around him, and saw her severed limb.

"What happened to my hand?"

"I promise to explain everything," he said, unable to keep from smiling.

She smiled back and they embraced one another. At length, Rook looked up and saw the familiar face of the visitor.

"Thank you, Jesus," Rook mouthed, tears welling up in his eyes.

The man smiled at him and gave a slight nod. Then He was gone.

# 42

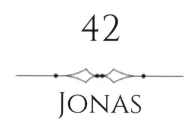

# JONAS

Jonas stared in awe and alarm at the two dueling wizards as they cast blasts of powerful magic at one another. He was not even aware of Rook's battle with XtaKal until he glanced over to see him cradling an unconscious woman in his arms. For a brief moment, he smiled in spite of the circumstances, knowing that Rook was finally reunited with his beloved. Yet his attention was called back to the dueling wizards when a ball of fire flew over his head; the heat of it scorching his hair.

Jonas glanced back and saw Methangoth cast another ball of fire at Galanor, who thrust out his staff to cast a bluish barrier out in front of him.

"You will never learn, Methangoth!" Galanor shouted.

"Stop trying to teach me, old fool!" Methangoth shouted in anger. "I will never stop trying to end you!"

He thrust out his hands to either side of him and a giant chessboard appeared between the two wizards. Jonas glanced about him, finding himself on the white side and standing beside a towering knight.

"I will give you a sporting chance," Methangoth shouted. "The victor gets the *Book of Aduin.*"

"I am done playing, Methangoth!" Jonas heard Galanor shout from somewhere to his right.

"Come now, Galanor," Methangoth said, with an evil grin. "It's been so long since we've played and I've missed the challenge."

"I will not play your games, Methangoth." Galanor said, irritably. "I have warned you countless times to leave this path and yet you keep choosing it."

Jonas heard the older man's staff strike the ground and the chessboard vanished in a flash of white light, leaving them standing some forty yards apart. Methangoth scowled at him.

"If you will not play the game, you are no longer the worthy opponent I seek."

"You're deceitful schemes and ploys will not deliver the book into your hands. You grasp at that which you may never touch."

Jonas saw Methangoth's eyes turn towards him.

"Oh, but I have touched and read the book. Even now it is within my grasp."

Jonas took a few steps backward.

The evil wizard thrust out his hand, but Galanor's barrier extended in front of Jonas and blocked the attack.

Jonas realized Galanor's mistake almost as quickly as Methangoth. A fireball blazed in the evil wizard's hands and he hurled it at the older man. Galanor reacted, but not quickly enough and though the fireball bounced off the barrier leaving the older man unscathed, his extension of the barrier weakened it. Jonas felt the heat of the blast even through the barrier and the sudden attack shook the very earth. Both he and Galanor stumbled and fell to the ground.

Shaking himself, Jonas was back on his feet in a flash, but Galanor was not so spry. In the blink of an eye, Methangoth was on top of him and driving his knee into the older man's chest. Jonas gasped in horror as a sword wreathed in red flames appeared in Methangoth's hand.

"The game is over, old fool! I've won at last!" Methangoth roared, bringing the sword down hard.

Galanor thrust his staff with both hands, deflecting the fiery blade, yet Methangoth had more than gravity on his side.

All at once, the world around Jonas changed. The passage of time itself seemed to slow or even stop entirely. The color seemed to drain from everything and the light grew dim. Fear gripped his heart and he shuddered. The figure of a man appeared before him, clothed in a grey hood and cloak. His outline seemed to glow with white light in the midst of the gloom. Jonas watched his approach, unsure of what to do. The figure stopped several paces away and seemed to look at him.

"Who are you?" Jonas asked, finding his voice.

"I've come to bring a light to your dark situation." The man said, pulling down his hood to reveal a pleasant face. Jonas gasped once again, remembering him as the mysterious man from the cave under Elmloch. He had the same brown hair that fell to his shoulders, a short brown beard, and the familiar kindness in his brown eyes.

"You were charged with guarding the *Book of Aduin* from evil hands," the man said, calmly.

Jonas glanced around at the frozen scene: two great wizards dueling, the City of Ethriel overrun with enemy soldiers and now lying in ruins, and he walked right into this fray.

"I am sorry," he said, hanging his head.

"No, Jonas," the man said, stepping towards him and laying a hand on his shoulder.

He glanced up and saw in the man's eyes compassion rather than accusation.

"You are the book's guardian and as such, you must become a loremaster like Galanor."

"But I do not have his strength or his power," answered Jonas.

"Do you think Galanor draws his power from within himself?" the man asked. "No, his power comes from obedience and courage. He obeys the Almighty and has the courage to do His will. You, Jonas, must be willing to take action."

Jonas was silent. There were several things he wanted to ask, but he could not find the words.

"You must find the courage to do what is right," the man said, more sternly. "And I will be with you always."

"Yes, but who are you?" Jonas demanded.

"Are you still in ignorance?" the man asked, patiently. "Remember this: before the world began, *I am.*"

Jonas gaped as the man vanished before his eyes and the world around him returned to normal. He glanced over and remembered Galanor's plight.

"No," Jonas whispered.

*Take action? What could he do against a wizard?* Jonas stood frozen in fear, his eyes wide as he watched Methangoth's blade edging closer to Galanor.

"No!" Jonas cried out, startling both himself and the two men.

He rushed forward, throwing caution to the wind. His sudden action drew Methangoth's attention. The evil sorcerer threw out his left hand and Jonas stopped in his tracks. His body felt trapped like a giant invisible hand had grabbed and held him in place.

Jonas's action did what he'd hoped and he watched as Galanor seized upon Methangoth's momentary distraction. He raised his hands above him and Methangoth was blasted backwards with the sound of a thunderclap. Jonas felt himself released from the invisible hand and he rushed forward toward the old wizard.

"Nice distraction," Galanor said as Jonas helped him to his feet. "But you're lucky he didn't kill you."

"I can't stand by and do nothing," Jonas replied. "Not anymore."

The old man smiled at him.

"You've grown much since we first met," Galanor said with a smile.

A rushing sound caught both of their attention. Galanor quickly pushed Jonas behind him and held up his staff just in time to block a blast of fiery arrows shooting towards them. Jonas took a few steps back as Methangoth flew at them, brandishing his flaming sword. Galanor quickly touched Jonas's blade and muttered something inaudible. At once his sword glowed blue and seemed to pulsate with energy.

"You want to help," the old man said, turning to face their foe. "Now's your chance."

With his staff in one hand and the pure white sword in the other, Galanor prepared for Methangoth's attack. This time, Jonas stood with him.

The dark wizard lunged at the older man, but Jonas attacked at the same moment. His blade cut into Methangoth's exposed shoulder.

"Impossible!" he cried, grabbing his shoulder and stumbling back.

"You will never learn," Galanor shouted. "When will you realize that a pawn, the weakest piece on the board, can become powerful once it has crossed the board."

Jonas watched the evil sorcerer's gaze dart between himself and Galanor.

"You wanted to play the game," the old wizard growled menacingly. "And it's your move."

Methangoth hesitated. For a moment, he stared at them both in disbelief then his hand dove into his robes. A heartbeat later, the evil sorcerer disappeared in a burst of black smoke.

Galanor sighed. His shining white sword vanished and the blue glow faded from Jonas's blade.

"He's gone for now," the old man said.

"What now?" Jonas asked, glancing about in expectation.

A deafening roar from high above them made Jonas cower in fear.

"Now, we must flee!" Galanor shouted over the din.

At that moment, several people came riding up on horseback from the city behind them. Jonas recognized two of them as Azka and Selena.

"Galanor!" Azka exclaimed in his deep voice.

He rode forward with the reigns of two other horses in his hands.

"Jonas, come!" the older man cried, running over and hopping astride one of the horses.

Jonas followed suit and they rode off towards the hills surrounding the city. Once atop the nearest hills, Galanor and Azka paused to look back. Jonas also turned and gazed at the once magnificent city. Fires burned all across the lower levels. His eyes fell upon a wide road leading up along the mountain slopes into the upper levels of the city, where even more fires blazed unchecked. He followed the main thoroughfare, the Citadel Way, until it terminated at a massive gate sitting at the edge of a wide plateau, high above the upper levels. Here sat the Citadel. The moment his eyes fell upon the ancient fortress, several fiery blasts hit the magnificent gatehouse. The stones crumbled under the massive barrage. Jonas and the others stared in sorrowful disbelief.

"Ethriel has fallen," Galanor said solemnly.

"And with it, the north," Azka said.

"No. There is still hope in the west," Galanor said, turning his horse westward.

"Where? In Elengil?"

"No. In Stonewall."

Galanor rode off westward, Jonas and the others in hot pursuit. As they rode, he couldn't help but wonder what power could possibly defeat the power of the dragon. Then, his mind was drawn to the memory of the man from the cave under Elmloch. *Before the world began, I am.*

# EPILOGUE:

# XTAKAL

Ben had witnessed the battle between Rook and XtaKal from behind part of the ruined wall. He'd watched in disbelief when Rook had cut off XtaKal's hand and the sword fell, embedded into the ground nearby. Coming out from behind the wall, Ben stared in wonder at the sword. He took a step towards it, and the sword pulsated with dark energy. It was strange, but he felt as if the sword was calling to him, or rather something in the darkness within the sword was. He took another step, then another. His hand was outstretched toward the hilt.

"Ben, no!" cried a strong commanding voice.

Ben stopped short and looked up. On the other side of the sword stood the strange visitor. His face, usually kind and welcoming, was grim and his eyes were stern and full of anger.

"You!" Ben exclaimed.

"Do not touch the sword, Ben!" The man said. "You saw what it did to Kinison's wife, Sarah."

Ben looked back at the sword.

"It will give you power, but at what cost?"

Ben's hand was outstretched again.

"Please, Ben," the man pleaded. "Don't touch the sword."

"I will not be told what to do with my life anymore!" Ben cried. "Not by my father! Not by you or anyone else!"

He grabbed the sword and drew it from the ground. At once, Ben fell to his knees as he felt the dark power surge up through his arm and into his body. He felt himself growing both taller and broader. Strength flowed through his arms and legs, the like of which he'd never dreamed or imagine. The hilt and his right hand were knit together and his clothes vanished, replaced by billowing black robes and hood. He got to his feet, realizing that he now stood over six feet tall. His arms were the size of tree limbs. He flexed his muscles and could not suppress a smile. *Never again would anyone dare to tell him what to do.* He looked up to see the stranger fade away, a look of deepest sorrow on his face. His revelry faltered for a moment, then a voice spoke inside his head.

"It doesn't matter," said the voice. "You don't need Him or anyone else. Together, we will do extraordinary things."

Ben looked down at the sword and a grin broke across his face. "I am XtaKal."

# APPENDIX

**The King and his house**

CORIN ARANETHON, King of Alethia, high lord of Ethriel, Lord Protector of the Northern Wilds, and Marshal of the North

- his wife and queen, RINIEL AURELIA ARANETHON, daughter of the late King Greyfuss Aurelia
- notable members of the Royal Guard
    - SIR ERIC TEAGUE, friend of Ben's father
    - LIEUTENANT LIAM
- important other members of the court
    - GALANOR, alleged wizard and last of the loremasters of Alethia
    - KINISON RAVENLOCH, honorary lord of Alethia and member of the Royal Guard, has not been seen in twenty years
    - SARAH RAVENLOCH, wife of Kinison, killed during the Second War of Ascension by Methangoth
    - AZKA, former member of the Assassins' Guild
    - ALYEN, sister of Azka

**The Council of Lords**
ARDYN THAYN, high lord of Stonewall
RNAL CYNWIC, high lord of Vedmore
ALASTER WARDE, high lord of Noland, Marshal of the South
PETER ASTLEY, high lord of Farodhold
SILAS MORGAN, high lord of Nenholm, father of Selena
JORDAN REESE, high lord of Elengil
JON GREHM, high lord of Abenhall
SIMON MOORE, baron of Ytemest
SAMUEL BRANDYMAN, baron of Ironwall

**Lesser lords of note**
GETHRIN WINDHAM, baron of Windham

**Other important groups**
GUILD OF ASSASSINS
GREY COMPANY, a mercenary army
SHADOW GARRISON

# ABOUT THE AUTHOR

R. S. Gullett has spent most of his life in Texas, growing up spending most of his adolescences and early adulthood imagining new fantastic worlds. A proud alumnus of Stephen F. Austin State University, he currently teaches United States history at a community college in Houston, Texas. It took him five years to finish writing *The Heir Comes Forth*, which was published in 2016; a very special day as it was also the same day his first child was born. As a historian, he loves to mingle the historical with the fantastical and places an emphasis on faith in all his writing.

38421348R00209

Made in the USA
Columbia, SC
08 December 2018